YULE LOG MURDER

"Is something wrong, Sergio?" Hayley asked.

He didn't answer her at first. He was still eye-balling the Yule log.

"Where did you get that red ribbon?" he asked.

"I'm not sure. Maybe the crafts store in Ellsworth. Why?"

"A red ribbon just like that was found in the pocket of Ryan Toledo on the night he was murdered."

"Well, that's not so unusual. You can find red Christmas ribbons everywhere this time of year."

"I know, but there is something else. The coroner found traces of chocolate and cream in Toledo's system that hadn't been digested, and there were also crumbs consistent with a chocolate Yule log on his clothing."

"Are you suggesting, and I certainly hope you are not, that Ryan ate one of my Yule logs right before he was killed?"

YULE LOG MURDER

Leslie Meier
Lee Hollis
Barbara Ross

KENSINGTON BOOKS
www.kensingtonbooks.com

KENSINGTON BOOKS are published by

Kensington Publishing Corp.
119 West 40th Street
New York, NY 10018

All Kensington titles, imprints and distributed lines are available
at special quantity discounts for bulk purchases for sales promo-
tion, premiums, fund-raising, educational or institutional use.

Special book excerpts or customized printings can also be created to fit specific needs. For details, write or phone the office
of the Kensington Special Sales Manager: Kensington Publishing Corp., 119 West 40th Street, New York, NY, 10018. Attn. Special Sales Department. Phone: 1-800-221-2647.

Kensington and the K logo Reg. U.S. Pat. & TM Off.

ISBN-13: 978-1-4967-1705-4
ISBN-10: 1-4967-1705-8
First Kensington Hardcover Edition: October 2018
First Kensington Mass Market Edition: October 2019

ISBN-13: 978-1-4967-1706-1 (ebook)
ISBN-10: 1-4967-1706-6 (ebook)

10 9 8 7 6 5 4 3 2 1

Printed in the United States of America

Contents

YULE LOG MURDER

Leslie Meier

Chapter One

"Well, I'll be," declared Phyllis Lundquist, waving a small slip of paper. Phyllis was the flamboyantly dressed and coiffed receptionist at the *Pennysaver* newspaper office, and the slip of paper was one of the order forms for classified ads that ran in every issue of the weekly paper that chronicled "Life as it is lived" in the tiny coastal town of Tinker's Cove, Maine. The form was usually used to advertise used furniture, used cars, and used baby gear, but this was clearly something out of the ordinary.

"What is it?" asked Lucy Stone, the paper's part-time reporter and feature writer. "Not another stuffed moose head?"

"No. It's a casting call for a feature movie to be shot at Pine Point. They want extras to play townsfolk. No experience necessary," said Phyllis, pulling off her reading glasses, which hung on a chain, and letting them rest on her ample bosom. The cheaters matched her hair, which was dyed bright orange and coordinated with her sweater, which featured an appliqued Thanksgiving turkey trimmed with oversized sequins that trembled with every breath she took.

"They're making a feature movie here in town?" asked Ted Stillings, the paper's publisher, editor, and chief reporter, who had just entered the office. His arrival was announced by the jangling of the little bell fastened to the door.

"Apparently, if this ad isn't a joke," said Phyllis, frowning suspiciously. "The check is signed by someone named Ross Rocket."

"That does sound suspicious," said Lucy, remembering various adolescent attempts to run prank ads.

"Only one way to find out," said Ted. "Lucy, drive over to Pine Point and check it out."

"I'm right on it, boss," she replied, "as soon as I finish writing up the new trash-recycling regulations."

"Now that's news we can use," said Phyllis, nodding approvingly and setting the suspicious ad aside.

An hour or so later, Lucy was driving along Shore Road, enjoying the million-dollar views of the spectacular Maine coast. Reaching the dizzying hairpin curve that wound high above a rocky cove, she gripped the steering wheel tight and concentrated on the road, remembering several fatal accidents that had taken place there. Once safely past the dangerous "Lovers' Leap," she flicked on the directional signal and turned through the open gate to Pine Point.

Pine Point was once the home of fabulously wealthy Vivian Van Vorst, but following her death, it had been inherited by her great-granddaughter, Juliette Duff. Juliette was a top model in New York, and visited the estate only occasionally, usually bringing friends along to enjoy the oceanfront views, riding trails, tennis court, and indoor and outdoor pools. The mansion, originally built in the Gilded Age, was still considered an architectural marvel for the clever way antique elements imported from Europe had been included without sacrificing modern conveniences and comfort.

Today, however, as Lucy followed the winding drive that led through the estate, she noticed the garden was filled with numerous white trucks and trailers, and lots of people were hurrying about, seemingly intent on serious business. Finding an empty spot along the drive, which was lined with all sorts of vehicles, Lucy parked her car and got out. She stood there for a few minutes, looking for somebody to approach, and finally spotted a young man with a familiar face, who was strolling along, seemingly studying a script.

"Hi!" she said, giving him a wave.

"Hi, yourself," he replied, pausing and waiting for her to catch up to him.

As she grew closer, Lucy realized the young man was Chris Waters, a leading Hollywood star she'd seen just a couple of nights ago on her TV, saving an entire platoon of soldiers from the Nazis. "Ohmigosh," she said, suddenly flustered. "I had no idea . . ."

He smiled, revealing a dazzling set of teeth. His skin, she couldn't help noticing, was a lovely tan shade, his square chin sported a stylish stubble, and his longish hair had blond highlights. He was tall, and she knew from the all-too-brief love scene in the film that he had an admirable six-pack under that puffy parka. His eyes were brown, and his expression was amused. "How can I help you?"

"I'm from the local newspaper," she began, feeling her face grow warm, "and we got an order for a classified ad, calling for extras, and I'm here to find out what's going on."

"We're making a movie. It's called *Guinevere* and it's a remake of *Camelot* from a feminist perspective."

"Wow," said Lucy.

"Wow, indeed," said Chris. "I suppose you want to talk to Ross, he's the director."

"Ross Rocket?" asked Lucy, remembering her earlier doubts. "He's for real?"

"Oh, he's real all right. He's the director, thanks to his wife, Juliette Duff. She's financing the film." He sighed. "And starring in it."

"Juliette's married?"

He nodded. "From what I hear, it was very sudden. One day they showed up at city hall, got married, and flew off to Italy for a honeymoon."

This was a surprise to Lucy. "There wasn't anything in the news."

"I guess that was the point. They wanted to avoid the paparazzi."

Lucy bit her lip. "I'm supposed to interview him. Do you think he'll talk to me?"

"He's over there," said Chris, pointing to a slight man in jeans, parka, and baseball cap. Strangely enough, he was talking with someone Lucy knew, her friend Rachel Goodman, who was busy nodding along and taking notes.

"Thanks for your help," said Lucy, giving Chris a

wave and hurrying across the frosty grass to the pair.

Seeing her approach, Rachel gave her a big smile. "Hi, Lucy! What good timing! Ross, this is my friend Lucy Stone, who works for the local newspaper."

"Nice to meet you," said Ross, who was a small, wiry man with a patchy beard and eyes set rather too close together. "I suppose you want to know what this is all about."

"Sure do," said Lucy. "This looks like a big story."

"Oh, it's big. It's *hu-u-ge*. It's gonna be great, fantastic, magnificent."

"Okay," said Lucy, responding to his enthusiasm. "Mind if I snap a photo or two?" She produced her phone and snapped away, making sure to capture both Ross and Rachel in the photo.

"Super," said Ross, stepping back. "I'll let Rachel fill you in. . . ."

"Oh, but, it would be better . . ."

"Sorry. Gotta run."

Lucy watched as he hurried off, then turned to Rachel. "So what's up?"

"They're making this movie, a new version of *Camelot*, and I got a phone call from Juliette Duff, asking me to help with the music. Ross is her husband and he's the director."

"You sly thing. You never told me. . . ."

Rachel smiled apologetically. "I wasn't at all sure about it. You know I've got my job with Miss Tilley, and I help Bob at the office, I didn't think I could manage it. But now that I've talked to Ross, it doesn't seem like it will be too much after all. It's not actually a musical, but the idea is to use local people for this one big scene where the townsfolk bring in a Yule log and sing carols for the nobles."

"I heard that Juliette is financing the film?"

"I don't know if that's for publication," said Rachel, looking serious. "She's the star, playing Guinevere, and Chris Waters is Lancelot."

"I already met him," admitted Lucy, with a smile, as she wrote it all down. "Any other big stars?"

"Just Chris," said Rachel. "He's the only one I recognized." She paused. "But they're all pros. It's not amateur hour."

"They're going to run an ad for extras in the paper this week," said Lucy.

"That's great. You're going to try out, right? You and Sue and Pam," she added, listing the group of friends who got together every Thursday morning for breakfast at Jake's Donut Shack. "It'll be fun."

Lucy struck a pose, lifting her chin and staring off into the distance. "I always wanted to break into show business. . . ."

"Well, this is your big chance," said Rachel, laughing.

The Thanksgiving turkey and the leftovers were only a memory, and preparations for Christmas were well under way, when the extras were finally called for filming some four weeks later. Lucy soon discovered that being a movie star, or even a lowly extra, involved a lot of waiting around. The stars waited in their cozy trailers, but Lucy and the other extras had to make themselves as comfortable as they could while remaining out of the way, but near enough to react quickly when they were called. Lucy and her friends, along with the others, had spent hours waiting to get their costumes and were waiting to rehearse in the mansion's ballroom. The ballroom was actually once the great hall at Scrumble Thornhill, an English castle, but had been transported stone-by-stone in the 1880s and rebuilt at Pine Point. Now it was crowded with dozens of extras and countless crew members, lights and cables that seemed to run everywhere, and cameras. There were even a few canvas deck chairs labeled with Chris's, Juliette's, and Ross's names, now unoccupied and awaiting their owners.

"This thing itches," said Pam Stillings, who was married to Lucy's boss, Ted. She poked a finger beneath her wimple and scratched her head. "I hope it's not used and full of cooties."

"That would certainly add to the authenticity of the scene," said Lucy, smoothing her long skirt. "People in the Middle Ages never bathed, they thought it was unhealthy."

"I wish they'd let us have a little makeup," said Sue Finch, studying her face in a small hand mirror and grimacing. "I'm afraid I look a little too authentic." She held out her hands, which had been stripped of polish, and grimaced. "That was a fresh manicure, you know."

"I wish they'd get started," complained Pam, with a big sigh. "I've got a million things to do. Christmas is almost here."

"Tell me about it," said Lucy, who had a big box of presents in her car destined for her son, Toby, and his family, who lived in Alaska. She knew she had to get them to the post office soon if they were going to arrive in time for Christmas. She was also uncomfortably aware that even though Ted had agreed to let her cover the movie shoot for the paper, this was Monday morning and she had lots of other stories to write before the Wednesday noon deadline.

She was looking about, hoping to spot Rachel, who was responsible for rehearsing the extras and might know the schedule, but instead caught sight of Ross Rocket. He was standing in front of a rough table that was laden with fake food meant to represent the feast provided for the townsfolk and was clearly furious about something. He had his hands crossed against his chest and was tapping his foot, rather like a school principal awaiting a wayward pupil. In this instance, the wayward pupil was Elfrida Dunphy, the cook at Pine Point. Everyone in town knew Elfrida, a former party girl who had five children by five different fathers, but had settled down after getting the plum job at Pine Point.

"What the hell is this doing here?" Ross demanded, pointing to a luscious Yule log cake that was set among the prop meats, breads, and fruit. The cake was frosted with fluffy pink icing, decorated with adorable meringue mushrooms and glistened with a dusting of sugary snow.

"It's the Middle Ages," he continued, "they didn't have fancy cakes and stuff. Am I right or what?"

"I wondered where that got to," said Elfrida, looking murderous as she picked up the offending cake. "Now I know and I've got a good idea how it got here. It sure didn't pick itself up and walk out of the fridge."

Elfrida marched off, carrying the cake, heading for the stairway that led to the subterranean kitchen area. She had just reached the doorway, when a bright feminine laugh rang out, and she turned her head, spotting her assistant, Bobbi Holden. Lucy knew Bobbi, who'd been in some of her daughter Zoe's high school classes, where she'd often been the ringleader for various mischievous pranks. She was a big girl, tall and carrying an extra twenty pounds, but had an easy laugh and an attractive, dimpled smile.

Bobbi, dressed in a shocking-pink mohair tunic and dark blue jeggings, was engaged in a lively conversation with Chris Waters, but sensing Elfrida's gaze, she quickly scurried off in the opposite direction. Elfrida watched her until she disappeared from sight, then ducked through the rather low, authentic medieval doorway to return to her kitchen in the great house's basement.

Ross, who'd turned his attention to Rachel, blew on the whistle he wore on a lanyard around his neck and everyone turned to him, waiting for instructions.

"Well, you guys look great, and I want you to remember you're simple folk in the Middle Ages. Put away those cell phones and eyeglasses, imagine you haven't eaten anything except gruel. . . ." Here he turned to his assistant, a serious young woman with a clipboard who followed him everywhere. "Do you know . . . does anybody know what gruel actually is?"

Receiving only a shrug in reply, he continued. "Well, the point is, you guys are hungry and you're bringing the Yule log into the castle, where it will be warm, and if you sing a nice song for the king and queen, you'll be given some food, which you really want. So the trick is to look hungry and famished and pathetic at the same time doing your damnedest to amuse and entertain your betters. So I'm turning this over to Rachel, here, who's going to teach you some old English carols, and don't worry if you don't know what the words mean, just sing along as if you mean it. Right? Right."

Rachel stepped forward, clutching a thick stack of papers, which she asked a few townsfolk to pass around to the extras. When everyone had the sheet music, she instructed them to begin on the first page with "Lo, How a Rose E'er Blooming." When everyone had the page, she blew on a pitch pipe, and they all began singing. They weren't very good, thought Lucy, but they probably did sound a lot like a bunch of poor peasants, hungry for some decent food.

The rehearsal lasted well past Lucy's usual lunchtime, and she was famished by the time the extras were finally released, but instructed to return Tuesday evening at six for filming. She grabbed a plastic-wrapped sandwich and a bag of chips at the Quik-Stop on her way to the office; by the time she parked the car, she'd eaten most of the chips and half the sandwich. She polished off the rest at her desk, followed with a warming cup of tea, which she made by heating a mug of water in the office microwave.

"Gosh, it was cold at that rehearsal," she told Phyllis as she dunked her tea bag. "I don't see why they couldn't put on the heat. And it would've been nice if they'd given us extras some lunch. They put out piles of food but it's only for the actors." She tossed the sodden tea bag into the trash and picked up the mug, wrapping it with both hands to warm them.

"The director's probably trying to keep it as authentic as possible," said Phyllis, when her phone rang and she picked it up. It wasn't the usual irate reader with a bone to chew; it was Elfrida and her voice came through the earpiece loud and clear, ringing through the office.

"You won't believe this," she began, sounding hissing mad, "that stupid Ross Rocket accused me of planting a fancy cake in with the fake food to sabotage his scene. Like I don't have better things to do, that's for sure. I'm cooking breakfast, lunch, and dinner for tons of people, plus Juliette's planning a big party this weekend and wants all sorts of fancy food like Yule logs and angels on horseback. I don't have time to blow my nose, much less plan stupid tricks, and besides, everybody knows it's Bobbi who's the troublemaker. She's the prankster. She's supposed to be helping me, but she's never around when I need her. She's always hanging with the actors instead of peeling carrots or washing dishes."

Elfrida paused for breath, and Phyllis clucked her tongue sympathetically. "What a shame, you used to love your job."

"That was when it was part-time, and I was able to keep track of my kids. Honestly, Aunt Phyl, I'm terrified what I'm going to find when I finally get home. Those kids are wild, they're turning into monsters."

Lucy and Phyllis shared a look. They both knew that Elfrida's five kids were a handful at the best of times.

"I don't know what I'm gonna do. Angie is supposed to be in charge, but she's only fifteen, and Justin's actually taller than she is, even though he's younger, and he won't listen to her because she's a girl, and little Chrissie's got a cough and I need to get her to the doctor. I've got an appointment at four-thirty, but I can't get away from work. . . ."

"I'll leave a bit early and look in," offered Phyllis. "I'll read them the riot act and take Chrissie to the doctor and pick up a pizza for supper."

"Auntie Phyl, you're an angel. . . . Gotta go." They heard Elfrida scream Bobbi's name; then the line went dead.

Back on set Tuesday evening, dressed once again in her wimple and long skirt, Lucy's mind was on the work she'd left undone as she made her way from the dressing tent to the lawn outside the great hall. She was missing the planning-board meeting, and would have to call the chairman for a recap tomorrow, there was a feature story about the high school's quarterback who'd been named to the All-State team, and there was already talk of a debt exclusion vote at the spring town meeting to fund a new patrol car for the police department. She was fretting, wondering how she was ever going to do it all, when Sue broke into her thoughts.

"Look, Lucy, it's like magic."

Lucy looked up and was amazed to see the lawn covered with sparkling snow.

"What? It didn't snow today. . . ."

"No, silly," said Pam, chiming in. "It's movie magic, it's fake snow."

"It's beautiful," said Lucy, gazing at the newly created winter wonderland, where snow draped the tree branches, icicles hung from the mansion, and it all glittered and shone in fake moonlight provided by theatrical lights.

"Okay, folks," said Ross, climbing on a step stool to address the crowd of villagers. "This is it, the real thing. We're shooting and it's going to go like this. You guys are going to proceed through the snow to the door of the great hall, following the men who are carrying the Yule log and singing that 'Make We Mery' song you rehearsed. They're going to knock at the door with the log, the door will be thrown open, and you'll enter the hall, singing your hearts out. Once you're all in, you sing 'Lo, How a Rose E'er Blooming' for Guinevere, the king thanks you for your song and for the log and invites you to join the feast, and you all cheer and smile and sing 'Good King Wenceslas.' Everybody got that? Cause we want to get it right the first time. Okay?"

There was a general murmur of agreement and lots of nods all round. The lusty lads who were carrying the Yule log picked it up, Rachel gave them a note, and they all began singing and tramping through the fake snow, accompanied by cameramen with handheld cameras. It was weird, thought Lucy, realizing that she was actually beginning to feel a bit like a goodwyf, eager to join the celebration. " 'Bryng us in good ale, good ale,' " she sang. " 'Listeneth, lordynges both grete and smalle. . . .' "

As the crowd reached the door, they stopped, as instructed, and the great log was tapped against the door; the door flew open and they gathered in the great hall, where King Arthur, Juliette as a gorgeous Queen Guinevere, and the other nobles were awaiting them. Once again, as Lucy took in the fes-

tively decorated hall and the beautifully robed nobles, she felt genuinely humbled and awestruck. It
was phony, sure, but it was darn effective. Even the
fake food, the piles of bread and glistening plastic
chickens, looked awfully good, since she hadn't
had time to eat any dinner.

"Welcome, all," said the gorgeously robed King
Arthur, stretching out his arms in welcome. There
was something familiar about him, and Lucy was
trying to place him. Was he the gangster who got
shot in the bank heist movie, or was he the wise
old stable hand who saw a winner in the kid's old
nag? She was leaning toward the gangster just as
Ross called, "Cut!" It was then that a shrill, pierc-
ing scream rang out. "What the hell?" said King
Arthur.

Chapter Two

"What don't these people understand about keeping quiet when we're working?" demanded Ross. "It's not like we're on a soundproof set or something." He marched off in a huff, shoving people aside as he went through the hall and banging his head on the low doorway before charging down the stairs. A few humorous glances were exchanged by the extras and King Arthur rolled his eyes.

"The sound guys could've fixed that," said Sir Kay, getting a disapproving stare from Juliette.

"He'd already called 'Cut,'" insisted the knight. "What did it matter?"

"Amateur hour," muttered King Arthur.

Juliette didn't respond, but stood silent as a stone, waiting for Ross's return.

Long minutes passed and people began to shift restlessly, eager to finish up the scene and get home to dinner. Someone behind Lucy wondered aloud, "What's taking so long?"

"You've seen him in action," said another. "He loves to chew people out."

It was then that they all heard a female voice screaming, "Help! Help! Oh, my God! Somebody! Call nine-one-one!"

"I think that's Elfrida," said Lucy. She hesitated a moment, but catching Rachel's eye, got confirmation for her own impulse to follow Ross downstairs and find out what was going on. Slipping through the crowd, she carefully ducked her head at the doorway and hurried down the stairs. Lucy had worked briefly at Pine Point some years earlier and knew her way around the mansion. She knew that the stairway was one of several that connected the ground-floor rooms to an old-fashioned service corridor lined with pantries, laundry, and kitchen. It was in this hallway, about halfway to the kitchen, that she found Ross and Elfrida standing over the prone body of Bobbi Holden, identifiable from that shocking-pink tunic.

Bobbi was lying facedown in the remains of the smashed pink Yule log cake. Ross and Elfrida were standing motionless, apparently in shock.

Lucy automatically reached for her cell phone, which she'd stowed in her jeans pocket, underneath the voluminous skirt. Finally extracting the device, she punched in 911, getting Jenny Kirwan, one of the town's emergency dispatchers.

"There's been an accident at Pine Point. Bobbi Holden has fallen and is unconscious. . . ."

"Help's on the way. Can you perform CPR?"

"I'll try," said Lucy. "We're in the basement corridor, outside the kitchen."

"Roger," replied Jenny.

Lucy listened anxiously for the siren signaling

that help was coming as she crouched over Bobbi's body, attempting to flip her onto her back so she could administer CPR. Bobbi was quite heavy and the smashed cake had made a gooey mess, so Lucy slipped as she struggled to lift the girl's shoulder, falling on top of her prone body. Seeing Lucy fall, Elfrida shrieked, covering her eyes and shaking convulsively.

"I could use a hand," said Lucy, but Ross remained frozen in place, his face ashen, nursing a bump on his forehead.

"Just leave her," he said. "You're not supposed to move an injured person."

"But I don't think she's breathing!" yelled Lucy, panicking and once again struggling with Bobbi's inert body.

"That's the siren, they're here," said Elfrida, and Lucy stood up and stepped back, making room for the two medics, who were hurrying down the long corridor. They were followed by the hulking form of Officer Barney Culpepper.

"Well, now that things are well in hand, I've got a movie to make," said Ross, letting out a long sigh as he started to leave.

"Hold on," ordered Barney, watching as the medics deftly flipped Bobbi onto her back, revealing a large chef's knife that protruded from her chest, soaking the fluffy mohair sweater with blood.

Elfrida covered her mouth with her hand and stepped back, meeting the wall and starting to slide down to the floor, her eyes rolling up into her head.

"You did this!" exclaimed Ross, pointing at Elfrida. "You hated her, and everybody knows it!"

Crumpled on the floor, Elfrida passed out.

Stunned and shocked, Lucy struggled with her emotions and tried to remain a detached observer. Bobbi was a dreadful sight, her face covered with Yule log cake and blood staining the shocking-pink tunic, which now seemed a pathetic attempt to dress attractively.

Ross was glancing furtively over his shoulder, like a trapped animal desperate to flee, but unable to find an exit, blocked by Barney.

The medics were too busy with Bobbi to attend to Elfrida, but she was already beginning to stir. Barney was on his radio, reporting the incident and calling for assistance.

Lucy became aware that her hands were sticky. She looked down and saw a mixture of blood and pink icing and wished that she could wash them, but knew they would be examined as evidence. Evidence in a murder case, because that's what she feared this must be: murder.

Elfrida started to sit up and Barney helped her to her feet, all the while keeping an eye on Ross. The director had apparently accepted the inevitable and allowed Barney to lead the three of them to the rear of the kitchen, where there was a large table and numerous chairs used for staff meals. The officer explained that the state police were on their way, and would need to take statements from the three witnesses.

"What about the extras?" demanded Ross. "I'm making a movie. I've got dozens of people upstairs. . . ."

"Have you got an assistant?" asked Barney, looming over the three who were seated at the table.

"Well, yes, but . . ."

"And a cell phone?"

Ross produced the latest-model iPhone.

"Call your assistant and say there's been an incident and nobody should leave the building until further notice."

"But . . . ," began Ross, only to be silenced by a look from Barney. He made the call, then sat mutely, fingering his fancy new toy. After a moment or two, he raised his head and glared at Elfrida. "Don't try to pretend you're innocent. You hated Bobbi. You made life hell for her, and everyone knows it."

Studying her, Lucy thought that Elfrida must be in her forties, but was still pretty. With her heart-shaped face and curly tendrils of blond hair, she looked as if she could have been painted by Botticelli, a modern Venus. She didn't respond to Ross's accusation, but bit her lip, tears glistening in her huge blue eyes.

Lucy sat quietly, with her gore-covered hands palms up on her lap beneath the table, trying to observe and remember as much as possible. Ross had fallen silent, but continued to glare at Elfrida, and Lucy sensed the tense atmosphere, so thick you could cut it with a knife. Horrified at the thought, she closed her eyes for a moment. When she opened them, Police Chief Jim Kirwan was entering the kitchen.

"The state cops are tied up, so I'm going to take preliminary statements." He pulled out a chair and sat down, producing a cell phone. "You don't mind if I record you? It's just procedure, to keep things clear."

"Okay by me," said Ross. "But let's make it snappy. I've got a film crew and dozens of extras sitting around upstairs and time is money, right? Besides, it's obvious what happened. The cook here stabbed Bobbi with her knife. That's how I found them. There was a scream, I came downstairs to investigate, and she"—he pointed to Elfrida—"was standing over the girl's body. End of story." He started to rise. "Now, can I go?"

"Not so fast, I need some info." He paused to adjust the cell phone, then turned to Ross. "Now who exactly are you?"

Lucy could practically feel the heat rising in Ross's wiry little body as he prepared to set this dumb cop straight. "What do you mean, who am I? I'm Ross Rocket! I'm directing this film. That's who I am, and I've got a scene I want to get shot, okay? So whatever you want to ask me, let's get on with it."

Chief Kirwan scratched his chin, as if he were pondering a big question, like maybe the origin of the universe. "How do you spell your name?"

"What sort of idiot are you?" demanded Ross. "Are you telling me you can't spell 'Ross'? It's a pretty common name after all. And 'Rocket,' like the spaceship."

The chief's lips twitched and Lucy guessed he was relishing the opportunity to exercise his authority. "It's just procedure. For the record." He leveled an extremely serious gaze at Ross, and the director shifted in his chair, squirming a bit. "Spell your name, and I'll need your address."

"Right." Ross spat the word, then proceeded to spell his name, letter by letter. His address, he said, was Pine Point in "whatever the hell the name of this crappy town is."

Kirwan was not amused. "That would be Tinker's Cove, Maine."

"Whatever," replied Ross.

"Do you have an ID? Like a driver's license?"

"Sure," said Ross, reaching for his wallet.

Lucy's hands were uncomfortably sticky, so she took advantage of Ross's hesitation to show them to the chief. "I don't know what you want to do about my hands," she said, holding them out. "I was trying to give her CPR. . . ."

Kirwan turned to Elfrida. "Have you got any Baggies?"

Elfrida was staring at Lucy's bloody hands, looking as if she might faint again.

Kirwan raised his voice, barking out the word: "Baggies!"

"I'll get 'em," said Elfrida, responding to his order. She stood up and, walking a bit mechanically, crossed the kitchen, opened a drawer, and took out a box of plastic bags, which she handed to the chief. He placed a bag over each of Lucy's hands, apologizing for the inconvenience.

"I know it's not pleasant, but your hands are evidence. Hopefully, it won't be too long. . . ."

"Do you mind?" demanded Ross, interrupting and sliding his California driver's license across the table. "Can we get on with this?"

"Sure," said Kirwan, setting the box of Baggies to one side. "By the way, are you all comfortable? Can I get you some water or something?"

"I could use some water," said Lucy, realizing her mouth was terribly dry, "and I'm sure Elfrida would like some, too."

"Righto." The chief ambled across the large kitchen to the watercooler, which stood by the doorway. He took his time filling two flimsy paper cups, which he carried back to the table and set in front of Lucy and Elfrida. Then he turned to Ross. "Are you sure you don't want some water?"

"No!" snapped Ross, rubbing the goose egg that had developed on his forehead. "I want to get this over with."

"Right," said Kirwan, seating himself and studying the plastic license. "This is a different name. Here it says Ronald Rosensweig, and the address is in Wrigley, California."

"Ross Rocket is my professional name, okay? And I used to live in L.A. before I met Juliette and we got married."

"L.A.? How come your license says Wrigley?"

Ross bristled. "Not everybody can afford to live in Beverly Hills, right?"

"So you lived in Wrigley and moved here when you got married, is that right?"

"Yeah."

"And how long ago was that?"

"A couple of months. Right after the honeymoon."

"Are you aware that state law requires new residents to apply for a Maine license within thirty days after arrival?"

Ross expelled a major sigh. "I was not aware of that. Are you going to arrest me or something?"

"I could cite you, but in the circumstances I guess I can overlook it." He handed the license back to Ross. "But I'd advise you to get this straightened out as soon as possible. The next cop might not be so forgiving."

"Thanks," said Ross, not really sounding grateful at all.

"Okay, why don't you start from the beginning?"

"Happy to," said Ross, who was fidgeting nervously and glancing from side to side in a manner that made him seem as if he felt guilty about something, though Lucy knew it couldn't be Bobbi's death, because he was upstairs directing the movie when they all heard the scream. "Like I said before, I was busy with the big crowd scene, we've got several dozen extras, when there was a scream. A woman's scream. I came down the stairs—"

"Why'd you go down the stairs?" asked Kirwan.

"'Cause that's where the scream came from."

"You didn't think it could've been outside or upstairs?"

"No. I was sure it came from down here, and I was furious because we were shooting and there should be silence on the set."

"Hmmm." Kirwan thought this over for a minute or two while studying Ross, who was rubbing at the lump on his head. "Okay," he finally said. "So what happened next?"

"I started to run down the stairs, but the door is low and I hit my head, got quite a whack. I sat on the stairs for a minute or two until the pain subsided, then I got up, and when I got out of the stairway, it faces one way, so you have to go back around to get to the kitchen, I saw this girl, Bobbi, on the floor and the cook here"—he pointed to Elfrida—"standing over her."

"What was Elfrida doing?"

"Screaming her head off."

"Was she saying anything?"

"I dunno. Maybe. It was just a lot of hysterical noise."

"Did you attempt to help Bobbi?"

"I didn't know what to do. I guess I was in shock or something. I was kind of frozen and then she came," he said, pointing to Lucy. "She called nine-one-one and she tried to turn Bobbi over, but she fell, right on Bobbi. I was feeling sick at that point, but the medics came, and when they turned Bobbi over, there was the chef's knife. I knew then that *she*"—he pointed once again to Elfrida—"must have murdered her. She hated Bobbi. She blamed her for anything that went wrong. She even blamed her for putting the cake, *that* bright pink cake that would have stuck out like a sore thumb in my scene, which would have wrecked it. That's why she killed her. It was about the cake."

"In what way?" asked Kirwan.

"I don't know. You'd have to ask her." He slid his chair back noisily. "Now, can I go?"

"No. Not without an escort and we're short-handed." Kirwan turned to Elfrida. "Did you know the victim?"

"Bobbi Holden," said Elfrida, speaking in a whisper. "She was supposed to be my assistant, to run errands and prep vegetables, that sort of thing."

"Family? Contact info?"

Elfrida paused, momentarily clueless, until the answer came to her. "Willis, he's the butler, he would have all that. He does the hiring and keeps the records."

Kirwan nodded, about to pose another question, when Barney Culpepper appeared in the doorway. "The guys from the state crime lab are here."

"What about the lieutenant?"

"He's on his way, should be here in half an hour."

"Great." Kirwan stood up. "Would you escort

Mr. Rosensweig upstairs so he can explain the situation to the cast?"

"Sure," said Barney.

"It's not Rosensweig," growled Ross. "It's Rocket. Ross Rocket."

"Mr. Rosensweig can tell them that a crime investigation is under way and everyone needs to stay in place until they are released by the police. You know the drill, get names and addresses from everybody."

"Right, Chief." Barney nodded. "After you, Mr. Rosensweig."

Ross got up and crossed the room, but paused at the doorway and turned around. Glaring at Elfrida, he lifted his hand and pointed at her. "She's the murderer," he insisted, once again accusing her. He turned as if to leave, but caught himself and stopped, still glaring at Elfrida. "And by the way, you're fired." Then he raised himself to his full height of five and a half feet and marched through the doorway to the hall, followed by Barney, who loomed over the slight director, nearly a foot taller and twice as wide.

Chapter Three

Kirwan seated himself at the table with the two women. He looked from one to the other, then settled his gaze on Elfrida. "You found the body, right?" He pointed his cell phone at her and asked for her name and position in the house.

Elfrida nodded, biting her lip, and identified herself. She was sitting up straight, with her hands folded on the table in front of her, and reminded Lucy of a schoolgirl who'd been caught talking in class. One of Lucy's hands itched and she started to scratch it, momentarily forgetting the bags that encased her hands until she felt the smooth plastic. A quick glance at Elfrida's hands confirmed what she already knew: The cook's hands were clean and free of blood. Of course, she thought, she could have washed them after stabbing Bobbi, and then faked the discovery of the body and the ensuing hysteria. Lucy studied Elfrida with new interest as she recounted the evening's events.

"I was working late, with Bobbi, making holiday

cookies for this party that Juliette is having this weekend. You can see, the stuff is all there. . . ." Elfrida waved her hand in the direction of a large, old-fashioned worktable that stood in front of the huge black range, once fired by coal, but since converted to gas. The table was covered with racks of freshly baked gingerbread cookies, as well as a large crockery bowl, rolling pins, and cookie cutters. The faint scent of ginger still lingered in the air.

"Anyway, Bobbi said she had to go to the bathroom and I said fine. I was taking a tray of cookies out of the oven, when I noticed Bobbi hadn't gone in the direction of the hall and the bathroom, but had gone back across the kitchen to the fridge. . . ." Here she indicated the antique white porcelain model on the opposite wall. "She was taking out that pink-peppermint Yule log cake, and, I admit, I was furious about it. I'd already gotten in trouble with Ross this morning when she put it on the prop food table and I figured she was up to no good. I yelled at her to put it back, but she just giggled at me, grabbed a knife from the holder—"

"Bobbi had the knife?" asked Kirwan, interrupting.

"Yeah. She grabbed it from that rack there." Elfrida pointed to a magnetized strip on the wall over a large wooden cutting block, which contained a number of knives. There was a gap just the right size for the chef's knife.

"Then she started running toward the door with the cake," continued Elfrida. "I started after her, but I slipped on a butter wrapper Bobbi must've dropped on the floor when she was mixing up the cookie dough." Elfrida sighed and rolled her eyes

at the memory, she didn't approve of such care-
lessness in the kitchen.

"I must've yelled when I fell down, I don't remember. Anyway," she continued, picking up her
story, "it took me a minute or two to get my breath
back and pull myself together and get up, but I
didn't have any broken bones, so I followed Bobbi
and, well . . ." Elfrida swallowed hard, and stared at
the doorway beyond which Bobbi's body still lay,
awaiting the medical examiner's inspection. "That's
how I found her, flat on the floor with her face in
the smashed pink-peppermint Yule log cake." She
shook her head sharply as if to clear away the
memory, then jerked her head upright, jolted by a
thought. "I don't think I turned off the oven." She
gave Kirwan a questioning look. "Can I do it now?
I don't think I'll be making any more cookies
tonight."

"I'll do it," he said, getting up and walking across
the large, old-fashioned kitchen to the stove, where
he paused in front of the vast array of black Bakelite
knobs.

"Fifth from the right," instructed Elfrida, and he
turned the knob. Then he turned around and studied
the table, where a circle of rolled dough remained on
the floured surface to be cut into gingerbread boys
and girls. He stooped and looked under the table,
where a crumpled butter wrapper seemed to verify
Elfrida's story.

"What did you think when you found Bobbi on
the floor like that?" asked Kirwan, returning to the
table and sitting down.

"I thought, served her right for taking the cake.
But when she didn't get up, I realized she was
hurt, and that's when I started screaming."

"Did you know she was dead?" asked Kirwan.

"I was afraid she might be. That floor is stone, it's hard, and I was worried about that knife. I knew for sure she was in trouble, but I didn't know what to do."

"So you yelled for help?"

"Yeah. Ross was already there, but he was just kinda standing there, staring at Bobbi and muttering, swearing. Then Lucy came and she called nine-one-one on her phone."

"What did you do then, Lucy?" Kirwan asked, moving the phone closer to Lucy to record her answer.

"Do you want my name and . . ."

"Oh, yeah. Sure."

"I'm Lucy Stone," she began, conscious that she had to be as accurate and complete as possible for the recording. "I'm one of the extras for the movie. After Elfrida yelled for help, I followed Ross Rocket down the stairs. You know I'm a reporter for the local newspaper and I thought there might be a story. I found Bobbi on the floor, just like Elfrida said. She'd been carrying a cake and it was smashed on the floor under her. Elfrida and Ross both seemed to be in shock, so I called nine-one-one. The dispatcher told me to perform CPR and I tried to roll Bobbi over, that's how my hands got covered with icing and, uh, blood. She was heavy and I slipped, I couldn't do it on my own, but that's when the EMTs came. Officer Barney Culpepper took charge and sent me and Elfrida and Ross into the kitchen."

"Right," said Kirwan, turning off his phone. "You two stay here," he said, getting up and leaving the kitchen.

"What a mess," said Elfrida, after he'd gone. Lucy wasn't sure if she was talking about the unfinished cookies and the floury baking mess that remained on the table, or the infinitely larger mess out in the hallway. One could be cleaned up in a matter of minutes with a damp sponge, but Lucy suspected the other presented a bigger challenge and would inevitably cause repercussions that would roil the town and inevitably destroy some lives. She thought of Bobbi's family, probably still unaware of their loss and the grief that awaited them. And then there was Elfrida, the sole support of five children, who'd lost her job.

"What about you, Elfrida? What are you going to do?"

"You mean, 'cause I was fired?" She shrugged. "I was about ready to quit anyway. Everything changed when Juliette married Ross and they started the movie. Until then, it was really just part-time, I made lunch on weekdays for the staff, just Willis and the gardener and the day workers. It was pretty simple, usually soup and sandwiches, sometimes a casserole or pizza. About once a month Juliette would come up from New York with friends, but even then they'd just want breakfast and lunch. They'd usually go out for dinner to one of these new locavore restaurants. They'd drive miles for free-range chicken and biscuits made from heirloom wheat grown in Vermont." Elfrida sniffed, she didn't approve of such nonsense. "I mean, I don't know what's the matter with good old King Arthur Flour, it's all I ever use."

"Me too," said Lucy. "So what's the story with Ross?"

"He's a first-class jerk," said Elfrida, "and the worst

part is that Juliette is absolutely gaga about him. Whatever Ross wants, Ross gets. If it's homemade pumpkin ravioli, I'm supposed to whip it up in fifteen minutes for lunch, like that's even possible. He turned the place into a three-ring circus, even before this crazy filming started. It was parties every night, all these supposedly fancy Hollywood bigwigs.

"Then he got Juliette to produce this film, and if you ask me, I think he's taking advantage of her. It's her money and she can spend it any way she wants, but I think he's bamboozled her, not that it's any of my business. My business is cooking up tons of food for the cast and crew. There has to be a table on set at all times with a variety of 'noshes,' that's what he called them. Bagels and cream cheese, lots of pastries and fruit and cookies, and a bunch of veggies, like beets and carrots, and something called protein powder for the juicer—and if you don't think that thing is a mess by the end of the day, you need to have another think. Plus there was still breakfast and lunch for everybody, plus dinner every night for Ross and Juliette and whoever they'd decided to include from the movie people. Oh, and don't let me forget the stars in their white trailers, they'd call up anytime and want this or that. 'Oh, I don't want to be any trouble,' they'd say, and then they'd ask if they could 'please have just a little salad with just a dash of balsamic vinegar, some edamame, and a bit of sushi on the side. And maybe an iced green tea, something like that, but absolutely no aspartame. I'd really love it if you could brew it up with a touch of organic honey. Is that okay?' "

Elfrida looked down at the table, then out at the hallway, now blocked from view by the closed door.

"You know what I regret? I should've put my foot down. It was way too much work and I was really overwhelmed, just trying to keep up with all the demands, but I should've insisted on a more professional kitchen. We need modern equipment, rubber matting, better ventilation, and a lot more staff. It's no wonder Bobbi fell, and I'm partly to blame. And you know what the worst of it is? She was an intern. Ross somehow convinced her he couldn't afford to pay her, but it was going to be a great experience, and now she's dead from an accident that didn't need to happen."

"Is that what you think happened? An accident?" asked Lucy, puzzled.

"Of course. She must've had the knife so she could cut the cake. I bet she was taking it to that Chris Waters, she had a thing for him. When I started to chase her, she must've panicked and slipped on that smooth stone floor and fell on the knife." Elfrida looked at Lucy with her big blue eyes, wide-open in an innocent gaze. "What else could have happened?"

"Well," said Lucy, speculating, "she might've met somebody in the hall who had an issue with her and wanted her dead. Can you think of anybody like that?"

"Oh, the wickedness!" exclaimed Elfrida.

"Very wicked indeed," said Lucy, "but it happens. It sounds like Bobbi loved pranks and jokes, and she might have gone too far with someone who decided they'd had enough."

"She was just joking, fooling around. Everybody

knew that, they didn't take it seriously. At least that's my impression. I'm not exactly in the loop, if you know what I mean. I'm down here in this antiquated relic of a kitchen, trying to keep up with . . ." She stopped, biting her lip. "Not anymore I'm not. Those days are over and I can't say I'm sorry. I only wish the state of Maine was a little more generous with unemployment benefits."

"If you can get them," said Lucy. "You're going to have to convince them you weren't fired, but laid off."

Elfrida's eyes grew wide. "He wouldn't, would he?"

Lucy knew that most local employers didn't fight unemployment claims, happy enough to be rid of difficult employees and aware that their former workers desperately needed the money, but she wasn't convinced that Ross would be so understanding. "Dunno," said Lucy.

"You're probably right, he's such a creep. Ross Rocket doesn't think about anybody except Ross Rocket." She sighed. "What am I gonna do?"

"If I were you," suggested Lucy, "I'd have a word with Juliette."

"Good idea," said Elfrida, brightening up. "I'll do that."

The door creaked a bit as it was opened, and both women turned to see Chief Kirwan returning to the kitchen.

"Can I go?" asked Elfrida. "My aunt is watching the kids, but it's getting late."

"Sorry," said Kirwan, looking rather uncomfortable. "I've been instructed to take you to the station to await questioning by a state police detective."

"Both of us?" asked Lucy.

"No. Lucy, you can go, after they check your hands, but they want to talk to Elfrida."

"What about my kids? Aunt Phyllis'll never be able to get them into bed."

"I can contact Child Protective Services. . . ."

"No. No. Don't do that!" exclaimed Elfrida.

"I'll swing by and help her," said Lucy, belatedly realizing she wasn't in a position to do that, considering the state of her hands. "You'll probably be home in a few hours."

"Is that right? Am I under arrest?" asked Elfrida.

"Let's say you're a person of interest."

"What does that mean? Do I have to go?"

"If you don't go voluntarily, then I will have to arrest you," said Kirwan.

Hearing this, Elfrida dissolved into tears. "I've never been arrested, I never even got a parking ticket."

"It'll be all right," said Lucy, who didn't believe it for a minute. Poor Elfrida certainly had means and opportunity to kill Bobbi, and the police had a possible motive, thanks to Ross's statement. She didn't think for a moment that Elfrida would hurt a flea, but she knew that once the police had a viable suspect, they were unlikely to continue investigating the murder any further. That meant that the real murderer would likely get away scot-free.

"Hang in there," she told Elfrida, "this will all get sorted out."

"Come with me," said Kirwan, taking Elfrida's elbow. As Lucy watched, he kept hold of her arm as he led her across the kitchen to the door.

At least he didn't handcuff her, thought Lucy, when a white-suited technician entered, carrying a tool kit. "Are you Lucy Stone?" he asked.

"That's me," replied Lucy, holding up her plastic-wrapped hands.

"I'll bet you'll be glad to get this over with," said the tech, opening his case.

"You'd be right," said Lucy, who knew it was really just beginning.

Chapter Four

After the tech was finished with her, Lucy went straight to the kitchen sink, intending to wash her filthy hands.

"No!" he barked, stopping her as she reached for the faucet. "This is a crime scene."

Lucy knew there was a staff toilet nearby, but guessed that was also considered part of the crime scene. She was pondering her rapidly diminishing list of options, when he handed her an oversized tidy wipe in a packet. "Give it all back to me, the packet, too."

"Thanks," replied Lucy, grateful for the wipe, which left her hands clean and lightly lemon scented. Squaring her shoulders, she started the climb to the great hall. By the time she'd reached the top, she already had thought of two ways to help Elfrida.

The first involved Rachel, whose husband, Bob, was a lawyer with a busy local practice. Most of Bob's work involved real estate transfers and wills, but he occasionally took on criminal cases. She hoped this was one of those occasions.

Ducking her head and stepping into the great hall, Lucy was stunned at the change in atmosphere. The make-believe movie set had been replaced by grim reality: The room was now filled with gilt ballroom chairs, where the cast members sat glumly, waiting to be released by the police investigators. Most were still at least partially in costume, though most of the women had removed their confining head coverings, and eyeglass wearers had put their glasses back on. Almost everyone was staring at a cell phone and Lucy knew word must be spreading fast that something unusual was going on at Pine Point, even if the senders weren't sure exactly what was happening. Scanning the gathered crowd, Lucy noticed that a feudal sort of ranking had been preserved as Ross and the film's stars, including Juliette, were gathered on and around the throned dais intended for the nobles in the scene, while the extras and crew had spread themselves throughout the hall. She soon spotted Rachel, who was sitting near the opposite wall, along with Sue and Pam.

She hurried over to them, where she was greeted with questioning expressions.

"What's going on?" asked Pam.

"Who got hurt?" asked Rachel.

"When are they going to let us go home?" asked Sue.

Lucy leaned close, speaking in a low voice. "Bobbi Holden's dead from a stabbing and the cops have taken Elfrida into custody. . . ."

"Elfrida!" exclaimed Pam. "She wouldn't . . ."

"Shhh," said Lucy, looking anxiously over her

shoulder. "I don't think I'm supposed to say anything. Elfrida insists she's innocent, that Bobbi fell on the knife, but they're taking her to the station to be questioned. . . ."

"Say no more," said Rachel, reaching for her phone and calling Bob, who quickly agreed to go to the station and protect Elfrida's legal rights.

"What about Elfrida's kids?" asked Pam, voicing Lucy's second concern.

"Phyllis was going to give them supper, but I don't know if she's still there."

Pam quickly called Phyllis, learning that she had gone home after settling the younger kids in bed and leaving fifteen-year-old Angie in charge. When she learned that Elfrida was detained by the police, she agreed to go right back to the kids for the night, if necessary.

"Let's hope it doesn't come to that," said Pam, speaking into the phone, but including the others in the conversation.

"Whatever happens, we'll cope," said Sue, who had been a preschool teacher and was still a part owner of Little Prodigies Child Care Center. "The kids come first."

"That's right," agreed Lucy. Now that the situation seemed to be under control, she was suddenly exhausted, completely drained of energy.

"Here, sit down," said Rachel, shoving a chair under her as she began to sag.

"So you've all been here this entire time?" asked Lucy, trying to pull herself together.

"Yeah," said Rachel. "Willis followed you and Ross downstairs and came right back up, locking everyone into the hall. He had some guys, estate workers I guess, bring in the chairs and we've been waiting. We're supposed to be able to leave once we give our contact info to the police, but so far nobody's come to collect it."

"They're shorthanded tonight," said Lucy, with a yawn. "The chief said the state police were delayed."

Lucy had no sooner spoken than she spotted state police detective Lieutenant Horowitz stepping into the hall, dressed as usual in an ill-fitting gray suit, and accompanied by two uniformed troopers. He looked tired, and Lucy guessed he'd had a long day. He paused, allowing a few minutes for the crowd to become aware of their presence. When the room was relatively silent, he cleared his voice.

Horowitz began by introducing himself, then went on to thank everyone for waiting. "I'm sorry about the delay, but I'm afraid it was unavoidable. As you may or may not know, we have had a suspicious death here at Pine Point."

A collective gasp from the crowd was followed by a buzz as people wondered aloud who had died.

"I am not at liberty to identify the deceased, as the family has not yet been notified."

There was a stir among the elite group gathered on the dais, and Lucy noticed Chris Waters take Juliette's hand. She was clinging to him, obviously deeply shaken, until Ross turned in their direction and she quickly snatched her hand away. Ross glared briefly at Chris, then turned his attention to Lieutenant Horowitz.

"It's getting late and there's no reason for us to detain you good people any longer," said Horowitz. "We will need to get names and contact information from all of you, but if you will simply form a line here, along the side of the room, the officers will have you out of here as quickly as possible. Thanks for your cooperation."

Horowitz left, ducking his head as he went down the stairs, and one of the uniformed officers took his place. "I'm Corporal Terhune, my colleague is Corporal Keller. You can expedite this process by having your ID ready, business cards, library cards, anything with your name printed on it. So let's get started."

The group shuffled across the room to form the requested line, many people leaned against the wall in obvious exhaustion. The line moved quickly, thank goodness, and Lucy and her friends were soon free to go home. She paused at the doorway and took a last look at the ruined set. Juliette was still sitting on the throne, all alone, a shimmering sight in gold brocade, with long blond hair. She was idly spinning a slim gold diadem on her fingers.

Stepping outside, Lucy walked down the driveway with her friends, losing them one by one as they reached their cars. She'd been late and her car was at the very end of the driveway, and as she walked along, she found she couldn't forget that image of Juliette.

It was almost iconic, she thought, remembering how alone Juliette had seemed when her beloved great-grandmother Vivian Van Vorst was dying. Juliette was not the only member of that family, but she had seemed to be the only one untouched by scandal as VV's children and grandchildren schemed and plotted to inherit the aged matriarch's vast fortune. In the end, though, Juliette survived a brutal attack in a parking garage and vanquished the greedy relations. She provided loving care for

VV and eventually became the well-deserved inheritor of the disputed fortune. But now, it seemed to Lucy as she clicked her key fob and watched her car light up, that Juliette's life had taken an unfortunate turn. Whatever had the beautiful model and wealthy heiress ever seen in someone like Ross Rocket? What had possessed her to link her fortune to his? That was the question that Lucy was pondering as she checked the interior of the car, reassuring herself that no carjacker lurked inside. That's when she noticed the box of Christmas presents for Toby's family, which she'd forgotten to mail. First thing tomorrow, she promised herself, as she made her way through the night to her home on Red Top Hill.

According to the clock on the dashboard, it was nearly eleven o'clock, but when Lucy rounded the curve and her house came into view, she was surprised to see that every window was illuminated. This was very unusual, as she and Bill were early risers who went to bed by ten, and the girls were usually either out or in their bedrooms, studying.

Even odder, when she pulled into the driveway, she was met by Libby, the family's Labrador, who was loose in the yard. Libby jumped up to greet her when she got out of the car, and Lucy happily scratched her behind the ears. "I'm happy to see you, too," she crooned, "but what are you doing outside this time of night?"

It was a worrisome development and Lucy held tight to the dog's collar as she approached the house. She had heard of home invasions and was fearful that something was not right, especially after she noticed a strange car parked some distance from the house. The dark sedan was partly concealed by a bushy fir tree, which seemed suspicious to Lucy. If they had unexpected company, why would a guest park so far from the house?

She seriously considered calling the police, which was the advice she had passed along from the police chief in numerous articles offering advice to women about staying safe when they sensed a dangerous situation. "If your gut tells you something's not right, trust your gut and give us a call," she remembered him saying, but considering the evening's events at Pine Point she figured the already short-staffed department would be hard-pressed to send an officer so far out of town. And then, when it turned out that Zoe or Sara had let the dog out and forgotten to turn out the lights, she'd feel absolutely ridiculous.

So Lucy straightened her shoulders, took a deep breath, and, still holding tight to Libby's collar, mounted the stairs to the porch. The gingham curtain on the glass panel in the kitchen door, which was usually pulled to the side, was tightly drawn tonight and blocked any view of the interior, so she said a quick little prayer and turned the knob. She opened the door and was immediately confronted by a snarling pit bull mix. There was no mistaking that bulldog snout, tiny cropped ears, thick neck, and muscular shoulders.

Libby was straining against her collar, eager to defend her turf from this intruder, and it was all Lucy could do to hang on to her. Seeing no option except retreat, she stepped back outside and pulled the door closed just as the growling pit bull leaped forward and slammed into it. This time, she decided, she really had to call for help, and was reaching for her phone, when the door opened and she was greeted by the smiling face of her grown son, Toby.

"Toby!" she exclaimed, throwing herself on him and hugging him for all he was worth. Toby lived in Alaska, with his wife, Molly, and their son, Patrick. Lucy hadn't seen them in over a year. "What are you doing here?" she asked, noticing her son had started growing a beard, like his father's.

"They came for Christmas," said Bill, stepping into the kitchen. He was followed by Molly and a very sleepy Patrick, as well as Sara and Zoe.

"They wanted to surprise you," said Zoe, smiling from ear to ear.

"They even hid their rental car," said Sara.

"Well, I was sure surprised," admitted Lucy, distributing hugs and kisses. "I guess you brought your dog?"

"That's Skittles," said Molly, who'd cut her hair short in what Lucy thought was a rather unbecoming style. "We couldn't leave him behind, so we brought him. He's a bit wound up from being in the crate on the plane."

"You don't mind having an extra dog, do you?" asked Toby. "I'll put him down in the cellar for the night."

"Skittles is my best friend," Patrick said as Lucy hugged him for the second time.

"Mind? Of course not," lied Lucy, who was wondering how they were going to manage two large dogs: Skittles was clearly aggressive, and Libby was determined to defend her home and people. "I'm just so happy to see you all." And a good thing, she thought, that she'd forgotten to mail that package.

"Well, now that Grandma's home, I think it's time for you to go to bed," said Molly, speaking to

Patrick and giving a nod toward the back stairs, which led from the kitchen to the second-floor bedrooms.

"Is everybody settled? Where's everybody sleeping?" asked Lucy.

"Patrick's got Toby's old bedroom, and Molly and Toby have the sleep sofa in the family room," said Bill. "You weren't here and that seemed best all 'round."

"Poor Patrick's beat, but he didn't want to go to bed before you got home," said Toby, ruffling his son's hair. "What took you so long?"

"Lots of retakes," said Lucy, unwilling to spoil the happy family reunion. "I'll tuck Patrick in," she offered, leading her grandson up the stairs.

Chapter Five

Next morning, Lucy woke up early, feeling like a little kid on Christmas morning. Her grandson was actually here in the house, not far away in Alaska, and she didn't have to worry about rogue polar bears or wandering glaciers. Here he was safe and sound, under her protective eye. Except, she realized, as she threw back the covers and wiggled her feet into her slippers, for the dogs. She certainly didn't trust Skittles for one minute, and even sweet and docile Libby would fight to defend herself and her people.

The empty bed and the sound of running water indicated that Bill was already up and showering in the upstairs bath, which Lucy knew could mean it would be unavailable for quite some time. She padded quietly downstairs to the kitchen, where she realized Libby was not in her usual place. Checking out the window, she saw the Lab was in her fenced kennel and assumed Bill had taken her out earlier.

She then visited the powder room, and when she emerged, she found Patrick seated at the breakfast table in his superhero pajamas.

"Good morning," she said, smiling ear to ear and ruffling his bed-head hair. "Did you sleep well?"

"Yes," he answered, rubbing his eyes, "but I'm real hungry."

Sweeter words had never been uttered, thought Lucy. The boy was hungry and she was a grandma with a well-stocked pantry. "What would you like for breakfast?"

"I usually have pancakes. I can toast them myself."

Frozen pancakes, thought Lucy, the one thing I don't have. She checked the cupboard for a box of Aunt Jemima, but didn't have that, either. That meant she'd have to make them from scratch, which she considered a major project, best undertaken on the weekend. "How about French toast?" she suggested, offering simpler options. "Or scrambled eggs?"

"Eeeuw," said Patrick, curling his lip. "I only like pancakes, and I watch *Scooby-Doo* while I eat them."

My goodness, thought Lucy, shocked at the idea. When her kids were little, the family ate a well-balanced, nutritious breakfast together at the kitchen table. It was only when the kids started high school and had demanding schedules and picky diets that they began foraging for themselves. "Oh, dear. The TV's in the family room, and I think your mom and dad are still asleep in there," she told him.

"Don't you have another TV?"

"No," said Lucy, unable to resist the temptation

to pry into her son's personal life. "How many do you have?"

"Four. I watch *Scooby* on the one in the kitchen."

A TV in the kitchen! Lucy was amazed. "Well, kiddo, I think TV's out, but I guess I can make you some pancakes. Do you like blueberries in them?" she asked, thinking of the wild berries she was hoarding in her freezer that were such a treat.

"Plain," said Patrick, in a rather firm voice that Lucy didn't think was appropriate in one so young, especially when speaking to his grandmother.

"I think you forgot the magic word," she said, employing a tactic she had frequently used with her kids.

"Magic word?" Patrick was puzzled. "What magic word?"

"Why, *please,* of course."

"So *please* is the magic word. What does it do?"

"It makes things happen," said Lucy, who was beginning to get annoyed despite herself. "If you want plain pancakes, you say, 'May I please have plain pancakes?' and then I just might make them for you."

"Don't you have frozen ones? They're the only ones I like."

"Okay," said Lucy, becoming aware that Skittles was scratching at the cellar door, demanding to get out. "Okay, let's start over. Do you want Cheerios or Raisin Bran?"

"Don't you have Cocoa Puffs?"

"No." Fearful that the dog would start barking and wake the sleepers, Lucy opened the door and Skittles came charging into the kitchen, running straight for the porch door. "It's Cheerios or Raisin Bran, period."

She reached for the leash that was hanging on its usual hook and attempted to attach it to Skittles' collar, but the dog slunk backward, out of reach. Lucy lunged, making a second try, but the dog reacted with a low, rumbling growl. What to do? She couldn't let the creature run loose in the yard, it might run off into the woods and get lost. Or worse, it might attack some jogger or tangle with a wild animal, like a deer or coyote, maybe even a black bear.

"Back you go," she said, opening the cellar door and instructing the beast in the firmest voice she could manage.

In response, Skittles lifted his leg and peed on the porch door.

Disgusted, Lucy opened the door to the family room, and Skittles bounded inside, eager to greet Molly and Toby. Lucy poured some Cheerios in a bowl, added milk, and set it in front of Patrick. Then she peeled off a long strip of paper towels, grabbed the spray cleaner, and got to work on the door.

Bill, freshly showered and dressed, found her on her hands and knees, scrubbing harder than absolutely necessary. "What happened?"

"Skittles peed on the door," said Patrick, giggling and dribbling milk down his chin.

"Where is he now?"

"I put him in the family room with Molly and Toby," admitted Lucy, getting to her feet.

"Won't he wake them up?"

Lucy actually hoped that was the case, but figured that was one thought best kept to herself. "I didn't know what else to do. He wouldn't let me take him out on the leash, and he wouldn't go back downstairs. . . ."

"Right." Bill poured two cups of coffee, one for himself and one for Lucy. "Here. Have some coffee and we'll figure this out."

Lucy sank into a chair at the kitchen table and wrapped her hands around the mug of coffee. Bill toasted some English muffins, poured glasses of juice, and joined her and Patrick at the table. This was better, thought Lucy, thinking that Patrick looked a lot like his father looked when he was a little boy, seated at this very table.

They were finishing breakfast when a rumpled Toby appeared with Skittles. He grabbed a parka from the hooks by the door and pulled it on over his pajamas, stuffed his feet into Bill's yard shoes, and let the dog outside, unleashed but insisting that he wouldn't go far. "He's trained to come when I whistle," he claimed as he ducked out the door.

Bill and Lucy were doubtful, and Bill decided to take Libby to work with him in his truck, which he sometimes did to have company when he was working alone. When Toby returned with a slobbering and excited Skittles, Bill suggested that he make use of the fenced kennel for the beast after he left with Libby.

"Thanks, Dad," responded Toby, availing himself of Libby's kibble to fill Lucy's favorite spatterware mixing bowl, "but Molly doesn't believe in confining Skittles. It was bad enough having to crate him for the plane."

"Well, just warning you, the town has a strict animal control regulation," said Bill, watching as the dog began gulping down the food. "If he gets in trouble, they'll put him down."

"Don't worry, Dad. Skittles won't get in trouble."

"Right," murmured Lucy, giving Bill a good-bye kiss. Then, passing child care duties off to Toby, she went upstairs to get dressed for work. She left somewhat reluctantly, wishing she could spend the day with Patrick, perhaps taking him ice-skating on Blueberry Pond or going to see the Christmas greens and decorations for sale at Macdonald's Farm Stand. But that was not to be, she thought somewhat resentfully, because she had to work.

As she drove the familiar route to the *Pennysaver* office, she reviewed the previous evening's events, preparing herself for a busy deadline day. When she arrived, setting the little bell on the office door jangling, she realized Phyllis had had a much rougher night than she had. The receptionist had dark circles under her eyes, she'd forgotten to wear her dangly Christmas-tree-light earrings, and her pink sweater didn't match her orange hair.

"Tough night?" asked Lucy, in a sympathetic voice, as she took off her jacket and hung it on the coat stand.

"You could say that, but it was the morning that really got out of hand. Honestly, I don't know how Elfrida manages to get all five kids up and fed and dressed for school."

"What do you mean? Didn't Elfrida come home?"

"No. The cops are still keeping her."

"That's not good," said Lucy.

"Tell me about it," said Phyllis. "So we missed

the school bus, but I managed to get the younger kids to school before the bell. Angie was late for high school, of course, but I told her to say there's been a family emergency and maybe she won't have to stay for detention. Wilf is pitching in and he'll meet the kindergarten bus and give little Arthur lunch." She let out a long sigh. "Of course, all of this is beside the point. The real problem is, we don't know what's happening with Elfrida."

"Well, we're a newspaper," declared Ted, who was already seated at his desk, staring at his computer screen. "We're gonna find out, right, Lucy?"

"We sure are," said Lucy, managing an encouraging smile. "I bet the cops will realize their mistake and she'll be back home in time for lunch."

"At the latest," said Ted.

"I sure hope so," said Phyllis. "This is something completely new to me. I know what to do if somebody's sick or dies, but we've never had any experience of crime in the family." She drummed her fingers on her desk. "I can't help being mad at Elfrida for getting herself in this situation. Just when I thought she was pulling herself together, taking good care of the kids and working at a real job instead of all that waitressing and housecleaning, she goes and gets involved in a murder."

"I don't think she did it on purpose," said Lucy, settling herself at her desk and reaching for her phone to call Bob.

"Sorry, Lucy," said his receptionist, "he hasn't come into the office yet. I tried his cell, but my call went to voice mail. Why don't you try again in a little while?"

"Thanks, I'll do that," said Lucy, going on to call

the district attorney, Phil Aucoin. There her call went straight to voice mail, which turned out to be full.

With a sinking feeling that things were not going well for Elfrida, she decided to try calling Officer Barney Culpepper, hoping he might be willing to share some inside information.

Her friend Barney, as it turned out, was being unusually cagey. "Sorry, Lucy, but I can't talk, I'm, uh, I'm on my way to the senior center to talk about charity scams during the holidays. Hey, do you want to cover it? It's good information. . . ."

"I'll have to get back to you on that," said Lucy. "I'm on deadline today."

"Oh, okay." Barney sounded disappointed. "Give me a call anytime."

"Will do," said Lucy, hanging up. She looked at Ted, and he nodded back, getting her unspoken message: No news, in this case, was decidedly not good news.

"Why don't you make a coffee run, Lucy," said Ted, "and get some donuts, too. I think we could all use a little sugar-carbo-caffeine lift."

"Good idea," she said, hopping to her feet, grabbing her coat, and hurrying out the door, avoiding Phyllis's questioning look.

Lucy enjoyed the short walk to Jake's Donut Shack, which was perched above the town cove parking lot. Most of the stores on Main Street were decorated for Christmas and there were little Christmas trees attached to every other light pole.

Jake's had the usual silver Christmas tree set out on the porch, and the music system was playing a selection of corny carols about grandmas run over by reindeer and the Hawaiian way of saying "Merry

Christmas." Lucy hummed along while she waited her turn at the counter, trying to decide whether she should get the eggnog donuts, or the chocolate-mint ones. In the end she opted for the plain home-style ones and regular coffees, figuring this was no time to experiment.

She was at the door, where she encountered Officer Sally Kirwan, making the coffee run for the police department. Lucy had recently written a feature story about the department's only female officer and figured she had some leverage, so she asked what was happening with Elfrida.

"Oh, Lucy, I'm not supposed to say anything, and this is completely off the record, but I know you work with Phyllis and she must be going out of her mind. . . ."

"You said it," encouraged Lucy.

"Well, the lab checked the knife for fingerprints and there were only two sets, Elfrida's and Bobbi's."

"That's to be expected, right?" countered Lucy. "They both worked in the kitchen and used the knife."

"That's not how the DA sees it," said Sally, whispering. "He's planning to charge Elfrida. The arraignment will probably be tomorrow, unless there are some new developments."

"I can't believe it," said Lucy, shocked to her core.

"Me either," said Sally, giving a shrug before stepping up to the counter.

The walk back to the office wasn't nearly as pleasant as the trip to the coffee shop, not least because she had to pause at the fire station as the town ambulance exited with lights flashing and siren blaring. Continuing on her way, Lucy didn't notice the sunshine or the festive decorations, but fretted instead about Elfrida. Should she tell Phyllis about the pending charges, or would it be better to wait, hoping that new evidence would emerge that vindicated Elfrida and implicated someone else?

That question was answered when she reached the *Pennysaver* office and Phyllis flew out, putting her coat on as she ran down the sidewalk to her car. Lucy stood there dumbstruck, holding the bag of donuts and the little cardboard tray with the coffees.

"Don't you want your coffee?" she yelled.

"No. I gotta run, it's Wilf," replied Phyllis, yanking open the car door and getting inside.

Lucy watched, horrified, as Phyllis pulled right out in front of a pickup truck, which swerved just in time and narrowly missed hitting her car. That didn't slow Phyllis down in the least. Lucy wondered if she'd even noticed the truck as she tore down the street, intent on reaching her husband.

"What's going on?" she asked Ted when she stepped into the office.

"Apparently, little Arthur left his bike on the porch and Wilf somehow got tangled up in it and fell. Rescue's on the way—"

"I saw the ambulance," interrupted Lucy.

"But now Phyllis has to meet the kindergarten bus and get to the hospital. I guess it never rains, but it pours."

"It's only gonna get worse," said Lucy, handing Ted a donut wrapped in a napkin and his paper cup of coffee. "Sally Kirwan told me, off the record, that the DA's going to charge Elfrida. The arraignment is tomorrow."

"Damn!" exclaimed Ted, burning his hand as he struggled to remove the plastic cap.

"Do you want ice for that?" Lucy asked as Ted stuck his finger in his mouth and sucked it.

"No. It's okay." He took a bite of donut, then slurped some coffee. "You know," he began, in a thoughtful tone, "I think our journalistic standards are slipping a bit here. We both care about Phyllis, and Elfrida, but they shouldn't be our focus. Bobbi Holden is the victim of a terrible crime, but we haven't given her, or her family, a thought. We've overlooked them while worrying about Elfrida, when for all we know the DA is right and she's a murderer."

Lucy chewed her lip thoughtfully while carefully prying the plastic lid off her coffee. "I don't believe Elfrida killed Bobbi, not for one minute, but I have to admit you've got a point. Bobbi's death is a tragedy that's going to affect a lot of people, and we need to address that."

"Good," said Ted, picking up his coffee. "You can get started on the obit. . . ."

"Me?" Lucy hated writing obituaries, since the job involved awkward and painful interviews with loved ones of the deceased.

"Yeah, you. You're much better at it than I am. People open up to a woman, you know."

Lucy sighed. "Ted, you know I have tremendous respect and admiration for you, but in this case you are a sexist pig."

"I know," he said, before popping the last bit of donut into his mouth.

Lucy glanced at the Seth Thomas clock that

hung on the wall above her desk and noticed that it was almost eleven. Deadline was twelve, so she had to get moving on the obit. Fortunately, she had Bobbi's mother's number in her Rolodex, because she'd done a story about her prize-winning recipe for Bird's Nest Pudding Pie. As she dialed the number, Lucy wished she was following up on that story, perhaps seeking an unusual holiday recipe.

The phone rang several times, and when it was answered, Lucy was relieved that the voice she heard belonged to someone much younger than Mrs. Holden. "Sorry, Lucy, but Auntie is too upset to come to the phone. I'm Nanette, Bobbi's cousin."

"Oh, Nanette, I'm so sorry about Bobbi. I know this is a difficult time for you all, but I would like to talk to you a bit about Bobbi and how you'd like her to be remembered."

"Oh, sure, Lucy. I know you'll write something nice."

Lucy swallowed hard, determined to set aside her early impression of Bobbi as an irresponsible prankster and to listen with an open mind. "So what was Bobbi like?" she began.

"We're cousins, you know. I'm about five years older, so I used to babysit for her sometimes, you know, when she was in elementary school and I was in high school. It was an easy job because all she wanted to do was watch TV. She was stagestruck at a really early age. I think it started when Aunt Harriet took her to see *Disney on Ice*. After that, she was always wearing princess costumes and singing songs from the movies. As soon as she could read, she got a subscription to *Entertainment Weekly*. I'm not kidding, she was a really advanced reader. When she got to high school, she joined the drama club. She starred in *Little Shop of Horrors*. She was in heaven when she got the job at Pine Point. She figured it was her big chance to break into show business. She was determined to catch the attention of a Hollywood insider who would recognize her talent, that's why she did all those practical jokes. To get attention."

"So she graduated from Tinker's Cove High School, did she go on to college?"

"Well, she got accepted at Emerson College in Boston, but she didn't get much financial aid, so she was working for a year to save up."

"I thought she was an unpaid intern on the movie," said Lucy.

"She was. She took a break from her job at the Queen Vic Inn so she could work on the movie. They were real nice about it."

"Now I need the names of survivors, family members."

"Well, there's her mother and father, Dick and Harriet Holden, my mom and dad, George and Sarah Walsh, me and my brother, Donald, and, oh, Nanny and Poppa, that's Stephen and Gloria Holden, and Grandma Walsh, her name is Audrey. I guess that's it."

"Well, if you think of something you want to add, just give me a call. I can usually put changes in until around three this afternoon."

"You've kind of got me thinking," said Nanette, her voice growing stronger. "I mean, I don't think that whoever did this should get off. It's a terrible thing and my whole family is devastated, especially Uncle Dick and Aunt Harriet. Bobbi was their only child, you know, and they adored her, you might

say they even spoiled her. That's not to say that Elfrida is the murderer, I know she's innocent until
proven guilty, but believe me, my whole family is
sure as heck determined that justice should be
done, and if she's charged, we'll do everything we
can to see she gets the maximum sentence."

Lucy knew that was no idle threat, as Harriet
Holden was a court stenographer, friendly with the
judges and attorneys at the county courthouse. It
was simply human nature that they would bend
over backward to support her through a difficult
time.

"Well, thanks for your help," said Lucy. "Once
again, I want to let you know how sorry I am for
your loss."

"Thanks," replied Nanette, with a little sniff.

After the call ended, Lucy turned to Ted.
"Bobbi's family is out for bear," she said.

"Can you blame them?" he asked.

"No, but I just hope they get the right bear, and
I'm not convinced it's Elfrida."

"Well, it's up to us to keep the pressure on and
make sure the cops don't miss something or someone. Right?"

"Right," said Lucy, vowing to make sure that no
stone was left unturned in the investigation. She
was going to do everything she could to figure out
who killed Bobbi, and she seriously doubted it was
Elfrida.

It was well past the noon deadline when the
week's issue of the *Pennysaver* finally went to press,
and Lucy was free for the remainder of the afternoon. Instead of heading home, however, she went
straight to the IGA to shop for groceries. She now
had two extra adults, a child who was a picky eater,

and a dog to feed, in addition to the usual crew. She zipped through the aisles, grabbing a gallon of milk, a couple of loaves of bread, a huge bag of dog kibble, salad fixings, potatoes, and a ham. Cruising past the frozen food, she threw in a couple of boxes of frozen pancakes.

Arriving home with her car full of groceries, Lucy was surprised to see Toby out in the yard, assembling a wire run for Skittles.

"What changed your mind?" she asked, watching as he perched on a ladder to screw in the hardware for the run on a corner of the porch. The coiled cable and remaining hardware were still in the package, lying on the ground.

"The dog officer stopped by," he said, looking down from his perch. "He saw Skittles out by the road and had some trouble trying to catch him. I don't know why he couldn't leave him be, it's not like Skittles was misbehaving, he was just kind of sniffing the mailbox post, but I guess that's against the law here in Maine."

"You know better than that, Toby," said Lucy, surprised at her son's attitude. "It's irresponsible to let a dog run loose, you can't predict what they'll do. What if Skittles got hit by a car? Or went after the mail carrier?"

"I guess you've got a point—but Molly's not going to like it."

"That's life," said Lucy. "Sometimes you've got to adapt."

"I'm not sure Molly got the memo," muttered Toby, grunting as he twisted the screwdriver. "Do you need help with the groceries?"

Lucy was surprised by the offer. "How'd you know I went shopping?"

"Just a hunch," he said, climbing down the ladder. "It's Wednesday, right?"

The spicy scent of chili met Lucy when she entered the kitchen, carrying a couple of bags of groceries. Sara was at the stove, stirring the pot, and Zoe was at the table, mixing up a batch of corn bread.

"Great idea, thanks for cooking," said Lucy, holding the door for Toby and the twenty-five-pound bag of dog chow he was carrying.

"We didn't think you'd mind," said Sara.

"And we found all the ingredients," said Zoe.

"Everybody likes chili," said Sara.

"Well, everybody except Patrick," said Toby.

"He can eat pancakes," said Lucy, flourishing a box before tucking it into the freezer.

Dinner was a lively affair, with all the family, except Elizabeth, gathered around the table. Lucy sent up a silent little prayer of thanks for her family, for their health, and for the dinner she didn't have to cook. Her eyes traveled around the long dining-room table, where Patrick sat between his two aunts on one side, Bill was at the opposite end, and Molly and Toby sat on the other side. She was overcome with gratitude and affection for them all. Even Skittles didn't seem so bad, now that he was restrained on the outside run.

She was spooning out seconds for Bill and Toby, when Molly put down her fork and dabbed her mouth with her napkin. "I guess I won't be getting meals like this in Germany."

"Germany? Are you all going to Germany?" asked Lucy, assuming that Toby had gotten a new job, or perhaps a fellowship of some sort, involving German fishery practices. "How wonderful for

Patrick to experience another culture, and maybe even learn German."

"Patrick's not going," said Molly. "I'm going to study German language and folk tales at Heidelberg. I'm actually flying out of Boston on the twenty-eighth."

Bill cast a concerned look at his son, who was staring at his plate. "Is this a separation?" he asked anxiously.

"Well, we'll be apart, but we'll still be married . . . ," offered Molly. Lucy noticed her daughter-in-law looked different, and it wasn't just the new hairstyle. It was the way she set her jaw, exhibiting a new, determined attitude.

"Patrick and I are going to be bachelors for a year," said Toby. "We're going to hunt and fish and play video games whenever we want."

"And I'm not gonna have baths anymore," said Patrick.

"Well, I'm not sure about that," said Toby.

Lucy was silent during this exchange, trying to understand why Molly would choose to leave her husband and son and go to Germany for a year. "Why, Molly, I didn't know you were interested in German folk tales," she finally said.

"I am, ever since I first read the Brothers Grimm," said Molly. "It's something I've wanted to do for a long time." She sighed, a long sigh, as if she was finally free of a terrible burden. "And more than that, I need some *me* time."

"Well," was all Lucy could say. She stared at the half-eaten servings of salad and chili and corn bread on her plate, picked up her fork, and put it back down. Suddenly she didn't seem to have any appetite.

Chapter Six

Next morning, Lucy couldn't wait to get together with her friends at Jake's to vent her frustration about Molly and the pit bull. As she drove down Red Top Hill, she wasn't sure which of the two creatures was most upsetting, but finally settled on Molly. Skittles, after all, was merely a dumb beast, but Molly had been blessed with understanding and a conscience, although Lucy definitely had doubts that her daughter-in-law had been listening to that still, small voice. At bottom, what she found most troubling was the effect Molly's departure would have on Toby and Patrick, and that's what she found herself saying when she joined her friends at their usual Thursday-morning table in Jake's Donut Shack.

"I'm terrified that this is the first step toward a divorce," she said as Norine filled her mug with coffee. "She can call it whatever she wants, a sabbatical or the junior year abroad she never got, or me time, but it's really just a separation." Lucy stared glumly into her mug, noticing the reflected light on the surface of the coffee.

"Usual all round?" asked Norine, who'd been serving the same choices to the friends for years: a sunshine muffin for Pam, yogurt and granola for Rachel, eggs and hash for Lucy, and black coffee for Sue. "Sure you don't want to try something solid for a change?" she asked Sue, pencil poised over her order pad, just in case.

"No thanks, not today," said Sue, who dodged the same question every week.

"I suppose you ate at home?" persisted Norine, narrowing her eyes.

"Actually, I did," admitted Sue, with a virtuous little nod. "I had a square of dark chocolate. It's supposed to be good for you."

"Chocolate for breakfast," scoffed Norine, rolling her eyes and marching off to the kitchen to deliver their order.

"You know what they say, eat dessert first," said Sue, with a naughty smile.

"I don't know if that's supposed to mean breakfast," said Lucy. "Not that I think little Patrick is eating any better. All he seems to want for breakfast are frozen pancakes, which he eats while watching TV." She took a sip of coffee and shook her head. "I really don't like the way things are going, and I don't understand why Toby isn't taking a stronger stand. He wasn't brought up to live like this—his whole attitude is very puzzling. Yesterday his nose was all out of joint because the animal control officer told him he couldn't let that pit bull run loose."

"I suppose things are different in Alaska," said Pam. "Things are probably freer, what with all that space."

"I have to agree with Lucy," said Sue, who was running a manicured finger around the rim of her coffee mug. "It's terribly rude to bring a dog along on a visit, unless you've cleared it in advance with your host."

"It sounds like Molly really loves the dog," said Pam, who was a sucker for anything with four legs. "And pit bulls are really unfairly maligned, they are awfully sweet dogs."

"It does make you wonder if Lucy's right and something is amiss in their marriage," said Rachel, who was a psychology major and never got over it. "This dog seems to represent masculinity and virility. . . ."

"Ohmigosh! You don't think Toby is, you know, having difficulties in the bedroom?" Lucy was horrified at the thought.

"It's definitely a possibility," said Rachel.

"He's much too young for that," said Pam. "I don't think anything's the matter. It sounds to me like Molly is just beginning to discover she's more than a wife and mother, and needs to develop her own interests and forge her own identity."

"That might present a real challenge to Toby," said Sue. "He might feel his masculinity is threatened."

"The male ego," said Lucy, thoughtfully. She remembered her mother's repeated warnings that a wife's first duty was to protect and preserve her husband's ego, advice that she'd thought was ridiculously old-fashioned.

"What about women? Aren't we supposed to have egos?" demanded Pam.

"Of course," said Rachel.

"Only occasionally," said Sue.

"I think I've misplaced mine. I'm going to have to look for it, and dust it off when I find it," said Lucy, getting laughs from the others as Norine arrived with their orders.

Lucy dug right in, and was stabbing her egg to let the yolk ooze over her hash, when her thoughts turned to Elfrida. "What's Bob got to say about Elfrida?" she asked Rachel. "They don't really have a case against her, do they?"

"Bob doesn't think so, but I guess the knife is pretty damning evidence, since it only has Elfrida's and Bobbi's fingerprints."

"A lot of people are in and out of that kitchen," said Lucy. "Anyone could have taken it, and there wouldn't be prints if they wore gloves."

"There's no smudges from gloves, though. Just the two sets of prints."

"Maybe it was an accident, like Elfrida claims," said Lucy.

Rachel picked up her muffin to take a bite, then reconsidered and put it back on the plate. "Bob says they will most likely arraign her today. He's hoping to get her out on bail."

Lucy's jaw dropped. "Are they really going to charge her with murder?"

"He's not sure of the charges, could be something lesser, like manslaughter."

"Golly," said Pam, stunned, and speaking for all of them. "Golly gee."

* * *

When Lucy got to the *Pennysaver* office later that morning, she found the door locked and the closed sign hanging in the window. After letting herself in and turning on the lights, she called Ted and discovered he was at the county courthouse.

"I'm staying here, waiting for the arraignment," he told her. "I need you to hold the fort at the office, since Phyllis is at Elfrida's place, taking care of Wilf and the kids."

"They ought to be at school now," said Lucy. "I'll give her a call."

The phone rang quite a few times and almost went to voice mail before Phyllis picked up the call. "Hello," she said, sounding breathless.

"It's me, Lucy. How are things going?"

"Under control, for the moment, since the kids are all at school," replied Phyllis. "Angie really stepped up and made sure they were dressed and even gave them breakfast—just cold cereal—but they all started the day with something in their tummies."

"How's Wilf doing?"

"Well, he had to have surgery, you know. They had to pin his leg together."

"Is he still in the hospital?"

"Are you kidding? They let him out yesterday with a bottle of pain meds. He's on the couch, pretty out of it and mostly dozing. I don't know how I'm going to manage later, though. He's got a follow-up with the orthopedist over in Gilead at noon, and little Arthur gets out of kindergarten at eleven-thirty."

"Don't worry, I'll fix something up. Toby's family is here for Christmas. . . ."

"You must be thrilled."

"Yeah," admitted Lucy, wishing she could actually spend some time with them. "It's a little crazy with such a full house, but I bet Patrick would enjoy a playmate for the afternoon."

"That'd be great, Lucy."

"I'll give Molly a call and get back to you."

"Good, 'cause I have to let the school know who's picking him up."

Lucy dialed Molly next, apparently catching her out running. "What is it?" she demanded, panting into the phone.

"Sorry to interrupt your run. It's just that my friend Phyllis needs some child care for her grandnephew and I thought it would be nice for Patrick to have someone to play with this afternoon. . . ."

"Are you crazy?" Molly's breaths were coming fast. "You want me to take care of somebody's grandnephew? What do you think I am? A day care center?"

Somewhat flummoxed, Lucy was quick to explain. "It's little Arthur, you know, Elfrida's little boy. He's a sweetheart."

"Elfrida!" Molly sounded like Queen Victoria being asked to receive one of the Prince of Wales's mistresses. "That slut! I can just imagine what her kid is like."

"Well, actually, Elfrida has really turned her life around. . . ."

"Then why can't she manage to arrange care for her child?"

"Well, she's in jail," confessed Lucy, realizing the gigantic flaw in her argument. "Not convicted, mind you, so we should consider her innocent. Actually, it's really just a big misunderstanding."

"No, Lucy." Molly was not about to yield. "I am

very careful about choosing Patrick's playmates and there is absolutely no way I will allow any child of Elfrida's anywhere near him."

Wow, thought Lucy. Not quite the reaction she expected. Of course, Molly did grow up in Tinker's Cove and had probably heard all sorts of gossip about Elfrida, probably from her parents. Jim Moskowitz was a successful insurance agent and his wife, Jolene, was very mindful of social distinctions.

Lucy's next call was to Sue. She didn't answer her phone, and since it was already ten past eleven, Lucy figured she'd better pick up Arthur herself. She called Phyllis as she closed the office and headed out to her car, asking her to alert the school.

"Oh, Lucy, you've got too much to do . . . ," protested Phyllis.

"It will be fine. I'll keep him with me at the office and you can pick him up on your way home from the doctor."

"Okay, thank you. You're a lifesaver."

"Nonsense, I'm just doing what anyone would do." Anyone, she realized, except her daughter-in-law.

Since it was lunchtime, Lucy decided to give Arthur a special treat and took him to the McDonald's out on Route 1, where he made short work of a Happy Meal. After he'd finished eating, he insisted on keeping the box, so he wouldn't lose the little toy figure that came with the meal. This was a child who was familiar with fast food, and knew how to protect his treasures from his siblings.

Back at the office, she settled him at the big

table in the morgue, supplying him with copy paper, pens, and colored markers she raided from the supply closet. Amazingly enough, she also found a box of Legos stashed there, probably donated for the holiday toy drive and somehow missed when the toys were packed up and sent to the food pantry to be distributed to needy families.

With Arthur happily occupied, she was able to work, planning the next issue's news budget. The investigation into Bobbi's death would undoubtedly be the front-page story and she decided to call Ted for an update from the courthouse.

"How's it going?" she asked, keeping her voice low so Arthur wouldn't hear. She figured Phyllis had probably been censoring the news, and had probably only told him that his mother was away, but would be home soon.

"Nothing yet," said Ted. "I guess the DA can't figure out what he wants to do."

"That's probably good," said Lucy. "Maybe they'll drop the whole thing."

"Uh, doesn't look like it," said Ted. "I see Bob's in the courtroom and so is the DA. Gotta go."

"Darn!" exclaimed Lucy, forgetting the little pitcher with big ears in the next room.

"Is something wrong, Lucy?" asked Arthur.

"No. Everything's okay." She went into the morgue to check on him, wondering if he needed a snack, or wanted to use the toilet, and saw he was busy drawing a picture. "Can I see your drawing?" she asked, looking over his shoulder.

"That's really nice," she said, recognizing the drawing as a portrait of his mother, complete with curly blond hair and blue eyes.

"It's Mom," he said, completing the picture by drawing a series of thick vertical black lines across his mother's face. "She's in jail."

Lucy was floored, she didn't know what to say. And how did he know about his mother's arrest anyway? "Who told you that?" she asked.

"Natalie. She's in my class." He paused. "Is it true?"

Lucy's heart was breaking for the little boy, with his Spider-Man T-shirt and freshly cut hair. She sat next to him and looked him in the eye. "It's true, but it's a mistake. Your mom didn't do anything bad, and lots of people are helping her."

"So they'll let her out of jail?"

"Yes. They'll let her out."

"When?"

"I don't know," said Lucy, wrapping him in a big hug.

That evening, Lucy was back on set. Ross wasn't satisfied with the previous day's shooting and was doing it over, barking orders to everyone and trying to hurry things along. Lucy had arrived late and, after quickly changing into her costume, was one of the last extras to go to the makeup area set up in the morning room. No one was there except one of the costume girls, who was chatting with the makeup guy.

"Where have you been?" asked the makeup man, choosing a bottle of foundation. "The call was for six o'clock sharp."

"Busy day," she replied, noticing the name Jimmy was tattooed on his wrist. "Are you Jimmy?"

"No. I'm Peter. Jimmy's my little boy. He's three."

"I bet he's adorable. I'm Lucy, by the way," she said, raising her face so he could apply the foundation. "So what's the mood around here? Are people upset after last night?"

"Subdued is the word, I guess," said Peter. He turned to the costume girl. "What do you think, Ray?"

"Well, I don't want to speak ill of the dead, but I've got to admit that things are a lot calmer without Bobbi's cute little pranks. She loved to switch the labels on the costumes, you know, and it was a real pain to keep things straight. One day she hid King Arthur's crown and it took hours before we found it hidden underneath his throne."

"Yeah," he agreed, applying eyebrow pencil to Lucy's brows. "She mixed up my palette a couple of times, and it was pretty frustrating to reach for a brown eyeliner and find it was blue."

"Did Bobbi have any real conflicts with anyone?" Lucy asked as Peter brushed her apple cheeks with dark powder, making her look somewhat gaunt.

"Make that everyone," said Ray, with a snort. "Ross isn't exactly calm and collected, if you know what I mean. . . ."

"He doesn't have it together, doesn't have a clue," said Peter.

"So every time one of Bobbi's little pranks caused confusion or delay, he'd absolutely lose it and blast whoever the poor victim was, even though it wasn't their fault at all."

"I saw that myself," said Lucy. "He was furious with Elfrida, the cook, about that Yule log cake on the banquet table, but she had nothing to do with it. It was Bobbi."

"Right." Peter put down the makeup brush.

"You're done, and I gotta say, you look very fifteenth-century."

"Thanks," said Lucy, hopping down from the stool she'd been perched on and hurrying outside to the lawn. The fake snow had been freshly touched up, erasing the damage caused by the previous night's comings and goings. It was almost as if Bobbi's death had never happened, thought Lucy, joining the assembled group of villagers.

The lights came on, Ross called action, and the extras began trudging toward the great hall, where the leaded-glass windows were glowing with light. As before, the scene was filmed by cameramen with portable cameras, who circled around the edges of the carolers, and Lucy found it was almost possible to forget this was all make-believe and to feel as if she were in another time and place.

The lusty lads toting the Yule log tapped it against the oaken door with its enormous wrought-iron hinges, the door flew open magically, and they proceeded into the hall, singing their hearts out. The lighting had been changed for this second take and the scene inside the hall took Lucy's breath away: Torches on the garlanded walls blazed brightly, the richly garbed nobles were splendidly arrayed on the dais, and a fire was glowing in the enormous stone hearth.

The scene had been rehearsed numerous times and Lucy knew exactly where she was supposed to stand, right in the middle of the assembled yeomanry who were gathered by the fire, grateful for its warmth after coming in from the cruel cold outside. Someone, or maybe several people, had gotten mixed up, however, and she found herself in the wrong place, right in front of the fireplace at the very moment the Yule log was thrown onto the hearth, releasing a spray of flaming cinders.

Determined to carry on like a showbiz trouper, Lucy ignored the uncomfortable heat and raised her voice in the ancient carol. "'Let none come into this hall, But that some meryment they bringe,'" she sang, enjoying herself. "'If they say they cannot singe, some other sport then they muste bringe,'" she continued, when she was suddenly thrown to the ground. She struggled to raise herself, but found she was unable to resist the strong arms that were rolling her on the hard stone floor. People were shrieking and she was practically smothered by a rug that was thrown over her; then dazed and confused, she was helped to her feet by Chris Waters.

"Oh, Lucy, what a close call!" exclaimed Rachel, hugging her.

"What happened?" she asked, rubbing her shoulder, which was beginning to ache.

"Your skirt caught on fire," said Sue. "Look!"

It was true, she discovered, when she looked over her shoulder and felt the coarsely woven fabric, now charred and partly burned away.

"Chris Waters saved you," said Pam. "Lucky you. A lot of women wouldn't mind rolling around with him."

"It wasn't as much fun as you might think," said Lucy, looking in vain for the actor so she could thank him. Her attention was caught instead by Ross Rocket, who was berating his assistant, a young woman in a white shirt and black jeans, with her dark hair pulled back into a neat ponytail.

"How do you explain this?" he was demanding, pointing to a chalk mark on the floor.

"I can't explain it," she replied, pointing to a stone flag several feet away. "I put the mark there." She paused. "Somebody changed it, and I suspect she's no longer with us."

"So that's how it's going to be? Every time somebody screws up, it's going to be poor Bobbi's fault? Well, I don't buy it."

The girl bowed her head in submission. "Okay, whatever you say, Ross. You're the boss."

"Darn right. So make the correct mark so we can salvage something from this disaster."

The girl bent down, chalk in hand, while Ross approached Lucy. "Are you okay?" he asked.

"I'm a little sore," admitted Lucy.

"You're gonna need a new costume," he said, sounding as if the incident was her fault. "You'll have to sit this scene out and we'll get you fitted tomorrow, okay?"

Before she could answer, he was striding off, taking his usual position at the edge of the set. "Okay, let's move on. Jolly yeoman singing, nobles beaming. Places, everyone."

Feeling somewhat shaky, Lucy seated herself in one of the director's chairs. She intended to leave and go home as soon as she felt stronger, but found herself watching the filming with interest. Until now, she'd been one of the actors, albeit only an extra, but she'd been focused on the demands of her part. Making sure she was in the right place and singing the right song had required a lot of concentration. But now, she was a bystander, fascinated by the process she was witnessing.

When she watched a movie, the scenes unfolded seamlessly, but that was not how the filming actually worked, at least not under the direction of

Ross Rocket. He interrupted the scene numerous times, usually to bark instructions to his wife, Juliette. As for Juliette, she didn't seem irritated when he repeatedly corrected her, and she maintained a professional attitude. In fact, her eyes rarely strayed from Ross, watching him obsessively as he interacted with other cast and crew members. Lucy hadn't noticed this before, but Juliette seemed to grow anxious whenever Ross consulted with the script girl. She wasn't exceptionally pretty, thought Lucy, but she was petite and bouncy, and wore tight tops that revealed quite a bit of cleavage. Even more of that impressive cleavage was revealed when she and Ross put their heads together and bent over the script.

A beautiful model like Juliette would seem to have little to fear from a less attractive woman, but Lucy knew that every woman was insecure about something. Juliette had long, glossy hair that Pantene claimed was "touchable"; she had wide-spaced hazel eyes with long lashes that Maybelline insisted were "voluptuous"; Revlon advised that any woman could appear to have "amazing" cheekbones, just like Juliette's, if they bought the company's amazing new bronzer. But Juliette was also whippet thin and nearly six feet tall, which looked great on a fashion show runway, but probably wasn't ideal when she was alongside Ross, who was a good six inches shorter.

Lucy's thoughts were abruptly interrupted when Ross finally shouted, "Cut," and dismissed everyone for the night. The schedule for the next day would be online first thing in the morning, he added, instructing everyone to check it and issuing dire warnings to latecomers.

Lucy had changed out of the damaged costume and was then heading toward her parked car when she noticed Chris Waters, also walking down the driveway.

"Chris!" she called, hurrying after him. "I just want to thank you. You probably saved my life."

"Are you okay? No burns?" he asked, those big brown eyes clouded with concern.

"I think I'll be a little sore tomorrow," she replied, shrugging. "That was quite a workout."

"I'm sorry, but I thought halfway wasn't good enough. All I could think about was getting the fire out."

"Believe me, I'm grateful," she said as they resumed walking along the tree-lined drive, which was lit by old-fashioned lanterns on posts. "It could have been so much worse."

"I'm just glad I was there. I wish I'd been there for Bobbi, you know?"

"Some people on set don't seem very upset about her death," said Lucy, remembering Ray and Peter's conversation.

"I know, and it upsets me. Bobbi was a nice kid and she didn't deserve to die just because she liked to get attention. That's what it was all about, you know. She wanted to be noticed."

"You're very perceptive," Lucy said as they approached her car.

"In this business, it's a curse," he said. "I wish I could be more like Juliette and let it all go, like the song. Not get bothered."

Lucy leaned against her car, fingering the keys in her pocket. "I'm not exactly a pro, but Ross doesn't seem to know what he's doing, does he? It's his first attempt at directing, right?"

"It's a shambles, that's what it is. I can't believe I let my agent rope me into this disaster. I could be home in New York, trimming the Christmas tree with my husband. . . ."

"You're married?" asked Lucy. "Millions of hearts will be broken if the news gets out."

"My agent works very hard to keep my marriage, and the fact that I'm gay, a big secret," admitted Chris. "It drives Karl crazy."

"Karl's your husband?"

"Yeah." Chris smiled. "He's a doctor. He doesn't like it that we can't be honest about our relationship."

"Well, I think he's a lucky man. Thanks again," said Lucy, clicking her fob and unlocking the car door. "See you tomorrow."

"Righto," said Chris. "We've had murder and fire, what can possibly go wrong tomorrow? Flood, famine, pestilence?"

"I sure hope not," said Lucy, climbing into her car and starting the engine.

Chapter Seven

When Lucy got home and mounted the porch steps, carrying a bag of last-minute stocking stuffers she'd picked up at the chain drugstore, she thought she glimpsed Bill through a gap in the window curtains, sitting in his usual spot at the kitchen table. He often sat there before heading to bed, catching up on the sports pages of the newspaper while eating a late-night snack. But when she stepped inside, she saw it wasn't Bill who was chewing on that chicken leg, it was Toby.

"Gosh," she said, with a big smile, "for a moment I thought you were your father."

"It's probably the beard."

Lucy set the bag down on a chair, hung her jacket on a coat hook, and crossed the kitchen, standing beside him and ruffling his brown hair. "More than that, I think," she said. "It was the way you're sitting, just like he does."

"Must be the genes," he said.

"Or the blue jeans," quipped Lucy, repeating a family joke.

"You try to escape, you even go to Alaska, but you can't escape those twenty-three pairs of little chromosomes. . . ."

Toby was smiling, but Lucy wasn't entirely convinced he was joking. "Some people would say you won the genetic lottery. You're tall, good-looking, intelligent. You've got twenty-twenty eyesight and you didn't even need braces. And don't forget, you're a white male with all the privileges that entails."

Toby groaned. "I know, Mom. I've heard quite a lot about that lately."

Lucy thought he probably had, and decided to change the subject. "So what did you have for supper?" she asked, opening the fridge and peering inside. "I didn't get any dinner."

"I don't know what they had here, we ate with Molly's folks. You sure are busy," observed Toby. "We came all this way, thinking you'd be thrilled to spend Christmas with Patrick. He's your only grandson after all."

Lucy took out a promising-looking plastic container and popped the lid, discovering some leftover chili. "I am thrilled, but I've got a lot going on right now," she said, wishing she'd had some advance notice of the visit. "I'll have more time this weekend, I promise," she said, putting the container in the microwave. "I can't believe Christmas is almost here."

"Don't do that," warned Toby. "The plastic poisons the food."

"I'll risk it." Lucy pushed the start button. "Hasn't killed me yet."

"You always were one to live dangerously." Toby leaned back in his chair, just like Bill often did.

Lucy watched the plastic dish go round and round in the microwave. "I don't go looking for trouble," she finally said as the machine beeped. She carefully removed her dinner, using a pot holder, and carried it over to the table, setting the hot container on a magazine that happened to be lying there. Then she poured herself a glass of wine and sat down, prepared to eat her late supper. She took a sip of wine, swallowed, and next thing she knew, the thought that she'd been repressing all day just popped out. "Do you really think it's a good idea for Molly to go to Germany?"

He got up and went to the fridge, grabbed a can of beer, and popped the tab as he returned to the table. "Don't you?" he asked, then tipped the can and took a big gulp.

"Well, since you asked, I don't think it's a good idea for a couple to go their separate ways."

"What if it was me, called to save the right whales? Would you feel the same way? Or what if the country was attacked and I joined the army? Folks in the military are routinely separated for long periods."

"That's different. Molly is not saving right whales, or the country, for that matter." Lucy took a big spoonful of chili.

"That's harsh. Molly sacrificed a lot so I could go back to school. She even put up with me switching majors, which meant she had to support me for an extra semester, and then grad school, too. And when this Alaska job came up, she didn't hesitate for a moment. She's always been there for me, and now that Patrick's in school, she feels it's her turn." He drank again. "How can I say no?"

"But you always stayed together," protested Lucy. She suspected Toby was merely repeating Molly's argument, which he'd heard over and over until he finally capitulated.

"I know," he said, sounding rather wistful. "We were fortunate to be able to do that, but the program Molly wants happens to be in Heidelberg."

"There's nothing here in the U.S.?"

"Sure, but not in Alaska. I'd have to give up my job and Patrick would have to change schools, and it just seemed better for us to stay put for the time being. And if she has to go off on her own, she figured she might as well get the best course of study, which is definitely Heidelberg."

"I see," admitted Lucy, scraping the last of the chili from the bowl. "But are you sure there isn't more to it than that?"

Toby set his beer down on the table. "Like what, Mom?"

Lucy searched for the best way to say what she was worried about, and it finally came to her. "Oh, you know. My mother used to call it the seven-year itch?"

Toby sat for a moment, then laughed. "Mom, you're too much," he said, getting up and shoving his chair under the table. "Too much," he repeated, bounding up the kitchen stairs.

But you didn't answer my question, thought Lucy, as she tucked the empty container and wineglass into the dishwasher. Didn't really answer it at all, she thought, picking up the bag of gifts and taking it upstairs for wrapping.

* * *

Phyllis was sitting at her desk behind the reception counter when Lucy got to work on Friday, but she wasn't quite her usual, colorful self. There was no bright sweater today, only a muddy brown turtleneck, and her hair, which she often colored with temporary dye to match her outfit, was just her natural light brown sprinkled with gray. The lack of color hadn't extended to the reading glasses perched on her nose, however, which were rainbow striped.

When the little bell on the door jangled, she turned to greet Lucy, but there was no smile. "Hi" was all she said.

"What's up?" asked Lucy, taking in this subdued version of Phyllis.

"Elfrida got bail, so she's back home, but she's got a monitoring bracelet and has to stay in the house, except for doctor appointments and meetings with her lawyer. She couldn't go to work, even if she still had a job." She sighed. "I don't know how she's going to manage to feed the kids without any income, much less pay Bob's bills."

"There's the food pantry, and Bob won't press for payment," said Lucy, hanging up her coat. "What about housing?"

"The house isn't much, it belonged to my sister, who died of breast cancer. She left it to Elfrida, so she owns it free and clear."

"That's a blessing," said Lucy. "What is Aucoin charging her with?"

"Second-degree," said Phyllis, her voice breaking.

Lucy went around the counter and wrapped her arm around Phyllis's shoulders, giving her a hug.

"Don't you worry, we know she's innocent, and the case against her will fall apart. I bet she doesn't even stand trial."

"But why would they charge her then? They must know something we don't. They must have some evidence, right?"

Lucy knew the DA was no fool and wouldn't bring charges unless he had evidence to support them, but didn't want to further dampen Phyllis's spirits. "Time will tell," she said, "but the important thing is to keep the faith and support Elfrida and her kids every way we can."

"The best way would be to figure out who really did kill that Bobbi."

"I know," said Lucy. "I know."

She gave Phyllis another encouraging squeeze and then went over to her desk, where she powered up her PC. When it finally allowed her to access her e-mails, she saw that Ross had kept his promise and posted the day's filming schedule. Right on top, in bold, was the news that extras were no longer needed. Checks would be mailed.

Not even a *thank-you* or a *job well done,* fumed Lucy, feeling rather disappointed that her film career was ending so abruptly. On the other hand, she admitted, she still had a lot to do to get ready for Christmas, and she would have more time to spend with Patrick and his parents. A mixed blessing, she conceded, as she scrolled through the e-mails, trolling for newsworthy items. She adored Patrick, even if she thought there was some grandmotherly work to do in the matter of manners, and it was always wonderful to reconnect with Toby. It was Molly who was the fly in the ointment, she thought, wondering what had happened to the sweet and bright girl Toby had married. She really couldn't understand Molly's decision to go to Germany for a year, essentially abandoning her little family. It was very troubling and it was a huge stumbling block in her relationship with her daughter-in-law, which until now had been loving and cordial. Truth be told, thought Lucy, as she repeatedly hit the little down arrow, passing up opportunities to donate to good causes and to take advantage of amazing sales, she really felt sick about the way Molly had changed.

The bell jangled, announcing Ted's arrival, but all Phyllis managed by way of greeting was a sad little nod. Lucy did a bit better, tossing off a curt little "hi."

"I guess I missed the memo. Is the world ending or something?" he asked, unwrapping his muffler.

"Ha-ha," replied Lucy.

"It's not ending, but it's certainly upside down," said Phyllis.

"Right." He hung up his jacket and strode across the room to the coffee machine and grabbed the carafe, carrying it into the tiny bathroom and filling it with water. Once he had the machine started, filling the office with the aroma of fresh coffee, he began rallying the troops.

"Things are indeed out of whack, but we're not giving up. When the going gets tough, the tough get going. So we're going to put the pressure on the DA and ask the tough questions. We're going to do a profile of Elfrida, highlighting the challenges a single mom faces and presenting the kids' achievements. Angie was on the dean's list last semester, if I remember correctly, and didn't one of the boys make the All-State band or something?"

"Albert. He plays French horn," said Phyllis.

"You know them best, Phyllis, so write up a list of everything you can think of, okay? Certificates, Scouts, karate belts, whatever. We want it all. And, Lucy, you can work on the single-mom angle, get some info from social workers, teachers, doctors. . . . I don't have to tell you, you know the drill. No one better than you. We'll have people out in the streets with pitchforks and torches, demanding justice for Elfrida."

It was a good plan, thought Lucy, who was more than willing to do her part, but there was a serious drawback. She recalled Molly's reaction when she asked her to let Patrick play with little Arthur and she knew that Molly wasn't alone in her opinion of Elfrida. A lot of people in town thought of Elfrida as a party girl with lax morals who hadn't been able to make even one of her several marriages stick. It wasn't going to be easy to change their minds, but she was certainly going to try. She was flipping through her list of contacts, looking for likely candidates to interview, when her phone rang and she picked it up.

Much to her surprise, the person on the other end of the line was Willis, the butler at Pine Point.

"What's on your mind?" she asked, hoping something newsworthy had prompted his call.

"It's Elfrida," he began. "Ross fired her, you know."

"I know. And even if he changes his mind, she can't work right now. She's under house arrest."

"Indeed," said Willis. "That's why I'm calling you. I remember that you and your friend Sue Finch were able to help out in the past. We just need help this weekend, even Ross knows he can't expect people to work on Christmas Day."

It was true. Lucy and Sue had worked at Pine Point years before, providing kitchen help for the funeral of Juliette's father, Van Duff. Van, who had been dressed as the Easter Bunny and was preparing to distribute treats to local children, was the victim of a murderous scheme hatched by a trusted employee.

"I'd like to help out," said Lucy, "but I really can't. Christmas is only days away and I have family staying for the holiday and my job here at the paper. Besides, I'm not the cook Elfrida is and I wouldn't know where to begin. I think you should call Sue, maybe she can help you."

"I already have," admitted Willis. "She said she's going to be busy this weekend distributing toys. She's apparently a toy captain for the food pantry's annual gift drive."

"Well, maybe a temp agency," suggested Lucy, noticing that both Ted and Phyllis were gesturing frantically. "Uh, hold on a moment," she said, hitting the button on her desk phone.

"What is it?" she demanded. "Do you know how distracting you're being? I could hardly focus on my call."

"It's Willis, right? And he wants you to work at the Point?" asked Ted.

"Yeah."

"Well, you should take the job."

"Are you crazy? I have a house full of family who've come all the way from Alaska for Christmas, who I've hardly gotten to see. I haven't written one Christmas card or baked a cookie. I haven't even gotten my Christmas tree up. . . ."

"Do it for Elfrida," urged Phyllis. "If you're at

Pine Point, you can investigate and find the real killer."

"I have worked there in the past, you know, and believe me, there is no time to investigate when you're chopping and mashing. Even Elfrida said she was overwhelmed by the workload."

"You don't have to do a good job, you just have to be there," advised Ted.

"And if you ask, you know Sue will help out, too," added Phyllis. "She has a soft spot for Elfrida's kids."

"Okay, but I can't do that and work at the paper tomorrow, too," said Lucy, who had agreed to work half a day on Saturday so she could take Christmas Day off.

"I know. I'll get Pam to come in, we'll figure it out," said Ted.

"And if I get stabbed?" demanded Lucy. "What then?"

Ted was philosophical. "Well, in that case, you'll definitely know who the killer is, right?"

Lucy hit the hold button, reconnecting with Willis. "After some reconsideration, it seems I can take the job."

"Great. I'll do everything I can to help, just let me know what you need and I'll get it for you."

"When do I start?"

"Tomorrow, eight o'clock. Is that okay?"

"Sure. I'll call Sue and see if I can convince her to help, too."

"That would be wonderful," said Willis, sounding very relieved. "Wonderful."

Sue wasn't at all surprised when Lucy called. "I've been expecting to hear from you," she said. "What did you tell Willis?"

"I said we'd be happy to help out. We're starting at eight o'clock tomorrow morning."

"Maybe you are, but not me."

"Sue, I'm begging you. I can't do it alone. And think of Elfrida, and those kids of hers. You know you're crazy about little Arthur."

"He was the cutest kid we've ever had at Little Prodigies."

"Well, maybe we'll turn something up that will keep his mommy out of jail."

Sue was suspicious. "Are you investigating or cooking? Or are you really just trying to avoid Molly?"

Lucy hadn't thought of the job in quite these terms, but she had to admit Sue might be right.

"All three."

Sue laughed. "A trifecta. I wouldn't miss it for the world."

In the past, when Lucy and Sue worked at Pine Point, they were instructed to use the servants' entrance on the side of the house. This morning, Lucy decided things would be different and marched right through the front door, where she encountered Willis in the hall. He was arranging a silver bowl of holly leaves on the hall table and Lucy braced for a reprimand, but none came.

"Thank goodness you're here," he said, giving the arrangement a final adjustment. "I'll take you down to the kitchen and get you started."

Willis led the way through the elegant dining room, pausing at the jib door that concealed the service stairs that led to the basement. "There's a lot for you to do," he said. "We'll need lunch for about sixty people, and Juliette is hosting a holiday dinner tonight for twenty-four guests. You'll find the menus on the bulletin board—but considering the situation, they are suggestions, only." He sighed. "Juliette is not the problem, she understands that things are difficult and compromises may be required, but Ross . . ." He sat down on one of the Jacobean side chairs that stood against the wall and Lucy noticed his face was ashen.

"Are you okay?" she asked. "Can I get you something?"

"I'm fine." He managed a wan smile. "Just tired. The last few days have been very difficult."

Lucy sat down beside him. "You must be exhausted."

"You have no idea. Everything's topsy-turvy, nothing like it was before Juliette got married." He stared at the Flemish still life of vegetables that hung on the opposite wall, above the Georgian sideboard. "I'm not getting any younger, you know, and these old bones tell me it's time to retire," he said, rubbing his knees, "but I don't want to abandon Juliette. I've known her since she was a little girl, you know, and I have to admit I've always felt very protective of her. Almost fatherly, you might say."

Lucy wasn't sure how far she could go, but figured she might never get Willis in such a chatty mood again. "Marriage is a big step, especially for someone as successful as Juliette. Do you think she's happy with Ross?"

Willis took his time before answering. "I think Juliette is happy, I believe she truly loves Ross, but I do worry that the feeling isn't mutual. I get the sense he married her for her money so he could get his movie made. The worst of it is, sooner or later Juliette's going to realize that she's been used. It will break her heart."

"I think she may be getting a clue," said Lucy. "I noticed her watching Ross like an eagle when he consulted with the script girl."

Willis lowered his voice. "It's not just the script girl, there's the wardrobe girl, and the actor playing Lady Clare, and I even saw him chatting up poor Bobbi." Willis hesitated, then decided to unburden himself, lowering his voice and leaning in. "He was actually pressing her up against a wall, leaning over her and whispering in her ear."

Lucy already had a rather low opinion of Ross, but she found this behavior shocking. "How did Bobbi react?" she asked, wondering if Bobbi might have threatened to expose his behavior, and if Ross himself had acted to eliminate that threat.

"She didn't seem to mind one bit," said Willis, pressing his hands on his thighs and rising from the chair. "I'm afraid this isn't getting lunch made, is it?"

He held the jib door open for her and followed her down the service stairs to the basement. As Lucy made her way down the stairs, she remembered someone telling her that Willis had left the great hall when the screams were heard. No one knew the ins and outs of the mansion better than Willis, and she wondered if he had taken matters into his own hands and killed Bobbi to protect Juliette. Reaching the bottom of the stairs, she turned and looked at him, a thoughtful expression on her face.

"Ah," he said, with a knowing smile, "I can only imagine what you're thinking. You're wondering if the butler did it."

"It did cross my mind," said Lucy, with an embarrassed little smile, "but I realize you didn't have time."

"Thanks for the vote of confidence," he replied, sounding rather offended. "I would think my integrity speaks for itself. I would never do such a thing."

"Not even for Juliette?" asked Lucy.

"Not for anyone," he said, marching on down the corridor to the kitchen. Lucy followed, relieved to find the hallway had been thoroughly cleaned and no trace of Bobbi's death remained. Pausing at the kitchen door, she discovered it was a huge mess: dirty pans, glasses, and dishes left on every available surface, along with assorted boxes of cereal, egg cartons filled with broken shells, plastic bread bags spilling their contents, jars of peanut butter and jelly, and half-empty milk bottles.

"I'm sorry about this," said Willis, "but people have been fending for themselves."

Lucy surveyed the chaos, dismayed. She'd expected to cook, not clean, but it seemed she'd have to do the latter before she could attempt the former. She was opening the cabinet beneath the sink, looking for cleaning products, when Sue breezed in.

"What the hell?" she declared, taking in the mess. She was standing, arms akimbo, still wearing her puffy winter jacket and carrying a tote bag, which Lucy knew contained her collection of knives, her *batterie de cuisine*.

"I'm sure glad to see you," said Willis. "Thanks for coming."

"Well, I'm going if this mess isn't cleaned up," declared Sue.

"I thought you and Lucy . . ."

"No way, Jose. This place has a cleaning staff, right? Well, let's see what they can do."

"Ross has them working on the set," said Willis.

"We'll see about that," said Sue, marching out of the kitchen. Willis followed, and Lucy noticed there was a new spring to his step.

She crossed the kitchen to the bulletin board to consult the menus posted there, learning that a variety of sandwiches and salads were expected for lunch. Easy peasy. Dinner was something else, beginning with a lump crabmeat appetizer followed by roast duck, pureed parsnips in zucchini boats, a mixture of steamed vegetables, with peppermint Yule log for dessert. It was clear that some compromises would have to be made, thought Lucy, hearing footsteps and voices in the hallway.

Next thing she knew, three young women arrived in the kitchen and got to work, setting things to rights. Sue came in right after them and joined Lucy at the bulletin board, studying the menus.

"What do you think?" asked Lucy. "Willis says we can make changes."

"Looks quite doable," said Sue, dropping her tote bag on a handy table with a *thunk* and shrugging out of her jacket.

"We'll definitely need something different for dessert," said Lucy. "Personally, I can't face another pink-peppermint Yule log."

Chapter Eight

It was almost ten when Lucy got home, and this time it was Bill who was sitting at the kitchen table, reading the sports pages and drinking a beer.

"Well, it's about time you showed up," he said, scowling at her.

Lucy was tired and looking forward to a hot bath; the last thing she wanted was a fight with her husband. "Didn't you get my message? I called and said I'd be late." She dropped her bag on a chair and shrugged out of her parka. "It's awfully quiet. Where is everybody?"

"It's Saturday night, the girls are out. Toby and Molly and Patrick are having dinner with her folks, and Patrick is sleeping over."

Lucy absorbed this last bit of news, trying not to feel jealous of Molly's mother, Jolene, who was no doubt spoiling Patrick with empty calories and endless TV shows.

"What were you doing all this time?" asked Bill, who was picking at the label on his beer bottle.

"They don't need extras anymore, at least that's what I heard from Jim at the hardware store."

Lucy sank onto a chair. "Sue and I are filling in for Elfrida, cooking for the crew."

"This late?"

"There was a special dinner, I think they were money people from Amazon. We made duck and cherries jubilee."

"Well, I'm glad somebody got a good dinner tonight," declared Bill, sarcastically. "As for your family, we had pizza."

Lucy tried to put on a brave front. "There's nothing wrong with pizza."

"Well, personally, I'm sick of pizza and chili. I'd like my wife to come home at a decent hour and cook a real dinner, like meat loaf and mashed potatoes. . . ."

"Poor you." Lucy rolled her eyes. "I'm not the only one who can cook, you know. There are five adults in this house, there's a ton of meat in the freezer, and the pantry is well-stocked. It seems to me that you ought to be able to cook up a chicken or a pot roast."

"How am I supposed to know what's in the freezer?" demanded Bill.

"You could look. . . ."

"What about tomorrow? Are you going to be working on Sunday?"

"Only a half day," said Lucy. "Elfrida's under house arrest. I'm sure they're working on getting a temp, but until they do, Sue and I have agreed to fill in."

"I don't get it. Why you?"

Lucy sighed. She really wanted to be soaking in that hot bath. "Because we did it before, and they need help right now." She looked at him, feeling her dander rising. "Because I want to do it, that's why."

"You know you sound an awful lot like Molly, don't you?"

Lucy was quick with a retort. "Maybe Molly's onto something."

Bill stared at his empty beer bottle. "You do know that Monday is Christmas Eve, don't you? What about presents and decorations?"

"I haven't forgotten," said Lucy, who knew only too well that Christmas was coming. "Actually, most of the shopping is done, I picked up gifts through the year. The girls can bake cookies and wrap last-minute gifts. You and Toby can put up the lights, Patrick will love trimming the tree. It will be a great Christmas."

"So you say." Bill got up and shoved his chair back, pointedly leaving the empty beer bottle on the table and heading upstairs.

Lucy picked it up, intending to toss it in the recycling bin, then put it back where he'd left it. Instead of following him upstairs, she went in the living room and settled on the sofa with a magazine. Feeling a bit chilly, she covered herself with an afghan and began flipping through the pages. She'd only read five of the ten reasons to cook with cast-iron pots when she fell asleep.

Waking sometime after midnight, Lucy wondered what she was doing lying fully dressed on the living-room sofa. Then she remembered her awkward conversation with Bill and decided she belonged in her own bed, sleeping beside her husband. She threw off the afghan and got up, stretched, and tiptoed upstairs. Bill was sound asleep, and didn't stir as she undressed and carefully slipped between the covers.

He and his truck were gone when she woke in the morning, and the closed door to the family room indicated that Toby and Molly were still asleep, but Sara and Zoe were in the kitchen, eating breakfast. She poured herself a cup of coffee and joined them at the table, still in her pajamas and robe. "I'm going to be busy today," she said as the mist cleared from her brain. "I need you both to help out."

"Sure, Mom," said Zoe, scooping up a spoonful of cereal.

"Do you really have to work on Sunday?" asked Sara, pulling a piece of toast from the toaster.

"I'm afraid I do. I'm helping out at Pine Point, because Elfrida's under house arrest. It's show biz and the filming must go on."

"Why you?" Sara was scooping avocado and spreading it on her toast.

"Because I did it before, and because Ted thinks I'll get a story out of it, that's why. And Christmas is in two days and Toby's here with his family and your father is tired of pizza, so you two are going to have to pick up the slack."

Sara sat down at the table, giggling. "I get it," she said. "Dad wasn't very happy last night, when you didn't come home for supper."

"What do you want us to do?" asked Zoe, pulling a memo pad out from under the pile of papers and mail that had accumulated on the table.

Lucy dug in her purse, still sitting on the chair where she'd left it the night before, and produced a pen, which she gave to Zoe.

"It would be great if you'd wrap some presents

for me, I'll leave them on my bed, along with the wrapping paper. The most important thing is dinner. Your father mentioned meat loaf, so I'll get some hamburger out of the freezer. You can use the recipe in *Fannie Farmer,* throw in some potatoes to bake, there should be salad in the fridge, also plenty of frozen vegetables. If you feel heroic, you could mix up some brownies with Patrick, when he comes home, and have them for dessert."

"Sounds like a Bill Stone Classic Dinner," said Zoe, writing it all down.

"That's the idea," said Lucy. "If all goes well, I won't be late today. We're just doing lunch." Lucy drank the last of her coffee. "For sixty."

Back at Pine Point, Sue put Lucy to work making dozens of sandwiches for the film crew's lunch while she baked a batch of oatmeal-raisin cookies that Juliette had requested. "We've got tuna salad, ham and cheese, and turkey breast for sandwiches, there's chowder thawing out in the slow cooker, and the cookies for dessert—that oughta hold them," said Sue, as she popped a tray of cookies into the oven.

Lucy spread a blob of tuna salad on a piece of whole wheat bread and slapped the sandwich together, then sliced it into two triangles with a big chef's knife. The knife, she realized, was very similar to the one that killed Bobbi.

A sudden yelp from Sue, who was pulling a tray of baked cookies from the oven, startled her.

"You okay?" she asked as Sue dropped the cookie sheet on the stainless-steel counter, making a clatter.

"The darn pot holder has a hole," muttered Sue, holding up the ragged scorched square of fabric.

"That is one sad pot holder," Lucy said, thinking she would have thrown it out long ago. She remembered that Elfrida had complained about the poor quality of the kitchen fittings, and this seemed to support her complaints. So did the limited counter space, which had Lucy and Sue vying for room to work. Sue's cookies were encroaching on Lucy's sandwiches, which meant they had to carry filled platters of food all the way across the kitchen and set them on a table. The very same table, thought Lucy, where she and Elfrida and Ross had been questioned by the police chief.

As she made the long trek for the fifth—or was it the sixth?—time, Lucy tried to picture the scene on the night Bobbi died. Elfrida had said they were making cookies, just like Sue was this morning. As she watched Sue plopping the dough onto the cookie sheets and shoving them into the oven, pulling out the hot sheets of cookies and setting them on the wire racks to cool, and then transferring the cooled cookies onto a serving platter, Lucy thought she looked busier than a one-armed paper hanger. No sooner would she pop a sheet into the oven, and then the beeper would sound, and she'd have to pull out the baked cookies.

Elfrida must have been even busier, scrambling to get finished so she could get home to her kids. Lucy knew what it was like to be focused on something, only to be interrupted by some sort of distraction. No doubt she would have been annoyed when Bobbi announced she needed to use the bathroom, and would have seen red when she saw her taking the Yule log cake from the fridge and took the knife.

It seemed obvious that Bobbi was taking advantage of the fact that Elfrida was very busy in order to pursue her own agenda, which involved the cake. She had either been planning to eat it herself, or, more likely, intended to share it with someone else. But who? Chris Waters came to mind, as Bobbi had been seen flirting with him. Had she hoped to surprise Chris with a treat, a special sweet snack? Thinking back to that evening, Lucy remembered that everyone, including Chris, had been involved in filming the big crowd scene. He wouldn't have been able to get away, but Lucy doubted that Bobbi would have thought so far ahead. She seemed to have been an impulsive sort who went full speed ahead, an unfortunate trait that hadn't worked out very well for her.

Bobbi hadn't even made it upstairs with the cake, which meant she must have encountered her killer in the hallway. The only person Lucy knew who'd actually been in the hallway was Ross, who had responded to Elfrida's scream. Elfrida claimed she'd screamed because she'd slipped on a butter wrapper when she attempted to follow Bobbi, which Lucy knew was definitely possible. That meant Ross might not have been quite as woozy after hitting his head as he claimed, and could have encountered Bobbi in the hallway, holding the cake and the knife. It would have taken only moments to seize the knife and use it.

But why? How much trouble was Bobbi, really? Sure, she had an unfortunate penchant for pranks, but that was hardly a motive for murder. There must have been something else, thought Lucy, but what? Blackmail? Willis had seen Ross behaving inappropriately with Bobbi; maybe Bobbi had threatened to go public with an accusation? That would have been no idle threat; these days the balance of power was shifting and a woman's claim of sexual misconduct could end a man's career.

"Lucy, what are you doing?" demanded Sue. "We need six dozen sandwiches."

Lucy realized she was just standing there, sandwich spreader in hand, instead of making sandwiches. "Oops, sorry," she said, getting on with her task.

Once lunch was prepared, Sue and Lucy were free for the day. Sue was planning to head over to the food pantry to help distribute holiday toys, and Lucy was planning on attending the visiting hours for Bobbi at McHoul's Funeral Home. Funerals were very popular in Tinker's Cove, combining the opportunity for fellowship and gossip with the added bonus of a generous collation afterward. Lucy couldn't stay for the service or the food and drink afterward, but that didn't matter to her. She was interested in the gossip.

As she expected, there was quite a crowd of people gathered at McHoul's, including many young people who had been classmates of Bobbi's at Tinker's Cove High School. Small groups of kids who'd gone to school with Bobbi were clustered outside, in the chilly December air, many puffing away on cigarettes. Older folks were inside, scattered about in the various tastefully decorated rooms, chatting mournfully. A few were studying photo collages featuring Bobbi with family and friends, leafing through family scrapbooks and signing the guest book.

Lucy joined the line of people waiting to express their condolences to the family and to view the body, lying in the open casket. This was something Lucy dreaded, but knew full well was the price of admission to the gathering. Harriet and Dick Holden were standing together, just in front of the enormous wooden casket that contained the body of their only child. As the line inched slowly forward, Lucy avoided looking at the body, but focused instead on the bereaved couple. Harriet was a full-figured, busy woman known for bringing cheer and home-baked cookies to the elderly residents of Pinewood Manor, but today she was dressed in pearls and a black dress, tearfully accepting the hugs and stilted words of her friends and neighbors. Dick, who was a heavy-equipment operator for the town highway department, was a large man with a booming voice, who held court at Jake's every morning when he dropped in at ten o'clock for coffee and two jelly donuts. Dick was the sort of man who would rather die than shed a tear in public, but his body language and choked voice made it clear he was holding a huge ball of grief inside that barrel chest.

When it was Lucy's turn, she gave Harriet a hug and mumbled how sorry she was; then she moved on to Dick and took his huge hand in hers, sharing a sad expression and a nod. Then she had to face the body, and paused beside the coffin. Bobbi was inside, and there was no doubt that this was Bobbi, except that her eyes were closed and she wasn't smiling and bouncing about. She was still, horribly still, which made her not at all like Bobbi after all. Suddenly overcome with emotion, Lucy turned away and struggled to compose herself.

"She was in my kindergarten class," said Lydia Volpe, giving Lucy's arm a comforting squeeze. "She was a little dynamo, so full of herself."

"It's awful when a young person dies," said Lucy, dabbing at her eyes with a tissue she pulled from her pocket.

"And it happens too often these days," said Lydia. "Opioids and guns, it's a killing field out there. I can't tell you how many funerals for former students I've attended lately. Such a waste."

"It is shocking, isn't it?" said Lucy. "And it affects so many people. If Elfrida goes to jail . . ."

"I know." Lydia nodded, her big brown eyes full of concern. "I had Angie, and Albert was in my last class, the year I retired. They're really good kids."

"It's not their fault their mother is a murderer," declared Sarah Walsh, joining the conversation. Sarah was Nanette's mother, and Bobbi's aunt, and bore a strong resemblance to her sister, Harriet. "Of course, even if Elfrida's in jail, she'll still be alive. They'll be able to visit and telephone, they won't lose her, like we've lost Bobbi."

"It's a terrible thing," said Lucy.

"You said it. It's terrible, and I know that Dick and Harriet want to see that justice is done. The whole family is behind them, you know. We've written to that judge, we don't think Elfrida should have gotten bail."

"I'd like to string her up myself," declared Nanette's brother, Donald, who was standing nearby with a couple of his friends. They were all young guys bursting with testosterone, spoiling for a fight, and Lucy could imagine them as part of a lynch mob.

"Well, Maine wisely did away with the death penalty over a century ago," said Lucy. "Let's calm down and see what develops. It may be that Elfrida is innocent."

"Innocent until proven guilty, that's how it's supposed to be," said Nanette, joining the conversation. "But believe me, if she's guilty, we're going to make sure Elfrida gets put away for life."

"I understand how you feel," said Lucy. "But I think the police may have been too quick to arrest Elfrida. They didn't really investigate anybody else."

"Like who?" asked Nanette, sounding rather doubtful.

"Well, Ross Rocket? Did Bobbi have a crush on him?"

"She was hoping he'd recognize her talent," said Nanette. "But I don't think she had a crush on him. Not like Chris Waters. She was wild about him. . . ."

"Everybody's wild about him," said Lydia, getting a few restrained chuckles.

"But what about Ross?" persisted Lucy. "They were seen together."

"She said he was her mentor," said Nanette. "She said he understood she was a creative personality, like he is, and he was interested in helping her develop her creativity. She also said that Ross told her his wife wasn't truly creative and didn't understand his needs, and that's why he liked talking to Bobbi."

"That's really interesting," said Lucy, thinking

that Ross's primary need as a creative was Juliette's money, and that he wouldn't hesitate to commit murder to keep it flowing.

"Yeah, so I think you can cross Ross Rocket off the list of possible suspects," said Nanette. "He liked Bobbi and he wouldn't have killed her, would he?"

"I'm sure you're right," said Lucy, who wasn't sure at all.

Drifting away from the group, she stopped to peruse one of the collages of Bobbi's life, struck by the number of photos picturing her in costume after costume. There was no doubt that Bobbi had loved performing, beginning at a young age and continuing right up until her death.

"She was in the Little Theatre production of *The Sound of Music* with Molly," said Jolene, stepping beside Lucy and pointing to one of the photos. "Molly was the oldest sister, I can't remember her name, and Bobbi was the cute little one. She stole the show."

"I didn't know Molly acted," said Lucy, turning to Jolene. Molly's mother was impeccably turned out, as usual, with silver-tinted hair and a black coat trimmed with fur.

"Just that once," admitted Jolene. "She had terrible stage fright. But little Bobbi loved performing, even back then." She glanced at the casket. "I just feel so bad for her folks."

"It makes you think," agreed Lucy. "We're awfully fortunate to have the kids home for Christmas, aren't we?"

"It's a real treat, and quite a surprise," said Jolene. "Showed up out of the blue, wanting a late lunch. Wouldn't you know, I sent their presents off to Alaska weeks ago, so I don't have anything to put under the tree for them."

"Good thing you were home that afternoon," said Lucy, feeling a certain satisfaction that she'd bested Jolene at her own game; she'd procrastinated and failed to ship the presents. "Nobody was home at our house."

"You are a busy lady, I've been trying to track you down," Jolene said as they made their way through the crowded rooms to the exit. "I've been wondering how we should divide up Christmas."

"I haven't really thought about it," Lucy said as they stepped outside into the cool, fresh air. "They're sleeping at our house, so we could open presents in the morning and have a nice breakfast. . . ."

"Then they'd come to us for Christmas dinner."

Lucy suddenly felt a big hole inside; she knew she couldn't monopolize Toby's family, but sharing wasn't going to be easy, especially since she'd had so little time with them.

"Maybe we could all do something together," suggested Lucy, knowing this was really a nonstarter. Bill didn't get along with Jim Moskowitz at all, and she suspected the feeling was mutual.

"That would be lovely, if only we could," said Jolene, smoothly. "We're going to have quite a full house with my brother and his family, and our dear friends who always come to us on Christmas. . . ."

"I understand," said Lucy, already shifting gears and planning to cook a special dinner for the whole family on Christmas Eve. Then she could have a relaxed Christmas Day with Bill and the girls, having leftovers for supper.

The two women had left the funeral home and

were walking toward the parking lot when Jolene stopped and took Lucy's arm. "I've been meaning to talk to you about Molly," she said, all in a rush, as if plunging into a cold swimming pool.

"Molly?"

"Yes. What do you and Bill think about this plan of hers to go to Germany?"

Lucy wasn't about to criticize her daughter-in-law, especially not to her mother. "Well, I don't think it's my place to think about it at all. Toby is fine with it."

"Is he? That's not good, is it?"

"He told me that Molly has always supported him, and now it's his turn to let her pursue her dreams."

"I don't buy it," said Jolene. "I know for a fact that she hated those Grimm fairy tales, wouldn't let me read them to her."

"People grow and change. I didn't know I'd like working for the newspaper until I started, and now I love it."

"And that awful dog. I don't trust him, especially around Patrick."

"Toby built a run for Skittles, so he's pretty much confined."

"Well, that's a mercy," declared Jolene.

"Maybe you could have a little talk with Molly," suggested Lucy, as they approached her car. "You're her mother after all."

"I've tried," said Jolene. "Believe me, I've tried, but once Molly has decided on something, well, that's it. She's very strong-minded."

"You should be proud of her," said Lucy, conscious of doing her best to spread good cheer. "She's a modern woman who knows what she wants."

"I suppose," admitted Jolene, warming to Lucy's praise. "And who knows, maybe she'll come to her senses, though I doubt it."

"If I don't see you, Merry Christmas," said Lucy, opening her car door.

"Isn't it great that we can say 'Merry Christmas' again?" enthused Jolene, jiggling her car keys.

"Absolutely great," said Lucy, who'd never signed on to the notion that there was a war on Christmas. On the contrary, she thought Christmas was a glittering, red-and-green, *pa-rum-pum-pum* assault on the budget that began before Halloween and didn't end until the last deeply discounted rolls of wrapping paper were replaced by cuddly teddy bears and heart-shaped boxes of candy for Valentine's Day. You couldn't escape it—the best you could do was to try to enjoy it.

Chapter Nine

Returning home, Lucy's arrival was announced by Skittles, who was barking his head off and straining against the lead that connected him to the new wire run. A Christmasy scene greeted her as Toby and Bill, both dressed in wooly plaid shirt-jacs, were busy stringing up tiny white lights on the porch roof. It was dusk and a light snow was falling, brightened by the glowing strings of old-fashioned colored lights that were wrapped around the bushes and were already shining. Inside the kitchen Zoe and Sara were baking spritz cookies under Libby's watchful eye, while Molly and Patrick were trimming a huge tree that filled at least half of the living room.

"Grandma! Look at the tree! Dad and I went to the woods and cut it down!"

"It's beautiful," said Lucy. "I've never seen such a full Christmas tree."

"It's so tall, I don't know how we're going to get this angel on top," said Molly, when Lucy joined them in the pine-scented room. She was holding a rather battered golden-haired angel whose halo was missing and whose gauzy wings were bent out of shape. "Maybe we should find something else?"

"We've had that angel since Toby was a baby," said Lucy, taking it and attempting to straighten the wings. She studied the tree, noticing that the top branches of the tree were indeed grazing the ceiling. Lucy considered clipping them, then decided to tie the angel to the topmost branch with a bit of string. She climbed up on a chair to perform this bit of magic, then stepped down to admire her work. "What do you think Patrick? How does she look?"

"Beautiful, she's all white and silver."

"You can't see the dings from down here," agreed Lucy. "What other treasures have you found?"

Molly was sorting through the plastic bin of ornaments wrapped in tissue. "This looks like something Toby made," she said, holding up a scallop shell painted silver that framed a school photo, probably made in first or second grade. "Gosh, Patrick looks just like him."

"He sure does," agreed Lucy. "So, Patrick, maybe you could make some ornaments like this tomorrow? I have the school photos you sent in the fall and you could use some of them. You could make one for me and one for Grandma Jolene."

"That's a great idea, Lucy," said Molly. "But we're going to be busy tomorrow. My folks are taking us to the holiday brunch at the Queen Vic, and then we're taking Patrick to see *The Nutcracker* ballet in Portland. Mom's been freaking out because she sent the presents to Alaska, so she came up with the idea of giving us a special treat. We won't be back until late, so we'll probably grab a fast-food supper on the way home."

"Wow, that is a busy day," said Lucy, dumbstruck that Jolene hadn't shared this information with her and abandoning her plan for a festive family dinner on Christmas Eve. She'd been bested once again, she thought, carefully hanging the shell ornament on a prominent branch. If only she hadn't been so busy with the movie and her job, she could have made similar plans for special holiday treats. As it was, she thought resentfully, she couldn't even get a day off. "I'm sure you'll have a good time."

Leaving Molly and Patrick in the living room, Lucy went back to the kitchen, where Zoe was popping the last tray of cookies into the oven, and Sara was already washing the bowls and cookie press. Dozens of the little buttery cookies were cooling on wire racks, others were piled on a platter. Lucy plucked one from the platter and nibbled on it, unleashing a flood of memories.

She remembered her mother, and even her grandmother, baking these same cookies. They'd always been part of Christmas. Her father, she recalled, awaited their appearance impatiently, saying it wasn't Christmas until he'd had spritz cookies and eggnog. Bill was a big fan, too, and after eating her mother's cookies, he had begged her to make them. Her first attempt hadn't been successful as she'd burned most of them, and undercooked the rest.

"These are perfect," she told the girls, taking another.

"Don't eat them all," admonished Sara, in a teasing voice.

"They're for Christmas," added Zoe, repeating Lucy's own words right back at her.

"Remember the year I hid all the Christmas cookies, saving them for Christmas Eve, and when I finally put them out, the dog ate them all?" asked Lucy.

"We're not going to let that happen this year," said Zoe, giving Libby a stern look. "No cookies for dogs."

Apparently abashed by Zoe's stare, Libby skulked over to her doggy bed and plopped down. She gave a mournful sigh and settled her chin on her paws.

"So what are you guys doing tomorrow?" asked Lucy.

"There's a holiday concert at the church, and afterward, we're going caroling to shut-ins," said Zoe.

"It's lots of fun, and we end up at Reverend Marge's house for mulled cider and fruitcake."

"Somebody usually spikes the cider and nobody eats the fruitcake," said Zoe, packing the cookies into plastic containers.

"That does sound like fun," said Lucy, realizing she'd better get the meat loaf and potatoes the girls had prepared for dinner in the oven. "I wish I didn't have to work."

Next morning, Lucy felt very sorry for herself as she drove to Pine Point. Even Bill, she'd learned at breakfast, was making merry, joining his friends in an old-timers' hockey game that would be followed, no doubt, by several rounds of beer at the roadhouse on Route 1. And if that wasn't bad enough, Sue had called to say she was sorry, but the toy distribution had been exhausting and she was too tired to work at Pine Point.

How was it, she wondered, that the whole world got Christmas Eve off except for her and the other poor unfortunates who were making Ross's movie? Didn't moviemakers take days off or was filming a 24/7 endeavor? That's the question she asked Juliette when she popped into the kitchen to say hi.

"It's just the way it is, Lucy," she began, climbing onto a stool at the makeshift island Sue had cobbled out of some high-top outdoor furniture. "Filming is so expensive that it's best to go full speed ahead, at least that's what Ross says. He is giving everybody Christmas off, but he's not happy about it. I'm ashamed to say I've been so busy I haven't had a chance to thank you for all your help. That duck dinner was fabulous, I don't know how you pulled it off on such short notice. Everybody loved it."

"That was Sue," said Lucy, who was elbow deep in a huge bowl of potato salad she was preparing for the crew's lunch. "I just followed orders."

"You're being too modest," insisted Juliette, helping herself to a pickle spear, which she pulled out of an open jar.

How does she do it? Lucy wondered. *She looks fabulous whether she's sitting on a throne, playing Queen Guinevere, or perching on a stool, eating a pickle.*

"I know it's Christmas," continued Juliette, "and you'd probably much rather be home with your family instead of feeding this bunch of ham actors."

"I was feeling rather sorry for myself," admitted Lucy, "but then I thought of Elfrida. I can't imagine what she's going through."

"You're right," agreed Juliette, pulling out another pickle spear. "I'm very worried about her

and her family. I made sure Willis sent her a sever-
ance check, even though Ross said not to." She
took a bite of pickle and chewed thoughtfully. "I
can't believe she stabbed Bobbi, it doesn't seem
like her at all," she finally said, waving the pickle
for emphasis. "I think Ross was too hasty and
shouldn't have fired her, but I did get him to agree
to have her back if she's acquitted, which I'm sure
she will be."

"Bobbi's family want to see her hang, and I
guess I can't blame them," said Lucy.

"They're grieving," said Juliette. "It's not going
to be a very happy holiday for them."

"Probably not ever," said Lucy. "Every year when
Christmas rolls around, they'll be reminded of
Bobbi's death."

"That's true." Juliette shuddered. "Easter is a lot
easier to avoid than Christmas. Ever since my dad
was killed, I make sure to get away somewhere for
Easter, someplace that doesn't remind me of what
happened. Last year it was Tokyo."

Lucy sprinkled some paprika on top of the
potato salad and covered the bowl with a sheet of
plastic wrap. "That's done," she said, putting it into
the fridge.

"What next?" asked Juliette. "Can I help?"

"Sandwiches, and you sure can," said Lucy, assembling several loaves of bread and packages of
cold cuts on the island. Juliette turned out to be a
fast worker, and between them they soon filled a
couple of platters with ham and Swiss, turkey, and
roast beef sandwiches.

"I've only got bakery cookies," said Lucy, producing a couple of plastic bins from the supermarket.

"Good choice," said Juliette. "It was baking cookies that started the whole mess, wasn't it?"

"Actually, I think it was the Yule log."

"Right." Juliette was busy arranging the cookies on a tray. "I had no idea there was so much tension between Elfrida and Bobbi. I really thought Bobbi was helping her."

"Bobbi's cousin told me that Bobbi was stagestruck from an early age. She was trying to get noticed so she'd be discovered, that's why she was making such a nuisance of herself. It all backfired, those pranks just annoyed people and made her lots of enemies."

"So that explains it," murmured Juliette, wrestling with the roll of ClingWrap.

"Explains what?" asked Lucy.

"I found her in my trailer with one of my wigs, I thought she was fooling around, probably going to try it on or something. She didn't act guilty or like she was doing anything wrong, she said she was checking on something for Ray, the costume girl. She put the wig back on the stand and said she'd tell Ray it was okay."

"Did you believe her?" asked Lucy.

"Not entirely," admitted Juliette. "But no harm was done, so I didn't want to make a fuss."

"Maybe you should have," said Lucy, loading the dumbwaiter with the platters of food.

Juliette was quiet, looking up at one of the windows set high in the subterranean kitchen wall. "Maybe," she finally said, shrugging. "At the time it seemed wiser to let it go." Then she was gone, slipping gracefully out of the kitchen like some sort of magical good fairy.

Lucy pushed the button sending the loaded

dumbwaiter up, then climbed the stairs that led directly to the dining room and began transferring the platters of food to the tables in the great room. As she carried the platters one at a time from the dining room and down the passage to the set, she thought about Juliette's ability to float about the house. She wondered if she'd managed somehow to slip away from the revels scene, perhaps through some secret stairway that only she knew about to make her way to the basement, where she'd stabbed Bobbi.

Ridiculous as it seemed, thought Lucy, she wasn't quite ready to eliminate Juliette from her list of suspects. Her comment about letting things go indicated to Lucy that Juliette wasn't happy about her situation, but didn't indicate what was bothering her. Was it her marriage to Ross? Or had making a movie turned out to be less fun than she thought it would be? Or was she really furious with Bobbi for intruding on her private space and messing with her things? Bobbi's murder didn't seem to have been planned, it seemed as if the killer had simply encountered her with a knife in her hand and decided to seize the opportunity to get rid of her. When she looked at it that way, Lucy thought, almost anyone involved with the movie might have done it, including the actors, the crew, and, of course, Ross.

Ross was the most likely, she decided, setting down the last platter of food. He was the only one who was seen in the hallway with Bobbi, the only one who had the opportunity to grab the knife and stab her. As for motive, at the very least killing Bobbi would get rid of a troublesome personality and restore some sense of calm to the movie set. There might well have been more, however, if Bobbi had seen Ross engaged in some unseemly behavior that she threatened to reveal.

It was all supposition, thought Lucy, stepping aside as the actors and crew began arriving and gathering around the table. "Sorry to bother you, but is there any mustard?" asked one of the knights, and Lucy hurried off to get the forgotten condiments, which were still in the basement kitchen. That chore done, her attention was caught when a cheer went up from a group of actors gathered around a screen, reviewing their performances. The buffet was going well, so she wandered over, curious to see the rushes for herself. Maybe she'd even see herself.

Joining the group, she saw they were indeed studying the revels scene. Fascinated, she watched as the Yule log was presented to the king and queen, who were seated on thrones surrounded by various knights and ladies. Then the screen went blurry and Chris Waters was pictured embracing Guinevere in a passionate kiss.

"Wow, Chris," commented the actor playing King Arthur. "That kiss didn't look like acting."

"Believe me, it was an Oscar-worthy performance," said the embarrassed actor, his face reddening. "I'm gay."

"Well, maybe you were in character, but Guinevere looked as if she was really into you," said another, causing a few chuckles.

"I guess that's why you didn't get that head shot in the revels scene," said a young woman Lucy recognized as the script girl. "You're supposed to be caught gazing at Guinevere."

"Ross doesn't know what he's doing," said Chris. "He cut the scene short, remember. He could've reshot it, but he probably forgot, didn't think it was important."

"Oh, right," said the actor. "Maybe he should have remembered to go to film school, maybe acting in B movies wasn't great preparation for directing."

That comment brought down the house as the group burst into laughter.

It wasn't as if the remark was actually that funny, thought Lucy. The laughter was a shared emotional release from a group of people who were under a lot of pressure. It was the sort of thing kids did when a mean teacher left the room for a moment, or when workers learned there wasn't going to be a holiday bonus this year.

Lucy checked on the buffet, which still had plenty of food, but looked rather unattractive, as some of the platters only had a few sandwiches. She rearranged the remaining food, consolidating the sandwiches on a couple of platters and stirring up the potato salad, then carried the empty platters into the dining room and put them on the dumbwaiter. Feeling a bit at odds, with time to kill until lunch was over, she decided to remind anyone who'd missed lunch that there was still plenty of food. Wandering through the various rooms of the mansion that were being used as staging areas for the shoot, she finally ended up in the library, which was the costumer's headquarters.

"Hi, Ray," she said, poking her head inside the doorway. It was one of her favorite places on the set, where the temporary racks of costumes, the sewing machines, and the ironing board gave a homey atmosphere. "There are still some sandwiches if you're hungry."

"Thanks, but I already ate. That potato salad is delish. Is it an old family recipe?"

"I got the recipe from Sue. It's the pickles that do it."

"Well, it's yummy." Ray was standing at a table, peering through a pair of eyeglasses with black frames at one of the knight's tunics. "You're a mom, right?" she asked.

"Guilty as charged."

"You do your family's laundry?"

"Yeah." Lucy couldn't imagine where this was going.

"Well, I've tried everything I can think of, but I can't get this stain out. It's grease, but it's not responding to my usual spot remover."

"I always use dish detergent," said Lucy, stepping up to the worktable to study the stain. "It's great on grease."

"Good idea! You're a lifesaver, this is an important costume and I don't have time to replace it."

"King Arthur's?" asked Lucy.

"No. Lancelot's."

"How on earth did he get grease on it?" asked Lucy, thinking that was the sort of stain Bill picked up when he was working on the car, or repairing a power tool.

"Food. You know, they eat in costume. I think this was icing, from a cupcake or something." She chuckled. "These actors are just like children. I found it stuffed in a crate of swords—you'd think he was a naughty little boy, ashamed of spoiling his new clothes."

"Somehow I never thought of him like that," said Lucy, thoughtfully. "He's always the leading man, the guy who saves the planet from the asteroid."

"Actors! They're all babies," said Ray.

"I'll get the dish detergent for you," said Lucy, heading back to the set to collect the remaining dishes from the buffet table. At the door she paused. "Are you sure it was icing?" she asked.

"Oh, yeah, no doubt. I had to scrape it off. It was pink, must've been peppermint. It smelled like a candy cane."

Peppermint, thought Lucy, remembering the stuff that stuck to her hands when she tried to revive Bobbi. The stuff, mixed with Bobbi's blood, which she'd been so desperate to wash off.

Don't jump to conclusions, she told herself. *There's probably a completely innocent explanation for the stain.*

"You won't believe this," added Ray, peering at her over her half-glasses, "but that naughty boy also lost his gloves and I had to order new ones. They're custom-made gauntlets, and, believe me, Ross is going to have a fit when he sees the invoice."

Chapter Ten

Lucy's feet were dragging as she returned to collect the leftovers from the buffet table. This was not how things were supposed to work out. Until now, all the evidence pointed to Ross: He'd had a motive, he had opportunity, and he had access to the murder weapon. Ross was obnoxious and horrible; he was overbearing and crude; she wanted *him* to be the killer. But this new evidence, the missing gloves and the stained tunic, was awfully incriminating. Even worse, the rushes were proof that Ross was not the only person who'd left the set after Elfrida screamed.

Or maybe not, she thought, surveying the messy table covered with mostly empty platters holding a few dried-out sandwiches and the smeared bowl containing a dab of potato salad. It wasn't difficult to believe that Ross had been jealous and petty enough to cut the scene. Or maybe he was simply such an inexperienced and clumsy director that he'd forgotten all about filming the knight's longing glance at his queen that was supposed to be the climax of the revels scene.

She began piling the platters onto a borrowed teacart, then impulsively decided she had to know for sure why Chris had left the set. Abandoning the cart, she marched through the great hall and out the massive door, crossing the lawn, which was still covered with fake snow, to the area where the trailers were located. Chris Waters was standing outside his, talking on his cell phone.

"Got to go," he said, seeing Lucy's determined expression.

"Tell me what happened," said Lucy, shivering and pulling her sweater tightly across her chest. The temperature had fallen and she wished she'd thought to grab her parka. "Tell me you didn't kill Bobbi."

"I wish I could," he said, taking off his jacket. "How did you figure it out?"

"The stained tunic, the missing gloves . . ."

He held out the jacket. "Here, put this on. You're freezing."

Lucy allowed him to drape the jacket over her shoulders, struck by his gentlemanly behavior. "I don't want to believe it," she said, imploring him to say he was innocent.

"I didn't mean to, you know, it was an accident. I wasn't looking for her. I was mad that Ross skipped my big moment—I'd been working on that longing gaze for quite a while and I'd really nailed it." He struck the pose and Lucy had to admit it was a triumph of expression that combined both love-stricken longing with a touch of guilt. "I couldn't believe it when Ross called 'Cut' and ended the scene. I was really mad, so I walked off set to cool off, then figured I might as well use the break to take a leak. That's why I went downstairs, I was looking for the toilet. I wasn't expecting to meet Bobbi or anything, but there she was, holding the cake. I didn't even notice the knife, she was all excited to see me. Her face lit up and she said something like, 'What a coincidence, I was going to bring this to you.'

" 'Why me?' I asked. 'I never eat cake. I've gotta stay thin, you know, and there's only so much you can do at the gym.' She laughed then and said, flirtatiously, that eating wasn't the only pleasure two adults could enjoy together.

"I'd had enough by then and told her she was only a kid and, besides, I'm gay. That's when she got kind of mad and started teasing me, saying a real woman could change that. That's when I noticed the knife, she was waving it around—"

Lucy interrupted. "Bobbi was waving the knife, pointing it at you?"

He nodded. "Yeah. Sort of teasing, but kind of threatening, too. I lunged at her and tried to grab it and down she went, falling right on the knife." He paused, a sick expression on his face. "I couldn't believe it. I was horrified. I tried to help her, to turn her over. . . ."

"Why didn't you call for help?" asked Lucy.

"I heard someone coming down the corridor and I panicked. I ran around the corner and into the bathroom, and after I'd calmed down, I slipped out the back door and back to the set. By then, it was pretty crazy. Everyone was upset and nobody seemed to have realized I'd been gone. It wasn't until I went back to my trailer to get undressed that I noticed that pink icing on my costume, and on my gloves, too. So I hid the tunic and I dropped the gloves in one of those Salvation Army collection boxes—they were warm gloves and I figured somebody could use them."

Lucy shook her head sadly. "You have to fess up," she said, "you can't let Elfrida go to jail for life for something she didn't do."

"I know." He nodded. "I've been trying to work up my courage. That's what I was doing, talking to Karl. He said he was with me one hundred percent, and I had to do the right thing."

"No way!" It was Ross, stepping out from behind the trailer, where he'd apparently been eavesdropping. "Nobody would believe that crazy story! And I'm not going to lose my leading man, we've gone too far in this project."

"What are you saying?" demanded Lucy. "You can't really believe this film of yours is more important than people's lives, can you? Elfrida has five kids, and you'd let her go to jail, even though she's innocent."

"Happens all the time," said Ross, dismissively. "But who says she'll go to jail? If she's innocent, she'll get off. It will be another unsolved case, and the movie will get a boost from all the publicity and be a huge hit."

Lucy couldn't believe what she was hearing, and neither could Chris.

"It will take more than sensational publicity to make this piece of crap a hit," he said. "Frankly, I'd rather go to jail than play one more scene in this pathetic travesty of a film."

"Oh, yeah?" snarled Ross, taking a swing at Chris. Chris swung back and the two men exchanged a few tentative punches. Lucy watched, horrified, not sure what to do. It almost seemed like they were playacting, practicing a scene, until Chris landed an uppercut that sent Ross reeling. Chris lunged at him and they both fell to the ground, rolling and grunting as each tried to gain the advantage. Fearful that the struggle was getting serious, Lucy yelled for help and two passing crew members pulled the two men apart. Ross marched off, nursing his jaw, and Chris apologized and expressed thanks to the two grips. Left alone, he turned to Lucy. "What now?"

"A trip to the police station?"

"Okay," agreed Chris.

When they arrived at the Tinker's Cove police station, Officer Sally Kirwan was seated at the front desk. Her face brightened when she recognized the movie star and she gave him a big smile. "What can I do for you?"

"Arrest me," said Chris, giving her the smile that made millions of hearts beat faster.

"I couldn't do that," she said, practically drooling. "You're Chris Waters."

"Not anymore, I'm not. I'm Geoffrey Christopher Waterstone and I'm here to confess that I accidentally caused the death of Bobbi Holden."

Sally gave Lucy a questioning look, getting a nod in return.

"I'd better call Uncle Jim," said Sally, crestfallen. "I mean the chief."

"That's one heck of story," said Ted, when Lucy called him from her car as she drove home. "Good work, Lucy."

"I think he'll get off pretty easily. . ." she said, sounding hopeful.

"That's if his story about it being an accident holds up," said Ted. "The important thing is that Elfrida is off the hook, and Phyllis can get back to work. And you, too," he added. "I want to see you in the office bright and early first thing tomorrow."

"Tomorrow's Christmas, boss."

"Uh, right. Wednesday, then. Have a happy holiday."

"You too. I'll see you Wednesday," promised Lucy, eager to leave Pine Point and get back to her real job and normal life. Although, she admitted to herself as she started the climb up Red Top Hill, things weren't really normal with Toby's family at the house, along with that awful hound, Skittles. Try as she might to understand and forgive her daughter-in-law, she was still angry with Molly over her plan to abandon Patrick and Toby, and she was finding it increasingly difficult to maintain a cordial relationship. Fortunately, she remembered that Toby's family had gone to the show in Portland with Molly's parents, so it would be a quiet evening with Bill, Sara, and Zoe. Maybe they'd even be able to find time to Skype Elizabeth in Paris.

Lucy's mood lifted as she turned into the driveway and saw her beloved house all lit up for the holidays; she was so happy that she failed to notice Skittles wasn't barking to announce her arrival. The driveway was rather crowded with extra cars, but it was dark and she assumed they belonged to Zoe's and Sara's friends, visiting after the caroling. Therefore she was quite surprised when she encountered Toby in the kitchen, along with Patrick, arranging holiday cookies on a plate.

"I thought you were going to *The Nutcracker* with the Moskowitzes," said Lucy, shedding her parka and hanging it up on the hook by the door.

"There's been a change of plan," said Toby, pouring eggnog into a number of glass punch cups. "We're all here instead."

"Jim and Jolene, too?" asked Lucy.

"Everybody!" said Patrick. "We're going to have cookies."

"Do you all want dinner?" asked Lucy, who had a ham in the fridge, which only needed to be heated up.

"Not sure," said Toby, lifting the tray of cookies and eggnog and carrying it into the family room.

Lucy followed and found everyone gathered around Jolene, who was sitting on the sectional sofa with a heavily bandaged leg propped up on pillows.

"What happened to you?" exclaimed Lucy.

"It was Skittles," said Patrick, in a very serious tone. "He bit Grandma."

"Oh, no," said Lucy, horrified. "How did it happen?"

"Well, you know, we were all going out together, so I brought Skittles along," Molly said. "Dad loves dogs and I thought he'd enjoy playing with Skittles. Their yard is fenced, too, so Skittles could get off the run and get some exercise."

"It was fine at first," said Jim. "Molly had one of those Chuckit! gizmos and I was throwing a tennis ball, and the dog was running and leaping, catching them right out of the air. But then Jolene came out and yelled something . . ."

"I wanted to tell him that it was getting late and we really had to leave, and the dog just went for me," declared Jolene, finishing her husband's sentence.

"It was really scary," said Toby. "He just turned and sprung at her and we couldn't get him to let go."

"He's never done anything like that before," insisted Molly.

"That's pit bulls for you," said Jim. "Once they bite, they just hang on."

"Oh, my God," said Lucy, her eyes wide. "How did you get him off?"

"Dad got a big pot of water and threw it at the dog," said Patrick.

"And Molly threw a blanket over him and we were all able to get into the house," added Toby. "He was pretty calm by the time the animal control officer came."

"So he's going to be put down?" asked Lucy.

"Oh, no. We can bring him home tomorrow, but he has to be confined for ten days, to make sure he doesn't have rabies," said Toby.

"It's really crazy because his shots are all up to date, so there's really no possibility that Mom will get rabies," said Molly.

"Better safe than sorry," said Jolene. "I told the doctor I'd like to have the shots, but she said I can have them after the ten days, if it turns out that I need them."

"It's a state law," said Jim. "I'm not usually one for excessive regulation, but I think this one is a good idea."

"Ten days," said Lucy, thoughtfully. "But isn't Molly leaving for Germany in a few days?"

"I was going to, but it's clear to me that I can't go now. I'm going to have to stay home and work with a pro to train poor Skittles. He needs me."

Across the room, for the first and possibly last time, Lucy's and Jolene's eyes met. The two grandmothers were in perfect agreement.

Sue Finch's Yule Log

Use a jelly roll pan lined with wax paper.
Cooking time 35–40 minutes. 300 degree oven

Ingredients:

4 eggs separated
¾ cup sugar
1 cup flour
1 teaspoon baking powder
⅛ teaspoon salt
¼ cup oil
⅓ cup orange juice
¼ teaspoon cream of tartar

Mix all together except for the egg whites and
cream of tartar, beat whites and tartar till stiff,
fold into mixture.
Pour into ungreased jelly roll pan.
Bake.
Have a clean dish towel ready, sprinkled with
sugar. Turn cake onto towel, peel off wax paper
and roll up.
When cooled and ready to frost, unroll and
spread frosting.

Frosting:

1 pint heavy whipping cream
½ cup confectioners' sugar
Cocoa to color
Combine and whip till peaks form.

Roll up Yule log.
Place on plate, finish frosting.
Grate a chocolate bar to finish it off.

Dear Reader,

Through the years I've written several Lucy Stone Christmas mysteries, and explored the various ways the Stone family celebrates the holiday. Christmas is always a special time for me and I try to express this in my books by including some of my favorite family traditions. For my family, and also for Lucy's, Christmas really begins when the tree goes up and is decorated with precious ornaments. Just like Lucy, I have saved those kindergarten treasures made by my children, who are now grown. We bake cookies, of course, and go caroling, and we go to church for the candlelight service. Stockings are hung, there are presents under the tree, and the whole family gathers for Christmas dinner.

Yule logs are not part of my family tradition, however, so when I was asked to write Yule Log Murder *I had to reach a bit, and came up with a new twist for Lucy and her family. This time, Lucy finds herself struggling to connect with her family because of her newspaper work, which involves investigating a murder, and also because she finds herself at odds with family members. A surprise visit by her son, Toby, with his wife, Molly, their son, Patrick, and their pet dog, Skittles, throws Lucy into a tailspin. I think we've all had holidays that turned out to be challenging, but in the end Lucy manages to keep Christmas rather well, and solves the murder, too!*

I hope you enjoyed reading Yule Log Murder *and that you will seek out other Lucy Stone Christmas mysteries.* Mistletoe Murder *was the first, when Lucy is a young mother moonlighting at a catalog store and begins her career in crime. Through all the books, now numbering more than twenty-five, I have followed Lucy's family through many holidays and family events, chronicling the kids' growth and evolving relationships. The fictional Stone family really seems like part of my own family, and I hope they will become part of yours.*

Wishing you a joyous holiday,
Leslie Meier

DEATH BY YULE LOG

Lee Hollis

Chapter One

As Hayley stood in her kitchen, a glass of red wine in one hand, and her cell phone in the other, which was pressed to her ear, she found herself fighting back a flood of tears. She was desperately trying to stay strong and pretend everything was perfectly fine, but she knew deep down in her gut why her son, Dustin, was calling. Her bottom lip quivered as she listened to him fill her in on the awesome blizzard that was raging right now over the Iowa plains and the city of Des Moines, stranding him at his dad's house, where he was spending the first few days of his holiday break. As he breathlessly explained how they were currently snowbound and without power or cell service and even, God forbid, Internet; as he marveled at how he had to call her on his father's landline like the old days before he was even born, because it was the only means of communication still working; as he reported that the Des Moines Airport had been shut down for the foreseeable future, since the most recent weather reports called for at least twelve more inches of snow before the storm would finally subside; as he explained all of this, the bitter truth had slowly come into focus.

Hayley's son would not be coming home for Christmas.

"Mom, are you still here?"

"Yes, Dustin, I'm here."

"Anyway, it doesn't look like I'll be able to get out of here for at least five or six more days, which means . . ."

"I know . . . ," Hayley said, sniffing.

"Mom, are you crying?"

"No, of course not."

"It's fine if you are," he reassured her.

"I'm not crying," Hayley insisted as a tear suddenly streamed down her right cheek. "It's just . . . this will be the first Christmas that we haven't spent together."

"I know, but we can celebrate when I finally make it home."

She heard someone talking in the background on the other end of the call.

"I'm on the phone with Mom," Dustin said. "I told her I'm going to miss Christmas and she's an emotional mess."

"Let me talk to her," Hayley heard her ex, Danny, say.

"No, Dustin, don't put him on—"

"Merry Christmas, sugarplum!"

"Don't call me 'sugarplum,' Danny. I'm upset enough already."

"Aw, you always were the sentimental type. Don't worry. I'll take good care of the kid and make sure he gets home in time for New Year's."

"Just don't let him gorge on too much—"

"We have plenty of supplies. I stocked up on frozen pizza and I got a whole pantry full of potato chips and pretzels I picked up at Costco."

"Junk food."

"Don't worry, I picked up a bag of veggie chips, too, for a little balance."

"Ever hear of a produce section, Danny?"

"It's the holidays, babe. No one is supposed to eat healthy."

"And don't let him play too many video games."

Dustin grabbed back the phone. "Hey, Mom, guess what? Dad let me open one of my presents early! He got me Resident Evil 7: Biohazard! Can you believe it? We've been playing it all day!"

Before she could respond, Dustin handed the phone to Danny again.

"So, did Gemma arrive yet?" Danny asked.

"She called from the Bangor Airport when she landed. She was going to pick up her rental car and drive straight home. That was about an hour ago. She should be here any minute."

"I hear she's not coming alone."

"That's right. I'm finally going to meet the boyfriend."

"Dustin says it's serious."

"From what I can gather, it appears to be. She hasn't told me too much about him," Hayley said, grimacing.

Ever since Gemma dropped out of vet school and moved to New York City to find herself, Hayley's relationship with her daughter had been slightly strained. They still talked on the phone every other day, but their conversations were mostly confined to the subject of Gemma's job,

waiting tables at a Chelsea eatery, and how she had
been dabbling more in cooking and was considering applying to a Manhattan culinary school.
Gemma couldn't decide if she wanted to be a chef
at a restaurant or write a food column, like her
mother did. Her ambitions far exceeded Hayley's,
however. Hayley was comfortable and happy just
writing her daily column for the local *Island Times*
newspaper in Bar Harbor, Maine. Gemma was eyeing her own column in *Bon Appétit* magazine or
starring in her own *Barefoot Contessa*–style TV show
on the Food Network, with a global Twitter following. But whenever Hayley broached the subject of
her daughter's personal life, Gemma made it clear
that topic was strictly off-limits.

She did spill a few minor details on occasion
about making new friends at her job and going out
to nightclubs on the weekends with "a couple of
girlfriends." There was also her roommate, with
whom she shared an apartment in Astoria, Queens.
She was Greek and an insomniac, so she was usually up all night making her grandmother's homemade hummus recipe and blasting the television,
watching gooey romantic-comedy movies on Net-
flix.

But when it came to dating, Gemma had remained mum.

Until recently.

About a month ago, while discussing her weekend plans, she casually mentioned she had met
someone at the restaurant where she worked. A guy
who came in with some buddies for dinner. He had
flirted shamelessly throughout the meal as she waited
on them, and scribbled his number on the back of
his credit card receipt after paying the bill. She was

debating whether or not she should call him. Well, by their next conversation, she apparently had, because she told Hayley they had met on the previous Sunday afternoon. He had taken her to an East Village Film, Performance, and Art exhibit at the Museum of Modern Art, and then they had spent hours getting to know each other over espressos at a nearby coffeehouse. After that, Hayley was able to squeeze out a few more details, but unlike when she dated in high school, Gemma resisted the urge to gush freely about her new beau.

And Hayley found that incredibly frustrating.

"Dustin tells me he's an actor," Danny said.

And then there was that.

Hayley had nothing personal against actors. But she had read enough magazines and watched plenty of E! Entertainment Television to know dating an actor was the equivalent of walking through a minefield. Inflated egos, innate self-centeredness, unchecked vanity, any one of those could blow up at a moment's notice. But Hayley hadn't even met him yet, so she was working hard in her mind to give him the benefit of the doubt.

"I always thought I'd make a good actor," Danny said.

Hayley pictured him saying that with a straight face. "You're always acting, Danny. You just don't get paid for it."

"Ouch. That hurt."

"The truth always does."

Hayley saw a pair of headlights turning into the driveway.

Her stomach did a flip-flop.

She was suddenly nervous.

"They're here, Danny. I have to go."

"Give our girl a kiss for me, will ya?"

"Sure thing. And tell Dustin I love him and miss him and can't wait for him to come home."

"You've always been such a softie. Bye, babe."

Hayley ended the call and placed her cell phone down on the kitchen counter. She quickly checked herself out in the mirror hanging in the hallway next to the staircase. Her eyes were bloodshot from crying, but there was little she could do about that now.

She took a deep breath.

Hayley heard footsteps on the front porch and then the door opened with a whoosh and Gemma burst in, her arms flung open for a hug.

"Merry Christmas, Mom!"

Gemma looked radiant. Fresh-faced and glowing, her hair beautifully coiffed and styled, she was dressed to the nines in a stylish Kate Spade quilted winter coat.

Hayley held her tight for a moment, and then as she stepped back to get another look at her daughter, she felt as if she might start crying again.

"Wow, look at you! New York suits you," Hayley said, her eyes brimming with tears.

"Oh, God, Mom, don't cry!"

"I'm just so happy to see you . . . ," Hayley said, sniffling.

When did she become so mushy and overly emotional?

She could only guess it had something to do with the empty-nest syndrome, now that both her kids were growing up and spending less and less time at home.

"Mom, I want you to meet Conner."

Gemma moved aside to reveal a strikingly good-looking young man, a few inches taller than Gemma, perfectly put together, wearing a very fashionable-looking black Burberry coat. He extended a hand and offered Hayley a warm smile.

"It's nice to finally meet you, Mrs. Powell."

His voice was deep and resonating.

"Please call me Hayley. And it's great to finally meet you too, Conner."

They shook hands.

"Is this your first time in Maine?" Hayley asked.

"No, I went to Indian Acres summer camp when I was twelve in Fryeburg."

"Maine in the summer is a whole lot different than Maine in the winter," Gemma groaned. "During the summer season, there are something like sixty restaurants to choose from in Bar Harbor, but in the winter, we have something like two."

Conner laughed. "Well, I'm just happy to be here."

There was more small talk.

Hayley made hot chocolate and they sat in the living room, and Conner complimented the Christmas decorations around the house and talked about how scary the bumpy flight from LaGuardia had been. Gemma stared at him, googly-eyed, as if he was the most wonderful man in the world, saying the most important and interesting things.

She was clearly smitten.

Meanwhile, Hayley silently sized him up as he talked about how much he admired Gemma and her decision to try and make it in New York, and how he had never met a girl with such a kind heart.

He struck every note perfectly.

There wasn't a red flag to be found.

He was even shy about discussing his acting career, explaining he was primarily a stage actor with a few obscure, but well-reviewed, Off-Broadway credits. Gemma had to drag out of him that he had appeared in a Shakespeare in the Park production of *The Merry Wives of Windsor* the previous summer, which was indeed impressive in Hayley's opinion.

Conner was not the vain, self-absorbed, chatty, shady character she had expected to meet.

On the surface, he appeared friendly, engaged, and very fond of Gemma.

There appeared to be absolutely nothing wrong with him.

So why did Hayley have the nagging feeling that there was something off about him?

There was no clear evidence.

Maybe she was just guilty of being the typical over-protective mother.

And yet, deep down, she just didn't trust this guy.

Chapter Two

"**I** once thought about pursuing acting as a career," Bruce Linney said as he lathered his blueberry pancakes with a healthy dose of maple syrup.

"Oh, brother, here we go," Hayley sighed, having heard this laborious tale more than once.

"I won Best Supporting Actor at the Maine State Drama Festival for my riveting performance in the musical *Godspell*," Bruce boasted proudly.

"It was rigged!" Hayley cried. "Bruce's father was a dentist, and two of the judges just happened to be his patients, and as I recall, your dad promised a big discount on new molars if they voted for you!" Hayley said, sipping her coffee.

Gemma and Conner were seated across from Hayley and Bruce in a booth at Jordan's Restaurant. The popular breakfast hot spot was one of the few eateries in town to stay open year-round, except for the month of February when the owners flew south to shake off the winter blues.

"Come on, Hayley, I deserved that award!" Bruce said before popping a forkful of pancakes into his mouth, maple syrup dripping down his chin.

Hayley mouthed silently, "No, he didn't!"

Conner smiled, shaking his head, and Gemma giggled.

"I actually won Best Actor at the National College Drama Awards my senior year for playing McMurphy in *One Flew Over the Cuckoo's Nest.*"

"When was that?" Hayley casually asked.

"It was 2014," Conner replied, winking at Gemma, who sat next to him, her eyes fixed on his handsome face, utterly enchanted by him.

Hayley's mind worked overtime.

Two thousand fourteen?

That would make Conner roughly twenty-five or twenty-six years old.

He was older than Gemma by about five years.

Certainly not an unreasonable age difference.

But it still rubbed her the wrong way.

Hayley hated herself for trying to find things wrong with this otherwise personable, friendly, ambitious young man.

"Why didn't you become an actor, Mr. Linney?" Conner asked.

"Call me Bruce, please. I don't know. Writing turned out to be more my thing. I used to watch a lot of cop shows when I was a kid and so I just sort of fell into crime reporting during college. But who knows? Maybe I'll get back into the whole acting game someday."

Hayley nearly spit out her coffee at that one.

Bruce shot her a sideways glance. "You know, we are technically dating now, so part of your job as my girlfriend is being supportive."

"You're right, Bruce. You should definitely follow your dream and become an actor. Ryan Gosling won't know what hit him!"

Bruce leaned in and bumped Hayley's shoulder with his own. "She loves to tease me."

"I can see that. You two make a nice couple," Conner said.

Hayley and Bruce hadn't been dating all that long. In fact, Hayley still woke up in the morning every now and then asking herself, *Is it true I'm actually dating Bruce Linney of all people?*

They had never been particularly close working together at the *Island Times* newspaper. They shared a brief history of once dating in high school, but Hayley hardly remembered any significant or lasting chemistry or attraction. It was only a few months ago, while working closely together, that she was suddenly struck, like by a lightning bolt, with a previously unthinkable thought—Bruce Linney was cute. And after a surprise kiss, which lasted longer than either of them had ever expected, they soon just fell into a relaxed, comfortable, slow-budding romance. A dinner here, a sporting event there, then eventually a romantic candlelight dinner for two at a quiet, out-of-the-way restaurant, and pretty soon she was cooking for him at her home. Now they were . . . Well, it was so hard to think about, let alone say it, but what the hell, now they were officially dating.

"You two make an adorable couple yourselves," Bruce said, returning the compliment.

Hayley kicked him under the table.

Bruce barely reacted, suppressing a wince as the pain from Hayley's shoe shot through his foot.

Hayley wanted Bruce to meet Conner in order to gauge his reaction to the young man from New York courting Gemma. She herself had severe reservations, even though she had only known him twelve hours, so she invited Bruce to join them for breakfast in order to get an unvarnished second opinion.

As it stood, he was definitely leaning toward Team Conner.

In fact, he appeared as if they were actually bonding.

Hayley could tell Gemma was loving every minute of it.

The more people who approved of her new beau was a good thing.

"How are your pancakes, Conner?" Hayley asked.

"Delicious, thank you," he said politely.

That was the moment Gemma picked up a crisp, almost burnt, piece of bacon and crunched on it before loudly announcing to the whole table, "Conner and I are moving in together."

Hayley dropped her fork and it bounced up off the table and clattered to the floor. The heavyset waitress, passing by, bent over and scooped it up, saying, "I'll get you a new one, Hayley!"

And then she was gone.

"I'm sorry, what was that?" Hayley asked.

"She's getting you a new fork," Bruce offered.

"I heard that, Bruce! I'm talking about what Gemma just said!"

"Oh . . . ," Bruce said quietly, realizing it was probably best to ease himself out of the conversation for his own sake.

"I said Conner and I are moving in—"

"I heard you!"

"Then why did you ask?" Gemma said, bracing for a fight.

Hayley felt sandbagged.

This bombshell was carefully planned.

Gemma clearly didn't want to break this news in the privacy of Hayley's home, because her mother would feel free to yell and overreact, so she covertly plotted and waited patiently until they were in a loud public setting before dropping the bomb.

It was a genius move.

Because as upset as Hayley was, she instinctively felt compelled to keep her voice down to an urgent whisper. "When did this happen?"

"Just a few days ago. Conner found a great deal on an apartment in Hell's Kitchen . . ."

"As great a deal as you can get in New York. It's still staggeringly expensive! I mean, seriously, for one month's rent, they'll probably want our first-born," he said, chuckling.

Hayley glared at him and his jocular chuckling ceased immediately.

"That was a really bad analogy. I didn't mean to imply Gemma and I are thinking about having children, because we're not. No way. It's just an expression."

Hayley ignored him and looked at Gemma. "Don't you think this is moving a little too fast?"

"No, Mother, I don't. It's not like we're getting married. We're just going to be sharing an apartment," Gemma said defensively, popping the rest of the half-eaten piece of bacon into her mouth.

"What about your lease in Astoria?" Bruce asked.

"I can get out of that easily. My roommate, Athena, drives me nuts with her constant complaining and insomnia and rigid rules, and frankly she's no big fan of mine anyway. She was thrilled when I told her I'm moving out, and she's already found another girl to replace me. It worked out perfectly."

Hayley turned to Bruce for some support, but he just shrugged helplessly. "She's twenty years old, Hayley."

Not helpful.

Not helpful at all.

He knew Hayley wasn't happy with him for that last comment, so he decided to just focus on eating the rest of his blueberry pancakes.

"It's a practical decision, Mrs. Powell," Conner said, leaning forward toward Hayley as he slid an arm around Gemma's shoulders, almost possessively in Hayley's opinion, though she suspected at the moment she might not be at her most objective.

"How is it practical?" Hayley asked.

"New York rents are ridiculously high for one person, so at least with two of us, we can take some of the burden off the other," Conner said calmly.

"How many bedrooms?" Hayley was quick to add.

"It's a studio," Gemma said softly, reaching for a glass of orange juice.

The waitress sailed by, dropping a clean fork off in front of Hayley and kept going.

"With a Murphy bed," Conner said. "The kind that comes down out of the wall?"

"I know what a Murphy bed is," Hayley said, trying to keep her voice even and emotionless.

So they would be sharing a bed.

In one room.

"It's a fifth-floor walk-up, so at least I'll get some

exercise, since I haven't had time to join a gym lately," Gemma blurted out.

There was a lull in the conversation.

Bruce was still stinging from the rebuke he got from reminding Hayley that Gemma was a legal adult. With his eyes downcast, he began gnawing on his own piece of crispy, burnt bacon.

Hayley took a deep breath.

As much as she resented Bruce for pointing out the obvious, she knew he was right.

Gemma was no longer a child.

Maybe it was time to let go.

She was just about to call a truce, and offer the young couple her support—however tepid it was—when Conner revealed his true self.

At least in Hayley's mind.

With a smug, smarmy smile, he added, "Besides, Gemma is a grown woman and can make her own decisions. It's not like you can stop her."

Hayley bristled.

Even Gemma was taken aback by the offhanded comment.

No one spoke for a full ten seconds.

Only Bruce managed to break the uncomfortable silence at the table by chewing loudly on his bacon.

Hayley had tried to give Conner the benefit of the doubt, but now it was official.

She not only didn't trust the guy, now she also didn't like him either.

Not one bit.

Chapter Three

Hayley's tree-trimming gathering at her house that evening was a quiet affair because the last thing Hayley wanted to do was give the impression she was competing with her BFF Liddy's far-more-elaborate annual Christmas party that was to be held the following evening. In fact, Hayley had purposefully used the word "gathering" because she didn't want to even utter the word "party." With Liddy too crazed and overwhelmed with her own party preparations to attend, that left Bruce; Hayley's brother, Randy; his husband, Police Chief Sergio Alvares; Hayley's other BFF, Mona Barnes; and, of course, Gemma and her new beau, Conner. All were crowded into her small kitchen, sipping spiked eggnog and watching as Hayley pulled a tray of piping-hot gourmet pigs in the blanket, or, in layman's terms, sausage in a puff pastry, out of her oven.

She had barely managed to set the metal tray on top of her stove, when she was instantly surrounded by her guests, all of them reaching in at once to grab one.

"Watch it, they're hot!" Hayley warned.

But no one listened, and Mona, who had plucked one from the tray with her chubby fingers, found herself suddenly tossing it around like she was juggling a ball of fire. She quickly popped it in her mouth to give her burning hands some relief. Unfortunately, she forgot to take into account that the appetizer would still be hot in her mouth and suddenly she was racing for the sink to spit out the food. She cranked the faucet on, and then lowered her mouth into the stream of tap water, gulping it down as if she had been lost in the Sahara for a week, dying of thirst.

Hayley grabbed some paper plates and quickly handed them out so everyone had something to hold their pigs in a blanket with, instead of their burning fingers.

"Hayley, you could have warned us!" Mona bellowed.

"You're right, Mona. How silly of me to assume you might not realize that when a hot appetizer comes directly out of an oven that's been heated to three hundred and fifty degrees, it might be a little more than warm. And when I actually said the words 'Watch it, they're hot,' was I speaking in a foreign tongue? Was it French, German, Spanish?"

"All right, don't get cute," Mona growled.

Mona gingerly poked at another one, making sure it had cooled down, before taking a tiny bite and chewing on it. "I have to admit, though, they're not half bad."

"Thank you. That's a rave coming from you,"

Hayley said, chuckling. "Be sure to write a Yelp review."

"Mrs. Powell, Gemma said you were talented in the kitchen, but I had no idea . . ."

"Flattery will get you everywhere, Conner," Hayley said, smiling.

The young man could be a charmer, that was for certain, but that didn't mean she had to like him.

Randy, however, was sold on Conner from the moment he met him.

Unlike Bruce, who had only dabbled in acting during high school, Randy had studied at the Academy of Dramatic Arts in New York for a brief time before his enthusiasm and determination flamed out. After a few years, he moved back to Maine and kicked around for a while, before opening his bar, Drinks Like A Fish. So when Randy met the handsome young actor, he felt an instant connection. It also didn't hurt that Conner was undisputedly good-looking. Randy could be a shameless flirt. Luckily, his other half, Sergio, was not the jealous type, despite his fiery Brazilian heritage. Sergio allowed Randy to have fun, bantering and teasing, just so long as at the end of the evening they left the party together as a married couple.

"So tell me more about your work, Conner," Randy said, beaming from ear to ear at Gemma, signaling to her that he definitely approved of her choice in a boyfriend.

Conner shrugged shyly. "I'm a stage actor at heart. Nothing fires me up like a live audience, hanging on your every word, your every movement, completely forgetting they're in a darkened theater because they are so purely in that moment with you."

Mona coughed, unimpressed.

Randy stared at Conner, mesmerized.

"That whole theater world is not for me. I would be too afraid I would forget the lines and look like a fool in front of all those people who paid so much money to come see the play," Sergio said in his thick accent, shaking his head.

"What are you talking about? You forget your words all the time," Randy joked, before leaning toward Conner with a sly smile. "English is his second language."

Sergio playfully swatted Randy on the back of the head with his open palm.

"I'd rather be a star on television. At least you get to do retakes if you mess up," Bruce said.

"I'm not a big fan of television," Conner said.

"What about movies?" Bruce asked.

Conner scrunched up his nose. "It doesn't have the same thrill as the rewards of being on stage. I'm not knocking it, it's just not something I'm all that interested in pursuing."

"But these days a successful actor has to be versatile enough to do it all. Film, TV, stage, Web series, not to mention have a Facebook account, a Twitter presence, and a ton of Instagram followers," Randy said breathlessly, outlining his own goals if he was back where Conner was now, just starting out.

There was something wistful about Randy as he interacted with Conner, as if thoughts of what might have been were suddenly bubbling to the surface. Hayley knew her brother loved his husband, his business, his family, and living in Bar Harbor, but she suspected there was always a little pang of regret deep inside him, wondering what might have happened if he had stuck with acting, what path his life ultimately would have taken.

"All right, can everyone clear out and give me some room to breathe, please? I still have to make my Yule log cakes and it's time to decorate the tree," Hayley ordered, shooing everyone out of the kitchen. "Make sure you have a full glass of eggnog. The decorations are in the boxes in the living room, so go get started."

She placed the rest of the pigs in the blanket on a ceramic plate with a reindeer design and handed it to Sergio. "Here, take these with you."

They all filed out, down the hallway, veering right into the living room. Hayley caught Bruce, who was the last to leave, by the arm. "I'm counting on you to supervise. Randy usually gets too tipsy on my eggnog and starts breaking the ornaments, and Mona has a tendency to drown the tree in tinsel!"

"I'm on it," he said, kissing Hayley on the cheek and dashing out.

She opened the refrigerator and removed a giant bowl of chocolate cake batter from the top shelf and set it down on the counter. Then she opened a cupboard and pulled down her mixer to whip the cream filling for the Yule log cake.

Gemma casually wandered back into the kitchen.

"Did you forget something?" Hayley asked.

"I just want to get your opinion. You haven't told me how you feel about Conner."

"Oh . . . I like him," Hayley lied, a frozen smile on her face.

Gemma studied her mother, trying to discern if she was telling the truth or not.

It was obvious Hayley was faking.

Gemma frowned, then asked, "Can I help with the Yule log cakes?"

"After making them all these years, I've got it down to a science. You don't have to hang out in the kitchen with me all night. Go rescue Conner from Uncle Randy's third-degree interrogation."

Hayley then searched a drawer for a big wooden spoon and noticed Gemma was still leaning against the counter, staring at her.

Hayley sighed. "Okay. I have nothing against Conner. I just feel moving in together is a big step, and maybe you're not quite ready for that kind of commitment."

"Like I said, it's more of a financial decision. New York is very expensive. I can't afford it on my own."

"I know, but—"

"I don't know what's going to happen between Conner and me down the road, but what I do know is I want to make a go of becoming a professional chef, with my own restaurant someday, maybe a line of cookbooks, or, who knows, perhaps a cooking show on TV or online. And I really feel like I should be in New York. It's a gut feeling I have, and I really want to give it my best shot."

"I'm proud of you, Gemma, and I want you to be happy doing whatever it is you want to do in life. But I thought you wanted to be a veterinarian."

"I thought so, too. But I'm allowed a few false starts while I figure out what it is I want to spend my life doing, right?"

"Of course."

"And right now, I really, really want to pursue

this. And maybe in five years I'll wake up one day and say to myself, 'You know what, I'm done with food' and I'll be on to something else, but I have time. I'm young."

"How on earth did I raise such a mature and thoughtful young woman?"

Hayley hugged Gemma tightly.

As they pulled away from one another, Hayley couldn't resist adding, "I'm still not sold on Zac Efron out there in the living room."

"Give him a chance," Gemma scolded. "He's a nice guy, Mother."

Hayley nodded, not entirely convinced.

"Now, let me help."

"I've got this. Trust me."

"And no one in town makes a better Yule log cake than you, but I'm talking about the presentation."

Hayley raised an eyebrow. "Presentation?"

"Look, every year all the neighbors rave about how delicious your Yule log cakes are, but when you deliver them, you drop them off in a plain old Tupperware container, and it's so boring!"

"Boring?"

"Yes, Mother, and then you spend half of January tracking everyone down to get the Tupperware back if they haven't bothered to return it on their own, or you just forget about it and have to buy new ones. Plus it's a real pain in the butt when you could just be a lot more festive with what you deliver them in."

Hayley folded her arms, suddenly curious. "What do you suggest?"

"Well, I picked up these cute little red-and-green baskets at a craft store in Brooklyn a couple of weeks ago. They're the perfect size for one of your Yule log cakes. How about we wrap the cakes and put them in the basket, and then we tie it to an actual Yule log with Christmas ribbon. That way, the neighbors can enjoy your cake in front of a fireplace while a traditional Yule log burns in the hearth."

"Who are you, Martha Stewart?"

"She wishes she could come up with something that clever!" Gemma boasted. "And if I've learned anything from all of those food competition shows I watch on a loop, presentation is everything!"

Hayley had to admit, it was an adorable idea.

And she really hated playing Tupperware detective trying to locate all of her containers after New Year's every year.

Maybe Gemma was onto something.

"So if you bake the cakes, I'll be in charge of wrapping and preparing them for delivery around the neighborhood and at your office," Gemma offered.

"Deal," Hayley said, reaching out and shaking Gemma's hand.

Mona sauntered into the kitchen. "You better go save your boyfriend, Gemma. Bruce is threatening to sing his opening number from *Godspell.*"

"Oh no!" Gemma exclaimed before rushing out.

Hayley poured the cake batter onto a paper-lined tray with the help of a wooden spoon.

"Randy's already dropped three ornaments on the floor, so you might want to think about cutting him off from the spiked eggnog," Mona said. "Any more of those piglet things?"

"Pigs in the blanket, and, no, I sent them all out

to the living room. Don't worry, I have a few more appetizers ready to go in the oven. Now that it's just the two of us, Mona, I have to ask . . ."

"No, I don't like him."

"Who?"

"The actor. There's something about him that rubs me the wrong way."

Hayley was grateful that finally someone agreed with her.

Mona was not a fan of Conner.

But it should not have surprised her.

Hayley had already strongly suspected Mona would be on her side, and so she felt validated knowing she wasn't the only one not cheering for Team Conner.

But asking Mona how she felt held very little risk because when it came to Mona and her strong opinions about people, one thing was perfectly clear—Mona Barnes pretty much hated everybody.

Chapter Four

Liddy Crawford's Christmas party was obviously the most anticipated social event of the entire holiday season in Bar Harbor. Liddy had once again tried to keep the guest list smaller this year by only mailing out seventy-five invitations, but more than two hundred people showed up, cramming into her house, devouring her food, and emptying her wine rack. The catering staff made a valiant effort to circle around to everyone and serve Liddy's carefully selected menu of appetizers. However, the waiters barely managed to feed just a handful of the hungry guests before having to retreat back to the kitchen with their empty trays to reload.

Hayley and Gemma volunteered to help out in the kitchen because Liddy's caterer was completely overwhelmed and on the verge of a meltdown. On the one hand, Liddy was flattered that her little soiree was widely popular with the locals, but on the other hand, she was taking down the names of those who had rudely crashed her party, some even arriving with tagalong friends she didn't even know.

The downstairs living room, dining room, and den were so jammed with people, Sergio feared the whole event was a fire hazard, but nobody seemed to care as they sang impromptu Christmas carols while Randy played the piano.

At one point, Hayley had to rush home and raid her own fridge for leftovers from her tree-trimming gathering from the night before so they could warm them up and serve to Liddy's guests, since the caterer was already dangerously low on food.

But the bottom line was, it appeared everybody was having a grand ole time, and Liddy's party was on course to go down in history as a memorable evening.

No one knew at the time, however, just how memorable it was going to be.

As Hayley rushed out a tray of Beef Short Ribs Empanadas to hand off to one of the college-aged waiters working for the caterer, she spotted a dark-haired woman in a slinky red dress, and too much makeup, slip through the front door and try to blend in with the crowd.

As Liddy zipped past her, Hayley reached out and stopped her. "We have another party crasher."

"Who?" Liddy asked, spinning her head around.

"Kimmy Bradford at two o'clock," Hayley said.

Liddy's eyes fell on the awkward woman desperately trying to act casual. "Oh, my God, what is she doing here?"

"Maybe she came as a plus one."

"No one would dare. Everyone knows I can't stand her!" Liddy growled. "And look at that dress. Could it possibly show any more cleavage?"

"Don't be catty," Hayley scolded, eyeing the even lower-cut party dress Liddy was wearing.

"Seriously, all that's missing is the embroidered scarlet letter," Liddy said, shaking her head.

Kimmy Bradford had what you would call a reputation in town.

She had always been a quiet mousy girl growing up, the daughter of a local minister, but after returning home from college in Portland with a teaching degree, she had transformed herself into a buxom raven beauty who could stop traffic. When she showed up for a job interview to teach English Literature, the high-school principal, who hadn't even recognized his former student, was so impressed with her assets, none of which actually involved teaching skills, that he hired her right on the spot. But sadly, Kimmy was only employed for two semesters before resigning under mysterious circumstances. A few gossips in town suggested Kimmy was forced to leave the school after it came to light that a few of her good-looking male students got a little too much attention than was proper, both morally and legally.

Kimmy was now a receptionist at the company where Liddy once worked before Liddy decided to quit and start her own real estate firm. Liddy claimed her animosity toward Kimmy had nothing to do with jealousy—because Kimmy was younger and prettier than Liddy—and as her closest friend, it was Hayley's job to take her word for it. Even though, deep down, she didn't believe it for a second.

"Are you going to tell her to leave?" Hayley asked.

"No, I'm not going to cause a scene at my own

party. And it's not like she's the only one who showed up without an invitation."

"I better serve these empanadas before they get cold," Hayley said, leaving Liddy's side and pushing her way through the endless throng of guests. She barely made a half circle around the room, when the last empanada was plucked off the tray by Ron Hopkins, the owner of the Shop 'n Save supermarket.

"Moonlighting for some extra cash, Hayley?" Ron asked before popping the empanada in his mouth.

"No, Ron, just helping out. A few more people came than were invited, so the caterer is a bit understaffed."

"Well, DeAnn and I were certainly invited," Ron announced loudly. "We would never be so vulgar as to crash, right, sweetheart?"

Ron's much younger wife, DeAnn, a petite blonde, attractive but with some pronounced worry lines on her forehead, nodded, uninterested in contributing any more to the conversation.

Hayley used to like Ron.

He once was a rather amiable, although beleaguered, friend of hers. Ron never really enjoyed owning a supermarket. He always wanted to travel with his first wife, Lenora, once his kids grew up and were out on their own. But when that day finally came, and he was officially an empty nester, Rob had a midlife crisis. He dumped Lenora and started dating a string of younger women, until finally settling on DeAnn, a single mother from Brunswick, whom he had met in a local bar one spring. DeAnn was in town for a golf tournament with her then-current beau, a married bank executive from Bangor. Once she and Ron connected, DeAnn sent the banker packing, back to his wife in Bangor, and by week's end she had moved in with Ron and enrolled her little boy at Conners Emerson grade school.

DeAnn seemed nice enough, but Ron, who had hung on to the store in order to support his new wife and stepson, never seemed the same as he was when they first met. Once a quietly charming, good, and decent man, he now struck Hayley as bitter and arrogant and sporting a superior attitude, never wasting an opportunity to show off his trophy wife, the one thing in his life that seemed to make him happy nowadays.

Ron suddenly noticed the worry lines on his wife's face, too. "Sweetheart, is anything wrong?"

DeAnn shook her head. "No, dear, I'm fine. Why?"

"You just don't seem to be having a good time. Do you want to leave?"

"No, you've worked hard all week. You deserve to have a little fun, and the last thing I want to do is spoil your evening by dragging you home early."

"Too late," Ron hissed as he spotted someone on the opposite side of the room.

"Why? What's wrong?" DeAnn asked, more worry lines finding their way to her forehead.

"Over there. Talking to Hayley's daughter. I'm reasonably sure he was not invited to this party. That creep is nothing but bad news."

This caught Hayley's attention. She turned to see a handsome young man, in a ratty white tank top that showed off his muscles and ripped blue jeans. It was a completely inappropriate outfit for the cocktail attire request that Liddy had printed clearly on her party invitations. He was chatting up Gemma, who held an empty tray in front of her, almost as if using it as a shield to keep the aggressive young man at bay. Gemma was smiling politely, but Hayley could tell she was not comfortable talking to him. Gemma kept trying to walk away, but each time she attempted to leave, he would block her with his body, keeping her in front of him.

Hayley instantly recognized him.

It was Ryan Toledo.

An old high-school classmate of Gemma's.

A bad boy who was always getting suspended for one infraction or another.

They were never close, but Gemma always tried to be nice to him.

Like she did with everyone in her orbit.

Years ago Hayley feared Gemma and Ryan might start dating, since as a rule, high-school girls tend to be drawn to good-looking, bad-boy rebels, but their relationship, luckily, never evolved beyond a casual friendship.

When Ryan reached out and suddenly gripped Gemma by the arm, whispering something urgently in her ear, Hayley had seen enough. She began moving through the guests squeezed together in such close quarters, trying to make her way across the room. She kept her eyes fixed on Gemma. Hayley could plainly see the tension in Gemma's face, despite the fact she was trying to maintain a good-natured, friendly demeanor.

By the time Hayley finally reached Gemma, she was close enough that she could smell alcohol on Ryan's breath, and instantly noticed his bloodshot eyes.

He still clutched Gemma's arm tightly.

"Gemma, I need you in the kitchen," Hayley said.

Gemma nodded and turned to Ryan, forcing a smile. "I have to go, Ryan. It was nice talking to you."

He still didn't let go of her arm. "But you didn't answer my question."

"Yes, I did. I'm already seeing someone, so going out with you is probably not a good idea right now. But I appreciate you asking."

"Come on, that guy? I saw him when you two walked in here. He's like a little mouse. You would do better with a real man," Ryan said.

Hayley stepped between Gemma and Ryan, forcing Ryan to finally let go of Gemma's arm, which he had held so hard Hayley could see the imprints from his fingers on her bare arm as Gemma withdrew.

Now even closer to him, she couldn't help but wince.

Ryan's breath reeked of alcohol.

Hayley had to turn away.

Ryan tried to shove past Hayley to get to Gemma again.

"Can I get a little kiss?"

"No!" a man's voice boomed.

Ryan slowly turned, focusing on the much smaller Conner, who bravely stood behind him, holding two glasses of punch.

"Says who?" Ryan laughed.

"Me," Conner said, standing his ground.

Ryan glanced at the two plastic cups full of red punch and then with his fists banged the bottom of them. The fruit punch flew out of the cups and drenched Conner's face.

"Mind your own business, bitch," Ryan snarled.

And then, Conner dropped the empty cups and pushed him.

Not hard, just as a warning, but it was enough to rile Ryan enough that he dove at Conner, knocking him to the ground, pummeling him in the face with his fists. Hayley and Gemma jumped in and attempted to drag Ryan off Conner, but Ryan was in some kind of zone, blocking out their screams. He wasn't going to stop until Conner was unconscious or dead.

As hard as they tried, Hayley and Gemma couldn't get Ryan under control as Conner covered his face with his hands, trying to protect himself from the onslaught of blows. The surrounding guests were so stunned and shocked by what was happening, none thought to intervene and help. Luckily, however, Sergio had just arrived a few minutes earlier. He was hanging by the piano, listening to his husband, Randy, bang out "Jingle Bells," when Kimmy Bradford noticed the commotion clear across the room. She immediately reported it to the police chief. He bounded across the room and the crowd parted like the Red Sea, allowing him to reach Ryan. Sergio was a big man, and after pushing Hayley and Gemma aside, he managed to get Ryan in a headlock. He applied enough pressure so that Ryan was finally forced to let go of Conner, who rolled over on his side in a crumpled heap.

"What the hell is the matter with you?" Sergio yelled into Ryan's ear.

Ryan, unable to breathe, slumped forward, about to pass out. But then Sergio released him and hauled him to his feet, holding him by a fistful of his tank top.

"Did you hear me?" Sergio said.

Ryan nodded slowly, but didn't speak.

"I'm taking you down to the station and booking you for assault."

Liddy suddenly appeared, eyes wide with fury, and screamed at Ryan. "I didn't invite you, I have absolutely no idea who you even are, and you ruined my party!"

Sergio clamped a hand on the back of Ryan's neck and began pulling him toward the door.

"Wait, I'm okay, let him go," Conner said, wiping away some blood around his nose with the back of his hand.

Sergio stopped and turned Ryan around to face Conner, who was back on his feet, being doted on by a concerned Gemma.

"You sure?" Sergio asked.

"Yes," Conner said. "It just got a little heated. No harm done. I don't want anyone arrested so close to Christmas."

"Well, I do! I want him arrested for trespassing!" Liddy howled.

Conner turned to Liddy. "Please, Ms. Crawford, let's just forget the whole thing and get back to having a good time at your wonderful party."

Liddy paused, then relented. "All right, if that's what you want. Wait. Who are you again?"

"He's my boyfriend," Gemma said.

"Oh, right," Liddy said, giving him the once-over. "Cute. And who's the sleazy outlaw?"

"Someone I went to high school with," Gemma said.

"Okay," Liddy said, turning to Ryan, who was still being held by Sergio. "Fine. I won't press charges, but at least get him out of my house!"

Sergio nodded and hauled Ryan over to the door and gave him the boot.

Hayley and Gemma rushed to the window and watched Ryan skulk away down the driveway and off into the woods across the road.

The party improved immeasurably from that point on, especially since most of the crashers cleared the room the minute the caterer ran out of food. Ron's wife, DeAnn, left shortly after the Ryan Toledo drama, complaining of a headache, but since it was barely after eight o'clock, Ron chose to stay behind for a while longer because he was enjoying the spiked punch and kept refilling his plastic cup. Kimmy Bradford disappeared soon after that. By ten o'clock, more guests had slowly melted away. Mona's younger kids, of course, ate too many sweets, like every year, and their sugar highs got so unmanageable, she and her husband, "Deadbeat Dennis" as she liked to refer to him, loaded them into their SUV to take them home. Conner asked Gemma if she would mind if he had Mona drop him off at Hayley's house. He was tired and wanted to get some sleep after his unexpected boxing match. Gemma offered to accompany him, but Conner insisted that Gemma stay and enjoy herself with her family and friends. He left after apologizing to Liddy for the tenth time for getting blood on her white Persian rug. Ron Hopkins also left around the same time to go home. So only the diehards were left around the piano to sing more Christmas carols—Hayley, Liddy, Randy, Sergio, Gemma, and late-comer Bruce, who had been busy filing a story at the office, and had to be brought up to speed on the dramatic events that had transpired earlier in the evening.

"Well, at least everyone will be talking about your party, Liddy," Randy said as the stragglers finished singing "Frosty the Snowman."

And he was right.

Liddy's party was going to be written about and talked about for years to come.

But not because a drunken suitor, who was vying for Gemma's attention, had attacked her actor boyfriend from the big city and had bloodied his nose.

No, the party would be remembered for something entirely different. Because not five minutes after Randy made that remark, Sergio's cell phone buzzed. When he answered the call, everyone immediately noticed the pale intensity on his face as he listened to whoever was on the other end.

When he hung up, Randy stood up from the piano. "What is it?"

"A body was just found in the woods not too far from here."

"What?" Liddy gasped.

Sergio turned to Gemma. "Ryan Toledo. Your high-school classmate."

Then he turned to Liddy, who had a puzzled look on her face. "The one we kicked out of your party."

Yes, this was going to be a Christmas party for the books.

Island Food & Spirits
By Hayley Powell

L ast week I hauled all the Christmas decorations down from the attic to sort through and get ready for my annual family tree-trimming get-together. Whenever the holiday season rolls around and the time comes to unpack all the ornaments and lights and garland and figurines, I can't help but daydream about all those Christmas mornings long ago when my now-fully-grown adult son and daughter were still two rambunctious, excitable little kids. I hate to admit it, but I'm a real softie, especially when I rummage through old cardboard boxes and happen upon the homemade decorations my kids made for me when they were in grade school.

I often think, "Where in the world did the time go?" But the real question should be: "Why in the world did I save every single decoration they ever made?"

I'm sure every mother knows some of those decorations and gifts created as projects in Art were downright ugly, something only a mother could love. But still, each one had a special memory attached to it.

In one box marked "Christmas Gifts from the Kids," I had to use both hands to pull out a giant glass bottle decanter! It was deep ruby red with fluorescent purple, yellow, and blue hearts all over it, and in glittery-gold, shiny letters on the front was printed the word "Perfume."

I immediately burst out laughing as I remembered the year I had received this awesomely tacky gift from Dustin when he was in the first grade. He was six, and I could never forget how excited he was to bestow such a valuable treasure upon me. He could hardly contain his excitement as he stood in front of the tree, bouncing eagerly from foot to foot, all the while trying to hold the heavy package in his tiny arms as he grinned from ear to ear. As I complimented the wrapping and began to open my gift, he stared intently at me, not wanting to miss a moment of my reaction to his carefully selected Christmas gift.

I should probably mention here, as some of you might not know, that every year our local YWCA holds a Children's Christmas Shopping Day on a Saturday in early December. All year long, people can donate gently used or never used items that are no longer needed or wanted so that all the children in town from ages five to eight can be dropped off to buy presents for their parents, siblings, and even grandparents. Volunteers escort the children around the rooms and gym of the YWCA that are filled with a variety of items that the kids can pick from to give away on Christmas morning. The volunteers then wrap and tag each gift, while the kids enjoy cookies and a movie until all the parents return to pick them up.

I was on the receiving end of quite a few interesting gifts from this lovely program over the years, so I was fully prepared to react with unbridled joy, no matter how hideous the gift! But even I had trouble on this particular Christmas morning not recoiling at what had to be the most enormous, grotesque perfume bottle I had ever seen in my life! To make matters worse, Dustin jumped up and down, yelling, "Open it up and put some on!"

Well, I could only imagine what kind of scent I would find inside this bottle, but I gamely unpeeled the foil wrapper off the top of the decanter and unscrewed the top of the bottle. As I slowly removed the top and the scent wafted out, I nearly passed out. It was an ungodly smell, so sour and overpowering. My eyes became watery, but Dustin, luckily, assumed I was crying because I was so moved by his thoughtful gift. Every facial muscle fought not to scrunch up in horror and I held the bottle with both hands because I was afraid if I spilled any on the floor, the smell would seep into the carpet and I'd never get the stench out.

I managed to convince my son I loved his gift, even though my performance would never rival Meryl Streep by any stretch of the imagination. My outspoken daughter, Gemma, however, saw no need to protect her little brother's feelings. She took one whiff and cried, "Mom, it smells like a dead skunk in here!"

Poor Dustin's eyes welled up with tears, though it could have been caused by the wretched perfume. I set the bottle down on the coffee table and ran over to him, hugging him close and assuring him that this wondrous, sweet-smelling perfume was the best Christmas present I had ever received. I chose to ignore his sister, who was dramatically pinching her nose closed while making loud, gagging noises.

After patting Dustin on the back and thanking him again for the lovely gift, I sat him down in front of his newly opened Christmas toys in an effort to change the subject. Luckily, he had a new train set to assemble, which kept his mind occupied for the rest of the morning, while I headed into the kitchen to make his favorite Christmas-morning muffins (and to open the kitchen window to get some fresh air inside the house). Baking also allowed me some private time to figure out a plan on how to replace the contents of the perfume bottle with a more palatable scent and to also enjoy a favorite Mom's Christmas Morning Cocktail.

Mom's Christmas Morning Cocktail

Ingredients

2 cups cranberry juice
1 cup orange juice
1 bottle Prosecco
1 orange slice
1 cup cranberries
1 cinnamon stick

In a two-quart pitcher, mix together your cranberry juice, orange juice, and Prosecco and stir.

Add the orange slice, cranberries, and cinnamon stick.

Pour into a chilled glass or chill a pitcher in the fridge for a while.

Pour into your favorite brunch glasses and enjoy.

Dustin's Christmas Morning Cinnamon Muffins

Ingredients
1½ cups flour
½ cup sugar
2 teaspoons baking powder
½ teaspoon salt
½ teaspoon ground nutmeg
½ teaspoon allspice
1 egg, beaten
½ cup milk
⅓ cup butter, melted

For the topping:
2 tablespoons brown sugar (or regular sugar if
    that's your preference)
½ teaspoon ground cinnamon
¼ cup melted butter

Mix your flour, sugar, baking powder, salt, all-spice, and nutmeg.

Add the egg and butter and milk into flour mixture and stir just until moistened.

Divide into a greased or paper-lined muffin tin.

Bake at 375 degrees for 20 minutes or until a toothpick comes out clean.

While muffins are baking, combine your remaining cinnamon and sugar in a small bowl and set aside.

Melt the butter in a small saucepan.

Remove the finished muffins from the oven and brush the tops of the muffins with the melted butter, then roll the tops in the cinnamon/sugar mixture.

Place them on a pretty Christmas platter, then just sit back and watch them be gobbled up in a matter of seconds.

Chapter Five

Ryan Toledo's untimely death was ruled a homicide a day later after the Hancock County coroner filed his autopsy report with the police. According to his findings, the victim had been bludgeoned to death. At first, no one in town seemed all that surprised or even cared much. In fact, the revelation that Toledo was savagely attacked in the woods and murdered was met with a collective yawn and didn't even warrant a front-page headline in Bar Harbor's two rival newspapers, the *Island Times* and the *Bar Harbor Herald*. Most people just assumed the kid had it coming. He had always been considered bad news and was probably mixed up with the wrong crowd since high school, hanging out with drug dealers and that sort. He was always up to no good, and most likely just crossed the wrong baseball-bat-wielding lowlife.

That was what people thought . . .

Then that evening after work, Hayley was making the rounds, delivering her chocolate Yule logs in the festive baskets tied with a red ribbon around a thick round actual Yule log. She stopped by Randy and Sergio's home to drop off the one she had personally made for them.

Randy ushered her inside, insisting she stay for a hot toddy. When Randy set Hayley's thoughtful Christmas gift down on the coffee table, in front of the fire, and went into the kitchen to make the drinks, Hayley couldn't help but notice Sergio. He was sitting on the couch, leaning forward and intensely staring at the Yule log.

"Is something wrong, Sergio?"

He didn't answer her at first.

He was still eyeballing the Yule log.

"Where did you get that red ribbon?"

"I'm not sure," Hayley answered. "Maybe the crafts store in Ellsworth? Why?"

"A red ribbon just like that one was found in the pocket of Ryan Toledo's jeans on the night he was murdered."

"Well, that's not so unusual. You can find red Christmas ribbons everywhere this time of year."

"I know, but there is something else. The coroner found traces of chocolate and cream in Toledo's system that hadn't been digested, and there were also crumbs consistent with a chocolate Yule log on his clothing."

"Are you suggesting, and I certainly hope you are not, that Ryan ate one of my Yule logs right before he was killed?"

"I wasn't suggesting anything until I saw this ribbon. It's exactly the same."

"Well, that's impossible, Sergio, because I hadn't delivered any of my Yule logs to anyone on my list before the night of Liddy's party. They were all wrapped and still at my house."

Sergio nodded, still considering the odd coincidence.

"How in the world would he have gotten his hands on one?" Hayley asked, suddenly worried.

"I don't know."

Then something struck Hayley, like a gut punch to the stomach.

"Wait . . . ," Hayley gasped.

"What?"

"Tonight when I went home from work to pack them up in a box for delivery, I was three Yule logs short. I thought I miscounted them, but maybe . . ."

"Maybe what?"

"Well, the night of Liddy's party, I was still at the office working on my column for the next day. Gemma called to ask if I would like her and Conner to get a head start and begin delivering the Yule logs to the addresses on the list. I told her not to bother, I would do it later. But maybe she decided to help me out anyway."

"I think we should go talk to Gemma," Sergio said, an urgency in his tone.

The hot toddy would have to wait.

Hayley drove Sergio in her car directly to her house. As they pulled into the driveway, she could see Gemma and Conner through the kitchen window, kissing each other in a way that made Hayley supremely uncomfortable.

She had to get over the fact her little girl was now a grown woman.

Hayley just wished she liked her choice of a boyfriend more.

* * *

Hayley and Sergio got out of the car and went inside the house, not exchanging a word. When they entered the kitchen, Gemma and Conner quickly separated, both grinning sheepishly, stealing furtive glances at one another, as if they had just gotten away with something.

Gemma instantly noticed the somber look on her uncle Sergio's face.

"What's wrong?"

"Gemma, did you deliver any of the chocolate Yule logs the night of the party?" Hayley asked, her heart racing.

"Oh, that's right, I totally forgot! I meant to tell you. Yes, Conner and I had some extra time before the party, so we delivered three of them. Didn't I cross the names off the list?"

"No, you didn't," Hayley said.

"Who did you deliver them to, Gemma?" Sergio asked.

Gemma stiffened, suddenly concerned. "Let's see . . . um . . . we took one over to Kimmy Bradford . . ."

"At her house?" Sergio asked.

"No, at the real estate office, where she works. She was very grateful and said she was going to try some when she got home to change clothes for Liddy's party," Gemma said.

"Are you sure?" Hayley asked.

"That lady is kind of hard to forget," Conner joked, a lustful look in his eye.

Gemma feigned indignation and playfully slapped him on the back of the head.

"Who else?"

"We took one over to Ron Hopkins's house. He was still working at the Shop 'n Save, but DeAnn was home and was very happy when we gave it to her," Gemma said.

"She told us she was a chocolate fiend," Conner added.

"And the third one?" Sergio asked.

"We swung by your office, but you had already gone home. Bruce was still there working, so we left one with him," Gemma said. "What's going on, Mom?"

When Hayley told Gemma the significance of her homemade chocolate Yule logs wrapped with red ribbon in a basket on top of a Yule log, the blood seemed to drain from her face and she suddenly looked ill.

"Are you saying the killer used the Yule log to bash Ryan's head in?" Gemma croaked.

"We didn't find a Yule log on the scene, just the ribbon and the traces of chocolate and cream in Ryan's system," Sergio said.

"Oh, my God . . . ," Conner whispered. "The killer probably took the Yule log with him to bury it or something, in order to get rid of the evidence."

Gemma gasped. "Mother, if people find out Conner and I were out delivering Yule logs that night, and it's true one of the Yule logs was used to kill Ryan, then he's going to be a suspect! I mean, everyone at that party saw him and Ryan fighting! They're going to think he did it!"

"She's right," Conner said, suddenly shaken. "And I left the party early with Mona and her family. They dropped me off at your house and I went straight to bed."

"And there was no one here with you at the time to corroborate your alibi because Hayley and Gemma were still at the party," Sergio said, never one to sugarcoat anything.

"Mother, you have to do something! You have to investigate and find the killer before Uncle Sergio arrests Conner!"

"First of all, Uncle Sergio is not going to arrest Conner, are you, Sergio?" Hayley asked.

Unfortunately, Sergio's dead-serious expression did nothing to alleviate the growing panic in Gemma's eyes.

Conner was definitely a suspect.

Hayley knew it.

Sergio knew it.

Gemma knew it.

And, most of all, Conner knew it.

Hayley also knew that the whole "innocent until proven guilty" rule didn't always apply in small towns, where the locals fed off salacious scandal.

No, Gemma was right. Although she harbored her own suspicions about Conner—and in her mind, his questionable character—Hayley was anxious to prove that the young man dating her only daughter, this total stranger whom she had only known for a couple of days, who was staying at her house with her family over the holidays, was not some cold-blooded, dangerous killer.

Chapter Six

"Hayley, could you come see me in my office, please?" Bruce asked, very curt and professional.

"Sure, Bruce, be right there," Hayley said before hanging up the phone and standing up from her desk. She walked around it and into the back bull pen of the office that housed most of the reporters who worked for the *Island Times*, as well as the editor in chief, Sal Moretti, Hayley's boss. He was currently battling a cold, which was making him far grumpier than usual. As she passed by his office, she saw Sal blowing his nose into an embroidered handkerchief with a Christmas tree on it. His wife loved arts and crafts and was constantly knitting and crocheting. She was always showing up at the office to hand out mittens and sweaters and scarves, and holiday handkerchiefs, apparently, from her huge pile of finished projects. Sal muttered to himself that he despised this time of year, the bone-

chilling winter months that made him more sus-
ceptible to the flu and colds.

When Hayley reached Bruce's office in the far
corner of the bull pen, and swung open the door,
she was surprised not to find Bruce sitting behind
his desk. After all, he had just called her moments
before. As she entered, the door slammed shut behind her, and before she had a chance to turn her
head, she was spun around and a man's lips smacked
against hers, two manly hands gripping her tightly
by both shoulders. When Bruce finally pulled away,
he sported a mischievous grin on his face, and gestured upward with his eyes. Hayley glanced up to
see a small mistletoe hanging down, taped to the
ceiling.

"Did you just stick that up there so you could get
me back here and have an excuse to kiss me?" Hayley asked, crossing her arms.

"You really are a good detective," Bruce answered with a wink.

"This is incredibly inappropriate behavior for
the office, Bruce," Hayley scolded.

Bruce shrugged.

They were officially dating, so he failed to see
anything inappropriate about it. Not like the office Christmas party a few years ago, long before
they were an item, when he drank too much spiked
punch and made a pass at Hayley by trying to kiss
her up against the old Xerox machine in the supply room. When that awkward and embarrassing
moment happened, it almost cost Bruce his job at
the paper. At the time, the last thing Hayley ever
expected was that only a few years later, he would
be her actual boyfriend.

Life was full of surprises, of that she was certain.

Bruce went in for another kiss, but Hayley stopped him with a firm finger to his lips. "Stop it, Bruce. What if someone walks in here?"

"So what? It's not like we're hiding the fact we're together anymore," Bruce whined. "Everybody knows."

"Yes, but I want to maintain a sense of professionalism," Hayley reminded him. "So no kissing at the office, understand?"

"Fine," Bruce sighed as he reached up and tore down the mistletoe. He stuffed it in the pocket of his khaki pants. "I'll keep it here for safekeeping until we get home and I put it up in your kitchen while you're making me dinner."

"Tonight is your turn to cook. I've been bragging to Gemma about your culinary talents. She wants to know if my judgment is clouded by infatuation," Hayley said, laughing.

"Great. The pressure's on," Bruce said. "Okay, I need to get cracking on my column. Want to grab some fried clams at your brother's place for lunch?"

"I can't. I have to go pick up a few things at the Shop 'n Save."

"Let me do that for you after work. I'm the one cooking tonight, apparently. You don't even know my menu yet," Bruce said.

"Okay, full disclosure, I'm not exactly going there to shop. I want to talk to Ron Hopkins."

"About what?"

"Well, at Liddy's Christmas party the other night, when Ryan Toledo showed up, Ron had a very negative reaction. He seemed very angry and upset that Ryan was there."

"I'm coming with you."

"Bruce, you don't have to do that. I'm just going to—"

"Hayley, the column I'm writing today is about Ryan Toledo's murder. I'm sorting through all the details, and I want to follow up on any lead that might shed some light on the story. You just gave me a lead."

"And you are the crime reporter for the paper, not me."

"Sometimes I'm not so sure," he said with a deadpan look. "We can slip out for an early lunch around eleven thirty."

"Okay," Hayley nodded before opening the office door to leave.

"Oh, one more thing . . ."

When Hayley turned back, she saw Bruce swinging the mistletoe by the string in front of her face, like a hypnotist trying to put her under his control. He quickly went in for one more kiss. Before she could stop him, his lips landed on hers again as Sal hustled by, struggling to put on his bulky winter coat.

"I'm going to the pharmacy for some cough medicine," he bellowed, before stopping, and taking in the sight of Bruce and Hayley in a lip-lock. "If I wanted to see all this, I would've stayed home sick today and watched *The Young and the Restless* with my wife!"

"Sorry, Sal," Hayley whispered sheepishly, before throwing Bruce an annoyed look, and scurrying back to her desk out front.

By lunchtime, Sal was coughing and snorting, his eyes were watery, and he was on his third embroidered handkerchief, this one with Rudolph

the Red-Nosed Reindeer on it. As he sucked down
his cough medicine, his mood soured considerably. Coincidentally, all of the reporters in nearby
cubicles discovered stories that needed to be covered out of the office. No one wanted to be
around Sal and risk getting sick right before the
Christmas holiday.

Bruce and Hayley drove over to the Shop 'n
Save, as planned, and found Ron in his office, on
his computer, reviewing his employees' time sheets.
Given Hayley's reputation in town for solving local
crimes, and Bruce himself was an investigative reporter, Ron was hardly surprised why they showed
up to see him. In fact, he was not the least bit reti-
cent about talking to them. It was as if he was relieved to finally get something off his chest.

"I had been mulling over whether or not I
should call Chief Alvares directly and tell him about
my run-ins with Toledo."

"What kind of run-ins did you have?" Bruce
asked.

"He worked here a few months back. I thought I
was being a good guy giving him a job. No one else
in town wanted to hire him. They were afraid he'd
steal them blind. But I took a chance. 'Ron,' I said.
'Be a Good Samaritan. Give the kid a break.' Well,
that turned out to be a boneheaded decision, believe me."

"I take it he wasn't exactly going to have his
photo put up by the checkout registers as Employee of the Month," Hayley said.

"You got that right. I tried him out as a stock
boy. Right off the bat, he goofed off during his

shifts, stole food from the shelves to take outside for his smoke break, and was downright rude to the customers. I gave him three warnings, which didn't do any good, so about a week ago, I fired him."

"How did he handle it?" Bruce asked.

"He didn't seem to care at all. He just shrugged, and walked out the door without saying a word. I thought that was the end of it, but then, about three days ago, he came back, and demanded he be paid for his last shift. I laughed in his face. He didn't like that at all, and things got pretty heated. Bethany, on register one, got her cell phone out to dial 911 if it escalated any further, but he finally gave up and barged out of the store."

"And that was it?" Hayley asked.

"Not by a long shot. The next morning, I showed up at six to open the store, and there was graffiti spray-painted all over the sidewall outside. Lots of four-letter words, threats against me and my family, obscene images, it was disgusting."

"Did you call the police?" Bruce asked.

"Of course I did! Officers Donnie and Earl showed up, took pictures, had me make a statement, and I told them it was that hoodlum, Ryan Toledo, who had done it. They said they would talk to him. Talk to him? I don't want them to talk to him! I want them to arrest him and throw him in jail! He's a menace to society! Do you know how much it's going to cost me to get all that crap scrubbed off? Anyway, that's the last I heard from them or Ryan Toledo. Until he showed up at Liddy Crawford's Christmas party."

"Ron, given your conflicts with the victim, you must realize—"

Ron interrupted Hayley. "That I'm a suspect? Of course I realize it! Hell, I wish I had been the one to bash that lowlife's head in, but I wasn't. Someone else got to him first."

"Any idea who that might be, if not you?" Bruce said, studying Ron's face, which was flushed red with anger.

"Not a clue, and I don't care. But just for the record, it couldn't have been me."

"Why is that?" Bruce asked, still not convinced.

"Because I stayed at the party until ten o'clock. Hayley saw me leave! When I got outside, I realized DeAnn had taken our car home earlier and I had too much of the spiked punch to drive anyway. I saw Mona Barnes loading her kids into her car, and I asked if she could give me a lift home and she did! I have the chocolate stains on my coat to prove it."

"Chocolate stains?" Bruce asked.

"Those wild kids of Mona's were eating chocolate candy and had it all over their grubby little fingers, and they got chocolate all over my coat."

"Why did you stay at the party after DeAnn left?" Bruce asked.

"Because I was having a good time. DeAnn suffers from migraines and she got one at the party. It was a doozy. She took a pill, but it didn't help, so she went home. I offered to go with her, but she insisted I stay. I've been working really hard lately and she said I needed to finally have a little fun, which was very sweet of her."

"Does DeAnn know Ryan Toledo?" Hayley asked.

"No! What possible reason would she have to associate with that scum?"

"Probably none. Just asking," Hayley said casually. "I assume she was there when you got home?"

"Of course she was. She left the party shortly after eight o'clock. I arrived around ten thirty. She was already in bed sleeping."

Hayley did specifically remember Ron leaving the party sometime after ten o'clock. If Ron was dropped off at home by ten thirty like he claimed, then it would have been extremely difficult for him to leave again, track down Ryan Toledo, bludgeon him to death in the woods by Liddy's house, and then flee the scene by the time the body was discovered around eleven.

Hayley could tell from Bruce's body language that he was now convinced Ron Hopkins was innocent of the murder, and at this point just wanted to get out of there and get his hands on some fried clams and tartar sauce at Randy's bar.

"Thank you for your time, Ron," Hayley said with a smile.

"When they do find Toledo's killer, I want to be the first one to shake his hand and congratulate him."

Hayley nodded, not sure what to say to that, and then she and Bruce left Ron to stew all over again about the pornographic graffiti that still marked up the sidewall of his store.

Chapter Seven

Hayley thought about the old saying "If you don't have anything nice to say about someone, don't say anything at all." She sat, off to the right, in the back pew of the Congregational Church, listening to Reverend Staples's sermon during Ryan Toledo's memorial service. When the reverend stopped talking after only two minutes, Hayley assumed he was going to sneeze or apologize for losing his place on his index cards, but, no, he was done, finished. There wasn't anything else he felt he needed to say. Just a quick recap of Ryan's brief, troubled life, and almost a Porky Pig imitation of "That's all, folks!" There wasn't much of a reaction in the pews, mostly because there were so few people in attendance. Hayley counted six, including Edie Staples, the reverend's wife, who always sat in on her husband's sermons. The other five people scattered around the mostly empty pews included Hayley; Gemma, who was seated next to her; Kimmy Bradford, who sat closer to the front, her face buried in a white handkerchief that contrasted with her low-cut black dress; Lenora Hopkins, Ron Hopkins's ex-wife, strangely enough, wearing a gaudy black hat with black roses sewn around the rim. She sat upright in a middle pew, staring straight ahead, a stoic look on her face. And, finally, there was Ryan's doddering, old aunt, Esther, who had driven down from Bangor. She appeared bored and kept checking her watch, anxious for the whole affair to mercifully come to an end. That was it. Ryan's parents were long gone, both having fled town years ago, his father to chase a woman he met while barhopping one summer night, and his mother on the run from the law for writing a slew of bad checks. Ryan's older brother, Timmy, his only sibling, was in the state prison after getting busted and convicted of running a meth lab out of his girlfriend's trailer in Bucksport.

Given how loathed the deceased was by many locals, it wasn't a surprise his funeral was so sparsely attended.

What was surprising was the number of expensive flower arrangements that surrounded the standard, low-cost closed coffin. Dozens of them.

As they made their way down the aisle to pay their respects, Gemma had turned to her mother and whispered in her ear, "I've never seen so many flowers and less mourners."

When they had reached the coffin in the front of the church, Hayley had bent down to check a few of the cards, and was surprised to discover that none of the cards had been signed. Nobody seemed willing to admit to sending flowers to Ryan Toledo's funeral, which struck Hayley as very odd.

"Now, please join us in the parlor for tea and coffee, as well as some of my wife's legendary, tasty baked goods."

Edie Staples loved baking cakes and cookies, which she always put out after a Sunday service or memorial. The trouble was, she was a terrible baker. Her sweets were always dry and tasteless. Most people tried to be polite and choke down a cookie or brownie, so Edie was under the impression she was a talented pastry chef ready to compete on a Food Network bake-off show.

Hayley and Gemma stood up.

"Mom, do you mind if I skip the reception? Conner's waiting for me at home," Gemma said, anxious to make her escape.

"No, go, I'll meet you there in a bit."

Gemma made a beeline for the door.

Hayley stepped into the aisle, intercepting Lenora Hopkins, who was on her way out. "Aren't you going to stay for some coffee and sweets, Lenora?"

"God, no," Lenora scoffed.

Hayley noticed Lenora's mascara was smeared from crying. "I wasn't aware that you and Ryan were close."

Lenora sniffed, trying desperately to remain impassive. "We weren't that close."

Hayley noticed Lenora's eyes now brimming with tears. "Oh, okay . . . you just seem a little upset . . ."

"I said we weren't that close!" Lenora wailed loudly, her voice echoing through the church, as she pushed past Hayley and out the door.

Reverend Staples gave Hayley an admonishing look as he gathered his notes from behind his podium. He had always suspected Hayley of being a troublemaker, ever since she was a rambunctious teenage girl, and so he was hardly surprised to see her now causing a commotion after his mini-service.

Hayley shrugged and nodded to Ryan's aunt Esther, whose cell phone was clamped to her ear as she sailed past Hayley.

"I'm on my way back now. The minister droned on and on for much longer than I thought he would, so now I'm probably going to hit traffic," she sighed.

Esther considers two minutes droning on and on?

Hayley made her way into the side parlor to join Reverend and Mrs. Staples and Kimmy, who had plopped down in a metal chair in the corner and was weeping softly. Edie Staples took a deep breath and crossed over to Kimmy with a plate of cinnamon cookies, but Kimmy waved her off. Edie snorted her displeasure, and marched away, insulted. When she spied Hayley, she headed straight for her, plate in hand.

"I'd love to have one, thank you," Hayley said, plucking a cookie off the plate and taking a bite. It was so hard she thought she might break a tooth, but she gamely chewed it and made a few obligatory moans to convince Edie that she found her awful cookies, in fact, yummy.

Sometimes a little white lie was necessary to keep the peace.

Edie was still stinging from Kimmy Bradford's rejection. She remained by Hayley's side, eyeing Kimmy and her lily-white bosom popping out of her frilly black mourning dress, disdainfully. "Can you believe she had the nerve to wear that to church of all places? Honestly, even the statue of Jesus on the cross had a surprised look on his face when she waltzed in, practically flashing her breasts!"

Hayley had no intention of encouraging this particular conversation with Edie Staples. "It was a lovely service."

"Yes, it was. I wish there had been more people here to appreciate the reverend's hard work to come up with just the right words."

Hayley struggled not to roll her eyes.

"But Ryan Toledo was a thug, so I'm hardly surprised my poor husband had to play to a nearly empty house."

As if the reverend's sermon was akin to a one-man Broadway show.

"You know, she paid for the service," Edie said off-handedly, gesturing toward Kimmy Bradford in the corner.

"Who? Kimmy?" Hayley asked.

"Yes. It costs money to heat the church on a cold day like this, and it's only fair I be compensated for the time and effort I put into preparing such a mouthwatering spread."

Hayley bit her lower lip to keep herself from laughing.

Edie eyed her suspiciously, so Hayley took another bite of the cinnamon cookie and moaned again. "Delish."

That was all Edie needed to suddenly consider Hayley a trusted confidante. Edie leaned in, and whispered under her breath, "When she came to meet with the reverend and discuss what she wanted for the service, I could tell she still loved him."

"Ryan?"

"Yes, well, we all know the history."

"I don't. Not really. I mean, I heard the rumors, like everybody else."

"They weren't just rumors. I witnessed the whole ugly affair firsthand, back when I was volunteering as a teacher's aide at the high school."

Edie stared at Kimmy, all by herself, sitting on a hard metal chair in the corner of the parlor, her hefty bosom rising and falling with each sob. "I knew she was trouble from the moment she came back to Bar Harbor after college. She had obviously changed from the sweet, quiet, flat-chested little girl she was during her high-school years. Suddenly, after four years away, she had transformed into this predatory vixen, with her revealing tops and her face caked with too much makeup, and those breasts, I mean really, they can't be real. What would her poor parents say if they were still around?"

Kimmy's parents were not dead. Her father, the minister who preceded Reverend Staples at the Congregational Church, retired after Kimmy went off to college. Her parents bought a camper and were currently touring the country, making an adventure out of their golden years.

"So you say you were volunteering at the high school when Kimmy left under mysterious circumstances?" Hayley asked, trying her best to get Edie back on point.

"There was nothing mysterious about it," Edie huffed. "She was summarily dismissed . . . for an inappropriate relationship with a student."

"Ryan Toledo?"

"Bingo. It was common knowledge amongst the

staff in the principal's office, although they tried to sweep the whole ugly situation under the rug."

"How old was Ryan?"

"Seventeen. His parents weren't around, and his older brother, who was acting as his guardian, didn't care one way or the other, so there was no one to raise holy hell about it. So Principal Harkins called Kimmy into his office and gave her an ultimatum—either she resign her position effective immediately or he would call the police and report her. Well, needless to say, Kimmy emptied her desk and was gone before the final bell. I had to fill in for her until a replacement could be found. It was a very stressful time."

So the rumors were true.

Hayley saw Kimmy struggle to her feet, cross over to Reverend Staples, shake his hand, and whisper a thank-you, before grabbing her faux-fur coat off a rack and rocketing out the side door.

Hayley spun around and smiled at Edie Staples. "I have to go! Happy Holidays!" And then she chased Kimmy Bradford out the door as Edie called after her, "Don't you want to take some of the left-over cinnamon cookies home with you?"

The door slammed behind her before Hayley could manage a response. She was singularly focused on catching Kimmy before she got to her car. But the only cars left in the parking lot were Hayley's Kia and Reverend Staples's Land Rover. Kimmy was halfway down the gravel path heading toward the sidewalk.

"Kimmy, wait up!" Hayley shouted.

Kimmy stopped, startled, and turned around to face Hayley. Her faux-fur coat was wide open, exposing her ample chest.

She didn't speak. She just stared at Hayley, waiting for her to talk first.

"Um, I noticed you didn't drive here . . ."

"No. I took a taxi because I was afraid I would get too emotional to drive. I'm going to walk home."

"It's freezing cold. And you live all the way across town. Why don't you let me give you a lift home?"

"You don't have to do that," Kimmy said.

She wasn't used to people being nice to her, not since she had left the high school under such a cloud of suspicion and scandal.

"That's very nice of you, Hayley, thank you."

As they walked side by side toward her car, Hayley felt a twinge of guilt.

This wasn't an act of kindness. Hayley wanted to get inside Kimmy's house to see if the Yule log Gemma and Conner had delivered to her at the real estate office was in her home. Because if it was intact, still wrapped in the basket and tied to the log with a red ribbon, then Kimmy Bradford would be in the clear for Ryan's murder.

When they pulled up in front of Kimmy's house, Kimmy casually asked Hayley if she would like to come in for a cup of coffee, half-expecting her to say no. Hayley jumped on the invitation, though, which seemed to surprise Kimmy. But she couldn't withdraw the invite, so she got out of the car and led Hayley to the front door.

Kimmy apologized for how chilly it was in the house, muttering an excuse about a faulty heater, but Hayley suspected she was conserving more than the average person, since she wasn't making nearly enough money as a receptionist to pay the hefty winter heating bills. Hayley followed Kimmy to the kitchen and glanced around in search of the Yule log, but did not immediately spot it. Kimmy filled a coffeepot with water from the sink and slid it into the coffeemaker, adding the grounds in the top and pressing the on button.

"So did you have a chance to try my chocolate Yule log?" Hayley asked.

"What?"

The question seemed to startle her.

"Gemma mentioned she dropped off one of my Yule logs to your office the other day," Hayley said as casually as she could.

"Oh . . . yes. Thank you. I haven't tried it yet. As you can imagine, it's been a very trying time. I haven't been eating much. I'm storing it in the freezer I have downstairs in my basement until I have a moment to enjoy it."

Hayley had a feeling that Kimmy was lying.

There was nothing overt about her manner.

She didn't twitch or look away when she said it.

It was just a feeling.

Once the coffee was ready, Kimmy invited Hayley into her living room. She also put out a plate of store-bought cookies that were far more scrumptious than Edie Staples's rock-hard, bland homemade treats.

Hayley was wondering just how she could manage to slip away and sneak down into Kimmy's basement to check the freezer to make sure she was telling the truth.

Finally the house phone rang, and Kimmy answered it.

"Mom, Dad, so nice to hear from you! Where are you, still in Arizona?"

Kimmy raised a finger, signaling Hayley she would be just a minute, and then wandered into the kitchen for a modicum of privacy.

Hayley wasted no time in setting her coffee cup down on a side table and jumping to her feet, quickly making her way to the door in the hallway that led down to the basement. As she descended the stairs, she could still hear Kimmy's muffled voice in the kitchen. She saw the freezer instantly and scurried over to open it.

There was no sign of the Yule log.

She rummaged through the frozen meats and TV dinners.

Nothing.

Her instinct was right.

Kimmy was lying to her.

The Yule log was gone.

When she closed the freezer, she noticed a board propped up against the wall.

It was covered with selfies of Ryan and Kimmy in private moments, photos of Ryan by himself smiling, Ryan shirtless, Ryan asleep. There were dozens of them tacked to the board.

It was like a shrine.

Downright creepy.

And it made Hayley shiver.

Kimmy was obviously still obsessed with him, which would explain why she used her own money—money she probably didn't have—to pay for his memorial service.

Was it out of devotion or guilt?

Was Ryan's death a crime of passion? Carried

out by an emotionally unstable stalker, with Hayley's real Yule log as the murder weapon?

Suddenly, from behind her, Hayley heard Kimmy's stern voice.

"What are you doing down here?"

Chapter Eight

Hayley spun around and gasped at the sight of Kimmy standing at the bottom of the stairs, gripping a large knife in her hand.

Hayley slowly backed away. "Kimmy, please put the knife down . . ."

Kimmy glanced down at the knife in her hand and smirked. "Relax, Hayley. I told my parents I had company and would call them back. I was just going to cut you a piece of my homemade cherry pie. Edie Staples isn't the only one in town who likes to bake sweets."

Hayley felt a wave of relief wash over her.

"I'm sorry, I didn't mean to freak you out," Kimmy said before noticing her loving shrine to Ryan Toledo in plain view. "I can see why you'd be so jumpy after seeing that."

"What you do down here is your own business," Hayley said, throwing her hands up.

"Then why did you sneak down here?"

She had a point.

And it was time to come clean.

"I was looking for the Yule log Gemma delivered to you at your office. You said you put it in the freezer down here and it's not there. Why did you lie to me?"

"Because I didn't want to admit to you that I regifted it."

"You what?"

"I gave it away. To Ryan. I know he loves chocolate, and I'd already put on a few unnecessary pounds after one-too-many holiday parties, so on my way over to Liddy's party that night, I left it on his doorstep with a little note."

A love note, no doubt.

"I thought he might appreciate it. I missed him terribly, so I invited him to come around on New Year's Eve for a little party I was planning on having. But I neglected to mention in the note that only two people were going to attend . . . me and him."

"Oh, Kimmy . . ."

"I know, I'm a damn fool. I've never gotten over him. After we got caught and I was forced to resign from the high school, it was only a few weeks after that when Ryan turned eighteen, so it was no longer a crime to be together. But I guess I was too intense, too much in love, and it scared him, because he dumped me. Since then, it's been a long road trying to get over him."

Kimmy noticed Hayley eyeing the shrine of photographs on the poster board.

"Obviously," Hayley sighed. "Did you talk to him when he showed up at Liddy's party?"

"Briefly. He was too focused on talking to your

daughter. I asked him if he got the Yule log, and he said no. He told me there was nothing on his doorstep when he got home, which isn't surprising, given the sketchy neighborhood where he lives. Anybody on the street could have swiped it."

Hayley nodded, still not sure whether Kimmy was telling her the truth or not.

"I didn't kill him, Hayley. I loved him. I still love him. If that Yule log I left at his house was the murder weapon, the killer could be anybody in town."

Kimmy was right.

The killer could have been lurking outside Ryan's house, stolen the Yule log after Kimmy left it on the doorstep, and then followed him to the party, waited outside until Ryan left, and then attacked him in the woods on his way home when he was all alone.

"I suppose I should be relieved," Kimmy whispered.

Hayley arched an eyebrow. "Relieved?"

"I've been burning up with jealousy for years. Finally, with Ryan gone, I may find some peace."

"What were you so jealous of?"

"Please, it was no secret Ryan got around, if you know what I mean. He was sleeping with a bunch of other women. He tried to be very discreet about it, but I knew."

"Were you spying on him?" Hayley asked carefully.

"I wouldn't call it spying," Kimmy snarled. "I mean, every so often I would drive by his house to see if he was home, or follow him every now and then when he took his Harley out, usually to the house of one of his girlfriends, but I would hardly call that spying."

Uh, yes, that would be the textbook definition of spying, Hayley thought.

"Did you know any of the girls he was seeing?"

Kimmy scoffed. "Yes, and they weren't girls, believe me. As you may have guessed from my own history with Ryan, he was attracted to older women, some much older . . . and married."

"I see," Hayley replied. "No wonder there were no signed cards on all those flower arrangements at the memorial service. They were probably from the married women in Ryan's stable who preferred to remain anonymous."

"Trust me. He was the Don Juan of Bar Harbor," Kimmy said.

Hayley was embarrassed to ask, but couldn't resist. "Was he that good?"

Kimmy offered a wistful smile. "Better than you could ever imagine."

"Wow. Who knew?"

"Certainly, none of their husbands," Kimmy said, not realizing Hayley's question was rhetorical.

The suspect list was growing by the minute.

The killer could have been any number of scorned lovers.

Or maybe a jealous husband who suddenly discovered his wife was having an affair with bad-news Ryan Toledo.

"So who are these women, if you don't mind me asking?"

"Currently there are three, that I know of. Lenora Hopkins was the only one who dared to show up at the funeral. Mostly because she's divorced and Ryan was of legal age, and she really didn't have any reason to hide the affair."

"And the other two?"

"Lacey Reinhart and Beth Sanford."

Hayley knew both women. Lacey Reinhart was the wife of Dan Reinhart, a high-level executive at one of the local banks. Beth Sanford was a travel agent and married to Stan Sanford, a city council member. Hayley instantly dismissed both Lacey and Beth as suspects, because Lacey was currently in the Bar Harbor Hospital for knee surgery and Beth was visiting relatives in Florida with her family. Of the purported three women involved with Ryan at the time of his murder, only Lenora Hopkins was both in town and able-bodied enough to carry out the murder.

Hayley wanted to speak with her right away. "I have to go . . ."

Kimmy raised the knife, stopping Hayley dead in her tracks. "Wait . . ."

Hayley stared at the knife, taking in a deep breath.

"Are you sure you don't want to stay for a piece of my cherry pie? I swear I'm a much better cook than Edie Staples."

"I don't doubt it, but let me take a rain check." Hayley smiled before gingerly passing Kimmy, who was still clutching the knife, and rushing up the stairs.

Fifteen minutes later, when Hayley rang the bell next to the front door of Lenora Hopkins's house, she braced herself for a chilly reception, given Lenora's rude demeanor at the funeral, barely two hours earlier.

The door flung open with a whoosh, and after sizing her up and down, Lenora scowled. "I was wondering when you'd show up here. You might as well come in."

Lenora waved her inside.

Hayley entered the front hallway and was led into the living room, where she was confronted by an oversized tree. It was weighed down by so many lights and ornaments, it looked as if it might topple over at any minute. Knitted stockings drooped from the fireplace and there was a small nativity scene on the coffee table.

"Sit down. I'll get us some coffee," Lenora said, trying her best to be a warm hostess, but coming off as just annoyed.

"No, thanks, I'm fine. So you were expecting me?"

"Yes. After I saw you at the funeral, I figured you'd start poking around. The police haven't arrested anyone for Ryan's murder yet. So given your reputation and how you like to insert yourself into every scandal that hits town, I figured it would only be a matter of time before you made your way here."

"My reputation precedes me," Hayley joked.

"I didn't say it was a good reputation," Lenora snickered.

Hayley decided to let that one go.

Lenora sat down on the couch and picked up a wool stocking she was knitting and began working on it, her needles clicking, as she got right to the point. "Ryan thought he was so smart. He actually believed that none of the women he was sleeping with knew about the others. But I knew all about his secret trysts with Lacey and Beth."

"Did it bother you?"

"Why should it? I wasn't planning to marry the kid. Listen, this is a small town and most of the men my age are taken or not worth my time. It got lonely after my divorce from Ron. I hired Ryan to do some yard work for me last summer, and I could tell he was interested in starting something. So I thought, 'Why the hell not?' I was single again and had needs, and he was young and had muscles and a pretty face. I wasn't foolish enough to think he was attracted to me. It was clear very early on that he was more attracted to the cash and gifts I showered upon him after our special afternoons together than in actually getting to know me. Although I can't speak for Lacey and Beth . . . maybe they were dumb enough to buy his load of bull crap."

If Ryan's murder was a crime of passion, then Lenora was certainly off the hook. Her affair with Ryan sounded more like a cold business transaction rather than anything remotely passionate.

"Lenora, what about Lacey and Beth's husbands? Do you think one of them may have found out about his wife's affair with Ryan and flew into a jealous rage?"

Lenora guffawed, dropping her half-knitted Christmas stocking in her lap. "Oh, Hayley, no! Are you kidding me? Have you been living in a cave? Dan Reinhart would be thrilled to know Lacey is getting some on the side because he's been so preoccupied with his own torrid affair with his secretary, Mimi Whitford. Dan's been looking for any excuse to divorce Lacey and marry Mimi. And as for Stan Sanford, let's be honest, Hayley, everyone knows Stan is gayer than a picnic basket! The poor man would be relieved, too, knowing Ryan was satisfying Beth in the bedroom so he didn't have to. How could you not know that?"

"I'm just not as plugged in as you to the town gossip, apparently," Hayley said.

"As for me, I didn't go to Liddy's party because I knew Ron and that sniveling new wife of his, DeAnn, were going to be there, so I went to another holiday cocktail party at my hairdresser's house. I stayed until well after midnight, and there were about twenty eyewitnesses there who saw me. And we had a grand time. I'm sure it was a far more memorable gala than Liddy Crawford's boring old party."

Despite Lenora's confidence, there was no way her hairdresser's gathering could possibly compete with Liddy's. Because at the end of the day, one of Liddy's guests had been brutally murdered, so it was certain her party was going to be the talk of the town for years to come.

And the killer was still out there on the loose.

Chapter Nine

When Hayley arrived home and entered through the back door, which led into the kitchen, she found Gemma pouring hot chocolate into three holiday ceramic mugs.

Hayley instantly noticed the strain on Gemma's face. "What's wrong?"

"Mona is here, and she's acting really weird."

"What do you mean, 'weird'?"

"I don't know. She showed up here, looking for you, and I told her you'd be home soon. I asked if she would care to wait, and she just sort of grunted and nodded and sat down in the living room. Conner's in there now, trying to make small talk, but she won't even look at him. I think she's being very rude."

"Mona's always rude," Hayley said, smiling, before reaching for one of the mugs of hot chocolate.

"Not like this," Gemma said, gently slapping her

mother's hand away. "Wait. I haven't topped it off with the whipped cream yet."

Gemma picked up a wooden spoon and scooped a dollop of whipped cream out of a bowl and plopped it down on top of the hot chocolate. She picked up the mug and handed it to her mother. "Would you go see what's gotten her so upset?"

Hayley took a sip of the hot chocolate. "I'm on it."

Gemma stopped her mother, picked up a dish towel, and wiped some whipped cream off her upper lip. "Thank you."

Hayley strolled into the living room, where she found Mona sitting upright in Hayley's recliner, her whole body stiff as she stared straight ahead. Not once did Mona glance at or even acknowledge Conner, who sat on the couch, awkwardly peppering her with questions about her lobstering business.

"So, do you haul the traps all by yourself, or do you have help?"

Mona managed a shrug, but refused to answer the question.

Hayley noticed Mona's white knuckles as she fiercely gripped the sides of the recliner.

"She has a few employees who help out, but Mona does a lot of the heavy lifting," Hayley said.

Mona whipped her head around. "Oh, good, you're home. Let's take Leroy out for a walk."

"Gemma and I already took him out when she got home from the funeral," Conner said.

"The dog's getting too fat. You feed him too much, Hayley," Mona growled. "Another walk will do him some good."

"Mona, what's gotten into you . . . ?" Hayley started to ask before Mona shouted over her.

"Leroy! Here, boy!"

Leroy bounded down the stairs, surprised to see Hayley. He had probably been sound asleep on Hayley's bed, his favorite napping spot, and didn't hear her come home. With his tongue panting and tail wagging, he ran into the kitchen and stood by his leash, which hung from a rack next to the dishwasher. Hayley's Persian cat, Blueberry, was perched under the kitchen table, his own tail flapping up and down, signaling his displeasure with all the unnecessary commotion.

Mona pushed herself up and out of the recliner, grabbed her coat, which she had flung on the floor next to it, and hurriedly shoved her arms through the sleeves.

"Nice chatting with you," Conner said, his tone dripping with sarcasm.

"Yeah, okay," Mona muttered, avoiding eye contact and pounding out of the living room toward the kitchen.

Hayley followed her, still utterly confused by Mona's strange demeanor. She yanked her own winter coat off the back of a chair, where she had deposited it after arriving home, and attached the leash to Leroy's collar. Mona was already out the back door, and Hayley and Leroy had to run to catch up to her.

They were halfway down the street, a good distance from the house, before Mona finally spoke.

"It's him," Mona said gravely.

"Him who?"

"Gemma's boyfriend."

"Conner?"

Mona nodded, her face a ghostly white.

"What about him?" Hayley asked.

Leroy was too preoccupied with a squirrel racing up the bark of a nearby tree to be interested in their conversation, but as he sprang forward, Hayley had to pick up her pace to keep up with both her dog and Mona, who seemed to want to just get as far away from the house as possible.

"He's the killer," Mona whispered.

"What?" Hayley exclaimed.

"Shhhh. Keep your voice down," Mona scolded.

"No one's around. What are you talking about, Mona?"

Mona stopped suddenly and snatched a fistful of Hayley's jacket. She stared intently at her and spoke slowly, to make sure Hayley heard every word of what she was saying. "I saw him on TV. On one of those Most Wanted crime shows my deadbeat husband, Dennis, watches all the time. They were saying he is some kind of serial killer who has been romancing young women all along the East Coast, from Maine to Maryland, for the past two years."

"Conner? Oh, come on, Mona . . ."

"I'm serious, Hayley," Mona said, clasping her jacket tighter. "I never forget a face, and I swear when they showed his picture on TV, it was him."

"Mona, that can't be . . ."

"According to the host of the show, that former FBI agent, you know, the cute one with the wavy black hair and dimples to die for, well, he said Conner wins the hearts of his victims by wining and dining them, and planning a future with them. Then, when they disappoint him, and they always disappoint him at some point, he strangles them and buries their bodies in the woods. So far, he's done away with three victims."

"This is preposterous, Mona, surely you're mistaken . . . Did they mention his name?"

"No, but he goes by a number of different aliases. And brace yourself . . ."

Hayley clenched her fists, not sure she wanted to hear this next part.

"They showed photos of his last three victims. All of them were pretty blond girls in their early twenties, with blue eyes . . ."

Hayley's heart nearly leapt into her throat.

The description matched Gemma to a tee.

"Let's just slow down here," Hayley said, catching her breath. "If all of Conner's victims were women, it doesn't make sense that he would kill Ryan Toledo."

"Oh, yes, it does," Mona cried. "His last victim, a girl he met in Providence, Rhode Island, was dating another guy, who got in his way. Conner mowed him down with his car, or so the police suspect. The poor fool survived, but is still in the hospital with a concussion and a bunch of broken bones. Anybody gets in Conner's way, he gets rid of them. Ryan tried getting in his way!"

"Look, Mona, I don't want to jump to any conclusions until we have a chance to talk to Conner . . ."

"Talk to him? What are you going to say? 'Mona saw your mug on TV and we know you're on the FBI's Most Wanted list for murder!' Then what? He probably pulls out a gun and shoots us all on the spot! I don't think it's very smart to confront him like that!"

"But what if you're wrong, Mona?"

"I'm not wrong. It was him!"

Hayley's head was spinning.

Liddy was usually the overdramatic one.

Not Mona.

Mona was never one for hysterics.

Or hyperbole.

And yet, here she was, standing in the street, crying at the top of her lungs, "Wake up! Your daughter is dating a cold-blooded serial killer!"

It seemed like such an outlandish notion.

How could that possibly be true?

No, Mona had to be wrong.

But what if she wasn't?

If there was the slightest possibility she was right, if that was Conner's photo on the Most Wanted show, then that meant her daughter was back at her house, alone, with a depraved criminal.

Hayley took off running back toward the house, dragging poor Leroy by the leash behind her. The poor dog was confused and disoriented by the sudden reverse in direction, as Mona hauled butt to keep up with them.

Island Food & Spirits
By Hayley Powell

Recently I attended my dear friend Liddy Crawford's annual Christmas party, which, as most of you probably know, is one of the most popular events of the holiday season. Well, this year was no exception. With all the festivity around me, I was amazed I had a rare quiet moment to myself. I found myself gazing across the room at my now-grown daughter, Gemma, who was having a grand time catching up with old friends.

Although my eyes saw a lovely, grown woman, so mature and self-assured, so full of grace and kindness, now in her early twenties, my heart could only see my daughter as she was at seven, sporting her favorite pair of denim shorts paired with her Power Ranger T-shirt. And it was not the pink ranger, mind you, whom she deemed too girly-girl, but rather the red ranger, the indisputable leader. Her hair was in a messy ponytail, and there were a few freckles splashed across her nose. When she smiled, she was missing a front tooth from a fall off her bike, which, unfortunately, happened while racing the neighborhood kids down the big hill near our house.

Gemma was always a competitive child, and a tomboy to boot. She loved collecting bugs, playing baseball with the boys, and she never missed an opportunity to build a fort in the woods with her posse. But with all that said, she was definitely still a daddy's girl.

Gemma and her dad loved to fish out on Eagle Lake in the summer, play board games like Operation and Battleship on a rainy day, but their absolute favorite times together were right after a fresh snowfall.

Gemma's favorite season of the year was winter, mostly since she was born in December during a raging snowstorm.

Gemma and her dad would bundle up in their winter coats, pull on their hats and gloves, and head out to engage in a snowball fight, erect a snow fort, or, most likely, build a snowman. Making a snowman was a tradition, something they did together since Gemma first learned to walk. Their early efforts were modest, but in just a few short years, they began getting more creative. This particular year, they decided to build their snowman at the bottom of our driveway for everyone to see as they strolled past or drove by our house.

The two worked hard for hours, creating the perfect snowman with all the trimmings. I must admit, I was quite impressed. There was a bright red stocking hat and a matching red scarf wrapped around its neck, walnuts for eyes, carrot nose, beads for its smile. They even put mittens on the branches they used for arms, and positioned them to give the impression that the snowman was waving to the cars that came down the street.

Gemma was so proud of their snowman that she gave him a name—Harvey. She was beyond excited when she heard cars driving by and honking their horns at Harvey. In honor of Harvey, who was becoming quite popular in the neighborhood, I decided to pay tribute by creating my own snowman in the kitchen. Gemma's favorite food was pizza, so I made a snowman out of pizza dough on a cookie sheet and served it to her and my husband, Danny, with some piping-hot cocoa to celebrate a job well done.

Unfortunately, the next morning, Gemma rushed into our bedroom, with tears streaming down her face, screaming hysterically, "Someone killed Harvey!"

I bolted out of bed, with my heart pounding and my mind roiling over and over with thoughts of "Who's Harvey?"

And then I remembered the snowman.

Trying to calm my fast-beating heart, I peered out the window, and, sure enough, all that was left of Harvey was a red stocking hat and scarf scattered in the middle of the road.

Danny came inside after having inspected the damage and promised they would build another one that very day.

I wish I could say that was the end of it, but, unfortunately, the same fate befell Harvey #2 the following evening. It was as if some serial snowman killer was terrorizing the neighborhood. But father and daughter were fiercely determined not to be deterred and to keep building.

That evening, Danny growled that someone was

running down the snowmen with his or her car and he vowed not to allow that to happen again. When I asked just how he planned on doing that, he just mumbled something under his breath and stalked out of the house. I shrugged it off and sipped my hot chocolate and went back to reading my arts-and-crafts magazine.

Well, it was sometime after midnight when Danny and I were jolted awake by a loud crash and commotion outside. We jumped out of bed, and Danny bounded down the stairs as I raced to the bedroom window to look down to the street.

Illuminated by the streetlight, I could see two teenage boys frantically trying to remove something from under their car, and it looked like the front end of the vehicle was pretty banged up.

A few of our neighbors' lights snapped on, and several people wandered out of their houses to see what was going on. Danny flew out of the house and confronted the panicked teens, who were still desperately trying to drag something out from under their car. From my vantage point, I could see Danny giving them quite a lecture, his arms waving about, gesturing toward our house as our neighbors all appeared to be nodding in agreement, caught up in his rousing speech.

Finally, with a little help from Danny and a neighbor, they dislodged what was under the car. I gasped as the realization of what had happened hit me, and I had to chuckle.

When Danny went outside before bed, he had taken some old cinder blocks, which we had in the garage, and stacked them up and rebuilt the snowman around them. So when the troublesome teens sped down our street late that night to once again destroy the snowman, they ran smack into a pile of cinder blocks and a couple of the blocks got stuck underneath the car after they toppled over from the impact.

I went back to bed, hoping Gemma wouldn't be too upset about poor Harvey #3's unfortunate fate. But I need not have worried.

The following morning as I came downstairs to make breakfast, I heard Gemma in the kitchen say brightly, "Good morning, Harvey #3!"

In the kitchen, Danny was sitting at the table, drinking his morning coffee, and he winked.

Apparently, I learned later, Danny had struck a deal with the teens. He wouldn't call their parents or the police if they replaced what they had destroyed. They spent two hours restoring Harvey #3 to his original glory. And I am proud to say we have had many more Harveys waving at passing cars over the years, and not one was ever a victim of a hit and run ever again. All our Harveys eventually just passed of natural weather causes.

Gemma's Christmas Snowman Pizza

For this recipe you can most certainly buy your favorite store-bought pizza dough and also your favorite store-bought pizza sauce to save time, especially during the busy holiday season.

However, I'm sharing my favorite pizza dough recipe, topped with a simple homemade Alfredo sauce.

Ingredients

For the Pizza Dough:

3½ to 4 cups all-purpose flour
1 teaspoon sugar
1 envelope dry yeast
2 teaspoons kosher salt
1½ cups warm water
2 tablespoons oil

Optional toppings you can use for the snowman's eyes, buttons, nose, mouth: sliced black olives, pepperoni, baby carrot, sliced sausage.

Using the dough hook on your stand mixer, combine your 3½ cups flour, sugar, yeast, and salt in the bowl of a stand mixer. While your mixer is running add the water and oil and combine until the dough forms a ball. If your dough is too sticky, add more flour a tablespoon full at a time until it comes together in a smooth ball. If your dough is too dry, add a tablespoon of water at a time until the dough comes together.

Remove your dough and place on a lightly floured surface and knead until it is in a nice smooth ball. Place in a lightly oiled bowl and cover with a towel. Let the dough rest for up to an hour.

For the Alfredo Sauce:

2 tablespoons butter
2 tablespoons flour
1 cup heavy cream
¼ cup grated Parmesan

In a saucepan on medium heat add butter and melt.

When the butter is melted, add the flour and whisk until a light blond color.

Add your heavy cream and whisk until there are no lumps and the sauce is smooth. (If too thick, you can add a little milk to thin it a bit.)

Remove sauce from heat and add the Parmesan cheese, whisking until all the cheese is incorporated into the sauce.

Remove your finished dough from the bowl and place on a lightly floured surface and divide your dough into three different sizes.

If you have made homemade dough, you could have a little too much to fit on the cookie sheet, so just remove some dough first and make an extra pizza on the side.

Shape and roll your dough pieces into the thickness you prefer for pizza and then place on a cookie sheet to make your snowman: big circle on bottom to small circle on top for head.

Spoon the Alfredo sauce on the pizza rounds and spread evenly with a spoon.

Add your mozzarella on all three dough rounds

and top with your preferred toppings to make eyes, nose, mouth, and buttons.

Bake at 400 degrees for 12 to 15 minutes, or until pizza is done.

Remove from oven and—voila—you'll have the cutest snowman pizza! Better take a quick picture for your friends because it will disappear faster than a real outdoor snowman will take to melt!

Gemma's Hot Chocolate

Ingredients

¼ cup cocoa
½ cup sugar
½ teaspoon salt
⅓ cup water
4 cups milk
1 teaspoon vanilla

In a saucepan mix your dry ingredients, then add the water, bring to a boil and boil for one minute. Add the milk, stir and heat to desired temperature. Remove from heat and add the vanilla. Pour into mugs, serve, and enjoy!

Mom's Special Hot Chocolate

Ingredients

Gemma's Hot Chocolate
1 ounce vodka
½ ounce peppermint schnapps

Pour a mug of Gemma's Hot Chocolate, add the vodka and peppermint schnapps, stir, then sit by a warm fire on a cold night and let your troubles melt away!

Chapter Ten

As she ran toward the house, huffing and puffing, arms pumping, Hayley wanted to kick herself for wasting so much valuable time chasing down dead-end clues, when, in fact, the real killer had actually been inside her own house the whole time! And now, because of her useless, stupid snooping, her daughter's life might now be in imminent danger!

Leroy, who trotted alongside her, desperately trying to keep up with Hayley's pace, started barking, as if he innately sensed trouble was brewing back at the house and was sounding the alarm. Behind her, Hayley could hear Mona wheezing and coughing as she struggled to stay close on Hayley's heels.

When they reached the house, Hayley could see Gemma through the kitchen window, standing at the counter, chopping something. She didn't immediately spot Conner.

Hayley tripped as she ran up the side porch

steps and stumbled, her knee banging hard against the wood railing. Despite the searing pain, she bit her bottom lip, pulled herself upright, and continued on into the house. Dropping Leroy's leash, she threw open the screen door and used her left shoulder to shove open the hardwood back door behind it.

Gemma, startled, dropped the knife she was holding in her right hand, which clattered into the sink. She whipped around, gripping a half-chopped carrot in her other hand. "Mother, you scared the bejesus out of me!"

"Where's Conner?" Hayley gasped, clasping a hand to her chest to catch her breath.

"He went to the store to pick up some wine for dinner," Gemma said, sighing, as she bent down to pet a discombobulated Leroy, who had passed by Hayley and was running in circles around the kitchen.

Hayley looked around, nervous. "Are you sure?"

"Yes, I'm sure."

"Thank God! I need a beer!" Mona yelled as she pushed her way into the kitchen and made a beeline for the refrigerator.

Gemma stood back up to face her mother. "Why do you look so upset? What's going on?"

"Listen, Gemma, we don't have a lot of time, so I'm just going to be direct and come out with it. I know this might come as a shock, and it's hard for me to find the right words to say what I have to say, but—"

"Your boyfriend is a serial killer!" Mona screamed.

Gemma stared at them incredulously. "What?"

Hayley sighed. "It's true, Gemma. I didn't want

to believe it at first, but Mona saw his picture on one of those crime-tip TV shows and she swears it was him."

"After how many beers?" Gemma asked, glaring at Mona and folding her arms.

"That was an unfair shot, Gemma! I used to babysit you and change your diaper when your mother and Danny used to go out on date nights. Show some respect. And for your information, I didn't have a drop last night because I had to pick up my kids from a Christmas party," Mona sniffed.

"What was the name of the show?"

"*FBI's Most Wanted* or *Most Wanted Files*, something like that."

"And if you saw the show last night, why did you wait until now to tell us?" Gemma asked.

"I don't know, maybe I was worried I got it wrong, but the more I thought about it, the more I realized it was him! It was definitely him!" Mona argued.

Gemma spun around and marched out of the kitchen.

"Gemma, where are you going? I think we should get out of the house before Conner gets home," Hayley called after her.

"I'm going to go get my computer."

Hayley and Mona exchanged confused looks and then followed Gemma up the stairs and into her room, where they found her already sitting on her bed typing on her laptop.

"What are you doing?" Hayley asked gently.

"Going to their website. Here it is," Gemma said, staring at the screen. "*FBI's Most Wanted Files.* You say you saw the episode last night?"

"Yes, and it was him, Gemma, I swear it. I never forget a face," Mona said, clutching the side of the doorway, almost afraid to enter.

"The episode isn't available On Demand yet. Do you remember the name of the guy they were profiling? I mean, it wasn't Conner Gibson, was it?"

"No, it wasn't that. It was another name, but I'm only good with faces, not names. Sometimes I even forget the name of my husband . . ."

"Dennis," Hayley offered.

"Yeah, him," Mona said.

Hayley sat down on the edge of the bed. "I'm sure a killer like that uses many different aliases."

Gemma closed her laptop. "Do you honestly believe what Mona is saying?"

Hayley nodded. "I've never seen her so certain about anything in all the years we've been friends."

Gemma spied something across the room. She jumped off the bed and walked over to a small desk and chair in the corner of her room. There was a black laptop case on top of the desk.

"What is it?" Hayley asked.

"Conner's computer. He was returning some e-mails earlier," Gemma said as she gazed at it, clearly debating with herself about something.

"Maybe there's something incriminating on there! Do you know his password?" Hayley cried.

Gemma eyed her mother warily and said in a soft whisper. "No . . ."

Hayley bristled. "Gemma Liddy Mona Powell, I have always been able to tell when you are lying, and that, right there, young lady, was a bald-faced lie."

"If we break into his computer and find nothing, then I've completely betrayed Conner, and I'll never be able to live with myself."

"If we don't break into his computer, and he slaughters us all in our sleep, then you won't have to worry about that because we'll all be dead, do you hear me? D-E-A-D!" Mona bellowed.

"Tell me the password, Gemma, and I will look on his computer so you don't have to," Hayley offered.

"I'll still be complicit by giving up the password."

"Is it a word, or a number, like a date, his birthday? What's his birthday?" Mona asked.

Gemma shook her head. "Forget it, Mona!"

"Wait a minute," Hayley said, her mind racing. "How did it come up, him telling you his password?"

"I'm not playing twenty questions with you, Mother," Gemma said. "I'm not saying another word."

"Why would he arbitrarily mention his password, unless . . . ?"

"Unless what?" Mona asked, dying to know.

Hayley shot forward, snatched the black laptop case off the desk, and ran out of the room before Gemma had a chance to move a muscle. Mona chased after her.

Gemma called after her. "Come back here! That computer does not belong to you!"

Hayley bolted down the stairs and into the living room, where she sat on the couch and set the case down on the coffee table. She quickly unzipped it and yanked Conner's laptop out. She fired it up, waiting impatiently for the log-in screen to appear.

When it finally did, there was a photo of Conner, one of his flattering headshots, and underneath that, a space to type in the password.

By the time Mona plopped down on the couch next to her, Hayley had already typed the word "Gemma" and tapped the enter button. Conner's home screen popped up with all his desktop files.

She had successfully gained access.

Gemma flew down the stairs and made a grab for the laptop, but Hayley scooped it up before she had the chance and held it against her chest.

Hayley looked at her daughter, who stood before her red-faced with anger, and said solemnly, "I'm sorry, Gemma, but we have to know."

Giving up, Gemma circled around the coffee table and sat down on the other side of her mother, unable to resist the chance to see what, if anything, her boyfriend was hiding.

First, Hayley scrolled down his list of e-mails.

Most were inquiries regarding possible acting opportunities, particularly an upcoming Broadway play that was holding auditions in a few weeks.

Mona grumbled, "I'm sure this whole actor identity is just one of many personas he uses to lure in his victims."

Gemma shot Mona an annoyed look and then she returned her attention to the computer screen. Hayley was now opening a folder marked "Monologues," which turned out to be just that, classic monologues for an actor of Conner's age: scenes from *Death of a Salesman*, *Fool for Love*, *The Glass Menagerie*, *The Importance of Being Earnest*, *The Cherry Orchard*.

Gemma began twisting her blond hair around her right index finger nervously. "See? There's nothing there! I feel so guilty! We never should have done this! I can't believe there was a small part of me that for a moment didn't trust him!"

Mona pointed at one of the files. "Click on that one."

It was a folder labeled "Gemma."

Hayley double-clicked on the folder and suddenly a collage of photos, all of Gemma, some in seductive poses, began filling the screen.

"Dear God, it's like the shrine I saw that Kimmy Bradford had in her basement of Ryan Toledo!" Hayley gasped.

"He's clearly obsessed with you, Gemma," Mona cried. "He's been collecting all these photos like a crazed stalker, waiting for you to disappoint him somehow, which will awaken the marauding killer living inside him, sparking a murderous rampage!"

"Mona, please!" Hayley said, swatting Mona on the shoulder before turning back to Gemma. "You have to admit, this is a bit disturbing."

"No, it's not," Gemma whispered.

Hayley sat back on the couch. "How can you say that? Did he take all these pictures of you?"

"No, he didn't!" Gemma wailed.

"Then who did?" Hayley asked.

Gemma buried her face in her hands and muttered, "I did."

"You?"

"Yes, me," Gemma sighed. "They're selfies. I took them with my phone. They're from my Instagram account."

"Insta-what?" Mona asked.

"I made a digital collage and sent them to Conner for his birthday," Gemma admitted. "For what it's worth, he loved it."

"So he's innocent of stalking, but you're guilty of trying to be a Kardashian," Hayley scolded.

"Mother, please, I'm not that self-absorbed. It was a silly gift, that's all," Gemma said.

Mona's eyes were fixed on the computer screen. She moved the cursor to an unmarked folder in the bottom left-hand corner of the home screen and double-clicked on it. What came up sent her spasming and gesturing toward the computer.

Hayley and Gemma stopped bickering long enough to see what was upsetting Mona so much.

Hayley's heart sank.

Inside the folder were dozens of photos related to a string of coed murders along the East Coast with links to all of the articles on the victims from the press coverage. It was exhaustive and comprehensive, a far cry from someone having just a casual interest in the crimes. This was a folder belonging to someone rabidly interested or, even worse, directly connected to the case.

"No . . . ," Gemma moaned.

"I knew it! I knew I was right!" Mona declared proudly.

Gemma jumped to her feet. "I can't believe it! I'm dating a depraved serial killer! I hate my life!"

"We should probably get out of the house before Conner gets home," Hayley said urgently, quickly ushering Gemma and Mona toward the kitchen to make a back-door escape.

But they had only made it to the kitchen window when Hayley saw a pair of headlights flash past as a car pulled into the driveway.

Chapter Eleven

"He's back!" Mona screamed, grabbing a spatula off the kitchen counter to defend herself.

"What are you going to do with that, Mona, hold it to his throat?" Hayley asked, shaking her head. "Now let's just stay calm."

They heard two car doors slam shut outside.

"Someone's with him," Gemma whispered.

"Maybe he doesn't work alone. He must need help getting rid of the bodies," Mona said, spinning around and rattling through the drawers for a sharper weapon.

They heard footsteps pounding up on the side porch about to enter the back door into the kitchen.

Hayley quickly began herding Gemma and Mona out of the kitchen, where Leroy waited for them in the hallway, tail wagging, oblivious to the impending danger. "Quick! Everybody out the front!"

They barely made it to the coatrack near the front

door when a man's voice stopped them in their tracks.

"Where do you think you're going?"

They all froze.

It wasn't Conner.

She whipped around. "Bruce!"

Bruce stood by the back door in the kitchen, his arm around Dustin, who had a big grin on his face.

"Don't you want to say hello to your son?" Bruce asked.

"Merry Christmas!" Dustin yelled as he pulled off his wool cap, took off his black leather gloves, and shook out of his winter coat. "I'm starving. What's for dinner?"

"Dustin, when did you—"

"He got in about an hour ago. He called me to pick him up at the airport because he wanted to surprise you," Bruce said.

"Surprise!" Dustin crowed, eyeing the half-made meat loaf on top of the stove.

"You scared us half to death!" Hayley scolded.

"He still may. I may be having a heart attack right now," Mona said matter-of-factly, clutching her chest.

"Are you serious?" Hayley asked.

"No, forget it, it's probably just a panic attack or gas." Mona shrugged.

"I kind of expected a bigger reaction when I got here, maybe a few hugs and tears, like when the kids in the military serving in Afghanistan or wherever show up and surprise their families at Christmas and the videos always go viral," Dustin said, arms out expectantly.

"Dustin! I'm so glad you're home!" Hayley wailed, eyes welling up with tears on cue.

"Can we postpone this teary reunion until later?" Gemma asked, her whole body shaking. "We need to let them know about Conner."

"Is that your new boyfriend I keep hearing about?" Dustin asked.

"Nice guy," Bruce added.

"Uh, I'd say that part's debatable," Mona said.

"I think we should call the police and have them waiting here for him when he gets back from the store," Hayley suggested, her mind racing.

"What if he shows up before they get here?" Gemma asked, nervously hugging herself to stop from shaking.

"Then we just have to act casual and pretend nothing is wrong until the squad car pulls up in front of the house, and then we'll look puzzled as to why they're here and then all calmly go outside, where they can arrest him," Hayley said.

"Arrest him? For what?" Bruce asked, confused.

Hayley sighed, collecting herself. "Some disturbing information has come to light about Gemma's boyfriend, and I don't want you to panic, but you should know that Conner is a . . ."

"Conner is a what?"

The question didn't come from Bruce or Dustin, but from the young man standing behind them in the back doorway.

Bruce and Dustin parted for them all to see Conner, holding a paper bag with two bottles of red wine.

Without missing a beat, Hayley sprang forward. "Conner is a dear for going out in this cold weather so we could have wine with our dinner. Thank you so much. What a thoughtful gesture."

Hayley knew her performance was painfully forced and phony, but she had committed to acting as if everything was perfectly normal. Everyone else in the kitchen stood about awkwardly, not knowing what to say.

Hayley took the bag from Conner, a big, fake, frozen smile plastered on her face. She set the bag down on the kitchen counter and took the two bottles out and summoned an obvious frown, making sure Conner could take note of her displeasure.

"Is something wrong?" he asked.

"What? No, it's nothing," she lied.

"You seem displeased," Conner said, turning to Gemma, who quickly slapped on her own bogus, strained smile.

"It's just that with the dinner we're having, I was going to serve a white wine . . ."

"Meat loaf? Usually you have red wine with that."

"Well, call me a rebel, I guess," Hayley said, laughing, eyeing Mona to join in.

But Mona just stood by the kitchen sink, gripping a carving knife in her hand, ready to attack if Conner made the slightest move toward her.

"I can go back to the store if you want," Conner offered.

"Only if it's not too much trouble. Let me get you some money from my purse."

Hayley reached for her purse, which was lying on the kitchen table, and began fishing through it.

Conner finally noticed Dustin. "Hey, I'm Conner. You must be Dustin. Your mom must be so happy you made it home for Christmas."

Conner stuck out his hand.

Dustin offered a limp handshake as he gaped at Conner.

Gemma tried signaling Dustin to stop staring, but he didn't catch it.

Because he was staring directly at Conner.

Hayley pressed some bills into Conner's free hand. "Take your time. There's no hurry. Dinner won't be ready for at least a couple of hours."

"Thanks," Conner said.

"Wait a minute! It just hit me! I know who you are!" Dustin gasped.

Conner looked at Dustin, confused. "I'm Conner, Gemma's boyfriend."

"No, I saw you on TV last night on *FBI's Most Wanted Files!*"

"Dustin, no!" Hayley screamed.

"See, I was right!" Mona cried.

"You're the actor who played the serial killer in the reenactment scenes!" Dustin said, slapping his forehead. "I knew I recognized you from somewhere!"

Everyone took a collective breath.

"Reenactment scenes?" Hayley whispered.

"Yeah, you were awesome hacking up all those bodies!"

"Thanks," Conner said sheepishly, shuffling his feet, clearly embarrassed.

Bruce tried not to laugh, but a tiny snort escaped through his nose.

As the realization hit Mona, her face turned a beet red, and she inched her way toward the back door past Conner. "You know, I need to get home to my kids! You all enjoy your meat loaf!"

And she was gone.

"That's the first time I've ever seen Mona rush home to her kids," Bruce remarked.

"You were on a TV show and you didn't tell me?" Gemma asked Conner.

Conner shrugged. "I didn't want to tell anyone I got the job, because I want to be a serious stage actor and those reenactment jobs are so cheesy and stupid, but my agent really pushed me to take the part because I looked so much like the real guy . . . Anyway, in the end, I took it because I needed rent money."

"I wish you had told me. I would have loved to have watched the show with you. And you should never be embarrassed about a paid acting job," Gemma said, hugging him. "I'm proud of you."

She kissed him softly on the lips.

Hayley instinctively cringed.

Not that Gemma was kissing Conner, whom she hadn't quite warmed up to yet.

More over the fact her daughter was a grown woman now, and she was having trouble accepting that.

Hayley cleared her throat. "Forget the white wine. Red's fine. Why doesn't everybody go into the living room and I'll warm up some hot chocolate and get this meat loaf in the oven."

Gemma led Conner and Dustin out of the kitchen.

Bruce turned and gave Hayley a playful wink.

Hayley initially believed they had successfully covered up the fact that they suspected Conner of actually being the killer, until she heard Conner in the living room.

"What's my computer doing down here? Were you looking through my files?"

"Um . . . ," Gemma's voice trailed off.

Hayley raced into the living room in time to see Conner bent down, looking at all the serial killer photos and articles on the home screen of his laptop.

"This was my research they sent me on the real guy to prepare for the role," Conner said quietly.

"Yes, of course," Gemma said, nodding. "I knew that."

"Did you actually think . . . ?"

Gemma's bottom lip quivered.

She was caught.

And there was only one thing left for her to do.

Blame her mother.

"It was Mom! She thought you were the real killer! It was her idea to hack into your computer. I wanted nothing to do with it! She forced me to give up your password! I never believed you were capable of such horrific, awful crimes! I never wavered, not once!"

Conner stared at her with a healthy dose of skepticism. "Maybe you should go into acting, too."

Gemma sighed.

She had given it her best.

Dustin howled. "I can't believe you and Mom thought he was a real serial killer!"

Bruce covered Dustin's mouth with his hand. "You're not helping the situation, champ!"

There was an uncomfortable silence for what seemed like an eternity, and then, without warning, Conner burst out laughing.

Hard.

Really hard.

To the point where he had trouble breathing.

A giant wave of relief suddenly swept over Hayley.

Especially when Conner put his arm around Gemma and drew her into him and kissed the top of her head between guffaws, to let her know it was fine.

That was the moment when Hayley had a newfound respect for this young man who had stolen her daughter's heart. And, apparently, she was now also aware of the fact that he was a damn fine actor to boot.

Chapter Twelve

"Where did you find it?" Hayley asked Sergio, who was on the other end of her cell phone.

"In the freezer," he answered.

"So Ryan Toledo lied to Kimmy Bradford?" Hayley said.

"Looks like it."

The news surprised Hayley.

But if this was true, then her list of suspects had just drastically narrowed.

While combing for clues to Ryan Toledo's murder, Sergio's officers, who had cordoned off the dilapidated shack on the outskirts of town that Ryan had called home, had come upon one of Hayley's homemade Yule logs tucked away in the freezer. Which, of course, meant that Ryan Toledo only pretended not to have received the Yule log Kimmy Bradford had left on his doorstep, along with an invitation to celebrate New Year's Eve with her. It was probably a halfhearted attempt to avoid the whole topic of Kimmy's desire to reignite their relationship.

Just pretend the Yule log and her note had been stolen by one of the roaming thugs in his ramshackle neighborhood.

Hayley ended the call with Sergio and sat down on a stool next to her kitchen counter. She had the whole house to herself. Bruce was at the office, and Gemma, Conner, and Dustin had driven to Bangor to do some last-minute Christmas shopping.

Hayley's mind raced.

This new revelation about Kimmy Bradford's Yule log meant that two of the Yule logs were now present and accounted for: the one given to Kimmy Bradford and the one given to Bruce. That left only one Yule log without an alibi: the one Gemma and Conner had delivered to Ron Hopkins's house.

But Ron had already been considered and discarded as a suspect.

However, his second wife, DeAnn, had not.

DeAnn had left Liddy's party early, complaining of a headache.

She would have had plenty of time to lie in wait outside, and bash Ryan over the head with the wooden log after he left the party, and still make it home before Ron did. But if she did attack Ryan in the woods near Liddy's house, what was she doing with the chocolate Yule log and the piece of wood to which it was tied with the red Christmas ribbon? It was unlikely that she went to the trouble of bringing Hayley's gift to Liddy's cocktail party, where there were going to be plenty of sweets already. Unless, of course, she was planning on murdering Ryan on his walk home and had already chosen the heavy log as her weapon. But that struck Hayley as implausible because traces of the chocolate Yule log were found in his system and the red ribbon in his pocket. Did DeAnn serve him the dessert before she whacked him over the head? It didn't make any sense.

There was only one way to get to the bottom of how this crime actually happened.

And that was to pay a visit to DeAnn Hopkins at her home.

Hayley hopped in her car and drove over to the sprawling, stately New England–style house Ron's profitable supermarket had bought for him. The sky began spitting snow and there was a grayness to the day as Hayley cautiously made her way up the icy, recently shoveled pathway toward the house. She stomped her boots to free them of snow and rang the bell. When DeAnn opened the door a few moments later, Hayley was met with a warm smile.

"Hayley, what a surprise, please come in," DeAnn said, motioning her to come inside. "You'll have to excuse the mess. I'm trying to get everything in order before Ron's parents arrive tomorrow night."

The house was already immaculate.

Hayley glanced in the living room and saw Eben, DeAnn's son from her first marriage, sprawled out on the couch, watching TV.

"Say hello to Hayley, Eben," DeAnn said in a singsong voice.

Eben grunted and raised a hand in the air as a greeting, but never bothered to tear his eyes from the television set.

DeAnn smiled tightly, embarrassed by her son's lack of manners, and pressed on. "Would you like some eggnog, freshly made?"

"No, thank you, DeAnn . . . I won't take up too much of your time . . ."

"First of all, I want to thank you for that delicious Yule log your daughter and her friend brought over to us the other night!" she effused.

"Actually, that was why I wanted to stop by . . ."

"After I got home from Liddy's party, Eben and I ate the whole thing together, didn't we, Eben?"

Eben raised his arm again, but probably didn't even hear her question.

"And we burned the log it came with in the fireplace, and it kept us so nice and warm. What a lovely idea you had of delivering the chocolate Yule log on top of an actual Yule log. It was so inventive, so clever."

"Thank you," Hayley said, then quickly added, "How are you feeling?"

"Excuse me?" DeAnn asked, a blank look on her face.

"The other night you left Liddy's party early because you had a headache."

A lightbulb seemed to go off in her head.

"Oh, right, yes, much better now. In fact, by the time I got home, it had gone away, so that's when Eben and I decided to split your yummy Yule log and watch one of those holiday movies on TV."

"I love those Hallmark Christmas movies. Which one did you watch?"

She appeared as if she was clicking off titles in her mind to decide which one she should say. "It wasn't a Hallmark movie. It was *A Christmas Story*.

Eben and I watch it together every year, ever since he was seven."

"Oh, I adore that one!" Hayley cooed. "The little boy, Peter Billingsley, is so darn cute. Of course he must be in his forties now."

"Yes, I suppose so," DeAnn replied, anxious to change the subject. "Now I insist you have a mug of my homemade eggnog. Make yourself at home and I'll be right back."

DeAnn scooted off into the kitchen.

Hayley casually wandered into the living room.

Eben's eyes were glazed over as he stared mindlessly at the TV screen.

"What are you watching?" Hayley asked.

Eben didn't flinch or move or acknowledge her in any way, so Hayley made a point of stepping in front of him and blocking his view of the television.

That stirred him to raise his head in silent protest.

He finally managed to look up at Hayley and make eye contact.

His eyes were droopy, and his mouth was turned downward in a disaffected pout.

Hayley tried again. "I just asked what you were watching?"

Eben shrugged. "The new *Blade Runner*."

"You're a sci-fi fan, like my son," Hayley said.

Eben was annoyed this woman in his house would not stop talking.

He struggled to keep up his end of the conversation, but did manage to say, "Yeah."

"My son is obsessed with all the Star Wars movies. He owns them all," Hayley said. "Don't say anything, but I bought him the latest one, *The Last Jedi*, on Blu-ray for Christmas."

"That's a good one," Eben said, his interest finally piqued enough to at least half-participate in the conversation. "I watched it the other night."

"What night was that?"

Eben shrugged. "The night my parents went to that party."

"Before you watched *A Christmas Story*?"

Eben scrunched up his nose. "*A Christmas Story*? Hell, no. I hate that stupid kiddie movie. They play it on a loop every Christmas and it drives me nuts. How many times can anyone watch it?"

"So you didn't watch it with your mother when she came home early from the party?"

"No . . . ," he said. "My mother rarely can sit long enough to last through a whole movie."

"Did you enjoy the chocolate Yule log I had sent over?"

Eben stared at her, vacantly, then summoned a half nod, before he returned his eyes to the TV set, deciding he shouldn't say anything more.

Hayley knew in her gut that the kid had no idea what she was talking about.

DeAnn suddenly appeared, carrying a tray of three piping-hot mugs of eggnog. She winced slightly at the sight of Hayley standing next to the couch talking to Eben, but quickly covered and set the tray of mugs down on the coffee table. She picked one up and handed it to Eben, who grabbed it from her and took a slug, before spitting it out on his sweatshirt.

"Mom, you could've warned me it's hot," he growled.

"Would you have listened?" DeAnn sighed.

Next, she handed one to Hayley, who blew on it to cool it down before taking a small sip. "Yummy."

"Why don't we sit down and enjoy these in my dining room, where we won't disturb the couch potato," DeAnn said, scooping up the remote and lowering the volume on the TV.

"What are you doing?" Eben whined.

"We have company," DeAnn said before seizing her own mug of eggnog and leading Hayley out of the room.

"DeAnn, I have to ask, did you like the cherry glaze I added to the Yule log this year? I was going for something different."

"Honest to goodness, it was my favorite part," DeAnn was quick to answer.

Hayley stopped in her tracks, gripping her mug of eggnog.

DeAnn noticed Hayley was no longer on her heels, marching toward the dining room; she stopped, turning back.

"Is something wrong, Hayley?"

"There was no cherry glaze."

"What?"

"I made it up. I didn't add a cherry glaze to my Yule log. I used the same recipe I use every year."

"Oh, okay, then I must have been thinking of something else."

"You never ate my chocolate Yule log."

"Hayley, I'm sure I have no idea what you mean. Of course I ate your Yule log. I just told you so. Eben and I—"

Hayley cut her off. "The reason there were crumbs from my Yule log found on Ryan Toledo's clothing, and traces of chocolate and cream in his system, was because he was the one who ate it."

DeAnn's whole body stiffened.

"He was here," Hayley whispered. "You and Ryan . . ."

"Keep your voice down," DeAnn hissed.

"You were one of his married cougars . . ."

"Stop it. I hate that term. It's demeaning. I'm not a cougar . . . We just . . ."

"You were both at the party," Hayley said as she tried pulling all the pieces of the puzzle together. "After he caused a scene and got kicked out, he was probably feeling dejected about Gemma rebuffing his advances and wanted to seek comfort with someone who actually desired him, so he must have texted you, or called you, and wanted to meet you . . . Am I right?"

DeAnn pursed her lips, but otherwise didn't move.

"So you feigned having a headache so you could bow out of the party early and hurry home to meet Ryan back at your place, knowing Ron was having a good time drinking the spiked punch and would stay a while longer."

DeAnn knew she was caught.

There was no talking her way out of this one.

Hayley had figured out too much already.

Her whole body stiffened as she spoke. "Yes, it was me. I killed Ryan. Congratulations. You caught me. Call Chief Alvares. You've solved the crime. Happy now?"

"But it doesn't add up. You were having an affair with Ryan. You wanted to be with him. What changed so suddenly that you decided to kill him?"

"He was drunk, and sometimes he would get rough, and it got to be too much for me. So I grabbed the piece of wood that came with your chocolate Yule log and knocked him over the head with it. I honestly just wanted to get him away from me. I didn't mean to kill him. It was just a horrible accident," DeAnn said flatly, laying out the details in a detached, almost resigned manner.

"So it happened here, and not in the woods?"

"Yes, right. I didn't want anyone finding his body here, so I dragged him to my car, drove back toward the direction of the party, and dumped him in the woods."

Hayley closely examined DeAnn's slight build and short stature.

"That would have been a challenging task, given that Ryan Toledo was almost twice your size," Hayley said.

"I was full of adrenaline. Sometimes you can be surprised by your own strength."

Hayley wasn't buying it.

She glanced into the living room at the tall, lanky figure of DeAnn's high-school-age son stretched out on the couch.

"Did Eben help you get rid of the body?"

"No, Hayley, he had nothing to do with it," DeAnn said, her voice strained, her hands shaking, trying desperately to somehow will Hayley into believing her.

Hayley stepped forward, closer to DeAnn. "He was here. He said so. Watching *The Last Jedi*, not *A Christmas Story*, which is what you tried to get me to believe. Mother and son home alone, enjoying a chocolate Yule log and a fun Christmas movie. No, that wasn't what happened. Why did you invite Ryan over to the house, knowing Eben would be here?"

DeAnn's eyes brimmed with tears.

"He wasn't supposed to be here, was he?" Hayley said.

DeAnn slowly shook her head, tears now flowing down her cheeks. "No. He was going to stay over at a friend's house, but he changed his mind at the last minute and stayed home. He didn't tell me. I thought Ryan and I would have the whole house to ourselves . . ."

"Ryan had a head start on you, so he arrived here first. He probably knew where you hid the spare key from his previous visits, so he let himself inside through the back kitchen door. He probably rummaged through your fridge, found the chocolate Yule log cake Gemma had dropped off earlier, and decided to eat it while he waited for you to show up . . . but Eben was home, and was in the living room, watching a movie, and when he heard someone in the kitchen and came in here to see if you or Ron had come home, he was confronted by a stranger, whom he had never seen before . . ."

Hayley stared at DeAnn for a moment to receive some kind of confirmation that her version of events was true. DeAnn simply sobbed and looked down at the floor, which was all the confirmation she really needed.

"Eben must have thought Ryan was a burglar and grabbed the only weapon within his reach . . . the wooden log that had come with the chocolate Yule log . . . ," Hayley said.

"I didn't lie . . . it was an accident . . . just a terrible, horrible accident. It wasn't Eben's fault. He's just a boy. He was only trying to defend his home. He didn't know . . ."

"You must have arrived moments later to find Ryan dead on the floor from a massive hemorrhage caused by the blow to his head. When Eben told you what had happened, you panicked. You didn't want to have to explain why Ryan was in your house, and you certainly didn't want your son going to jail for murder, so instead of calling the police, you had Eben help you move the body to the trunk of your car. The two of you drove him out to the woods near Liddy's house and left him there for somebody else to find, so nothing would be connected to you. You hoped the police would focus on Conner, given the fact that he had a fight with Ryan in front of dozens of witnesses at the party."

DeAnn covered her face with her hands and bawled.

"What did you do with the log Eben used to strike Ryan?"

DeAnn tried wiping the tears off her face with one arm as she gestured toward the fireplace with her free one. "I told you, we burned it in the fireplace."

"And came up with the story that you and Eben had spent the whole evening watching a movie. Only you forgot to get your movies straight."

Eben suddenly appeared.

He was at least six feet two inches standing up and he towered over Hayley, almost menacingly. "Does she know, Mom?"

"Don't stay another word," DeAnn warned. "Not until we call a lawyer."

Chapter Thirteen

Upon hearing the news of his wife and stepson's arrest, Ron Hopkins immediately put his store manager in charge of the supermarket. He took an indefinite leave of absence in order to help his family with their pending legal battles, which loomed over the upcoming new year.

Hayley felt awful about the whole nasty business. It was, after all, an accident, but according to Sergio, there would certainly be charges brought, most likely involuntary manslaughter for Eben and obstruction of justice for DeAnn for her role in orchestrating the cover-up. It was going to be a gloomy, sad Christmas for the beleaguered Hopkins family. Hayley held out hope that at least in the case of Eben, there would be no jail time and he would be able to put this whole sordid episode behind him and move on, especially with so much of his life still ahead of him.

This was one time Hayley's insatiable need to dig and dig until she uncovered the truth had been far from satisfying. She had wondered in the hours after DeAnn's full confession to the police if justice, in this case, had really been served. Did her dogged pursuit of the facts ruin a family? She shared her troubled thoughts with her brother-in-law, Sergio, but he assured her that she had done the right thing. The truth has a way of coming out eventually, and for Ron Hopkins, for DeAnn, and, yes, even for Eben, it was best to deal with the consequences now instead of later when the guilt and regret would have undoubtedly eaten away at them, perhaps causing even more damage.

Still, as Christmas Eve finally arrived, Hayley decided to leave a Christmas card in the Hopkinses' mailbox. The lights were on inside, and she assumed they were home, having heard Ron posted bail for both DeAnn and Eben earlier that day. In the card, she simply offered her help if they needed it.

She didn't expect to hear from them.

But she had to leave the door open.

When Hayley arrived home, pulling into the driveway, she could see through the kitchen window Gemma and Conner preparing dinner together. They looked happy and content, and that was the moment Hayley knew she had to say something.

She got out of the car and marched inside the house through the back door, which led into the kitchen.

"There you are! We were getting ready to send out a search party!" Conner said with a warm smile as he spotted her entering and kicking off her boots and coat.

"Sorry, I had an errand to run after work," Hayley said, returning the smile. "Something sure smells good."

"I'm making a turkey dumpling stew for dinner," Gemma said, moving to the stove and stirring the pot on the burner with a long wooden spoon.

"It's been a Christmas Eve tradition at my family's house for years, so Gemma thought since I wasn't going to be with my own family, she'd make a batch here."

"I think that's a lovely idea," Hayley said.

She could hear Dustin and Bruce in the living room in the midst of a competitive video game, yelling at each other and trying to distract one another in order to score more points.

Hayley's whole family was gathered together for the holiday, and for that, she was so grateful. She felt her eyes welling up with tears, and she tried to fight them back, but she couldn't, and the waterworks soon started.

Conner was the first to notice, because Gemma was checking on a loaf of bread baking in the oven.

"Mrs. Powell, are you okay?" Conner asked.

"Yes, I'm fine," Hayley said, sniffing. "I just get overly emotional this time of year."

Conner instinctively walked over and enveloped her in a hug.

Hayley almost resisted at first, still hanging on to her first impression of him when he arrived, but then she wrapped her arms around him and hugged him back. She knew in her heart he was sincere in his efforts to comfort her.

And she was now seeing him in a whole new light.

"I'm sorry . . . ," she choked out.

"For what?" he asked, leaning back to look at her, with a truly puzzled look on his face.

"For everything, Conner, for everything . . ."

Gemma had shut the oven door and was watching the scene between her mother and boyfriend, completely mesmerized.

"Oh, that," he said, laughing. "Please don't worry about it. I would've suspected me, too."

He could have blamed her, even used the situation to drive a wedge between her and Gemma, but he was letting it go, and she was grateful for that, too.

Hayley gave him a gentle peck on the cheek. "You're a good man, Conner. You be sure to take care of my girl in New York City."

"It will be my number one priority," he assured her.

"Merry Christmas, Conner," Hayley said.

"Merry Christmas," he replied.

"Enough with the lovefest," Gemma said, "Let's eat."

And as they sat down to enjoy Christmas Eve dinner, Hayley counted the many blessings in her life.

And she found herself crying all over again.

Bruce, who was sitting next to her, squeezed her hand to let her know he was there for her, and she imagined in her mind a future Christmas with Bruce by her side, in this very house where she raised her children, when Dustin and Gemma would come home with their own families to celebrate Christmas.

And hopefully with good health and a little luck, there would be many, many more of those memorable holidays to come.

Merry Christmas, everyone!

Island Food & Spirits
By Hayley Powell

Last night after my daughter, Gemma, and her new beau, Conner, headed back to New York City after spending Christmas in Bar Harbor, and my son, Dustin, scooted off to play some new video game at a buddy's house, and my own beau, Bruce, headed home to work on his column for Friday's edition of the *Island Times*, I decided to treat myself to a nice cup of my brother Randy's homemade mulled wine and a generous slice of leftover Yule log cake. I settled into my recliner in front of a roaring fire, with my cat, Blueberry, curled up on my lap, my dog, Leroy, at my feet, and replayed once again in my mind the happy memories of our family Christmas together.

There was a strong sense of familiarity as I thought about the last few days, a slight feeling of déjà vu or something like it, and then it suddenly dawned on me. I lifted Blueberry off my lap, raced to my computer, and began searching my files for past Christmas columns I had published in the *Island Times*.

And suddenly it was there, right in front of me: a column I had written a few years ago, when my kids were still living in the house and I was a single mom, doing my best to raise them.

I had written about a dream I had one Christmas Eve, a dream set far in the future. I remembered when I wrote that column the dream seemed so fantastical, so far away, but now with the passage of time, I could actually see my future life as depicted in the dream starting to slowly take shape.

I breathlessly read through the column, amazed at the details, some of which I will excerpt here:

> *I quickly fell into a deep sleep and dreamt of a Christmas future, and I'm happy to report that I looked pretty darn good for it being about twenty or so years from now. Just a few gray hairs. Not too many wrinkles. I guess that's why they call it a dream.*
>
> *I was married again. That was my first shock.*
>
> *My husband and I were sitting in our living room and waiting for our guests to arrive on Christmas Eve. We were sipping on a lovely bottle of Off the Vine wine made from our very own Bar Harbor Vineyard, which we had purchased some years back when the original owners decided to retire; and with the help of a few of our friends and family, we were all enjoying a little bit of extra yearly income and loads of great wine at our disposal to share with friends and family.*
>
> *The first to arrive was one of my oldest friends, and still one of my two BFFs, Liddy, who had scored a huge multimillion-dollar*

sale on a mansion on the island that once
had been owned by a former TV producer a
few years back.

She was now retired and traveling the
world and had recently brought back one of
her latest acquisitions—a stunningly good-
looking young man from Costa Rica, "young"
being the operative word. I wasn't even sure if
he was old enough to drink the wine we were
serving.

Next to arrive was my other best friend,
Mona, with a few of her grown children who
still lived on the island, and she was carrying
a newborn baby in each arm, but I am relieved to say they were her grandchildren. I
was starting to lose count of her grandchildren that her offspring were constantly providing for her, but she was thrilled and proud
of each and every one of them.

Next was my brother, Randy, who still
owned his bar, Drinks Like A Fish, but it had
become so popular he had bought up two more
properties and now had three highly successful watering holes for the locals and visiting
tourists to frequent.

He was still with his husband, Sergio, who
was as handsome as ever (although I have to
admit, Liddy's new boy toy gave him a run
for his money).

Sergio was still the chief of police for Bar
Harbor. Poor Officer Donnie was waiting patiently for Sergio to hand over the reins to
him, but my brother-in-law loved his job so
much that he wasn't quite ready for retire-
ment just yet.

My son, Dustin, soon arrived. He looked to be in his early thirties and had grown quite tall and very handsome. Hanging on to his arm was a lovely woman, his fiancée, Destiny.

Mona's grandchildren ran eagerly to Dustin as he was bearing copies of his latest successful video game, a futuristic James Bond–type adventure, which, of course, I never understood. But to no one's surprise, he became a popular video game designer in California, where he and his future bride resided.

Last, but not least, the door flung open again and in breezed my daughter, Gemma, who had grown into such a beautiful woman! I'm proud to admit she had followed in her mother's footsteps, or at least a small footprint of it.

Gemma had chosen not to go to vet school, and instead moved to New York City, where she was now a well-known food writer. The restaurant world clamored for her to come try out their delicious creations in hopes they would get a glowing review in the food magazine that published her columns. But, of course, in true Gemma fashion, she was a tough critic, with a fierce reputation, in the close-knit but competitive group of top-ranked food writers. She rarely gave rave reviews. You had to knock her off her feet. If you did, then your restaurant was suddenly on everybody's radar, and reservations became near impossible to get. My husband and I dined at most of them, thanks to my powerhouse daughter's many connections.

*I would like to take at least a sliver of credit
for her impeccable palate. But whenever I did,
I would get that withering look she used to
give me as a teenager: Oh, Mom!*

*Following behind her was her adoring
businessman husband who thought the world
of his food critic wife, and my equally adorable two twin grandchildren, Jack and Dan-
iel. Somewhere in their names, I feel there was
a loving nod to their grandmother there.*

I stared at the computer in a state of shock. It
was so prescient, like a psychic prediction slowly
coming true. Gemma moving to New York to start
a career in the food industry. Dustin following his
dream to be a video game designer. And me . . . so
resolutely single at the time I had the dream, but
now . . . this awesome future husband with our fabulous vineyard . . . Could it possibly be . . . ? Oh,
my God, I need another glass of Randy's Crock-Pot
Mulled Wine and an extra piece of Christmas Yule
Log, stat! Happy New Year, everyone!

Randy's Crock-Pot Mulled Wine

Ingredients

1 bottle (750ml) Merlot
2 cups apple cider
¼ cup honey
1 orange, zested and juiced
5 whole cloves
4 cardamom pods
2 cinnamon sticks
1 star anise
¼ cup brandy
Orange slices and extra cinnamon sticks for garnish (optional)

Add your wine, honey, apple cider, orange zest, and orange juice to your Crock-Pot. Stir to combine. Add the cloves, cardamom, cinnamon, and star anise. Cook on low until warm for about an hour. Stir in the brandy.

Ladle into mugs and garnish with orange slices and cinnamon sticks, if you like.

Keep your Crock-Pot on the warm setting for a nice mulled wine. This can be doubled, tripled, or more, just adjust accordingly.

Hayley's Christmas Yule Log

Ingredients

For the Yule Log:

½ cup butter
1 cup semisweet chocolate chips
5 eggs
1¼ cups sugar
1¼ cups flour
1 teaspoon baking powder
¾ cup water

For the Filling:

6 ounces cream cheese, room temperature
1 cup powdered sugar (more for your towel later)
1½ cups your favorite whipped cream

Preheat your oven to 350 degrees. Prepare an 11 x 17 pan or a half-sheet cake pan by spraying it with cooking spray or greasing pan and adding parchment paper.

In a microwave bowl, melt your butter and chocolate chips in 30-second increments, stirring until smooth and set aside.

In a stand mixer, beat the eggs on high until nice and frothy. Keep the mixer on low and slowly add the sugar. Now slowly add the chocolate mixture and mix until blended.

Sift the baking powder with the flour, then on low speed alternate adding the flour mixture and water a little bit at a time, ending with the flour, and mix until it is just incorporated, you don't want to overly mix.

While your cake is baking, sprinkle lots of powdered sugar on a clean dish towel.

When the cake is done, remove it from oven. Do not cool, but immediately turn it out onto the dish towel. Starting on the short end of the towel, roll the towel and cake up together. Now allow to cool completely.

Prepare your filling by mixing your cream cheese on high for four to five minutes. Gradually add the powdered sugar until well blended. Fold in your whipped cream.

Carefully unroll your cake. Remove towel and spread the filling all over cake and gently roll it back up (without towel). Refrigerate at least one hour before slicing and serving with some warm mulled wine to your friends.

Note: This is the basic cake, but please feel free to frost and/or decorate your rolled cake any way you want and to be as creative as you like!

LOGGED ON

Barbara Ross

Chapter One

"It looks like a mousse," my sister, Livvie, said. Charitably.

"It looks like something a moose left in the woods," her husband, Sonny, corrected. "An unhealthy one."

Page, my ten-year-old niece, leaned in toward the disaster sitting on a board on the countertop. "At least it must taste good." She dipped a finger in the mess and popped it in her mouth. "Yuck."

"There's the final verdict." I used a big kitchen knife to sweep it into the garbage bin. "Tomorrow I try again."

The crease between Livvie's big amber eyes deepened. "Maybe you should try something a little less challenging." It was a gentle suggestion, well-intentioned.

I shook my head. "Nope. Bûche de Noël, it is."

"Okay, then." She turned to her family. "Let's go. It's a school night. Sonny, can you get Jack?" Their ten-month-old was asleep in a portable crib

in my old bedroom upstairs. I'd made the Yule log
cake, or, rather, I'd attempted to make the Yule log
cake, at my mother's house. The tiny kitchen in
the studio apartment over Gus's restaurant, which
I shared with my boyfriend, Chris, couldn't have
handled the complicated dessert. Of course, as it
turned out, neither could I.

"Sure," Sonny said. "Then we'll light this baby up."

While I'd measured, mixed, and baked, Sonny,
Livvie, and Page had strung lights outside the
house. My mom had grown up motherless, in an
apartment in New York City, and never had been
one to go over the top at Christmas. All my life a
simple Maine-made evergreen wreath had graced
our door, nothing else.

But the year before, the Maine Coast Botanical
Gardens, up the peninsula, had started a new holiday tradition. Called the Illuminations, they adorned
a huge swath of their 128 acres with five hundred
thousand colored bulbs. It had been successful beyond their wildest imaginings. The first year, sixty
thousand people showed up. But when those people had driven down to our little town of Busman's
Harbor, looking for dinner and perhaps a place to
stay overnight, they'd found the sidewalks rolled
up and the town in darkness. The only place to eat
in the off-season was the dinner restaurant Chris
and I ran in Gus's space. But we catered to locals
and Gus was anti-signage, so most people missed us.

This year the Tourist Bureau had persuaded two
of the larger restaurants to stay open every night
until New Year's. The town had strung lights along
the stretch of two-lane highway from the gardens
into the harbor, and they'd attempted to persuade
all the year-rounders to decorate their homes. My

mother was suddenly into it, consulting with Sonny about what kind of lights to buy and where to put them on the house.

While Sonny was gathering Jack, Livvie again tried to talk me out of attempting the Bûche de Noël.

"Julia and Jacques assured me that this flour-less chocolate roulade would make a perfect cake layer for my Yule log," I told her.

"Julia Child and Jacques Pépin were both considerably more experienced bakers than you are," Livvie pointed out.

I shook my head, unmoved. "You have cookie day." Livvie was the field general of the family Christmas cookie-making efforts. "And Mom gives out her strawberry-rhubarb jam." Made when the fruits were fresh in the spring, the jars were festooned with bright green ribbons and delivered to neighbors, friends, and relatives when the holidays arrived. "I need my own thing." I'd been back in Busman's Harbor for almost two years and had decided to make it my home. I needed my own contribution to our Christmas traditions. Livvie was the family baker. I was not. I admit the Yule log cake was an odd choice, but I had my reasons.

"Julia Child said she never changed the recipe for her Bûche de Noël—only for the cake, the filling, and the frosting," Livvie said. I squinted at her, my best daggers stare. She shrugged. "I'm just saying."

"Let's go! Outside." Sonny charged down the stairs, ten-month-old Jack in warm footie pajamas held to his shoulder. My mother hurried after them.

"So exciting," she said as we slipped into our

coats, stepped into our boots, and went out the big mahogany front door.

"Ready?" Sonny handed Jack to Livvie and disappeared around the side of the house. We stood in the road, shivering. "One, two, three!" Sonny shouted.

Merrily-colored miniature bulbs outlined the front of the house, showing off its distinctive Victorian features, including the deep front porch, the mansard roof, and the cupola at the top. We gasped appreciatively, then clapped.

"Bravo! You've outdone yourselves." Mom ran to Sonny and gave him a hug as he returned to the front yard.

"The lights are on a timer," Sonny instructed. "They'll come on at four every day, and go off at midnight."

I turned in the road, taking it all in. While many of the houses of seasonal residents around town were completely dark, Main Street had always been home to year-rounders. Up and down the road, every house twinkled against the night sky. Across the street, the Snugg sisters' B&B had white lights outlining the gingerbread on their porch. One block down the hill all the town stores, including Gordon's Jewelry, Walker's Art Supplies, and Gleason's Hardware, were decorated to the nines. Our days were short in coastal Maine. Dark came early. The lights made me feel so happy. They were everywhere.

Except one house. Mrs. St. Onge's. It was at the top of the harbor hill, next to my mom's. Set back from the street, the overgrown house was always dark and foreboding, and now, the only one on our block not lit up. It was like a black hole sucking up all the happiness on the street. I shivered and turned away. Back toward my family, smiling and laughing. Back toward the light.

"You don't have to do this." My boyfriend, Chris Durand, stared over my shoulder at the mess I'd made on Gus's countertop. Rather than humiliating myself yet again by attempting the Yule log cake at Mom's house, I'd waited until Gus finished lunch service so I could make the cake in the quiet of the restaurant kitchen. This time I'd tried a traditional sponge cake, but once again I'd foundered while trying to roll the base and filling into a log.

"I want to do it," I insisted through clenched teeth. "Your family is coming for the holiday. It's my tribute to your French Canadian heritage."

Chris's green eyes looked straight into my blue ones. "Honey, it's lovely what you're trying to do. But I guarantee you, the only rolled cake in our house while I was growing up was wrapped in cellophane and baked by Drake's."

"I want to make a good impression."

Chris wrapped his arms around me, kissing the top of my head. "I'm more worried about the impression they're going to make on you." He stepped back and brushed flour off his flannel shirt. "I need to get to work."

Our restaurant, Gus's Too, served dinner to guests Wednesday through Monday. Gus had talked us into opening the winter before as a place for locals to gather in the evening. Chris was a gifted home cook. I'd grown up in the food business and had come home to run my family's company, the Snowden Family Clambake. Gus's Too was intended for casual dining, but also as a place where a couple could have a date night, or a family could celebrate a special occasion.

I'd worried about our lack of experience, and about how working and living together 24/7 would affect our relationship, but we'd done more than survive, we'd thrived. So this fall, once the clambake was done for the season, and Chris had finished closing all the summer homes and cleaning their yards for his landscaping business, we'd opened Gus's Too again. This year we had more competition, with Crowley's and the dining room at the Bellevue Inn open until New Year's, but they were mostly aimed at the tourists who'd come to the Illuminations. We still had our niche with the locals.

I looked at the cake, which resembled a log that had fallen into the sea in a storm and broken up on the rocks, and swept it into the garbage. This was getting expensive.

Chapter Two

"That smells promising." Mom drifted into the kitchen as I lifted the large, flat pan with the sponge cake on it out of the oven. I was back, trying again at her house. It did, indeed, smell delicious, and the dent I made when I pressed it with my thumb sprang back, giving me hope that its texture was right. It would have to cool before we found out if it had worked. I put the cake to the side to cool and began work on the filling.

Mom put the teakettle on and sat at the kitchen table. "You're not used to failing," she said.

"What are you talking about? I've failed at plenty of things."

"Not many things you've set your sights on."

"Are you calling me a sore loser?"

"I'm calling you a person who never showed the slightest interest in baking, who has spent an inordinate amount of time and money making a cake." The teakettle whistled and she rose, mug and tea bag in her delicate hands.

"Or *not* making a cake, as the case may be," I said.

I turned on her standing mixer to make the filling, drowning out any additional comments. To my surprise, she didn't leave with her tea, but settled again at the table. When the filling was done, I poured a cup and sat across from her.

"If you really want to learn to make this cake, why not ask for help from someone who knows what they're doing?" she asked.

"If you mean Livvie," I answered, "I want this to be my thing."

"Not Livvie." My mother shook her head. "She's never made a Bûche de Noël. I'm talking about Mrs. St. Onge, next door."

Involuntarily, my gaze drifted out the kitchen window, through the trunks of the pines that divided the properties. The St. Onge house was set much farther back on its lot than Mom's house. I could only see a corner of the ugly mustard-colored stucco. "No, thank you."

"Don't be stubborn, Julia. When you were little, Mrs. St. Onge used to contribute a Yule log cake to the Festival of Trees opening party every year. It was something to see, with icing bark, and meringue mushrooms, and surrounded by spun-sugar moss. People in the gym would jostle to get close and ooh and aah over it. It looked like a limb cut from an enchanted forest. And then they'd serve it and the taste . . ." Mom closed her eyes and swallowed. "I remember it still. Now *that* was a Bûche de Noël."

"I don't remember any of this."

"You and Livvie were too busy playing tag with the other kids around the decorated trees."

"That was years ago. We don't even know if she can make one anymore."

We were silent for a moment. Then Mom said, "I wonder how she's doing."

We'd lived next door for almost thirty years, but relations between us and our neighbor had never been warm. Mrs. St. Onge wasn't friendly. She didn't mix. Scrubby pines grew against her house, blocking the first-floor windows. She was the kind of neighbor who turned off her lights on Halloween, pretending not to be home. When we were children, Livvie and I and our friend Jamie, whose parents' property backed onto our own, had dared each other to go onto the St. Onge property. We'd take a running start, touch one of the pine trees that lined the drive, and yell, "I did it!" and then fly back to the safety of our yard as fast as our feet could carry us. As we got older, we'd extended the game to touching a pillar on the front porch. I had been terrified, but there was nothing more motivating to a ten-year-old than a double dare.

"She's had someone coming since the early summer," I said. From the clambake office on the second floor of Mom's house, I'd seen the odd-shaped sea-foam-green car arrive three mornings a week. A woman about my age, with light brown hair, had stepped out determinedly and marched to the house. Often she and Mrs. St. Onge would leave and then return with groceries or other shopping.

"So I've seen," Mom replied. "And there's a relative who visits regularly. A young man. At least I've assumed he's a relative."

We were trying to feel better, assuring ourselves

that our elderly neighbor wasn't alone over the holidays.

"I haven't seen the caregiver in a while," I said. "Not since Thanksgiving at least. But then, I haven't been in the clambake office as often, since we shut down at Columbus Day and reopened Gus's Too."

"I haven't seen the young man lately, either. Of course, I've been busy at the store." Mom was in her second winter working at Linens and Pantries, the big-box store in Topsham. After a rocky start she'd found her footing and been promoted to assistant manager. The holidays were the busiest time and she worked a lot of extra shifts.

My mother went to the window. "I hope she's okay over there." She turned to me. "Julia, why don't you take her a jar of my Christmas jam and make sure she's all right? If she is, you can ask her to help you with the Bûche."

"We'll see," I answered. "I think this one is going to work."

Later, I discovered my sponge cake was, indeed, spongier, and I did manage to roll the thing. But instead of a tight log, it sat on the board looking vaguely egg-shaped.

"Perhaps you could frost it in a pastel color and save it for Easter," Mom suggested.

"Okay." I admitted defeat. "I'll get the jam. I'm going."

I didn't cut across the lawn. I walked down our front walk, out to the sidewalk, and then down Mrs. St. Onge's long driveway, cradling the jam jar with its bright green bow in my gloved hands. The strawberry-rhubarb jam was my mother's tradition. She made it every year in the spring with rhubarb from our garden and strawberries purchased at the farmers' market. The truth was, my mother was a terrible cook, and throughout our child-hoods, Livvie and I had crept around the neigh-borhood, dying of embarrassment, passing out jars of grayish sludge. In recent years, Livvie had subtly taken charge of the jam-making, while somehow letting Mom keep the illusion that the project was hers. The jam I held was lovely, deep red, and Christmasy with its green bow.

An uneven flagstone path led from the drive to Mrs. St. Onge's front porch. The pines that sur-rounded the steps left just enough of a gap to get to the door. I rang the doorbell and waited, fight-ing an impulse that went back to my childhood to turn and run.

There was a scrabbling inside, barely audible through the heavy door, which shuddered open, revealing Mrs. St. Onge, blinking at me through her glasses. The lenses were thick and convex and made her light blue eyes look like a bug's. "What's this about?" she asked, those eyes tracking from my face to the jar and back again. She'd been tiny when I was a child and had been getting tinier ever since.

"I've brought you my mother's Christmas jam, Mrs. St. Onge. I'm Julia Snowden, from next door. I'm not sure if you remember."

"Well, you'd better come in, then." She shuffled back from the doorway, leaning on a wooden cane. "Put it in the pantry. Top shelf on the left. You'll see where. Through there."

I did as I was told, passing from the living room, with its beige wallpaper with pink roses, through a small passage into the old-fashioned kitchen. I found the pantry without difficulty and, glancing up and to the left, spotted about twenty years of my mother's Christmas jams, some with fading bows still attached. I left the new one with its brethren and turned to find Mrs. St. Onge standing directly in front of me just beyond the pantry entrance.

I smiled my bravest smile. "Mom and I haven't seen your regular visitors in a while. She wanted me to check to make sure you're okay."

Her sour expression didn't change. "Visitors? I never have visitors."

I cleared my throat. "I thought, well, this summer and fall, I saw someone coming regularly, in a sea-foam-colored car?"

She shook her head. "I did have a girl from the elder services who came in to help me clean and do my errands. Gwyneth, her name was. Called herself Gwyn."

I looked around the kitchen. It had two small windows, dark wood cabinets, and looked like it hadn't been updated in fifty years, but it was spotless. "But Gwyn's not coming anymore?"

"No. Quit three weeks ago. Didn't show up the Monday after Thanksgiving, and that was that."

"Did you call the elder services office to find out—"

"Wasn't interested. Don't need her. I'm fine on my own."

I wasn't sure how she could be. "Do you drive? How do you get—"

"Never learned. Never cared to. Mr. St. Onge

drove me, until he went to a better place. Now I make do. Take taxis."

That made sense. One of Chris's three jobs, four now with the restaurant, was driving a cab he owned. It kept him jumping evenings during the tourist season, but in the winter most of his fares came from taking older people to the supermarket.

"My mother says you had another regular visitor, a young man." I continued to press.

"My grandnephew, Bradley. He lives with his parents over in East Busman's Village and is kind enough to visit an old woman from time to time."

"Has he been here recently?"

She shrugged her thin shoulders. "Can't expect a young man to stay interested in an old bag of bones like me."

"So who is looking in on you, Mrs. St. Onge?"

"I don't need no 'looking in on.' Never have, never will." She paused. "Mr. Eames comes regular to take my trash to the dump and do things that need doing around the house."

When she said it, I remembered Mr. Eames and his rattletrap truck. He was an elderly man with a bent posture and massive forearms. All he needed was a corncob pipe to have looked exactly like Popeye the Sailor.

"Okay." I backed slowly through the kitchen doorway toward the front door. "But can I pick up some groceries for you? Is there anything you need?"

She followed me, leaning more heavily on the cane. "That's nice of you. Come over next time you do your shopping and I'll give you a list, and some money. And I'll pay you for your trouble, of course."

By this time I was almost to the door. "No, no, no. I couldn't take your money. It's no trouble."

"It most certainly is trouble. I insist on paying for your service, or I won't let you do it."

I put my hand on the doorknob. "I won't take your money, but there is one way you could repay me. Mom says you make an amazing Bûche de Noël. I'm trying to learn. Will you teach me?"

That brought her up short. "A Bûche de Noël, do you say? I used to make half a dozen every Christmas season. Gave them to relatives for their celebrations." She paused. "I can't manage carrying the heavy pans and bowls, what with having to use my cane, but I reckon I could teach you if you supplied the muscle."

"Yes, please. We have a deal. Can we start soon?"

"Come back in the morning. I'll give you a list for the supermarket with my little items and the ingredients we'll need. We'll bake the base when you come back."

I practically danced. "Thank you, Mrs. St. Onge. Thanks so much. I'll be back at nine o'clock tomorrow."

Chapter Three

The next morning I made my way across the frozen grass to Mrs. St. Onge's house. When she answered my knock, she was up and dressed and had her list all ready. Aside from the ingredients for the Bûche, the list was spare—tomato juice, a loaf of bread, oatmeal, and some luncheon meats. Aside from the eggs, which were on the part of the list labeled "Cake," there wasn't much protein. When I attempted to ask, "Is this all?" she cut me off with a wave.

Before I went to the supermarket, I drove ten miles out of my way to the elder services office to inquire how they'd managed to leave an old lady at home, unsupported, over the holidays. It hadn't snowed yet, but with winter looming, I thought the practice was dangerous.

The middle-aged woman who agreed to speak to me was appropriately cagey about answering my questions about Mrs. St. Onge, citing client confidentiality. She was more forthcoming about her

employee, or rather former employee, Gwyneth.
"Up and quit. No notice. Didn't even have the
nerve to tell me. Her mother, Mrs. Hillyer, er . . ."
The woman paused, recognizing she'd revealed
Gwyneth's last name, then hurried on. "Her mother
called for her. Can you imagine? Twenty-nine
years old and her mother has to call to say she's
quit." Like the magnet filings within an Etch A
Sketch, the woman's sharp features slid into a
"these young people today" expression. Then she
seemed to realize I was close in age to Gwyneth
Hillyer and therefore unlikely to agree my entire
generation was an irresponsible mess. "Whatever,"
she muttered.

"Are you looking for someone new for Mrs. St.
Onge?" I asked.

"Yes, yes," the woman answered, apparently forgetting her concerns about my neighbor's privacy.
"Maine has the oldest population in the country
and our county has the oldest population in
Maine. As soon as I get through the approvals and
can hire someone, I'll add your neighbor to our
list. These things take time."

In the meantime the holidays would pass and
the winter weather would arrive full force. I thanked
her for her time and said I would check in again.

She didn't thank me for that.

I did the grocery shopping at a Hannaford I
passed on the way back to Busman's Harbor. It was
larger than the one on our peninsula and I felt
more certain they'd have everything I needed. I
stowed the bags in the back of my new, used Subaru Forester. The ancient Caprice I'd bought the

year before had made it through the previous winter and most of the summer, far beyond its life expectancy. After nine years in Manhattan, it had taken me a while to come to terms with needing a car, but now that I had a reliable one that could handle our Maine weather, I adored it.

I parked in the St. Onge driveway and made two trips carrying bags to the front porch, then rang the bell. I heard the clump of Mrs. St. Onge's cane coming across the living room.

"Come in, then."

I dragged the groceries into the kitchen and put the personal purchases away under Mrs. St. Onge's exacting supervision. When she directed me to put the oatmeal on the third shelf in the pantry, I did as she asked. Or so I thought.

"Not that shelf! The one below it!" She'd appeared in the doorway to the pantry so quietly I jumped. She glowered at me, her cane raised like she was about to fence with me.

"Sorry." I moved the offending box.

"Not the third shelf from the top, the third from the bottom. Why would anyone store the oatmeal with the soups? Stupid girl!"

I began to have an inkling why Gwyn had left without a good-bye.

At the old woman's direction, I left the bags containing the ingredients for the cake out on the counter. Once the groceries were stowed, she went to work wordlessly, lifting a ceramic bowl out of a lower cabinet and filling a saucepan with water.

"Let me help." I moved forward, hands out to take the pot. Carrying heavy things was the part of the job she'd said she couldn't do.

"I can do it." She'd left her cane by the sink to

carry the pot with both hands, limping awkwardly
as she moved toward the stove on the other side of
the kitchen. She limped back, picked up the ceramic bowl, placed it on the pot, and turned on
the burner.

I grabbed my notebook from the Snowden Family Clambake tote bag I always carried and began
to write. "Place ceramic bowl on pan of water. Turn
on heat," I wrote.

"I'm turning on the oven to three hundred fifty
degrees," she said over her shoulder. She measured out a quarter cup of milk and poured it into
the bowl. Then she tossed in what looked like a
quarter stick of butter. I dutifully wrote down the
measurements and instructions, putting a question mark after the butter. I'd try to confirm the
amount with her later.

While the milk and butter heated, Mrs. St. Onge
slowly made her way back across the fake red brick
of the linoleum floor. She opened a bottom cabinet and bent to lift out a bowl, the bigger sibling of
the one on the stove.

"Let me get that." This time I insisted. Both
bowls were beige with a navy blue band around
them. My mother had the same set. The big one
weighed a ton.

"Set it on the table," Mrs. St. Onge instructed.

I did as I was told. The old woman rooted
through the grocery bags, pulling out the cake flour,
baking powder, and salt. "There's a flour sifter in
the cabinet over the icebox," she said. "Get it down
and sift three quarters of a cup of flour into the
big bowl. Then add a teaspoon of the baking powder and a quarter teaspoon of salt and whisk it to-

gether. The whisk is in the drawer next to the sink."

"I'm glad you know the measurements so precisely," I said. "I was worried you've been making the Bûches for so long you did it all by eyeball."

She grunted. "I cook by eyeball, as you say. Cooking is art. Baking is science. You have to measure."

While I whisked, I attempted to restart the conversation about Gwyn Hillyer. "So the woman from elder services who helped out, she just stopped coming?" I didn't want to admit I'd been to talk to the caregiver's supervisor.

"I told you that yesterday. Didn't need her in the first place." Mrs. St. Onge pursed her lips in distaste. "She was a most unpleasant girl. Had her own ideas about how things should be done."

The greatest sin of all.

As we talked, she got two more bowls from the cupboard, the middle sizes from the set we were using. With a quick hand and deft flick of the wrist, she cracked an egg on the side of one bowl, and then separated it, putting the white in one bowl and the yolk in the other. She separated two more eggs as efficiently. "Get the beater. In the drawer," she directed.

I found a hand beater in the drawer next to the sink. My mother had one, in case of a whipped-cream emergency during a power outage, she said. But how likely was that? I'd never used it.

Mrs. St. Onge pushed the bowl containing the egg whites forward. "You beat these. I'll add the sugar." I went for it, turning the handle quickly, while she fed a quarter cup of sugar into the egg

whites a tablespoon at a time. Soft white peaks
formed on the mixture just about the time my arm
went numb.

"And you said your nephew stopped coming.
Why is that?"

Mrs. St. Onge took the beaters from me and
shook the egg white that clung to them into the
bowl. She limped over to the sink to rinse and dry
them. "Grandnephew," she corrected. "I don't
know why. He just did. Who knows why anyone
does anything? Being honest, I'm glad. Always pes-
tering me, asking about my parents and grandparents." She stopped washing and, standing up as
straight as she was able, pushed air out through
tight lips in exasperation. "The past is better left to
rest, I find."

"You said he lives in East Busman's Village," I
prompted.

"Lives with his parents, my late sister's son and
his wife. Why would a man, a successful accountant, thirty years old, live with his mother and father? Time he got married and settled into a place
of his own."

"Did you say that to him?" I began to suspect
why the grandnephew wasn't coming around so
much anymore, either.

"'Course I did," the old woman allowed. "Though
why anyone had to say it, I don't know. Plain as the
nose on his face. He needs to get out of his parents' house."

The pot on the stove was simmering by then.
Mrs. St. Onge turned off the burner, leaving the
bowl on top of the pan. She returned to the table
and, with that wrist movement I so envied, she
added two more complete eggs to the bowl that

contained the egg yolks. Then she put the beaters into the bowl, turning the handle vigorously, pausing only to occasionally sprinkle in the contents of a half cup of white, granulated sugar. I wrote madly in my notebook.

"Do you see your grandnephew's parents, then?" I asked. "Your nephew and his wife."

Mrs. St. Onge raised her voice against the din of the metal beaters hitting the side of the ceramic bowl. "No. I don't like him much. Pushy man. Thinks he's the boss, even when he's in my home. And that wife. She's a milquetoast. Can't abide people who don't speak their minds." Mrs. St. Onge was certainly speaking her mind, and I could see why she and her nephew weren't close.

"And their name is?"

"Woodward. Richard and Whatshername Woodward."

"What's her name?"

"That's what I told you. I can't remember. Something soft and unmemorable."

I doubted a woman still as sharp as Mrs. St. Onge would really forget the first name of her nephew's wife, the mother of one of her most consistent visitors and someone who lived in the next village.

Mrs. St. Onge left the beaters and went back to the stove, banging the cane with each step. This time, when she stuck her finger in the bowl, she counted out loud, "One, one-thousand, two, one-thousand," until she got to ten, then jerked her hand away.

After a longer time than I could have turned that crank, she dragged the beaters across the surface of the bright yellow mixture. They left tracks across the top, and she pronounced it done. She ordered me to get a big rubber spatula from the drawer, grabbed it from me, and then folded the egg whites into the egg yolks a third at a time.

Then she grabbed the sifter and sifted the flour mixture into the wet ingredients, occasionally stopping to fold it with the spatula.

"Can I do that?"

"You're not ready," she snapped.

I might have been getting a lesson, but it definitely wasn't hands-on.

"Stick your pinky finger in that," she said, indicating the bowl containing the milk and butter on the stove.

"What?"

She repeated the instruction and I did as I was told. The mixture was hot and closed around my finger. "Count," she commanded. "One one-thousand, two one-thousand."

I counted, until I got to ten, one-thousand. "Ouch!" I snatched my pinky out of the bowl, hurried to the sink and ran cold water over it. Was this her revenge for my request to be more hands-on? She was as prickly as a cactus, no doubt about it. I considered ending the lessons after today and trying to make the cake on my own. But three failures had taught me I needed the help.

"Perfect temperature," she said with satisfaction. "It should remain hot enough you can't stand to hold your finger in it for more than the count of ten." She folded the milk mixture into the rest.

When she was done, she lined a rectangular cake pan with parchment paper and poured the mixture in.

"How big is the pan?" I asked.

"The perfect size for a Bûche de Noël," she answered.

I wrote down "10 x 15?" She popped the pan in the oven, slammed the door, and set the old-fashioned timer on the stove for twelve minutes.

I gathered all the bowls and utensils, put them in the sink, and began washing before she could beat me to it. She collapsed in a kitchen chair, took off her glasses, and rubbed her eyes. It was obvious the cake-making had worn her out.

I'd finished drying the last item in the dish rack just as the timer dinged. Mrs. St. Onge removed the cake from the oven. It was golden and beautiful and smelled like heaven. She loosened the sides of the cake with a sharp knife, covered the top with a clean dish towel, and flipped it onto the kitchen table. She shimmied the pan off the cake and then gingerly peeled off the parchment paper. Then she slowly rolled the whole thing, towel and all, into a log shape and put it on a cooling rack.

"That's it for today," she announced. "We'll do the filling tomorrow."

"Okay. Is there anything else I can do for you?"

She looked around the neat kitchen, peering through her thick glasses. "The parlor could use some dusting." She gave me a cloth and feather duster and set me to it. The knickknacks on the mantel, the side tables, and the back of the old upright piano were covered in a thin gray coating, the kind of soot you got with an old burner when the oil heat first came on. I wondered how well Mrs. St. Onge could actually see. As I worked, I got madder and madder at the caregiver and the relative who had abandoned her. She might be tough to deal with, but that was no excuse.

I dusted the dining room while I was at it and returned to the kitchen. The old woman sat in the kitchen chair, eyes closed behind the distorting lenses. "Anything else I can do?" I asked.

She opened her eyes, shook her head vigorously, picked up her cane, and stomped to the front door. If she'd handed me my hat and said, "What's your hurry?" I couldn't have been more thoroughly dismissed.

When I was on the front porch, the heavy door slammed behind me. She was difficult. Curt. Not warm. The opposite of warm. But that didn't mean she should be left alone by her family members during the holidays. I got in my Subaru and pulled out of the drive. It was time to find out what was up with these Woodwards.

Chapter Four

I found the address for Richard Woodward in East Busman's Village on my trusty phone. East Busman's was a charming little enclave a few miles out of town. It sat on a thin peninsula that jutted into the Gulf of Maine. In the center of town was a mill-pond, with a small waterfall at one end that had originally supplied the mill's power. A swath of green parkland surrounded the pond, originally used for grazing cows. Even though the grass was brown and the leaves had fallen off the maples, it was still a beautiful sight.

I didn't have any trouble finding the Woodward house. It was undoubtedly visible from outer space. The front yard hosted a human-sized Santa in a sleigh who nodded his head and waved. The reindeer were all there too, also full-sized, which was big. On the roof was a deep red banner that proclaimed, "Merry Christmas!" in marquee-style lights, which were lit even now in the middle of the day. There was a wreath on every window, and a larger one on the door. I threaded my way through the reindeer and knocked.

"Hello. Merry Christmas." The trim blond woman at the door was in her midfifties, dressed in a well-fitting kilt, white blouse, and red cardigan, with an appliqué wreath on the lapel. She had to be Whatshername.

"Merry Christmas," I said, offering my gloved hand. "Julia Snowden. I'm a neighbor of your husband's aunt."

She took my hand with a firm grip and shook it. "My name is Julia too. Julia Woodward. You'd better come in."

I smiled as I crossed the threshold, remembering how Mrs. St. Onge had described Mrs. Woodward's first name as "soft and unmemorable."

"Let me take your coat. Richard! Company!"

While Mrs. Woodward hung my coat in the closet in the small front hall, I had a moment to look around the living room. It was, if possible, even more Christmasy than the yard. A tree that reached to the ceiling dominated the space, decorated with expensive-looking, one-of-a-kind ornaments and white lights. An elaborate train track circled the base of the tree twice, and two trains chugged away, passing each other with perfect timing at the switch-over. One train was driven by Santa, its cargo cars laden with presents. The other train had passenger cars filled with townspeople in Victorian dress.

Every shelf on the built-ins around the fireplace held a Victorian Christmas scene of people, houses, and trees; and on the base cabinet nearest me was a large crèche with the infant Jesus, Mary, and Joseph, the Three Kings, and more shepherds, donkeys, and sheep than I could count. I stepped forward to examine it. The figures were made of wood and the individuality of their features and expressions made me sure they were hand painted. Joseph was the tallest at about a foot. Mary held the infant Jesus in her arms. Her expression wasn't that of a virgin or a saint. It was the look of a new mother, exhausted, elated, suffused with joy.

"I made them," Mrs. Woodward said. While I'd been dazzled by the show in the living room, Mrs. Woodward had evidently slipped into the kitchen because she emerged with a tray holding three Santa mugs, a Santa pitcher, and a small plate of Christmas cookies.

Quickly I put Mary back in her place in the crèche. I'd been so entranced, I hadn't realized I had picked her up. "You painted them? They're lovely."

"Carved and painted." She put the tray on the coffee table in front of the sofa. "When Richard retired from the Navy, I thought he should have a hobby. I bought him all these wood-carving tools and such. He never showed the slightest interest, so rather than waste the money, I took it up."

"You're very talented."

"Thank you. Richard turned his hand to this." She gestured around the room, taking in the tree, the Victorian villages, the trains.

"It's amazing."

"He'll be happy to hear that. He is quite traditional about Christmas. We were about to have some lovely hot chocolate. Please join us. Richard! Cocoa!"

Her husband came down the stairs into the room. He held himself erect and didn't use the handrail. Like his wife, he was tall and trim and dressed in wool, in his case gray slacks and a bright red pullover. He had a most impressive mustache, gray like his thick head of hair.

"What ho," he said, greeting me. "Who have we here?"

"Julia Snowden," I said, offering my hand as he came toward me.

"Julia is a neighbor of your aunt's," his wife informed him.

"Oh." His smile vanished, replaced by two deep wrinkles over his nose. "Her." He welcomed me nonetheless, gesturing that I should sit on the sofa. His wife poured the cocoa and they took the chairs on either side of me. We were all a little crowded in the space, and I sensed that the arrangement of the furniture had been condensed to make room for the tree.

"Which house do you live in?" Mrs. Woodward asked, her tone neutral and polite.

"My mother's house is number forty-three, next door on the right as you face Mrs. St. Onge's house from the street."

"The beautiful yellow house with the mansard roof and the cupola. I've admired it often," she said.

"What brings you here?" Richard Woodward sat ramrod straight in his chair. His friendly demeanor had vanished.

"My mother and I had noticed your aunt was well-looked after over the summer and fall. She had a caregiver from elder services who called on her several times a week, and a man—your son, I believe—who visited often."

"Our son, Bradley," Mrs. Woodward confirmed.

I cleared my throat. "But since Thanksgiving, the situation has changed. The caregiver has quit her job and elder services has been unable to replace her. And your son seems to have stopped checking in."

"Bradley is on a business trip," Mrs. Woodward said. "He's a CPA with Jenkins and Anton downtown. They've sent him out to California to do a job. It's not clear how long he'll be there. He's working long days and with the time difference we haven't spoken. I'm sure he would have told his Aunt Odile all this. He's quite fond of her. He wouldn't have left her wondering."

"Perhaps she's gone gaga and forgotten he's told her," Richard suggested. "Or more likely, she's complaining to you about Bradley for the sake of complaining and knows perfectly well he's away on business."

I didn't have anything to say to that and we all sipped our hot cocoa in silence for a moment. It had a rich, chocolaty flavor and the heavy Santa mug kept it warm.

"You're concerned about Aunt Odile," Mrs. Woodward said.

I hesitated. It wasn't my family, or truly any of my business. "With both the caregiver and your son gone, I'm worried about your aunt's well-being. Of course, my mother and I are happy to look in on her. She's teaching me some baking, which will give me an excuse to go over every day for the next few days, but after that, and with the holidays approaching . . ." I let the rest of the sentence hang. Surely, there were few people more invested in Christmas than the Woodwards. And surely, Christmas was a time for family.

"Aunt Odile is my late mother's sister," Mr. Woodward said. "When I retired from the Navy and we moved back to the area, we tried"—he hesitated—"to have a relationship with my aunt. She made it clear she wasn't interested. Finally, after several years of miserable holidays and visits, we gave up. Bradley, for whatever reason, persists. He likes her and finds her stories of growing up speaking French at home, and whatnot, fascinating. I find them tedious. She's hypercritical. Hates everything we do. Everything we care about."

"We did have a few lovely holidays together," Mrs. Woodward said. "Thanksgivings and Christmases. She used to bring the most beautiful Bûche de Noël."

"Except the last time, when it practically killed us," Mr. Woodward reminded her.

"You don't know it was the Bûche," his wife cautioned. "There were lots of dishes that day."

"You and I were the only ones who ate dessert. Bradley said he was too full. Aunt Odile said she'd already had plenty of cake at home. They were fine, and you and I were so sick with intestinal distress we didn't even have the strength to go out by New Year's. I know it was the cake."

Mrs. St. Onge's cake had made them sick? I didn't need her mentoring to achieve that. History suggested I could do it on my own.

Mrs. Woodward sighed. "In any event, during that visit, things were said that cannot be unsaid. By either party. Bradley will be back before Christmas. We'll make sure he calls on his great-aunt."

Her husband grunted his agreement. "Funny you're the one who's conciliatory," he said to his wife. "She treated you worst of all."

I hadn't thought the reference to Whatshername had been a memory lapse.

"What are you going to do?" Mrs. Woodward raised her hands, palms out. "She's old and she's alone, and Bradley cares for her."

I said my good-byes, assuring them I'd look in on their aunt until their son returned.

Mrs. Woodward walked me to the front door. As I struggled into my coat in the small front hall, I noticed the wall opposite the coat closet was covered with dozens of photos of boys at all ages and stages. "Do you have other children?" I asked.

"No. They're all Bradley."

I looked more closely and indeed they were. Every single one. The wall was like a shrine. I said good-bye, left the house, wove my way between the eight flying reindeer, and got back in the Subaru.

I was late getting to the restaurant. Gus had left for the day after lunch service, leaving the place meticulously clean, as always. Chris and I tried to meet his standards before we closed up every night, but we usually failed in some way only the hawk-eyed Gus could notice.

Chris had gotten there ahead of me and the smell of slow-cooked short ribs filled the open kitchen. It was important for the two of us to do as much prep ahead as possible. We had a strong list of reservations, and the stores on Main Street would be open late for holiday shopping as well. And who knew, maybe some of the people going to the Illuminations at the botanical gardens might find their way to our door.

"Hey, beautiful."

I went to Chris, presenting my cheek for a quick kiss, mindful that his plastic-gloved hands were arranging halibut cheeks for seasoning and baking later. "Salad station prep?" I checked on my assignment.

"Please."

I washed up and got to work. "I made the base of a Bûche de Noël with Mrs. St. Onge this morning," I told him, making conversation. " 'I made' is a bit of an exaggeration. Mostly I watched."

"The woman who lives next door to your mom?" His tone was skeptical.

"Do you know her?"

"She and her husband used to go to our church," he answered. "When I was a kid, I was terrified of both of them. Always with the sour expressions on their faces."

"I don't remember him. I think he died before we moved to our house. I was terrified of her as a kid. Livvie, Jamie, and I used to dare each other to run to their porch, tag it, and run away. Did your family know them well?"

"Not well. I think my dad was friendly with them, or maybe it was my granddad. Or maybe they worked together or came from the same village in Canada. You know how that is."

The conversation fell off. Chris concentrated on his prep. As I rinsed and chopped, filling the stainless-steel bins with the salad fixings, I thought about my visit to the Woodwards. Had they really become sick from Mrs. St. Onge's Yule log cake? Their digestion woes were more likely psychological than physical, a long-sought excuse to end an unhappy relationship. But would that have affected them both?

My mind traveled to their son, Bradley. Jenkins and Anton was a fine accounting firm, the biggest in the area. They took care of the taxes and other accounting needs of many local businesses, including the Snowden Family Clambake. They also did the personal taxes for lots of wealthy retirees. But what business would they have that would send a junior associate like Bradley Woodward to California for a weeks-long stay? Perhaps some kind of continuing education course? A local retiree who still had a business in California? Either explanation felt like an improbable stretch.

Impulsively, I stepped away from my salad prep, walked into the bar, and took my cell phone out of my tote. I found the number for Jenkins and Anton and placed a call.

"Jenkins and Anton, CPAs," the receptionist chirped.

"Hi, Joan. It's Julia Snowden. Can I speak to Mr. Anton?"

"I'm sorry, Julia. He's not here. He and Mrs. Anton are in Hawaii." This, I knew. The accountant went away for the first three weeks of December every year, grabbing the last days of leisure before his busy season began on January 1, and roared on until the middle of May. "Is there someone else who can help you?" she asked.

"Mr. Anton said if I ever needed anything while he was away, I could speak to his associate, Bradley Woodward." This was a total lie. I didn't know if Bradley had ever worked on our account. I held my breath.

"I'm so sorry," Joan said. "Bradley's on vacation too."

"On vacation?" Not on a business trip, as his parents had told me.

Fortunately, Joan took the surprise in my voice to have another meaning. "Normally, we coordinate vacation coverage," she assured me. "But Mr. Woodward had a sudden opportunity to use a friend's house in Costa Rica, and you know how crazy our winter season will be."

So he wasn't in California, as his parents had said, either. "That's okay. It isn't urgent."

"I'll leave Mr. Anton a message you called."

I thanked her and ended the call, hoping that by the time the accountant called me after his return, I'd have thought up a reason for placing the call in the first place.

Chapter Five

I felt some of the old feelings of trepidation as I walked up the flagstone path at Mrs. St. Onge's the next morning, but I shook them off. A lovely—okay, maybe not lovely—but certainly a harmless old woman was helping me learn to do something important to me. The only feeling I should have was gratitude.

Mrs. St. Onge answered the door on my first knock, blinking at the sunlight through her thick glasses. "Come in, come in." Her tone was almost cheerful. "Best get started."

She had all the ingredients and equipment we would need laid out on the kitchen table, as well as a double boiler sitting on the stove. I shrugged out of my coat and hung it in the back hall. By the time I returned to the kitchen, she'd already started. I whipped out my notebook and stood behind her, hastily writing down everything I saw.

"Melt -?- ounces chocolate with two tablespoons of water in the top of a double boiler," I wrote.

While Mrs. St. Onge was occupied with the stove, I snuck over to the trash and found the wrapper for the chocolate I'd bought the day before. "Four ounces, semisweet chocolate." I amended what I'd written. Meanwhile, Mrs. St. Onge had moved relentlessly on. She put six tablespoons of sugar and three tablespoons of water in a saucepan and put the heat under it. She stirred it with a wooden spoon as the sugar dissolved. She popped a candy thermometer into the mixture and left it to boil. I documented every step.

"My goodness, you are good at this," I said, trying to keep up.

"Time was when I used to make six or seven of these a season," she answered.

I wasn't confident I could make even one of these complicated cakes. "My mom said you used to bring a Bûche de Noël to the Festival of Trees. She said it was breathtaking—beautiful and delicious."

For the first time since I'd been coming, Mrs. St. Onge smiled, obviously pleased. "That was one. The rest were for family."

The chocolate had melted. She turned off the burner and took the top pot off the double boiler. "We'll let that cool." She separated three eggs, putting the yolks in the big ceramic bowl with the blue band around it, which we'd used the day before. She handed me the bowl and a whisk and said, "Have a go."

I beat the yolks with the whisk until Mrs. St. Onge grabbed the bowl from me, tsk-tsk-tsking as she did. She put it in the crook of her arm and used the whisk at about twice the speed I had managed. I wondered about her upper-body strength.

Mrs. St. Onge had been old all my life. Or at least
it seemed so. I'd never not thought of her as the
old lady next door. I was in good shape. The Snowden Family Clambake demanded hard, physical
work, and schlepping trays full of dishes and sacks
of Maine potatoes around Gus's Too was no picnic, either. But elderly Mrs. St. Onge had me beat
on this whisking thing by a mile.

A few minutes later, when the egg yolks were
thick and pale yellow, she handed me the bowl and
whisk. "You go at it now," she said. "This next part is
about your speed."

She checked the candy thermometer, nodded
in a satisfied way, and took the sugar and water
mixture off the stove. She fed the hot sugar ever so
slowly into the eggs while I whisked.

"Why did you stop making Bûches?" I asked.

"Used to make one for my cousin Annie Gre-
nier and her husband," she answered. "Nasty piece
of work he was. She never said, but I think he used
to hit her. Felt so bad for her, I thought she should
have something to brighten her holidays. She always loved my Yule log cakes."

"But you don't make one for her anymore?" I
was semi-prying, but she'd brought it up. She
could have easily pleaded old age and avoided my
question.

"She moved to Florida. He's dead. Heart attack.
At Christmastime. They say the last thing he ever
tasted was my Bûche de Noël. Died with a smile on
his lips."

"Well, um, er . . ." What could I say to that? It
was a shame he was dead? Maybe, if he did hit his
wife, it wasn't. The whole upper part of my arm
was numb by that point. I didn't know how much

longer I could go on whisking. The cake-making exercise had taken on a crazy tilt. Doing the complicated recipe with hand tools felt like an insane degree of difficulty added. Just across the driveway, my mother had a perfectly good standing mixer with a whisk attachment.

"I used to make a Yule log cake for my husband's brother, Claude. Never married, and no wonder. I never met a more miserable miser. Al and I asked him for some help with the down payment on this house. Turned us down flat. Said Al was shiftless and useless." She sighed. "Of course, he was. But that's another story."

"But you no longer make a Yule log cake for your brother-in-law?"

"Dead," she said. "Dead as a doornail. Massive stroke. Over the holidays. He was such a miserable SOB it took them a week to find him. Good riddance, I say. I save the money I used to spend on the ingredients for cake for the so-and-so."

I was momentarily left speechless by her holiday horror stories. "Still, I'm sure there are people who used to get your cakes who miss them," I finally ventured.

"Then there was Auntie Amalie," she said. "Terrible person. Lived in a big house out on Mussel Point with about a hundred cats. Mistreated them, she did. Neglected them. The last time I went there was to deliver her Bûche. I felt so bad for those cats. I called the Humane Society and reported her and they took them all away. She died right after. Gastrointestinal distress, they said. Soaked in her own evil juices, I said."

I had nothing to say to that.

Finally she signaled I could stop whisking and I

gratefully set the heavy bowl on the table with the whisk in it. I pumped my arm three times to get some feeling back.

"So you don't give away any Bûche de Noël any-more because—"

"They're dead," she answered. "All dead. Every one of them." She said it with neither sadness nor bitterness. In fact, I thought I detected a bit of rel-ish. She took the whisk from the mixture and put it in the sink. Then she handed me the hand beater with a cheery "Get to it." I turned the han-dle while she fed twelve tablespoons of softened butter into the mixture, one tablespoon at a time, not putting the next one in until the previous was completely blended. At least the motion required by the beater was different from the one for the whisk.

As I worked, I thought about all Mrs. St. Onge's dead relatives. How she hadn't had a nice word to say about any of them. And how the Woodwards had gotten sick after they ate the Yule log cake. I hadn't been inclined to believe Mr. Woodward that the cake had been the cause of their illness, but after Mrs. St. Onge's stories about the relatives and all the cakes, I was having second thoughts. Yesterday the ingredients had been in sealed pack-ages, since I'd just brought them from Hannaford. But today we'd used the sugar from the box opened the day before. What if it had rat poison in it, or some other deadly substance?

"Keep going," Mrs. St. Onge said when the last tablespoon of butter had been absorbed into the mixture. I turned the beaters around so I could power them with my other hand and did as she said. I reminded myself that the old woman wasn't

making a cake for my family. She was showing me
how to make a cake for my family. They weren't
going to eat this one. Then I shook myself—liter-
ally—to loosen my constricted shoulder muscles.
What was I thinking? Mrs. St. Onge was a harmless
old lady. Not a nice old lady, but a harmless one, I
was sure. *Sheesh.*

After five more minutes Mrs. St. Onge said,
"Stop," and I did. She lifted the cooled chocolate
off the stove and stirred it into the mixture. "We'll
set this aside for now," she pronounced. "We don't
want to fill the cake too long before we eat it, or it
will get soggy. Come back tomorrow morning.
We'll make the icing and fill the cake then."

For the first time in my life, I had no desire to
lick the beaters.

I did the dishes we'd dirtied and then asked her
as I had the day before, "Is there anything else I
can do?"

Her brow creased, adding vertical wrinkles to
her already prominent horizontal ones. "I've noticed a lot of Christmas lights on the street. Even
your mother's house is all lit up. She never used to
do that."

I explained about the Illuminations show at the
botanical garden and the town's efforts to light a
cheerful path from the gardens into the harbor.

Mrs. St. Onge was silent for a few moments after
I finished, taking it all in. "There are some old
Christmas lights and things in the cellar," she said.
"Will you bring them up?"

"Sure. Where in the basement?"

She led me across the kitchen to the cellar door.
"In the front room," she said. "Somewhere over

near the washer. Look there." When I'd opened the door and stood with my foot hovering in the air over the top step, she grabbed my arm. "Look in the front room," she repeated. "They'll be somewhere there. Don't go in the coal bin. No need of that. Nothing of value stored in there."

I nodded to show I understood and flipped the light switch at the top of the stairs. The glow that came from below was faint.

The basement wasn't as scary as I expected. It was relatively warm and dry. The furnace was an old octopus of a thing, with arms going out everywhere, no doubt covered with asbestos. My parents had the same one when we were little. It had long since been replaced. While I stared at the old beast, it rumbled to life.

A tiny puddle of water had collected on the concrete floor in front of the washer. A drip fell slowly from the brittle black hose connecting the machine to the faucet. I turned the cranky handle and shut off the water.

Rummaging through the boxes piled next to the ancient washing machine and dryer, I found one filled with holiday candles with old orange light bulbs, and a few other light strands of the same vintage. I pulled the box toward me and set it on the floor, carefully avoiding the puddle.

On the way back to the stairs, I looked at the wooden wall that divided the basement, reserving about a quarter of it for the old coal bin. I was dying to peek inside, if only because Mrs. St. Onge had asked me not to, but I summoned up as much self-discipline as I could and marched back up the stairs instead.

Mrs. St. Onge was at the top, one hand on her cane, the other on her hip, waiting for me. "Ah, good. You found them."

"There's a slow leak in your washer hose. I shut the water off."

"Mr. Eames will take care of it the next time he comes. He'll be working in the cellar anyway."

I pointed at the box of lights. "Shall we put them up?"

"Tomorrow. We've done enough for today."

Once again I was dismissed.

As I made my way across the lawn to my mother's house, my thoughts ping-ponged through the stories of the relatives, suddenly dead at the holidays. Good grief. No wonder Gwyneth Hillyer and Bradley Woodward had fled without saying good-bye, and immediately after Thanksgiving. They'd been in fear for their lives.

I didn't really believe tiny Mrs. St. Onge was responsible for all those deaths, did I? Of course not.

But still, Gwyn Hillyer's sudden departure was odd. As a professional caregiver, Gwyneth would be used to cantankerous old people, and she'd probably been in creepier houses. At least Mrs. St. Onge's was tidy.

Despite the rigors of the morning, I had several hours before I had to be at Gus's Too. I decided to pay Gwyneth's parents a visit.

They were the only Hillyers who popped up in an online directory. They lived on Holly Hill Farm Road, about midway up the peninsula. I'd never heard of the street, but my GPS found it, no problem.

The road was long and winding, taking me far from our two-lane highway past a couple of houses and then to a sign—HOLLY HILL FARM. My Subaru bumped up the rutted road to the top of a hill, where the view of Townsend Bay spread out before me. The farm was big by coastal Maine standards, with pastures of brown grass and the stubble of harvested hayfields that rolled down to the water. I stopped in front of a white outbuilding with a sign that said HOLLY HILL FIBRES ARTES. On the door was a lush wreath and another sign that said, OPEN. PUBLIC WELCOME. It seemed like the place to start.

There was a large red barn, a little way off, and when I got out of the car, I could hear, and smell, the presence of sheep. On the other side of the white outbuilding stood a charming cottage. I almost lost my nerve as I approached the fiber shop. What was I going to say to these people? *In for a penny, in for a pound.* I pushed the door open.

Inside the building the walls were washed white and the room was bright. A woman worked at a spinning wheel and another at a loom, while three others sat knitting. Along the walls were displays of knitted and woven goods and yarns in the most luscious colors—deep pinks, purples, blues, and greens.

"Merry Solstice!" A woman rose from the loom. She had beautiful high cheekbones and long white hair. She wore a loose, ankle-length dress, the vanilla color of fine wool. "I'm Holly Hillyer." She had the same fine-boned build I'd observed Gwyn had as she walked in and out of Mrs. Onge's house all those mornings. "What can I help you with today? A gift for someone special, perhaps?"

I stared at the shelves of yarns and handmade

goods. "Handmade by Holly Hill!" The light had finally dawned. "You're famous."

She beamed. "Not as famous as all that."

But she was. Through a doorway I hadn't spotted before, I saw three more women packing boxes that would be sent all over North America and even farther, holiday gifts for knitters and fans of handmade gifts.

I extended my hand. "Mrs. Hillyer, I'm Julia Snowden. I've come about your daughter."

Holly Hillyer looked around the room. All conversation had ceased and the other women looked at us with pointed curiosity. "Of course, of course. I'm always happy to meet Gwyneth's friends. Let's go someplace where we can talk more privately." She threw a cranberry red shawl around her shoulders and headed for the door. Outside she turned not toward the charming house, but toward the red barn.

Inside the barn smelled of wool, hay, and manure. There were dozens of sheep, most wearing capelike garments, which made me smile. Some were tall and rangy, with long strands of curls peeking out beneath their capes. Others were short and fat like little clouds, with tight frizz across their foreheads. There were white sheep, beige sheep, chocolate-brown sheep, two goats, and an alpaca.

Mrs. Hillyer caught me smiling at the sheeps' capes. "They keep the fleece clean until we shear it in the spring." She greeted each sheep. "Hi, Lulu. Hi, Jane. Hi, Cora, Flora, and Dora." She smiled at a group of the cloud-shaped ewes that were huddled together.

"Do they all have names?"

"Every one. Names and genealogies and person-
alities, believe it or not."

At the back of the barn, the big door was open,
looking out over the dead grass and hayfields.

"Beautiful, isn't it?" she asked.

"Yes, but also a little sad. So brown and dead. It
must be gorgeous in the summer."

"Winter isn't the season of death," she corrected
gently. "It's the season of life, when the sheep grow
their fleece and little lambs in their wombs."

"That's an interesting way to see it."

"It's the truth."

I looked up at the barn loft, filled with bales.
"All this hay comes from your fields?"

"That's what farming sustainably means. We
keep our flock to a size that the farm can feed
them, grazing in the warm weather and hay in the
cold."

A mountain of a man entered the barn, six foot
six, at least, and big. He had a trimmed white
beard and long, wiry white hair barely controlled
by a ponytail. He wore tall rubber boots and a
large brown coat. "Joyous Yule!" he boomed, making his way over to us.

"Julia, this is my husband, Odin. Odin, Julia is a
friend of Gwyn's."

I didn't correct her.

"Always happy to meet a friend of our Gwynnie's." He pumped my hand with his enormous,
gloved one. "What brings you out?"

"I'm trying to get in touch with Gwyn. Is she
here?"

"She's visiting a school friend in Portland." Mrs.
Hillyer held her hand beside her mouth, miming a

whisper. "She's had a bad breakup," she confided. "Perhaps you've heard?"

"No," I answered honestly. "We haven't been in touch."

"She needed a little R and R," her father said.

"So she quit her job?" It seemed like an extreme reaction.

"Why would you ask that?" Mrs. Hillyer was clearly surprised.

"Because I stopped at elder services—"

Mr. Hillyer cut me off, thank goodness, since I didn't know where I was going to go from there. "No, no. She's taking a break. She'll be back to it in a few weeks."

"She's had a bad breakup," I repeated, absorbing the information.

"Yes. She and Tree have been together since they were children," Mrs. Hillyer told me. "They were homeschooled right here at the farm. We thought they'd always be together. It was written in the stars." She looked so downcast, I thought she might cry.

Mr. Hillyer covered her delicate hand with his gloved paw. "Now, love. You don't know they won't get back together."

Mrs. Hillyer shook her head. "I don't think so. This is really it. Gwynnie was devastated. *Devastated*."

"So you didn't call the elder services office for her to give her notice?" I said.

"By the goddess, no!" she exclaimed.

I didn't know where to go from there. They'd told quite a different story than the one I'd been told by Mrs. St. Onge and by the woman at elder services. I didn't want to alarm them unnecessarily. I thought they'd been lied to, probably by their daughter. "Can I call Gwyneth?"

"She's taking a connectivity cleanse," her mother said. "She took her cell phone with her, but she turned it off. She needs to heal while she's away."

"You haven't heard from her since she's been gone?"

"Just the once," Mr. Hillyer said. "To let us know she'd arrived okay and was turning off her phone."

There didn't seem much more to say. Holly walked me back to my Subaru. It was midafternoon, and I could already feel the chill that would come with sunset. "Almost Solstice," she said brightly. "In a few days the sun will start its trip back to us, bringing light and warmth. My Gwynnie will be back too, bringing light and warmth with her as well."

I nodded. "Yes, of course. Happy holidays."

"Happy holidays to you and yours," she said, and waved good-bye.

Chapter Six

The restaurant was quiet when I walked in. Gus had almost finished cleaning up for the day. But he took one look at my face and fixed a cheese sandwich to heat on the grill.

"Thank you, Gus," I said, sitting at the counter.

"You look like you could use it. Coffee?"

The coffeemaker was clean, the pots empty. I didn't want him to make a new one for me.

"No trouble to make it," he said, as if reading my thoughts. He put a filter in the machine and filled it with coffee. Then he took one of the pots to the sink to fill it.

"Trouble in paradise?" he asked when he returned.

"What?" It took me a moment to realize he was asking about Chris and me. "No. No trouble there. Well, a little. His whole family is coming for Christmas, so I'm nervous about that."

"No reason to be nervous. You're a catch. They'll figure that out pretty quick." He pulled the grilled cheese sandwich off the grill and cut it in half with a quick crack of the knife. He put it on a plate in front of me and then fetched us both steaming mugs of coffee. He stood across the counter from me. Gus rarely sat down in his own place. "So if it's not your love life, what is it?"

"You know my mother's next-door neighbor?" I started.

"The Carters?"

"Other side."

He nodded. "Odile St. Onge."

"Yes, her." I gathered my thoughts. "She's been teaching me to make a Bûche de Noël."

"A what de what?"

"A classic French Yule log cake."

"Oh. Like the ones she used to bring to the Festival of Trees celebration."

"Exactly. Anyway, I'm concerned she's gotten a little isolated. She had a caregiver checking her from elder services, but that woman's recently quit . . . or gone on vacation, or something. And she had a grandnephew who also came by. But he's on a business trip . . . or something."

"So you're worried she's alone? You think she can't take care of herself." His great white eyebrows swept over his nose in a challenging squint.

"Er." I was treading on thin ice. No one knew how old Gus was, except Mrs. Gus. They had a son in Arizona and a daughter in California, both with families of their own. He opened his restaurant at five every morning for the lobstermen and fishermen, seven days a week, every month of the year except February, when he and Mrs. Gus visited their kids out west. If anyone from elder services or anywhere else tried to check on him, I didn't want to think about the consequences. "Well, you know, she's a widow, she's alone," I stuttered.

"A widow?" Gus's squint deepened. "She tell you that?"

"No, I always heard—"

"She's no widow, at least that I ever heard. That miserable Albert took himself off one night. Disappeared."

"Really? When was this? What happened?"

"Long time ago." Gus took a swallow of coffee. "A couple of years before your parents bought their place. There's not a lot to tell. One day Albert was there—being rude to customers at his job at Gleason's Hardware. Living in that ugly house. And the next day he was gone." Gus stared off in the middle distance, remembering. "Around this time of year, it was. The holidays."

Another disappearance around the holidays? "There must have been some speculation around town about what happened to him."

"Some said he had a girlfriend in Rockland, he'd run off with her."

"Did you believe them?"

Gus shook his head. "Nah. I never did. A mean old bird like Albert. It was hard to believe he'd gotten one woman, let alone two. I was more in the camp that thought that miserable jerk had finally crossed the wrong person and skedaddled out of town. But it's all gossip and guesswork. No one knows. Except possibly Odile." He looked up and saw my questioning expression. "I assume she took care of it, one way or another, though whether she divorced him or had him declared dead, or something else, I don't know. People around town started referring to her as a widow, and she never bothered to correct them. That's probably why your family thought she was. Either way, he's never been back. I've never heard tell that anyone saw him again. Good riddance, I say. She's better off without him."

"And those were the only rumors? He ran off with another woman, or he was being chased by bad guys?" *No one ever suggested his wife killed him, with a cake, for example?*

"Most I ever heard, and I hear a lot in here." Gus looked me in the eyes. "Did that help at all? My best advice is, if you're worried about Odile St. Onge, don't be. That lady can take care of herself."

That's what I was beginning to worry about. Was she taking care of herself with terrible consequences to the people who crossed her?

I swallowed the last bite of sandwich and chased it with the last sip of coffee. "Thanks, Gus. If Chris arrives while you're still here, can you tell him I'll be right back? There's something I want to do real quick."

"Sure thing, Julia. I hope I've set your mind at ease about Odile St. Onge."

I fast-walked over the harbor hill to Busman's Harbor's ugly brick town-hall-police-station-fire-house complex. In the off-season we had so few officers working, they were always out answering calls or on patrol. But I knew from experience the best time to catch my friend Jamie Dawes was at shift change at three o'clock. If he'd worked days, he'd probably still be finishing up reports. If he was working evenings, he might not have gone out yet.

The civilian receptionist was gone for the day, so I walked right in. I found Jamie at one of the two desks all the officers shared. His partner, Officer Pete Howland, sat at the other.

"Julia?" Jamie looked up, his brow furrowed. "What are you doing here?" It wasn't a greeting appropriate to our status as each other's oldest friend. If he'd seen me on the street or at Gus's, he would have smiled and given me a hug. But, as far as he was concerned, my presence in the police station could only mean there was a problem. A problem in general, and, in particular, a problem for him.

"Hi," I said. "Don't look so happy to see me."

"Is this a social visit?" His voice was cautious.

"No," I admitted. "Well, sort of."

"Spill it," he ordered.

So I started the story. I didn't get far.

"Wait. You're learning to bake some kind of cake at old lady St. Onge's house?"

"A Bûche de Noël, yes. And I don't think you're supposed to call her that, now that you're a grown man sworn to protect her." From across the aisle Howland snorted.

Jamie was the lucky kind of blond who had dark brows and dark eyelashes framing his sky-blue eyes. In the summer he tanned, as did my auburn-haired sister, much to my pale-skinned annoyance. But he wasn't tan now and a slight blush rose in his cheeks. "Go on" was all he said.

So I explained about Gwyneth and Bradley and how they were both gone, neither one reachable,

having told conflicting stories about their where-
abouts. I kept the stories about the cakes and the
dead relatives to myself. I didn't want him to think
I was a total loon.

"I don't get it," Jamie said when I finished.
"What do you want me to do?"

"You don't think it's odd?"

He gave an exaggerated shrug. "Maybe. Maybe
it's a little odd. But police don't investigate odd. In
this town we'd never have time to do anything
else."

"I guess," I admitted. "But that's not all. Did you
know Mrs. St. Onge's husband disappeared suddenly?"

"I thought she was a widow."

"I heard that," Pete Howland said. He didn't
apologize for listening to a private conversation.
But then, he was sitting five feet away, so how
could he not have? "My parents used to talk about
him. Al St. Onge. A real SOB, apparently."

"Did your parents say what they thought happened to him?" I asked.

"Gambling debts, my dad thought. Owed someone lots of money."

"Do these two missing people know one another?" Jamie asked.

"They might." As far as I remembered, Gwyneth
Hillyer had come to Mrs. St. Onge in the mornings, while Bradley Woodward had visited in the
evenings, perhaps on his way home from the office. But they might have met. Either at Mrs. St.
Onge's or around. Busman's Harbor was a small
town.

"Julie, we're talking about adults," Jamie said.
"Neither has been reported missing. They're most

likely exactly where their parents told you they are. She's in Portland, visiting a friend, and he's on a business trip."

"Then why did the receptionist at Jenkins and Anton tell me Bradley was on vacation in Costa Rica? And why did the woman at elder services tell me Gwyneth's mother had phoned to say she quit her job?"

"I don't know. Information gets mixed up in offices all the time. It certainly does around here. And by the way, lying to your parents isn't a crime, either."

Jamie looked tired and more than ready to be finished with his workday. I stood up, pulled on my gloves, and said good-bye and thank you. It was almost dark. Chris would be wondering where I was.

Gus's Too was crowded that evening. As the calendar clanked closer to Christmas and the nights grew longer, more people, too busy from holiday preparations to cook, or simply in search of company to ward off the darkness, came for a night out.

Chris and I had no time to speak beyond the placing of orders and the curt acknowledgment they'd been received. But later, after the diners were gone and the place was cleaned up, we gathered at one of the little tables in the bar for a well-deserved beer, our little ritual.

"You're awfully quiet, Slim," Chris observed.

I'd drunk half my beer without saying a word. "Sorry. I was thinking about Mrs. St. Onge."

"What about her?"

The story came tumbling out, and not in a particularly coherent fashion. It was only because he knew me so well that Chris was able to follow along.

"So you're saying, what, that Odile St. Onge is a serial poisoner?"

Am I? No, that's ridiculous. "You have to admit it's suspicious. Three of her relatives die after eating her cake. Her husband disappears. Mr. and Mrs. Woodward get deathly ill. And now Gwyn Hillyer and Bradley Woodward have disappeared too. Every single one around the holidays."

"She's old. Her relatives from the same generation are old too. Old people die, with some regularity."

"Gwyn and Bradley aren't old."

"Julia, Mrs. St. Onge probably weighs eighty pounds soaking wet. Even if she poisoned them, what did she do with the bodies?"

"That's where Mr. Eames comes in!" The thought struck me at that moment. "He's the trashman. He gets rid of the bodies."

Chris was quiet. Finally he said, "Then don't go back."

"Just don't show up?"

"No. Call and make an excuse. You're too busy. It's Christmas."

I thought for a moment. "But I really want to learn to make a Bûche de Noël."

Chris held out his arms, bent at the elbow, palms up. He swayed back and forth, miming a scale. "Learning how to make a cake no one expects or has asked for," he said when one hand was higher, "spending time alone with a serial killer," he said when the other was.

The thought of the old lady sitting at her kitchen table, so small and alone, surrounded by cake ingredients, waiting . . . it was too sad. *What if I'm wrong?* "I want to go back."

"Then you don't think she's poisoned anyone."

I took a long pause. "No, I guess I don't."

"Good, but just in case I want you to phone me before you go in and right after you leave, okay?"

"Okay," I agreed.

"Good. Finish your beer and let's get to bed. Tomorrow promises to be even crazier than today."

Chapter Seven

I felt small and scared when I walked up Mrs. St. Onge's flagstone walk the next morning, the way I'd felt when I approached the house as a child. We'd had a hard frost overnight and the brown grass on her lawn was tinged with white, which gave the yard an otherworldly feeling. *Grow up,* I told myself. *Don't let your imagination run away with you.*

It didn't help that when Mrs. St. Onge answered my knock, she was holding a large kitchen knife. "You're late." She turned on her heel and clumped toward the kitchen on her cane. Despite my qualms I scurried after her. I'd come too far on this Bûche de Noël journey.

In the kitchen the old woman had arranged on a cutting board the remaining chocolate I'd bought three days before: five ounces of bitter-sweet chocolate—"not unsweetened!!!" she'd specified on her list (exclamation points hers), and four

ounces of quality milk chocolate. Mrs. St. Onge
made quick work of them with the big knife, chopping the thick slabs into nickel-sized pieces. I had
pulled my notebook from my Snowden Family
Clambake tote and wrote furiously.

The old woman turned to the stove, measuring
out three quarters of a cup of whipping cream and
three tablespoons of butter and putting them in a
small saucepan. She turned on the heat and handed
me a wooden spoon. "Stir until the butter melts,"
she directed.

I moved the spoon carefully as the butter began
to send yellow rivulets into the white cream. "Did
Gwyn know Bradley?" I asked, keeping my tone
conversational.

"Did who know who?" she replied, though I had
a feeling she knew exactly what I was asking.

"Did Gwyneth Hillyer, the woman from elder
services who came to help you, know your grandnephew, Bradley Woodward?"

"Of course not!" she snapped. "Why would they
know each other?"

"I thought maybe because they both came here—"

She shook her head. "One's a servant. The
other's family. Why would I introduce them?"

Calling Gwyneth a servant was inappropriate,
given her role, but I kept quiet. "Butter's melted,"
I said.

"Turn off the heat and bring it over here."

Feeling a little like a servant myself, I brought
the saucepan to the kitchen table and placed it on
a pot holder. "Stir," Mrs. St. Onge commanded,
and so I did while she fed the chunks of chocolate
into the mixture. When the last one was melted,
she poured the mixture into a bowl and covered it

with a dish towel. "That will need to sit for an hour or so, to cool," she said. "Then we'll fill the cake and ice it."

My heart gave a little leap that we were finally, finally to this place. Today I was going to see our Bûche de Noël. I washed the saucepan and spoon. "Anything else I can do while we wait?" I asked.

"The decorations you brought up from the basement yesterday. Do you think you could put them up?"

"Of course!" I went to the box in the living room and sorted through the tangle of plugs and wires. In addition to three strings of old lights, there were a half-dozen sets of three attached candles, complete with orange bulbs, enough for each of the front windows. I plugged them into a living-room outlet one at a time and was astonished to find they all worked.

Mrs. St. Onge hadn't left the kitchen.

"I'll put these candles in the windows," I called to her.

"Fine."

The living room had two big windows facing Main Street. I set up the candles there, but the pines around the front porch were so overgrown, I wasn't sure anyone would be able to see the decorations from the road. The second story would be more successful. I gathered the remaining four sets and went up the stairs.

There were two bedrooms at the front of the house, each with a double set of windows, side by side. I looked into the first room. It had a neatly made bed, and was clearly unoccupied, a guest room, I assumed. There was an outlet under each window. I plugged both sets of candles in, made sure they worked and then turned them off. It was the middle of the morning, too early for the lights. I wondered if Mrs. St. Onge would come up the stairs to turn them on in the evening. I set the candles on the windowsills and went into the next room.

The second front bedroom was also unoccupied, another guest room. I entered, noticing the twin bed with its ancient chenille bedspread. When had someone last slept there? Setting up the candles was quick work. Then, as I turned from the windows, I noticed the closet door on the other side of the room was ajar. Scolding myself for being nosy, I peeked inside. There were several articles of men's clothing, neatly ironed khaki pants and blue work shirts. Surely, Mrs. St. Onge hadn't kept them since her husband had left, before I was born?

On the pole, apart from the other clothes, was something that made me inhale noisily with surprise. A neat, sea-foam-green winter overcoat, the size a small woman would wear. Gwyneth Hillyer was a small woman, and, if her car was any indication, she had a predilection for sea foam green. It seemed like too big a coincidence. The coat had to be hers. Wound around the top of the hanger was a beautiful knitted scarf, like the ones her mother sold, and hanging out of the pocket was a pair of knitted gloves. I was tempted to put a hand in the pockets, to check to see if there was any indication of the owner, or a receipt that might tell me when the coat had last been worn, but I hesitated.

"Time to fill the cake!" Mrs. St. Onge called up the stairs.

"Coming!" I closed the door to the closet, wishing I could close the door to my careening thoughts as easily.

In the kitchen, the old woman had everything we would need laid out on the table, the original cake in the plastic container, the bowl of filling, the icing, and the platter. She unwound the cake from around its tea towel. To my astonishment, it was supple and didn't fall apart.

"Go to the pantry and get the jar of my home-made raspberry jam," she directed.

Dutifully, I trooped to the pantry and located a single jar of unopened raspberry jam next to the jars of my mother's strawberry-rhubarb, which stood like silent soldiers, guarding it.

"Ah, the secret ingredient," Mrs. St. Onge cried when I returned to the kitchen.

Is this where the poison is?

"Spread a thin layer on the cake," she said. "And then cover it with the filling."

I did as I was told. My mouth watered as I worked. I was dying to taste the filling, but my mind flashed to the dead relatives and I resisted. What if she wanted me to taste the cake when we were done? I imagined us each sitting down with a cup of coffee and a slice of the cake. I wouldn't touch mine until she'd eaten hers.

"Gwyn Hillyer is a small woman, right?" I said.

"Who?"

"The woman from elder services." *Really, this game is getting frustrating. She knows who Gwyn is.*

Mrs. St. Onge glared, clearly unhappy with the question. "I suppose she was. Never really noticed her."

"And you're sure you haven't seen her since Thanksgiving?"

"Nope. Why do we keep talking about this?"

When I was done spreading the filling, she rerolled the cake, tighter this time, and put it on a long, white platter. Unlike all my efforts, it looked like a perfect log. She selected a large carving knife from the block and cut off about three inches of each end of the cake at an angle. Then she reversed the pieces, so the log had an angled cut at each end. "There," she said with satisfaction, "now we ice it."

That wasn't a task she was prepared to let me do. I watched in wonder as she smoothed the dark chocolate icing on the cake, working it to the texture of bark, without getting any on the platter.

"This town thing," she began, "the reason we're all going crazy this year with lights and decorations, explain that again."

So I repeated the information about the botanical gardens and the Illuminations and how the lights around town were meant to welcome visitors, and let them know we were open for business.

"That must be something to see," she said. "I wish I could go."

My heart sank. She might be a serial poisoner, but she was old and alone at the holidays. "My whole family's going tonight," I told her. "Would you come if I can get another ticket?"

I expected her to turn me down. She'd lived next door to us all my life, and I couldn't remember a single social occasion we'd spent together.

"I would enjoy that very much," she replied. "Thank you."

"Do we test the cake now?" Perhaps I would be dead and wouldn't have to explain my impulsive invitation to the rest of my family.

"No, no," Mrs. St. Onge answered. "Tomorrow we make the meringue mushrooms and spun-sugar moss. Then we eat it."

"His name is Tree?" My sister, Livvie, sounded skeptical.

I hugged my cell phone to my ear. I was in the clambake office on the second floor of Mom's house. Mom was at work and had turned the heat down, so I was still wearing my winter coat.

"Tree what?" Livvie asked.

"That's what I'm trying to find out."

"I don't know him," she reported, though I'd gathered that. "Nor his brother, Stump, his sister, Willow, or his uncle, Dutch Elm Disease."

"I'm hoping maybe you know someone who does. I'm looking for an address, work or home."

"Hmm. Let me think. How old is he?"

Gwyneth Hillyer was in her late twenties and her mom had said she and Tree grew up together. "Around your age, I think."

"He didn't go to our school. I'd remember a Tree."

"Homeschooled."

"Hmm," she repeated. "Let me get back to you."

Within fifteen minutes Livvie called back with a last name, Smith, and work address for Tree. She'd called the person she knew who was mostly likely to know a person named Tree, and though that person didn't know him, she'd called the person she thought was most likely. In a small town there were only ever two degrees of separation.

Tree worked in a garage a ways up the peninsula. That was all Livvie's informant knew. Her network had been fast, but not expansive.

The sea-foam-green coat in Mrs. St. Onge's guest room closet had unnerved me, along with her tales of dead relatives. But I'd pretty much run out of places to go to find out what was going on. Bradley Woodward's parents insisted he was fine and on a business trip. His office insisted he was fine and on vacation. Gwyneth Hillyer's office said she'd quit. Her parents said she hadn't; she was in Portland, visiting a friend, while nursing a broken heart. A heart broken by Tree, who was the only person I had to turn to at this point.

Clyde's Garage was a ramshackle affair. The building, a small office with an adjacent three-bay garage, sided with crumbling asbestos shingles, had a distinct lean to it. Though the weather was freezing, the garage doors were open and I could see an old Volkswagen Beetle up on a lift. In the other bays sat a two-door Thunderbird convertible, and a classic, forest-green MG from the 1950s, my fantasy car.

The man who ambled out of the garage to greet me had sandy-colored hair, long enough to be tucked behind his ears. The name on the chest of his coveralls said, "Clyde."

"Hello, I'm looking for Tree Smith."

"I'm Tree." He lifted a greasy hand, showing me why he didn't offer to shake mine.

"Did you buy the coveralls used?"

He glanced down at the name on his chest and laughed. "No. I bought the garage used. I put the old owner's name on my work clothes because it cuts down on a lot of unnecessary explanations." He noticed I couldn't tear my eyes off the MG. "Do

you have a classic car you need fixed or restored?"
He looked pointedly at my Subaru, the most common car in Maine.

"No," I admitted. "I'm here about Gwyneth Hillyer."

He stepped backward, putting a little more distance between us, and his friendly smile disappeared. "What about Gwyn?"

"I'm trying to get in touch with her. I was hoping you could help."

He put both hands up in a gesture of surrender. "Not me. I'm the last person you should be asking. She made it clear she didn't want to hear from me."

"Because she was so devastated when you broke up with her?"

"When I broke up with her? I don't know who you've been talking to, but she broke up with me. Months ago. So I think she's definitely over it."

Gwyn broke up with him? That's not what the Hillyers led me to believe. "I talked to her parents, actually."

His wariness dissipated a bit and he smiled again. "Look, Holly and Odin are lovely people. After my mom had enough of going back to the land, and decided to go back to the city, where there are jobs and people and homes heated with fuel you don't have to chop, Holly practically adopted me. I know the Hillyers want me to be the son they never had. But the truth is, if Gwynnie and I were going to make it permanent, we would have done so a long time ago. I love her, but I've never been in love with her. She broke up with me because she decided she wanted to go for it, you know, love with a capital *L,* passion with a capital *P.* The truth is, she did us both a favor."

We stood for a couple of moments while I absorbed what he'd said, and thought about what to ask next. "Her parents say she's visiting a friend in Portland. Do you know who that is or how to get in touch? She's not answering her cell."

The wariness instantly returned. "Who did you say you were?"

"I'm a neighbor of a woman Gwyneth cared for when she worked for elder services." I knew the answer wouldn't satisfy him. How could it? And any elaboration would only make things worse.

"When she worked for elder services? Doesn't she anymore?" I didn't answer and he went on. "I'm not comfortable giving you her contact information without her permission."

"I totally understand. But if you don't feel you can call her, could you ask one of her friends to? Or maybe if you have a sister or someone?" I remembered the imaginary siblings Livvie had given him, Stump and Willow.

He shook his head. "Since my mom left, it's only ever been me and my dad, and he's pretty useless. I don't want to harass Gwyn or send friends to do it. Like I said, she did us both a favor. I'm sure she's fine."

"I'm sure she is too." I gave him the most reassuring smile I could muster. "One more thing, did you work on her car?"

He smiled, relaxing again. "I gave it to her. It's a 1971 BMW, sea foam green. Her favorite color."

"You invited who?" My brother-in-law, Sonny, stood, hands on hips, staring me down.

"I invited Mrs. St. Onge from next door to join

us tonight at the Illuminations." I held my ground. What choice did I have? The invitation had been made and accepted. I'd already called the botanical gardens and secured a ticket for her.

"Remember when we used to be terrified of her?" Livvie asked.

"Not helping," I warned her, though I wasn't sure I still wasn't terrified of Mrs. St. Onge. Behind Livvie, Mom and Page were putting on coats, boots, hats, mittens, and scarves. Jack was already in his snowsuit. Getting ready to go out took forever at this time of year.

Sonny sighed loudly when he saw I wasn't going to give up. "She's your responsibility. You need to help her around the gardens. She's not slowing us down."

"She uses a cane," I said, "but she's in pretty good shape. The show's in the upper gardens, which are accessible. They have wheelchairs there. If we have to, we'll use one. Besides, it's not a race. You're supposed to stroll and enjoy the lights."

Chris moved behind me and put a hand on my shoulder, a show of solidarity. "We'll be responsible for her."

The tickets had been purchased for a Tuesday night, so Chris and I could go. Gus's Too was shuttered on Tuesdays, our night off.

With the addition of Mrs. St. Onge, there were too many of us for one car, even Livvie's ancient minivan. Mom went off with the four of them, next to baby Jack, strapped in his car seat, with Page in the way-back.

Mrs. St. Onge had her wool coat and gloves on and her pocketbook in hand when she opened the door. I was pleased to see the orange candlelight

glowing in all the windows. "My, you're a good-
looking one," she said, peering through her thick
glasses at Chris. I was used to the reaction. My
mother had at first maintained he was "too good-
looking for his own good," though they were fast
friends now. He helped Mrs. St. Onge down the
walk and into the backseat of his cab. "Going in
style," she said approvingly.

The parking lot at the gardens was a madhouse,
which felt a little weird, since it normally wasn't
open after dark. Chris helped Mrs. St. Onge from
the cab and we made our way toward the show, she
with one hand on his arm and the other on her
trusty cane.

The rest of the family was waiting for us by the
ticket desk, Jack in his pack on Sonny's back, and
everyone appropriately bundled up against the
cold. The garden employees were timing people's
entrance, letting in small groups every few minutes. I hoped our family would be its own group,
but when I glanced across the lobby, there was another couple obviously waiting, ready to go. Bradley Woodward's parents. Their eyes darted around,
searching the crowd. Finally Richard Woodward's
landed on his aunt. He turned and whispered
something to his wife, his thick mustache brushing
against her pink cheek. A suggestion to visit the
gift shop, perhaps, so they could catch another
group? But it was too late. Mrs. St. Onge had spotted them. He saw her looking at him and squared
his shoulders, as if facing something that required
all his courage. Like a firing squad. He took Mrs.
Woodward by the arm and brought her over.

"Aunt Odile," he said when they got closer.
"Merry Christmas."

She stared through her glasses, and for a moment I thought she couldn't place him. He was in an unusual setting, she hadn't expected him, and they hadn't seen each other in a few years. But then she got it. "Merry Christmas, nephew," she said, "and you," she added, turning to her nephew's wife.

My stomach wound into a tight ball. I was scared it would come up that I had visited the Woodwards, asking questions about their son and his relationship to Mrs. St. Onge. How would I explain to her what I'd been doing? What if she tried to introduce me to them? I thought about slipping into the ladies' room.

But then, the man at the door to the gardens called our group, and we all shuffled forward. Neither Mrs. St. Onge nor the Woodwards seemed anxious to prolong their conversation. "Merry Christmas to you, my good sir!" Richard Woodward greeted the man at the door. "Merry Christmas."

We passed through into the garden. My exhale of relief was like the air going out of a balloon. Across the upper gardens hundreds of thousands of little lights winked and blinked, outlining the trees and plants in shimmering colors. As we watched, the shapes changed, moving and dancing before us. We started down the garden path and our new vantage point opened into a whole new scene. Lights bounced off the garden pond, an upside-down reflection of the scene above. I was entranced. Chris moved us along, an arm around my shoulder, the other hanging firmly on to Mrs. St. Onge.

The Woodwards led the group; Mr. Woodward,

apparently our official ambassador, greeted everyone with a cheery "Merry Christmas!"

Couples cuddled on benches in the corners,
children's laughter echoed through the trees. The
smells of kettle corn, cocoa, and pine needles filled
the air. We lingered on the path, taking it all in.
The Woodwards had moved ahead of us. The tension drained out of my shoulders.

But then, as we turned the next corner, I spotted an enormous man in the group across the way
from us. I could see in the reflection of the light,
he wore a great white coat with lamb's wool curling around the cuffs and lace-up boots with lamb's
wool ringing their tops. Some kind of evergreens
looped around his head, coming across his forehead and back around his long white hair. Odin
Hillyer. He was unmistakable. My eyes searched
the crowd and I found what I knew I would. Next
to him was a petite woman in a flowing white cape,
wearing the same evergreen crown over her long
white locks. His wife. And next to her, Tree Smith,
known around his workplace as "Clyde."

"Great."

I didn't realize I'd said it aloud until Chris said,
"What?"

"Nothing." I hoped it was exactly that. *Nothing.*

My family continued to ooh and ahh about the
lights as we shuffled along the twisting paths.
Every corner we turned held a new vista, a new surprise. I relaxed again, caught up in the holiday
magic. The Hillyers' group was well ahead of us. I
doubted they would even see me. And, presum-
ably, they wouldn't recognize Mrs. St. Onge. She
was just some woman their daughter might have
told them about.

But then, as fate would have it, our paths crossed in a figure eight.

"Hello," Mrs. Hillyer called to me. "You're Gwyneth's friend." I stole a quick look at Mrs. St. Onge. She was deep in conversation with my mother, and appeared not to have heard. I stepped forward from our little group to greet Mrs. Hillyer, but I didn't get the words out.

"Merry Christmas, my good sir," Richard Woodward shouted, still in his role as our group's official greeter.

"Happy Solstice," Odin Hillyer boomed back at him.

Richard Woodward stopped so short, his wife bumped into him, and my mom bumped into her. "I said 'Merry Christmas' to you, sir."

Odin Hillyer put his hands on his hips, which spread out the great coat, making him appear even more enormous. "And I said 'Happy Solstice' to you."

Mr. Woodward didn't move, trapping the rest of us behind him.

His wife put her hand on his elbow and murmured, "Now, dear," with absolutely no effect. Woodward cleared his throat. "I think, basking in the pleasure of this beautiful display"—he gestured in a circle, indicated the lights—"we should honor the reason for the season and include the name of the—"

"Solstice," Odin roared. "The happy day the sun begins its return to bring us longer days, warmth, and food. Every tradition you have, you stole from us"—his sweeping arm took in all the lights—"including this one. The solstice is the reason for the season." His wife, too, snuck up behind him, muttering a "Not now, Odin," also to no effect.

"The lights represent the star in the East, you ignorant savage," Mr. Woodward jabbed.

"The lights represent the turn of the sun. The star of your show wasn't even born in the winter, but in the spring when shepherds slept in their fields by night. Believe me, I know sheep and I know their seasons."

Even in the reflected glow of the LED lights, Richard Woodward's face was crimson. "Why, why, you . . . ," he sputtered. And then he pulled back his arm and socked Odin Hillyer right in the nose.

There was a gasp from the crowd that had gathered. While we'd been standing there, the tour had backed up considerably behind us. Hillyer's hands flew to his nose in surprise. Woodward was tall and fit, but Hillyer was a giant. It was like a Labrador retriever lunging at a Saint Bernard when their paths crossed in the dog park. Though dogs would never be motivated by such a stupid argument.

Recovering himself, Odin wound his arm back, ready for a roundhouse punch. His wife screamed, "No!" and Chris and Tree jumped between the antagonists, hauling them to separate corners as they struggled to get free. In the melee, all four of them fell to the cold, hard ground, where Hillyer and Woodward continued to kick at one another.

Sonny looked ready to jump into the fray, but Livvie pulled him backward, using Jack's pack, reminding him he was strapped to a ten-month-old. I threw my arms around Mrs. St. Onge, who stood openmouthed watching the fight, and moved her out of the way, while Mom pushed Page behind her and away from the fracas.

At that point, security arrived and, well, dot, dot, dot, we were all thrown out. We Snowdens protested we hadn't been involved, but with Chris lying on the ground on top of Richard Woodward, it was too hard for the security people to make fine distinctions.

Our group left the gardens deflated. Mom offered hot chocolate at her house in an attempt to salvage some festive feeling, but Livvie said no, they'd take their kids home. Mom rode back to town with Chris, Mrs. St. Onge, and me, while Livvie's family took off for their house up the peninsula.

At her front door, Mrs. St. Onge turned to Chris and me. "I apologize for my nephew. He's always been a terrible hothead who thinks he's the only person in the right. Someone needs to take him down a peg or two."

There seemed to be nothing to say to that. We said our good nights, and she closed the door and turned off the porch light before we were off the front steps.

Chapter Eight

I turned up on the St. Onge doorstep at the appointed time the next day. Despite the scene the night before, I was feeling more confident and centered, less afraid my Yule log cake teacher was a murderer. If anything, Richard Woodward's aggression showed he did have issues. Perhaps his aunt was right to cut him out of her life. As long as she hadn't poisoned him too. Or any of the others.

The oven was already on, at a low temperature, when I entered the kitchen. Mrs. St. Onge stood over the large ceramic bowl with the broad navy stripe around it. Beside it were two large eggs. "I took them out of the icebox to bring them up to room temperature," she said.

Once again she separated the yolks from the whites, using that deft flick of the wrist. She added a pinch of salt to the whites and handed me the manual beaters. I understood my cue and turned the crank. When foam began to appear in the bowl, she slowly added a third of a cup of granulated sugar. I turned the beaters around so I could use my other arm and kept pumping until stiff peaks began to form. Then Mrs. St. Onge added a third of a cup of confectioners' sugar and a teaspoon of distilled vinegar, while I wondered, once again, why we were doing this with manual tools.

When the mixture was dense, with stiff, glossy peaks, the old woman at last said I could stop. She had me fill a pastry sleeve while she covered a baking sheet in parchment paper. Then she showed me how to make the quarter-sized dots of meringue that would be the mushroom caps. She let me work on my own for a while, with, I have to admit, mixed results. "That's okay, dear," she said, looking over at the sheet, "mushrooms are very irregular in nature too." She counted the mushroom caps and then set me making the inch-long (well, they were supposed to be an inch long) cones that would form the mushroom stems. When I was done, she dusted the caps with unsweetened cocoa, using a sieve, then put the tray in the oven. "These will have to bake quite awhile," she said, "before we can put them together. While that's happening, you'll make the spun-sugar moss, but first, let's have some tea."

She put the kettle on while I washed the bowl and beaters. Soon we were seated at the kitchen table.

"It was nice of you all to take me to the Illuminations last night," she said.

"I'm sorry we didn't get to see all of it."

"My nephew has been like that since he was a boy. Never could control his temper." I didn't know where to go from there and was happy when she continued the conversation. "I remember when your parents moved in next door." Behind the thick glasses she'd closed her eyes and turned her face toward the ceiling. "You were a toddler and your mother was pregnant with your sister."

"That's right. I was two. Before that, we had an apartment in town."

"Your father was a lovely man. My Al was gone by then, and your dad always helped me out, shoveling snow from the walk or taking my trash to the dump. Once he even chased a bat out of the house for me."

I couldn't recall any of these things, but they didn't surprise me. My father had been that kind of man. I noticed she said her Al was "gone." Only days ago that statement would have confirmed my belief that he was dead. But then again, maybe he was.

When we finished the tea, I asked, "Is there something else I can do while we wait?"

"We'll do the spun-sugar moss."

During my research phase I had watched the famous video of Julia Child making the spun-sugar moss, but it had never occurred to me that we would attempt it. I picked up my notebook, eager to document the process.

Mrs. St. Onge was rummaging in a cupboard for a saucepan. When she found it, she combined a cup of sugar, three tablespoons of corn syrup, and a third of a cup of water in the pan. She put it on a burner on the stovetop. When the sugar had dissolved and the mixture was clear, she turned the burner up to boil and popped the candy thermometer we'd used on the first day of our baking project into the pot.

Was it really only three days ago? It seemed like

we'd been making this cake for a lifetime. Four days ago I didn't know the Hillyers or the Woodwards or Tree Smith. I'd thought Al St. Onge was dead. And I'd thought Mrs. St. Onge was an old lady with a house I'd been afraid of as a child.

When the mixture was caramelized, Mrs. St. Onge took it off the stove; then she took a broom from the kitchen closet. She wrapped the broom handle in parchment paper, securing it at each end with twine. She stuck a fork in the caramelized sugar and lifted it, pulling up a mass of thick, threadlike strands.

"Come with me." She led me out to her tiny back porch, where she balanced the broom horizontally between one of the railings and a wooden kitchen chair. She bustled back inside. I waited, not knowing what to do. I shivered and hugged myself, exhaling visible puffs of moisture into the cold air. I had a sweater on, but hadn't grabbed my coat as we came out the door. Mrs. St. Onge returned with a white sheet and bent to spread it under the broom.

"Let me do that." I tried to help her, but she had neatly covered the porch floor.

"Do this," she commanded, and sticking the fork into the saucepan, she lifted a bit of the caramel from the saucepan and waved it over the broom handle. The mixture spun itself into a long sugary thread that hung from the broom, catching the morning light. "You finish," she instructed. "Too cold out here for me."

This was the thing she was going to let me do? So far, my cooking lessons had been closer to demonstrations, but at this tricky juncture she was leaving me on my own? I squared my shoulders and looked at the broom handle. I probably didn't have long before the mixture cooled into a giant wad. I lifted the fork and flicked.

And missed the broom entirely.

"Darn it." I tried again. And missed again. I couldn't imagine Mrs. St. Onge's reaction if she came out to see one strand of sugar moss on the handle, the rest in puddles on the sheet. I tried again, and this time the thread caught. The next one was also a success, and I kept flinging that sugar until the pot was empty and there were long caramel threads up and down the broom handle.

"I'm done!" I entered the back door and called out in triumph. I couldn't believe I had succeeded.

Mrs. St. Onge gave no sign of being impressed. "Time to put the mushrooms together" was her only response.

I was glad to be back in the warm kitchen. A small pan of brown liquid bubbled on the stove and the room smelled of chocolate.

"What's that?" I asked.

"You'll see."

"No. I meant, what are the ingredients besides chocolate?" But it was useless. I was never going to get a detailed recipe out of Mrs. St. Onge.

She put the baking sheets with the meringue caps and stems in the center of the kitchen table and lifted the pot from the stove. She made a small hole in the flat side of one of the caps with a paring knife, filling it with a dollop of the melted chocolate. Then she fitted one of the cone-shaped meringues into the hole, turning it into the stem. A bit of the chocolate oozed out the sides, and she used the knife to spread it out, drawing veins so delicate on the underside of the cap, it looked like a real mushroom. I was astonished by her artistry.

She pointed to indicate I should sit down and pushed the baking sheet in my direction. Evidently, I was to assemble one myself. I got my own knife from the drawer by the sink. All the happy adrenaline from my triumph over the spun sugar left me. What kind of a mess was I going to make of this?

Hand shaking, I made the small hole in the cap, then filled it with chocolate. When I put the stem in, I saw it was way too much. The chocolate came out and filled the cap. I spread it around so the underside of the mushroom was entirely brown. Weren't there some like that? I followed her lead, putting the finished mushroom back on the parchment paper, took a deep breath, and took another cap.

In the end Mrs. St. Onge did six and I completed four. You could easily tell who did which. Mine looked like mushrooms freshly picked that hadn't yet been washed. Mushrooms that had a disease that left them misshapen. Mrs. St. Onge's looked like an illustration from a book. "This is what a mushroom should look like," the caption would say. "Healthy and beautiful."

"Should I get the spun-sugar moss?" I asked when we finished.

"Leave it. We'll put everything together and taste the cake tomorrow. We'll each have a big slice."

While I wasn't anxious to prolong the lessons, I was happy to put off the tasting. I made a few notes in my notebook, finishing the instructions for the day, though I still didn't know what was in that chocolate mixture, exactly. I washed the remaining pans and utensils and put them in the rack.

"Anything else today?" I asked.

Mrs. St. Onge glanced toward the kitchen garbage can, its lid poking up from the wadded parchment paper beneath it. "If you could take the garbage out to the shed? Mr. Eames will take it to the dump."

I extracted the plastic bag from the can and tied it, then located a fresh one and relined the can. I put on my coat and hat, I wasn't going to be caught outside without them again. I grabbed my tote bag, then said my good-byes. I figured after I hit the shed, I'd walk across the yard to Mom's.

On my way past I smiled at my shimmery sugar strands. The shed was open and there was plenty of room in one of the cans. It made for quick work. But as I spun around to go, the old garage on the property popped into my field of vision. As far as I was concerned, it was as creepy as the house. It had two bays, one closed up tight, but one of the double doors to the second bay was slightly ajar. I went over to investigate.

The windows in the old garage door were above my height-challenged eye level, but I could see into them by standing on my tiptoes. One of the bays was empty, but when I stood on my toes and looked into the other one, I gasped. There was the sea-foam-green BMW I knew so well. The one I'd watched Gwyn Hillyer park in the St. Onge driveway so many times over the summer and fall. The one Tree Smith said he'd given her.

What was going on? Should I go back inside and confront Mrs. St. Onge? I pulled out my phone and took a photo of the back of the car and the license plate, then crept out the way I'd come in.

"Hey, you, girlie! Whaddaya doing in Odile's garage?" Mr. Eames slammed the trash can down on the driveway. He wore a navy peacoat and a squashed hat with earflaps.

I jumped a mile. "I-I-I've been helping Mrs. St. Onge with some baking."

"In the garage?" His skepticism was warranted. For the first time I noticed his truck, an oversized pickup with wooden slats extending the height of the bed. I'd been so absorbed with the sea-foam-green car, I hadn't heard him drive in.

I forced a smile. "No. In the kitchen. I came outside to make the spun-sugar moss." I pointed to the back porch. When he didn't respond, I continued. "I noticed the garage door was open and came over to close it."

"From the inside?" When he put his hands on his hips, his massive forearms bulged under his coat. "You better not be giving Odile a hard time. She's a friend of mine and I see to it nobody messes with her. *Nobody*," he repeated. The menace in his voice made the hair on my arms stand up.

"I'm just going," I managed to rasp.

I walked across the backyard and past him as slowly, and with as much dignity, as I could, but once I passed the line of pines, my feet took off under me, running like the wind, back to the safety of my childhood yard, just as I had all those years ago.

Chapter Nine

"**N**ope. No cars reported stolen." Jamie turned from his computer monitor to face me.

"I told you. Nobody knows the car's missing, so they wouldn't have reported it stolen. The Hillyers think the car is in Portland with their daughter, Gwyneth. But it's not there, and I'm pretty certain she's not, either. Won't you at least come look at it?"

"What reason do I have to snoop in Mrs. St. Onge's garage, looking for a vehicle no one has reported stolen?"

"You could say you had a hunch."

"It's not TV, Julia. This is my actual life and my actual job. We don't go crashing around on private property for no reason."

I let out a snort of impatience. Why was no one concerned about Gwyneth Hillyer and Bradley Woodward except me? "How about this?" I tried again. "Your property abuts Mrs. St. Onge's, just like my mom's does. Maybe, after work, in an unofficial capacity, you could wander over, like a concerned neighbor, and look in her garage?"

"And then do what? It's not that I don't believe you that the car is there, but I don't have any cause to believe it shouldn't be. You're the one going to that house for cake-baking lessons every day. Why don't you ask Mrs. St. Onge about it yourself?"

I hadn't been certain, until that moment, I was going back to Mrs. St. Onge's the next day. "Can you do one thing? I have the plate number." I pulled out my phone and brought up the photo I'd taken of the back of the car. "Can you run the plate and find out who the car is registered to?"

Jamie sighed. "I'm not supposed to." But he turned back to the monitor, brought up a new screen, and typed into it. I sat perfectly still. I didn't want to do anything that might make him change his mind. He turned back to me. "Nineteen-seventy-one BMW, green, registered to Gwyneth Lillian Hillyer, Holly Hill Farm Road, Busman's Harbor, Maine."

"See I told you. And what if I told you a coat the exact same color of that car was hanging in Mrs. St. Onge's guest room closet?"

He stood up. Clearly, it was time for me to leave. "I'd say I believed you entirely. And that having a green coat in your guest room closet is not something that attracts the interest of the police."

"I don't think you should go back."

Chris and I worked in the restaurant on dinner prep. Tonight would be busy, the traditional Busman's Harbor shopping evening called Gentlemen's Night. It used to be the time when men went out and bought presents for their wives or sweethearts, but it had evolved into a whole family event, when the stores stayed open late and offered free gift-wrapping. The previous year for many of the shoppers, a new stop had been added to the evening, dinner at Gus's Too. We would be slammed.

"It's the only way to find out what's happened to Gwyn and Bradley. No one else seems to care."

He paused in his knife work. "I can't stop you. She's a little old lady, and I'm sure you can take her. Just promise me you won't eat or drink anything while you're there."

"I promise." It would be hard to wiggle out of tasting the cake, but I agreed with Chris. It was too dangerous.

There was a knock at the kitchen door. Chris and I exchanged puzzled glances. It was too late in the day for deliveries. The knocking persisted. I wiped my hands on my white apron and opened the door.

Holly Hillyer stood there, a tiny figure in her off-white cape. Her eyes were red and swollen. "Come in, come in. What's wrong?" I led her past Chris, his eyebrows raised in a question, into the restaurant and sat her at one of the little tables in the bar. She'd composed herself somewhat by then, but I fetched a glass of water and some cocktail napkins from the bar to use as tissues.

"Mrs. Hillyer, what's the matter?"

She drew a deep breath. "You're not a friend of Gwyn's, are you?" Her tone was sympathetic, not accusatory. "You came to see me, and then you went to Tree, because you think she's in trouble."

I kept my voice calm. There was no use alarming the poor woman, who was already overwrought, with my theories and guesses. "I don't know if she's in trouble. I was concerned when she quit working for elder services so abruptly."

"If you're not friends, how did you find out she'd quit her job?"

Well, that was the rub. "Gwyn worked at the home of my neighbor, Mrs. St. Onge."

"*That woman!* She is so difficult. Did you know, before Gwyn, she had three caregivers who quit after a couple of days each? When I heard that, I warned my daughter not to go to her, either. But Gwyn has a way with seniors. She believed she could befriend the woman and truly help her."

"To all appearances, at least from what I saw from the window of my office in my mother's house next door, Gwyn did help her."

"Yes, it's true. Gwyn does have a way. She told me most of the time the two of them got on fine, but then, suddenly, Mrs. St. Onge would turn on her, berate her. Always over something trivial, like she put a particular kind of food away on the wrong shelf in the pantry."

I remembered how Mrs. St. Onge had lost her temper when I'd put the oatmeal on the wrong shelf. Wielding her cane like a sword. "Did the temper tantrums ever get physical?"

"No. Not that Gwyn ever said. Why do you ask that? You think that woman has done something to her, don't you?" Holly Hillyer was plainly terrified.

What did I think? That Mrs. St. Onge had done something to Gwyn. Or Mr. Eames had. Probably the two of them together. "I take it you still haven't reached Gwyn at her friend's house in Portland?"

A tear slid down Mrs. Hillyer's nose. "No. She does this, she takes connectivity cleanses, when she turns everything off. At first, I didn't think anything of it. But after you came to the house, I kept trying to call her. I didn't know her friend's exact address, but I tracked her down on Facebook and we finally spoke this afternoon. She was surprised to hear from me. She doesn't know where Gwyn is, hasn't talked to her in ages." Mrs. Hillyer began to cry again. "I'm worried something is terribly wrong."

I leaned across the table, tapping it with my finger for emphasis. "You need to tell the police Gwyn is missing. Tell them her car is missing too."

She looked up sharply. "How do you know that?"

"If Gwyn's not in Portland, her car probably isn't, either."

Mrs. Hillyer nodded and blew her nose. "I will. I'll go straight to the police station. I wanted to make sure you didn't know anything before I did."

I remembered the way I'd been treated by Jamie, who was a friend. In the evening there were only two officers on duty and they would be busy with the crowds shopping on Gentlemen's Night. I didn't think Mrs. Hillyer would get much of a hearing.

I put my hand on hers. "I know it will be hard, but you should wait until tomorrow morning to go to the police. Ask for Officer Dawes. He'll be on duty then. He's a friend and he's aware that I've been worried about Gwyn."

She hesitated. I couldn't blame her. But I didn't want her to go through all the rigamarole I had about missing adults not being missing. Jamie knew right where the sea-foam-green car was. He would help her out.

She stood to go, pulling the beautiful cape around her. "Thank you."

I stood as well and gave her a quick hug. "There's a woman in East Busman's Village you should visit. Her name is Julia Woodward. You can't miss her house. It's got eight full-sized reindeer on the front lawn. Her son is also missing, and I think his disappearance is also connected to Mrs. St. Onge."

Her face went as white as her cape, but she said, "I will."

"There's one more thing. Mrs. Woodward is the wife of the man your husband had the fight with in the botanical gardens. I want you to know that so you're not surprised when you see them."

Holly Hillyer's eyes opened wide in surprise, but she shook the reaction off. Nothing was going to stand in the way of her hunt for her daughter. "I understand," she said and went out the back door.

After she left, I went back to work. Diners would be arriving at any moment. Holly Hillyer had come to see me because she thought I might know something. Did I "know something"? I had questions, but no answers. Where were Gwyneth Hillyer and Bradley Woodward? Why was Gwyneth's car in Mrs. St. Onge's garage, her winter coat hanging in Mrs. St. Onge's closet? I was positive the person who had called Gwyn's boss and given Gwyn's notice was Mrs. St. Onge. Was it because she alone knew Gwyn wasn't coming back?

I wasn't looking forward to going to the ugly stucco house in the morning. But as Jamie had said, if I wanted answers to my questions, there was only one way to get them. I had to ask Odile St. Onge.

Chapter Ten

The smell of brewing coffee hit me in the face when Mrs. St. Onge opened the heavy front door. "I made us a pot of coffee," she said. "To enjoy with our cake."

The Bûche, in all its glory, was on a platter in the center of the kitchen table. Despite my fears and distractions, the cake was breathtaking. Mrs. St. Onge hadn't waited for me to add the meringue mushrooms and spun-sugar moss to the plate. I had a momentary pang, wishing I'd seen her remove the long strands of caramel from the broom handle. My cooking lesson hadn't even risen to the description of demonstration when it came to that phase.

I had to admit that the platter looked amazing. The Yule log was so appetizing. It didn't look real, in the sense that you'd expect to see it on a woodland floor. Instead it looked like a log in an animated cartoon, so beautiful and perfect. I expected pastel butterflies to swoop through the air, and wobbly-legged fawns with giant eyes to appear at the edge of the room.

"It looks too good to eat." I meant it. I had no intention of eating that cake.

"Nonsense," Mrs. St. Onge huffed. "The coffee's not up yet. It'll be a few minutes."

A reprieve. "Is there anything I can do for you in the meantime?"

"You could take that box with the rest of the Christmas lights back down the cellar."

The cellar. I shivered and nodded my agreement. It was a way to put a showdown over the tasting of the cake off for a few more minutes. Subtly (I hoped), I slipped my tote bag over my shoulder. I wasn't going to be the girl in the horror movie who went down into the creepy basement without her phone.

"Don't go in the coal cellar," she reminded me. I was sure the coal cellar was dark and creepy. She didn't have to tell me again.

I humped the box down the stairs.

I stowed it by the washer, where I'd found it, and turned to go. But as I moved toward the stairs, I was drawn to the wooden wall that separated the coal bin from the rest of the basement. I had to see what was back there, and why Mrs. St. Onge had warned me, twice, specifically not to go in.

I took my phone out of my tote bag and peeked around the wall. I wasn't surprised to see that part of the basement had a dirt floor. It wasn't unusual. What was unusual was the state of it. The dirt was loose, not hard-packed, as I would have expected after years of disuse. And it had been recently raked, the tine marks sharply visible in the soil. And, in the dim light from the small, high windows, I spotted two indentations in the freshly raked soil. Each the size of a body!

I ran for the stairs, knees shaking, breath shallow. Mrs. St. Onge loomed at the top.

"What do you take?"

It took me a moment to realize she was asking about my coffee. "Milk, please." I could barely hear my voice over the beating of my heart.

She took a bottle of milk from the refrigerator and poured some into my mug. She carried each one to the table, one at a time, because of her cane. "Come. Sit." Then she sat.

I tore myself out of the basement door frame and forced my feet across the floor. I couldn't take my eyes off the Yule log cake. "It's awfully early in the m-morning for cake," I stammered.

"Nonsense," the old woman repeated.

I sat down across from her, my phone on the table next to me. "The cake is so beautiful. Perhaps I should take it home to my family."

Mrs. St. Onge picked up a big carving knife. I tried not to flinch as she neatly cut off one end of the cake. "There," she said. "An end cut. People always fight over those. They have the most icing."

The icing! That has to be where the poison is.

She placed the slice on a pretty china plate, with the icing end up. She added a meringue mushroom and passed the plate across to me. "You must taste the cake. Otherwise, when you make your own for Christmas Eve, how will you know if it turned out right?"

If I live that long . . .

Suddenly it all came rushing at me. The dead friends and relatives, the acutely sick Woodwards, the missing Gwyneth and Bradley, Holly Hillyer pleading with me with tears in her eyes to find out what had happened to her daughter, the creepy Mr. Eames and the freshly raked dirt in the basement. My fork fell from my hand, clattering on the top of the old kitchen table. I darted out the back door without even stopping for my coat while Mrs. St. Onge called after me, "What's wrong, dear? Come back!"

Once I was in the backyard, I didn't know where to go or what to do. Dashing to my mother's always-unlocked kitchen door was the obvious solution. But something held me back. I turned instead toward the garage.

The sea-foam-green BMW was still inside. I flung open its door.

The interior was unnaturally neat. I couldn't see much in the dark of the garage, but Gwyn hadn't been one to leave Dunkin' Donuts cups on the seat or dry cleaning hanging in the back. Shivering from the cold and the adrenaline, I tugged at the glove box, which fell open with a *bam*. I stuck my hand in and pulled out the registration. Gwyneth Hillyer. Of course, it was. I had known that all along. But there was something else in the box. Something glossy and thin. I put my hand in again and pulled out a brochure for an all-inclusive resort in Aruba. Why on earth would Gwyneth Hillyer, daughter of the sheep-farming, solstice-celebrating Hillyers, have a brochure for such a place? And in her glove box.

And then it all fell into place. I had been an idiot.

I was still squinting at the brochure in the dim light of the garage when the door I'd come through burst open.

"Put that down!" Jamie commanded. "It could be evidence."

"It is." I kept ahold of the brochure. "But not evidence of a crime."

As Jamie and I left the garage, I heard a car door slam on the street and then another. Holly Hillyer ran up the driveway, followed by Julia Woodward, her lips pulled back in a frantic look.

"Officer! Officer! What's happened to our children?" Mrs. Hillyer shouted.

By that point I had reached Mrs. St. Onge's back porch. "Come inside," I said. "All of you."

Jamie shot me a questioning look, but he nodded and we all went through the back door.

Mrs. St. Onge was exactly where I'd left her, sitting at the kitchen table. She'd finished half the coffee in her mug and had eaten her entire slice of cake. My untouched slice and full cup of coffee sat at the place across from her.

Holly Hillyer ran into the room. "Where is my daughter? What have you done with her?"

Mrs. Woodward clenched and unclenched a leather-gloved hand. "If anything has happened to my Bradley—"

I stood in the center of the room, grateful to be out of the cold. "Bradley is fine," I said. "And Mrs. St. Onge knows where he is. Where both your children are."

Mrs. St. Onge picked up her mug and took a slug of her coffee, apparently unconcerned about the appearance of a uniformed cop and two frantic mothers in her kitchen.

Jamie spoke up. "Mrs. St. Onge, if you can tell

Mrs. Hillyer and Mrs. Woodward something that will reassure them about the location of their children, I would suggest you do that."

The old woman returned her cup to the table. "I promised." She crossed her arms defiantly.

I sat in my place across from her, then reached out and put my hand on her arm. "It's okay to tell now," I said. "There's nothing anyone can do to change things."

Mrs. St. Onge put her hand to her chin, considering. "Okay. Why doesn't everyone sit down? This is going to take a minute."

The worried mothers collapsed into the other two kitchen chairs, while Jamie remained standing by the stove. I addressed our hostess directly. "To put everyone's mind at ease, tell us first, are Gwyn and Bradley okay?"

"I believe they are better than okay. I believe they are excellent."

Both mothers exhaled noisily.

"And why do you believe that?" As I asked the question, I laid the brochure for the resort on the table.

"Have they . . . run off together?" Mrs. Woodward's voice was shaky.

"They have eloped," Mrs. St. Onge said. "They are taking a long honeymoon."

"What!" Both women jumped from their chairs as if pulled by puppet strings, staring at each other in disbelief.

"They're married," Mrs. St. Onge repeated.

"I never." Mrs. Hillyer sank back into her seat.

Mrs. Woodward fished a handkerchief out of her coat pocket and dabbed her eyes. "I always pictured Bradley's wedding day. I'd wear a blue silk suit and a corsage and stand in the church, bursting with pride as he said his vows." She held the handkerchief to her nose. "All that's gone now."

"I have a million questions." Mrs. Hillyer seemed to have recovered somewhat. "How did they meet? Were they even dating? Gwyneth never mentioned Bradley's name. Until a few months ago, I thought she was going to marry someone else."

"They met here," Mrs. St. Onge said. "I arranged it. Gwyn would come in the morning to run my errands, take me to the hairdresser and such. Bradley often stopped by in the evening to check in on me and chat on his way home from work. They're both such lovely people." She fixed their mothers with a beneficent smile. "You've done very well with them." She picked up the big knife off the table and cut three more slices off the Yule log cake. "Julia, will you fetch coffee for my guests? There's plenty more in the pot. And plates and forks, please."

I did as instructed, and refilled Mrs. St. Onge's cup.

"My goodness, this cake is delicious," Mrs. Hillyer said. Mrs. Woodward used her fork to divide her slice into bite-sized pieces, but she had yet to put one in her mouth.

Finally I picked up my own fork. Unless Mrs. St. Onge was planning a mass murder, I was safe. I took a big bite of the cake. The taste exploded on my tongue. My taste buds danced in happiness. The texture was perfection, the cake springy, the filling smooth and rich, the icing creamy and flavorful. All that work, all the worry, all the expense, every bit of it had been worthwhile.

"You were saying, about the kids." Mrs. Hillyer returned us to the matter at hand.

"Ah, yes." The old woman returned to her tale. "Seeing Gwyneth as frequently as I did, naturally we talked about this and that. One day she seemed down, so I asked what was going on. She told me she had to break up with the boyfriend she'd been with for years. She loved him like a brother, but there had never been any passion. The problem was, in addition to changing the habits of years together, her family loved him too. Loved him like a son already, and she hated to disappoint them.

"Every day when she arrived, I asked if she had ended things with the young man yet. It took about a month, but she finally did it. Afterward, she was like a different person, like a weight had been lifted from her shoulders."

A single tear ran down Holly Hillyer's cheek. "I had no idea."

Mrs. St. Onge continued. "In the meantime I'd been seeing Bradley almost every day. What a fine man he is. But I could tell he was lonely. Busman's Harbor is a small town and he was having trouble meeting his match."

From across the room I heard Jamie let out a breath. He, too, was having trouble finding someone to share his life with.

"So one morning when Gwyneth took me to Hannaford, I left the case with my second pair of glasses under the seat in her car." The old woman grinned at her cleverness. "I called Gwyn and asked her to stop by on her way home from work and drop them off. Of course, I still had my main pair, I can't see a thing without them, but I didn't tell her that.

"As I hoped, she arrived while Bradley was visiting and I invited her to stay for tea. They got to talking, you know the usual things, what do you do, where'd you go to school. After they left, I happened to peek out the window and they were still in my driveway, still talking.

"I'm not sure what happened after that, I assume some dinners, maybe other activities. The autumn is so beautiful in Busman's Harbor, a wonderful time to fall in love. They never told me what was going on, but I noticed they both were much happier. Perhaps you noticed too?" Mrs. St. Onge looked at each of the mothers in turn.

"No," Mrs. Woodward admitted. "Bradley seemed the same to me. Even though he lives with us, he works so hard, we barely see him. He was late at the office so many evenings this fall. Oh—" She stopped, realizing Bradley hadn't been at his office, at least not every night.

"I thought Gwyneth was unhappy this fall," Holly Hillyer said. "Still suffering from the fallout from Tree breaking up with her. That's why I wasn't surprised when she said she wanted to get away for a while."

"The unhappiness came later," Mrs. St. Onge said. "Things progressed rapidly. The young people were deeply in love. They wanted to make a future together. But they were afraid. Afraid of disappointing you. They feared you and your husbands would never approve of the match."

"Of course, we would!" Mrs. Hillyer declared.

"Why wouldn't we?" Mrs. Woodward demanded.

"There are perhaps some differences in values, goals, religions?" the old woman suggested.

The mothers continued to protest.

"Two nights ago your husbands were rolling around in the dirt, slugging each other," she reminded them.

"Well, maybe," Holly Hillyer admitted. "Maybe we wouldn't like to have our daughter marry a man in a gray flannel suit."

"Men like my Bradley made this country great." Mrs. Woodward's voice rose to a squeak at the end of the sentence. "Bradley is a fine man and will be a wonderful provider. Any family should be grateful to have him as a member."

"Men like your Bradley grind people up and leave them like trash by the wayside, like Mrs. St. Onge, here."

"Well, I wouldn't say—" Mrs. St. Onge protested, glancing around the dated but cozy kitchen.

Mrs. Hillyer didn't let her finish. "My Gwyn is a caring nurturer. A person who puts other people's needs before her own. I hope your striver son doesn't take advantage of that."

Mrs. Woodward jumped out of her chair. "My son is a perfect gentleman!"

"My daughter is a paragon of virtue, a beacon to those in need." Mrs. Hillyer was out of her seat as well. I glanced at Jamie, wondering if he would intervene, but he seemed to be focused on not laughing out loud.

Mrs. St. Onge rose too. "This is the point!" She moved between the women, stomping her cane harder than necessary with each step. "This is what they were afraid of. Can you imagine trying to plan a wedding with you two? And your husbands are worse." She waited. Both women had the good grace to look embarrassed. "So I urged them to elope."

"You what?" Holly Hillyer cried.

"How could you?" Julia Woodward wailed.

"Sit down," Mrs. St. Onge directed. They did, and so did she. "I was young once. I was young and in love. With a man who was perfect. The right age. The right job. He was even Catholic. But he wasn't French. He was Irish, or his parents were. My father forbade me to see him." She took off her glasses and rubbed her eyes, remembering that long-ago time. "I argued some, but I gave in, like the obedient daughter I was. Later my father introduced me to Al, who was a miserable human being, but he was French, from my father's hometown in Quebec Province. We married, to both our great regret. I have spent my whole life wondering what would have happened if I'd stood up to my parents. What if I'd had the courage of my own convictions?" She paused. "Gwyn and Bradley worried so much about how they would introduce their families, how they would plan a wedding. I told them to skip past all that. Get married, I said. Take the longest honeymoon you can and spend time together, just the two of you. Deal with the rest of it when you get back."

Mrs. Woodward looked away, blinking tears from her eyes. Holly Hillyer stared at her empty cake plate. "Did my Gwynnie really believe we wouldn't love her, no matter what?" Her voice broke. Behind her, Mrs. Woodward stifled a sob.

"And all those relatives who died after eating your Yule log cake?" I asked.

"Three. Three people," she corrected. "Each of

them old with serious medical conditions. Many people die around the holidays."

Just as Chris had said. "And Mr. and Mrs. Woodward getting sick after your last Christmas together?"

"The oyster stuffing!" Mrs. St. Onge gasped. "I was so sick myself."

"You think it was the stuffing?" Julia Woodward's eyebrows rose in surprise. She still hadn't touched her cake.

"It must have been. I didn't eat any cake that day. I was sick for days afterward. I didn't tell you because we never spoke again after that Christmas." Her voice was thin and hurt.

"No, we didn't," Mrs. Woodward agreed. "But we should have."

"What happened to your husband?" I asked Mrs. St. Onge.

"Left me. Left me for another woman up in Rockland. And I say good riddance. We never were happy."

"And the men's clothes hanging next to Gwyn's overcoat upstairs?"

"I do Mr. Eames's laundry in exchange for help around the house." She blushed and I wondered if their relationship was merely a simple exchange of labor.

"And the depressions and the freshly raked dirt in the coal cellar?"

"Mr. Eames is going to finally pour me a concrete floor and add insulation. The cold comes up from there something terrible in the winter. He's been trying to even it out to get ready, but he's had a devil of a time. Some old clay pipes have collapsed under there, and it keeps leaving ruts. It's giving him fits. That's why I asked you not to go in there. I didn't want you to walk around on it and make it worse."

"And you're the one who called elder services and gave Gwyneth's notice," I said.

"She wanted to take a little leave in addition to the vacation she was due, in order to spend the longest possible time with Bradley before tax season began. They wouldn't let her take the time off, so she left rather than have a major confrontation on the eve of her wedding. She and Bradley met here, and she left her winter clothes and car. After they were gone, I called elder services to tell them she'd quit."

"She'll find another job," Mrs. Woodward assured her son's new mother-in-law.

"I'm not sure she'll look for anything," Mrs. St. Onge said. "Bradley makes a good living. Gwyneth wants to volunteer at the senior center, and they plan to get started on a family right away."

The mothers stared into one another's eyes. "We're going to be grandmothers!" they cried, and fell into a hug.

Jamie drained his coffee. "I don't see anything criminal happening here. Congratulations to you both."

Chapter Eleven

Christmas Eve dinner was a triumph, with a first course of Chris's unforgettable spaghetti with lobster sauce, followed by Livvie's baked haddock, with more side dishes than we could possibly consume. The dining-room table, extended by all three of its leaves, groaned under the many platters. Gus and Mrs. Gus joined us, as well as our across-the-street neighbors and honorary great-aunts, Viola and Fiona Snugg. Sonny's father and brother were with us, as they had been since our families were joined together. New at the table was Chris's family, including his brother and his niece, Vanessa. Page and Vanessa were best friends, and I could tell Page was relieved to have another kid in the mix after ten years as the only one. It was Jack's first Christmas with us as well, and he sat in a high chair wedged in at a corner of the table.

The other new person attending was Mrs. St. Onge. Bradley and Gwyneth had dropped by during cocktail hour, and given everyone their best.

They were living next door while they waited for the lease on the apartment over Gleason's Hardware to start on January 1. They were to spend Christmas Eve with Bradley's family, after spending the Solstice with Gwyn's. There had been initial enthusiasm about the families spending part of the holidays together, but negotiations had broken down over menus and timing, and mandatory precelebration worship attendance.

Gwyn told me all this with a sigh. "It's not as bad as I feared," she said. "It'll all work out." She looked around Mom's crowded house. "But I wish we could be together, like your family."

I didn't tell her that Chris hadn't spoken to his family for over a decade, or that Sonny's brother had been in rehab for a drug habit, or that when Livvie had gotten pregnant with Page, while still in high school, it had devastated my parents. Life was complicated, but she already knew that. Better to savor the good times.

At dinner the wine flowed and we all ate too much. The grown-ups talked and talked. Finally the kids could stand it no longer, and Page asked if they could be excused.

She and Vanessa went into the living room, where they engaged in shaking the presents under the tree, speculating about the contents. There were only a few more hours to go, and they could barely stand it. Freed from the high chair, Jack tagged along, crawling rapidly toward the tree. When he was three feet away, he pushed to standing, something he was getting quite adept at. One by one, the adults fell silent as we watched. He was so taken by the sparkling lights and beautiful ornaments, he seemed to forget he couldn't walk, and took one step forward and then another and another. I turned and saw a tear track down Livvie's cheek.

When he reached the tree, Jack shot a hand out, grabbing the strand of the lights and pulling it as hard as he could.

"Dad!" Page wailed. "He's—"

But Sonny was up, out of his chair already, sweeping Jack into his great arms. "That's enough, buddy. Be gentle with the tree." Jack laughed as his dad lifted him into the air.

When the dinner plates were cleared and the coffee served, I brought out the Bûche de Noël, holding the platter for all to admire. Everyone applauded. The moment was just as I'd imagined it.

In the end I hadn't been able to make the cake by myself. After two more failed attempts, I returned to Mrs. St. Onge and begged for help. She let me do more of the actual baking than she had the first time, though she kept a wary eye on me. Bradley had returned to work, but Gwyn was there and she helped too.

"I'd love to learn to make one of these," she'd said.

"Perhaps you will be the family member to carry on my legacy," Mrs. St. Onge told her.

The cake tasted as good as it looked, as I knew it would. After every crumb was eaten, my mother raised her glass. "To old friends and new," she said. "To the youngest and the oldest. Whatever you believe, may you experience the healing and hope that comes with the holidays, and may you know that after the darkness always comes the light."

"Hear, hear," we all said. "Hear, hear."

Odile St. Onge's Yule Log Cake

For those of you who tried to follow along as Julia and Mrs. St. Onge made the Bûche de Noël, I have included the recipe here. However, I do not urge you to make it. I deliberately picked the most complex recipe for each element I could find, and then added a few more twists. I wanted to give the two women plenty of time together so the relationship and the plot could play out. My niece Julia, who does make a Yule log cake (and for whom Julia Snowden is named), recommends doing it over multiple days.

If reading this story has given you a taste for Yule log cake, I urge you to make friends with a local baker and put one on order. When you get it, curl up with a cup of coffee, a slice of cake, and a good book.

For the Cake Base

Ingredients

¼ cup milk
2 Tablespoons butter
¾ cup shifted flour
1 teaspoon baking powder
¼ teaspoon salt
5 eggs
¾ cup granulated sugar

Instructions

In a bowl over a saucepan of water, heat the milk and butter until the butter melts. Remove the pan from the heat, leaving the bowl on top to keep warm enough that a finger can remain in the mixture for no longer than 10 seconds.

In a separate bowl, whisk together the flour, baking powder, and salt.

Separate the yolks and whites of 3 eggs. Beat the whites until they are foamy; beat in ½ cup of the granulated sugar, one Tablespoon at a time, until soft peaks form.

Beat the egg yolks and remaining two complete eggs and remaining ¼ cup of granulated sugar until the batter leaves ribbons on surface when the beaters are lifted, about 5 minutes.

Fold in one-third of the whites, then fold in remaining whites. Sift dry mixture over top, then fold in. Pour in milk mixture, then fold in until blended.

Line a 15- x 10-inch rimmed baking sheet with parchment paper. Spread the mixture in the pan.

Bake in 350°F oven about 12 minutes until golden and cake springs back when touched.

Loosen the edges with knife. Put a flour-dusted dish towel over the cake. Top it with tray larger than pan. Flip it over and lift off the pan. Starting at a corner, peel off the paper.

Starting at short side, roll up the cake in the towel. Cool it on a rack.

For the Filling

Ingredients

12 Tablespoons unsalted butter, softened and divided into one Tablespoon chunks
6 Tablespoons sugar
4 ounces semisweet chocolate
3 egg yolks

Instructions

Melt semisweet chocolate with 2 Tablespoons water in the top of a double boiler set over simmering water over medium heat. Stir to combine, then set aside to cool.

Combine 6 Tablespoons sugar and 3 Tablespoons water in a saucepan; cover and bring to a boil over medium heat, swirling pan several times until sugar has dissolved, about 1 minute. Uncover and continue to boil until syrup reaches 236°F on a candy thermometer, about 5 minutes more.

Beat egg yolks in the bowl of a standing mixer with the whisk attachment on high-speed whisk about 3 minutes or until thick and pale yellow.

Reduce speed to medium and gradually pour in hot syrup. Beat constantly about 10 minutes until mixture cools to room temperature.

Beat 12 Tablespoons butter into the egg mixture, 1 Tablespoon at a time, waiting until each is completely incorporated before adding more; continue beating for 5 minutes or until thick and smooth.

Stir in cooled semisweet chocolate and set aside to cool.

To Assemble the Cake

Gather the cake base, the cooled filling, and a jar of raspberry jam.

Carefully unroll the cake base from the dish towel.

Spread a thin layer of raspberry jam over the base.

Spread the filling over the base.

Roll the cake into a log, starting at a short side.

Starting 1 inch from one end of cake, cut on a piece on the diagonal so it is about 3 inches on the long side. Do the same on the other end. Reverse the pieces, so the diagonal cuts face out, giving the appearance of a cut branch.

For the Frosting

Ingredients

¾ cup whipping cream
3 Tablespoons unsalted butter
5 ounces bittersweet (not unsweetened) chocolate, chopped
4 ounces milk chocolate, chopped

Instructions

Bring cream and butter to boil in medium saucepan over medium-high heat, stirring to melt butter. Remove from heat.

Add both chocolates; whisk until melted.

Transfer to medium bowl. Let cool at room temperature until thick enough to spread, about 1 hour.

Spread the frosting over top and sides of cake and pieces. Using the tines of fork, draw circles on cake ends to resemble tree rings. Draw the fork along the length of the cake to form a bark design.

Jewel Brooch Cookies

Since I've included one holiday recipe I've urged readers not to follow, I thought I would also include an easy one you'll enjoy.

Many people make these sorts of cookies and call them by various names, including gems. This version came to me from my grandmother and I think they are particularly good.

Ingredients

1 cup, plus ½ teaspoon floor (yes, really, that's what the recipe says)
⅓ cup sugar
½ cup soft butter (Note: ½ cup, not ½ pound. That is the only way you can screw this recipe up)
1 egg yolk beaten with a fork
½ teaspoon vanilla

Instructions

Mix flour and sugar. Cut in butter like a piecrust. Add egg yolk and vanilla.

Mix with fingers until dough holds together. Place in refrigerator for 20 minutes.

Roll into balls the size of a marble and set on parchment-lined cookie sheet 1 inch apart.

Make an indentation in the center of each ball with your thumb. Fill the indentation with any jam or jelly. (I use raspberry and apricot.)

Bake at 350 degrees for 15 to 20 minutes or until golden brown.

Makes about a dozen cookies, depending on the size of the balls. I almost always double the recipe.

Dear Readers,

I hope you enjoyed reading Logged On, as much as I enjoyed writing it.

When Kensington asked me to write Nogged Off, for Eggnog Murder, the first collection one of my novellas appeared in, along with stories by Leslie Meier and Lee Hollis, I was thrilled. I pulled out all the stops, including every tradition from my little Maine town: Santa coming to town on a boat, Men's Night, the Festival of Trees, and the Saturday when everyone shops in their pajamas. After all, who knew if I'd ever get the chance again?

And then I did.

Luckily, by the time this second opportunity came around, my part of Maine had added a new tradition. The Coastal Maine Botanical Gardens had started Gardens Aglow, decorating the gardens with five hundred thousand LED lights. It is spectacular.

I have changed the names slightly here, to the Maine Coast Botanical Gardens and Illuminations, because the actual event is much less rigid than I portrayed. You do need tickets, but you can wander to your heart's delight. And I have never, ever seen a fistfight. I urge you to go if you have a chance. You will not regret it.

If this is your first meeting with Julia Snowden and the Maine Clambake Mystery series, she made her debut in Clammed Up, when her sister, Livvie, calls her back to Busman's Harbor, Maine, to rescue their family's failing clambake business. There are six books in the series, soon to be seven when Steamed Open comes out later this year. In each of the books, Julia gets involved in solving an actual murder, not just one she imagines.

I'm always happy to hear from readers. You can write to me at barbaraross@maineclambakemysteries. com, or find me via my Web site at www.maineclam bakemysteries.com, on Twitter @barbross, on Facebook www.facebook.com/ barbaraannross, on Pinterest www.pinterest.com/barbaraann ross and on Instagram http://www.instagram.com/maine clambake.

If you read Yule Log Murder *over the holidays, I hope you accompany it with a nice slice of Yule log cake. And if you make a Bûche de Noël—you are a better baker than I am!*

Merry Christmas, Happy Solstice, and a Happy New Year!

Barb